His early career in the construction industry took Richard V. Frankland abroad to Zambia and Jordan. Returning to England, he worked for a Japanese trading house administering civil and industrial engineering projects.

In early retirement he read for a Masters degree in Maritime Studies before being encouraged to complete his first novel, *A Cast of Hawks*, which he had started some years earlier. *Shadows in Sunshine* is his third book in the Ian Vaughan thriller series.

Apart from writing, Richard gives talks on maritime and local history, occasionally finding time for sailing and watercolour painting.

SHADOWS IN SUNSHINE

Also by Richard V. Frankland

A Cast of Hawks
Vanguard Press, 2010
ISBN: 9781843866077

Batsu
Vanguard Press, 2012
ISBN: 9781843868590

Richard V. Frankland

SHADOWS IN SUNSHINE

To Kate and Nick
Hope you will enjoy the plot.

Best wishes

Richard V. Frankland

Vanguard Press

ISBN: 978-1-84386-968-9

*Vanguard Press is an imprint of
Pegasus Elliot MacKenzie Publishers Ltd.*
www.pegasuspublishers.com

First Published in 2015

**Vanguard Press
Sheraton House Castle Park
Cambridge England**

Printed & Bound in Great Britain

Acknowledgements

This book could not have been written without the generous exchange of cultural information given about the people of Madeira. These include Dr Francis Zino for his information about the Desertas and other aspects of the Madeiras and Susan Smith, whose information and advice concerning locations was invaluable. I must also thank Carla Camacho and the management of the Vidamar Hotel for allowing the use of the hotel's name in scenes within the plot. I should also like to thank Bruno Silva, whose support and linguistic assistance has been greatly appreciated, and Susie Coelho and Luz Goncalves, whose patience and understanding when responding to my many questions has brought greater depth to this work.

Regading my insight into the workings of Britain's Consulates I must thank Mrs Joy Murray Menezes MBE, Madeira's Honorary British Consul, for her clear presentation of her current responsibilities.

In writing I am continuously learning new things and again have been priviledged to meet experts in their field who have been generous with their time and information. Lieutenant Commander Hamish Frazer RN, then of *HMS Illustrious*, provided an excellent guided tour of the ship and explanation of her final role together with confirmation that my plot would be a practical possibility. In addition, I should like to thank the captain of *HMS Illustrious* for allowing my visit to take place. Though a sailor myself, new to me is the sport of sailboarding, but thanks to the patience and careful explanation of the sport's equipment and its characteristics, I am now much wiser; for that I must thank Jon Popkiss of Kai Sports Ltd.

As with all my books, my deepest thanks go to my wife, Sandra, and daughter, Caroline, without whose assistance this work would have been much the poorer.

To the beautiful island and delightful people of Madeira.

CHAPTER 1
THE BRIEFING

Scaling the wall, Vaughan dropped down the other side, landing in a parachute roll that brought him back onto his feet, just in time to parry the first two vicious and painful blows. In mid-air he had seen the man leap from cover towards his landing point and had prepared himself for the unpleasant reception. Regaining his balance, Vaughan immediately went on the attack with a barrage of punches and kicks intent on breaking through his assailant's defences. The sight of others arriving at the edge of the clearing made Vaughan hesitate for just a moment, enough to allow his attacker an opening to launch another brutal assault. It was when the man's last punch got past Vaughan's left arm block that things changed. The blow struck Vaughan painfully on the chest just above his heart, sending him backwards off balance on his left leg. The attacker, thinking to follow through his advantage, took a step forward with his right leg. Seeing the opening, Vaughan, pivoting slightly on his left foot as he toppled back, lashed out with his right foot, kicking the man in the groin, to be rewarded by a loud agonised cry from the man, who fell to the ground doubled up in a ball of pain. *Got you, you bastard,* thought Vaughan, and swiftly regaining his balance took some pleasure in delivering a second kick, striking his victim hard below the ribcage winding the man. *That's payback.* Breathing heavily and with heightened senses induced by the rapid adrenaline rush, Vaughan fell on his attacker and with his left leg trapping the man's arms, grabbed his chin in his left hand and clasped the back of the man's head with his right; one hard twist of the head would snap the spine like a twig. Vaughan could see the man's neck muscles strain and a look of fear form in his eyes.

Two of the watching group rushed forward, in what would have been a vain attempt, to prevent Vaughan from completing the coup de grâce; stopping in their tracks the instant he released the hold, both wondering what would happen next.

"The next move would have been to break the neck," Vaughan said coldly, before standing quickly and stepping away from his unarmed combat instructor, resisting a satisfied grin.

Sergeant Instructor McClellan rolled onto his hands and knees and slowly forced himself to his feet, blowing hard through his teeth. He was of the old school, that taught the self-preservation and killing skills of unarmed combat by the method of inflicting pain. The pain was such that it guaranteed rapid learning and in the preceding weeks all those undergoing training at 'The Manor' had received a lot of pain from the sergeant.

"What are you doing... this evening... Mr Vaughan?" the sergeant asked, still fighting for breath.

"Studying code grouping notes, why?" Vaughan replied, dabbing at a split lip, now fearing that the sergeant wanted a return match in the gymnasium.

"Meet me... in 'The Lazy Miller' after dinner, I'll stand you enough beer... to give you a hangover for a week. That was the best reaction move... I've seen since a guy called Strachen... passed through here, and that was three years ago... at least. You also followed the golden rule... never lose your temper... it slows you down," panted the sergeant, still bent, hands on his knees, trying to recover.

Aware of the anger he had still been feeling as he had seen the sergeant leap towards him, Vaughan smiled inwardly. Was that the difference he wondered, was his anger something he could coldly control? To lose his temper was, yes, different, irrational, not controlled. Was it that cold anger that had enabled him to efficiently kill Murata and the sadistic Fumiko Hamaura in what seemed a lifetime ago?

*

That morning Ian Vaughan had woken as usual five minutes before the bedside alarm was due to go off to yet another Monday at 'The Manor'. Pulling the bedclothes aside he had swung his legs out of bed onto the cold stone floor of his spartanly furnished room. Stretching and yawning he had reached across to the bedside alarm clock and switched it off before it could ring. A mood of depression still hung over him like a dark cloud, generated by his weekend with his daughters. It was not their fault. Any child subjected to the subtle indoctrination that his, soon to be ex-wife, was so capable of, would be in fear of their father. It had taken a court action for him to even be allowed to see them once a month, and at each visit he had become aware of their changing feelings towards him. Nothing a court could do would change that. It was up to him to win back their affections, but he was determined to do that without resorting to bribery and the type of antics Sarah was employing. Her words were still ringing in his ears. "Why a court chooses to allow someone as dangerous as you to look after two young girls for a weekend is beyond me," she had said as he had collected the girls the previous Friday afternoon.

Taking her to one side, out of earshot of their daughters who were sat in his hire car, Vaughan had said firmly, "You make anymore statements like that to me or about me, in front of the girls, and I will take all the steps in my power to have them removed from your care. It is not me that is dangerous, and what

15

little danger they were in from Hamaura has been dealt with. He is secured in prison with assurances that he will never be released, so just you drop the dangerous man lines when referring to me, understood?" He had frightened her; he saw that at the time. *Damn, another reason for her to terrify the girls, no doubt egged on by that bitch, Rebecca.*

Pulling on boxer shorts, tracksuit and trainers he had left his room and made his way downstairs, and leaving the old manor house by the butler's corridor gently jogged across the courtyard and out into the grounds. Normally he would have waited for the rest of the group under training to gather, before going on the morning run, but today he had wanted to be alone. Taking the level path between North Wood and the lake he had run at a gentle pace until he got to the boundary wall, and then increased speed as the path swung away from the lake and began to wind its way up the hill through the wood to the assault course. His depression had turned to anger, more at himself for rising to the bait and threatening his wife, than at her inflammatory remark. So it was with some considerable aggression that he had charged at the climbing net, tyre trip course, rope climb, bars and barbed wire crawl tunnel before tackling the wall.

*

"Are you running back with the rest of us?" asked Sergeant McClellan, interrupting Vaughan's thoughts.

"No, I'll carry on clockwise, see you at breakfast," Vaughan replied, now just irritated by McClellan's intrusion into his personal gloom.

Without looking at the others, Vaughan jogged off up the slope back into the wood heading for the north boundary at the top of the rise. Here the wall gave way to a high chain link fence topped with coiled razor wire. The view through the fence was stunning and Vaughan stopped to admire it and get his breath back. The now familiar sound of horse's hooves had him looking round to see a fine chestnut stallion cantering along the track the other side of the fence. *Here she is again,* he thought, as the young lady rode past, smiling at him and waving. She had become almost a regular part of the group's morning routine as they ran along that section of the course. Each day the sighting of her had brought admiring comments and some less honourable remarks. Vaughan returned the smile and waved back, then turning on his heels, started to run down the hill to 'The Manor', his mood now considerably lighter than before.

Seated in the midst of his group at breakfast listening to Bowen's latest joke about getting to heaven from Scotland, Vaughan was surprised to be given a note by the last arrival, Mannings. "They asked me to give you this," he said, shrugging his shoulders indicating that he knew nothing else about it. "Jesus, Vaughan, we thought you were going to kill Mac this morning."

"Most of us wish you bloody had," said Graham, with some feeling. Graham was one of those that at best would be put behind a desk, but would probably be given alternative career advice.

Vaughan tore open the envelope and pulling the note from inside read it, then glanced at his wristwatch. "Got to go guys, I've been summoned."

Isabel Handley, the Director's secretary, surreptitiously studied Vaughan over the file she was pretending to be reading. She had read his file, and was well aware of his previous exploits. An interesting man, and brave too.

The buzzer on her desk sounded. "You can go in now Mr Vaughan," she said, a little breathlessly. "The Director will see you now."

In the Training Director's office, Vaughan was invited to take a seat on the chair, set in the middle of the spacious office, that made him feel exposed whilst sitting there.

"Apart from your appalling ability with languages we think that you have reached a sufficiently good standard to move onto operations. You did your stint of dangerous stuff before joining us, so you can expect something pretty boring as your first official field op," said J.T. Marshal, the Director of Training. "I know I am repeating something that you have already been told, and that is, that most of what SIS does is watch and report and occasionally make contact with sympathetic people working for those 'less friendly' states. In fact the more 'friends' you make in those areas the better."

Ian Vaughan nodded. "Yes, we were given very clear briefing on that area of our work." He didn't like Marshal, something about the man and the way his eyes constantly ranged over Vaughan's body from head to toe, and that whining, almost sneering, tone of voice, made his skin crawl.

"Sometimes a bargain needs to be struck that may offend your code of ethics. Be aware that you very rarely know the whole picture or what plans are in place for the future. Mention your concerns by all means, but never act without agreement from your controller. Independent action is not acceptable so separate your personal ideals from those of the Service and you will do well. Mix them up and you could well end up out in the cold."

Vaughan left Marshal's office half an hour later feeling uncomfortable about his future and wondering whether his conscience would become his downfall. *Obey the last order, that is the rule, and the last order was to collect my train ticket, weapon and start packing.*

His evening with Sergeant McClellan was both hilarious and highly educational. The stories of those who had passed and those who had failed in training were mainly very amusing and sometimes sad, but all were a lesson in themselves.

"You know that they try and break you while you're here. Don't think that because you passed you are accepted. They won't trust you for years and maybe never will," McClellan said, slurring his words slightly as the bell sounded for last orders. "Too many trained men have been turned, for them to give you their full confidence. At first you won't like it, but as time passes you get used to the way they work; for what it's worth, I think you'll do okay. Come on, drink up, we've just got time for another."

*

The following morning Vaughan found it difficult to keep up with the group on the morning run. On arrival back at 'The Manor' the previous evening he had drunk a pint of water, and each time he got up during the night he repeated the treatment, but he still had a sore head and uneasy stomach. He stunned the group by eating an enormous cooked breakfast washed down with three cups of black coffee, after which he felt a little better. There were no goodbyes, no one expected any, he just checked that he had not left anything behind, threw his case and sailing bag into the back of his van and drove out of the grounds and through the springtime countryside to Taunton. Near the station he found the industrial estate and the warehouse where he had been instructed to leave his vehicle; then, with sailing bag over his shoulder and pulling his suitcase, he walked to the station and boarded the London train.

He had not seen her on the platform and was surprised that in an almost empty first-class carriage she chose to sit opposite him. Her face was familiar and one that Vaughan classified as 'county beauty'. Vaguely searching his memory he wondered whether he might have seen her photograph in one of the coffee table magazines at 'The Manor', then somewhere in the back of his mind alarm bells rang. 'Miss County Magazine' smiled, one of those flattering smiles that suggested she wanted to become immediate friends. Vaughan struggled not to respond, managing instead to give her a brief smile in return before opening his current copy of 'Yachting Monthly' and starting to read the letters section.

Some five minutes must have passed before she said, "Excuse me keep looking at you, but have we met before? Your face is so familiar, I feel sure we have met."

"No, we have never met, or at least, never been introduced. I have a very good memory for faces and I can assure you that I would have remembered yours," replied Vaughan, pleasantly, before lowering his eyes again to the magazine.

"Those are nasty bruises on your face, have you been in an accident?" she asked, her expression one of apparently genuine concern. Her question made him look at her more closely noting that the eyes were seductively warm.

"My own fault, I came unglued from some equipment in the gym yesterday. More embarrassing than painful," he replied with a quick smile before returning his gaze yet again to the letters page. *What the hell is this? Why the over-familiar concern, surely she's not picking me up. Is this Sarah's last-ditch attempt to justify stopping me having any contact with Louise and Clare? Get a grip, how the hell would she know that I would be travelling on this train. She doesn't even know I've been in training at 'The Manor' come to that.*

Surreptitiously he reached in his trouser pocket for his mobile phone and by feel unlocked it, dialled six ones followed by five threes and pressed send. After allowing time for the number to be dialled he pressed the 'end call' button and waited. *I wonder whether this trick will work.*

"Do you work up in London?" she asked.

Looking up from his magazine Vaughan was about to answer when his mobile rang. "Oh, excuse me, I must answer this," he said, having pulled the phone from his pocket and studied the screen. "Charlie, old chap, where are you?" he said to the quick-thinking DELCO switchboard operator.

"Greenways florists, how may I help you?"

Vaughan turned his head away from the woman, apparently trying to get a clearer signal. As he did so he pressed the 'end call' button and switched the phone off. "Ah that's better where did you say you are?" he paused. "Oh you got the earlier train after all, which carriage are you in? I'll come and join you," he paused again as if listening to the reply, "Right, hold on there I'll come along to you."

Looking across at 'Miss County Magazine' he said, "Please excuse me I must join a friend." *Why am I running? Is it really this bloody divorce, or nerves about what awaits me?*

Hurriedly gathering up his belongings he left the carriage and worked his way back down the train. In the corner of the buffet car he switched his phone back on and dialled the number again, and this time waited for the operator to say something.

"DELCO Publishing."

"Seven three seven eight two seven, Harrier," he said, quoting the last six digits of his mobile number and temporary codeword. "I dialled in a few minutes ago, thanks for calling back, I needed an excuse to get away from someone being a little too friendly."

"Understood, call if you need any further assistance." With that the line went dead.

Vaughan moved on until he found a second-class seat opposite a man of similar age to himself. Stowing his luggage in the rack he sat and started a casual conversation with his new travelling companion. Looking out of the window at the countryside flashing by, he saw some horses in a field and made the link. He smiled. *So, that was why I was given a first-class rail ticket. Very clumsy for a honey trap, I would think.*

*

A week later Vaughan eased his rapidly numbing backside to another position on the hard plastic chair and idly looked at a yellowing bruise on the back of his left hand as a smile crept over his face at the memory of Sergeant McClellan.

"Out of the confusion of the Arab Spring uprisings in North Africa," Ian Vaughan's attention snapped back to the present and this, oh so long briefing; "climaxing with the brutal demise of Muammar Gaddafi and many of his close supporters, we have made a contact, which we and the FCO believe is worth pursuing, and indeed, giving support to." The speaker hesitated, "Do you find this amusing?"

"No just er pleasantly fascinating," Vaughan lied, removing the unconscious grin from his face.

"Oh," the speaker replied, in that surprised tone that suggested he felt flattered by the reply.

Ian Vaughan watched as the pompous, pasty-faced little man with the lank greasy hair, bad breath and a strange odour of fish about him studied the ceiling, no doubt seeking heavenly guidance for the next passage of his sermon.

"Fortuitously, the man we have come to know as Walid al Djebbar arrived in Benghazi towards the end of the fighting with offers to try and negotiate a peaceful settlement and launch a programme of reconciliation." Tristan Allsopp-Stevenson paused again. "There were moments when we thought it possible he would succeed, but as you know, that was not to be. It was during this time that we learnt he was actually Tunisian and was active in the 'Jasmine Revolution'." A superior smile crossed Allsopp-Stevenson's face as he detected that Vaughan did not recognise the name given to the revolution. "The overthrow of the former government of Tunisia," he said intently, almost preening himself. "He is a member of a desert nomadic style family living near the border with Libya and Algeria, in the Tataouine province." Allsopp-Stevenson produced a large pink handkerchief, blew his nose loudly, and then mopped the perspiration from his forehead. "We think that he is of Berber heritage, which seems to give him cross-border affiliations that have enabled him to attract a very large rural support base across southern Libya, Algeria and Tunisia. It also appears that the current tensions between Morocco and Algeria have not deterred him from making powerful friends in Morocco, who are apparently willing to work with the Algerians in stabilising the region." The pink handkerchief was pulled out again to mop the pasty brow. "Currently he has been busily drumming up support for a North African Unification Conference to discuss the prospects of forming a political, trade and military alliance; from what we understand, it would be a cross between OPEC and the EU."

Ian Vaughan's eyebrows raised in surprise at the concept. "From the point of view of the region he sounds too good to be true. Is he that well connected that he, and it appears he alone, can pull this together?"

"Obviously we, together with the French and Italians, are indicating our fullest support, though French support for the former Tunisian President, Ben Ali, and Italy's anger over illegal immigration has, shall we say, restricted the number of avenues we have available at this time."

"Where does the US stand in all of this?" Vaughan asked.

"Oh they are in full support as well. Strangely, we have heard that Al Djebbar has warned the American State Department not to make any offers of arms; any of the oil and gas exports, under the scheme he is proposing, are to be paid for in cash." Allsopp-Stevenson smiled to himself, obviously finding the information amusing. "Needless to say from the European perspective we find Al Djebbar's comment encouraging. Rumours emerging from his numerous talks indicate that he is intent on restricting military activity to the region's southern borders with the rest of Africa, with the intention of controlling cross-border migration. Should he be successful, it would greatly relieve the strain on European countries such as Spain and Italy, who are currently struggling to handle the influx of economic migrants, refugees, call them what you will."

"This is all very fascinating, but where do I fit into this?"

Allsopp-Stevenson looked disappointed that his lecture was being short-circuited. "I am coming to that." The pink handkerchief appeared again, to mop the now furrowed brow. "Intelligence reports just in, confirm that sufficient parties in the region have indicated a willingness to attend or be represented at a conference. Despite offers from us and the French it has been decided that the island of Madeira is to be the venue."

"An interesting choice. A small island in the middle of an ocean would make security a lot easier than here or in Paris."

"Possibly, but it also severely restricts our diplomatic opportunities. The PM was hoping to entertain some delegates and set up a series of discussion groups. This can hardly be done when the delegates are isolated on a, as you say, small island in the middle of an ocean." Allsopp-Stevenson sounded as if the decision had been a personal insult to him. "Any significant diplomatic mission sent to the island would be too obvious and it has been agreed amongst EU members to avoid a circus that would disrupt what Al Djebbar is trying to achieve."

It was Vaughan's turn to smile, "So I still don't understand why I'm here."

"We have decided that you, being an unknown in the 'security agent' and diplomatic world, are to be teamed up with Arthur Claremont to make 'friends' with Al Djebbar and an Algerian delegate named El Alami." His lecturer emphasised the titles, 'security agent' and 'friend' by holding up both hands and waggling stubby forefingers as if to mark apostrophes in the air. "Arthur Claremont retired to Madeira two years ago having worked in our embassy in Algiers for two full tours. El Alami and he became friends and we would expect Claremont to know of the visit and be in contact during El Alami's stay on the island." After another flourish of the handkerchief Allsopp-Stevenson continued, "Much against FCO advice and, I might add, my own, the Commodore has chosen you to be the friendly contact with Al Djebbar. Your entrée is through an Oxford University friend of Al Djebbar called Charles Stanthorpe-Ogilvey; apparently they sculled together and shared an interest in dinghy sailing. Both were reading Philosophy, Politics and Economics, Al Djebbar obtaining a first."

"A very bright boy then," said Vaughan.

"Highly intelligent, educated in France before coming to Oxford; speaks fluent French, faultless English, as well as several of the North African dialects." Allsopp-Stevenson gave Vaughan a look of utter distain. "We have arranged for you to meet Stanthorpe-Ogilvey tomorrow. He will brief you on their friendship and others in their group at university. Take a notebook with you, he is now quite senior and does not have time to waste."

"Neither have I," replied Vaughan, annoyed by his comment.

Desperate to demonstrate his vast knowledge of North African politics and tribal relations Allsopp-Stevenson plunged back into his specialised subject keeping Vaughan bored, amused, irritated and occasionally interested for the next hour and a half.

"You cannot afford to meet with Al Djebbar unprepared," said Allsopp-Stevenson as he began the final stage of his lecture, "He would expect a friend of Charles Stanthorpe-Ogilvey to have followed world events and be reasonably knowledgeable about the current North African situation."

"You have not mentioned Islamic fundamentalism in the area," Vaughan said, looking curiously at his lecturer.

"I have been saving the potential threats to last," Allsopp-Stevenson replied, annoyed at being prompted. "On our radar is a man called Mohammed el Kamal al Bashir, a Libyan who was forced into exile some twelve years ago. We lost sight of him, but think that he went first to Pakistan then Afghanistan. His return to Libya is probably inspired by Taliban interests intent on destabilising the region by radicalising the Libyan youth. He brought with him several followers, most of whom received training in either Pakistan or Afghanistan. In the folder I will give you before you leave are photographs of the man and some of those close to him." More brow mopping followed before Allsopp-Stevenson raised his head and carried on. "The few still loyal to the late Muammar Gaddafi do not appear to pose a threat to the conference. Their initial objective is to regain control at home and as such the Libyan delegation is limited to those with interests in oil and one or two of their military personnel, interested in what Al Djebbar has to say about border security. Another threat to the conference comes from Russian interests. They see European influence, increasing post Arab Spring, particularly in Libya, where Europe played a strong supporting role in the removal of the old regime. We believe that Russia fears

European investment in gas field development and transportation, threatening their interest in increasing domination of the wholesale energy market. Already they are firmly established in Algeria and since 2010 have been negotiating to expand their gas production interests in that country."

"Surely the conference will not get into such economic detail?" queried Vaughan, realising almost instantly the stupidity of his comment; was it frustration with the length of time his lecturer was taking? Vaughan couldn't decide.

"The region's only major revenue is from oil and gas. Any discussion relating to economic co-operation cannot fail to have implications concerning the future development of those commodities," replied Allsopp-Stevenson pompously, jumping on Vaughan's apparent naivety. "There are some Russians living in Madeira, two of whom may have ties that could bring them into play during the conference. They will probably try to contact the Algerian delegation and 'make proposals' shall we say." Again the stubby fingered hands were held high to mark the emphasis. "That is only to be expected, what we are anxious about is any move on Russia's part to extend their interests into Morocco where there is a growing interest in exploration and development."

Vaughan left SIS headquarters, with his head spinning, following the intensity and volume of the information presented. Jammed in his briefcase were notes of the briefing, supplied by his knowledgeable lecturer, and a folder of photographs to memorise. Now sat in the DELCO Publishing Offices he started work reading the notes.

The DELCO offices were really a front to disguise the location for field operatives reporting in or meeting with senior staff, and to work with MI6/SIS intelligence analysts. It had been decided that for this operation his cover was to be that of an author currently writing a pilotage book entitled 'A Tramp's Guide to the Islands of the Atlantic' which, it was hoped, would cover any coastal sailing whilst in Madeiran waters, without people guessing the real reason for his presence.

"Your arrival problem is solved."

Vaughan spun round in his chair. He had not heard Lieutenant Penny Heathcote enter the room.

"I thought it was already sorted. I fly to Funchal and charter a yacht," he replied.

"I didn't think that an author writing 'A Tramp's Guide to the Islands of the Atlantic' would be credible if he arrived by plane, and the Commodore agreed."

"What solution have you found?"

"Lifted aboard 'Lusty' as far as the Algarve then dropped in the water for the last few days. We thought your own boat would be best, just in case you bump into someone who knows you. We assumed that your boat was back in the water."

"Yes it is. You're chartering her?" he asked frowning, annoyed at their apparent presumption.

"Oh er yes," she replied, looking a little taken aback by his question and reaction.

"By 'Lusty' I assume you are referring to *HMS Illustrious*?"

"Exactly, she is due to leave Portsmouth in six days, heading for Gib. I have arranged for you and your yacht to be lifted aboard in the early hours of Tuesday morning," informed Heathcote, briskly.

"No pressure then," Vaughan replied, sarcastically.

"South-westerly winds 4 to 6 forecast for the next few days. That should get you from Dartmouth to Portsmouth in good time. I'll arrange for some euros to be waiting for you onboard; you will need to provision for a week, we don't want you having MoD stuff in your galley when you get to Madeira. You are being issued with a company credit card; be careful how you use it, we have the Public Accounts Committee to answer to, so read the rules carefully." Heathcote placed a brown folder on the table.

"Here is a full set of charts," she said, patting a large cardboard tube stood on end by the door. "They are up to date, just make sure, during the voyage, that you mark your sailing passage on them and write up a log as if you had sailed all the way."

"Yes Ma'am," Vaughan said. "Is it possible to have weather information for the voyage covering say, the last two weeks?"

The pretty lieutenant with the amazing red hair gave him a sharp look. "I will see what I can do and get it aboard *Illustrious* ready for you."

"That would be great, thank you," he replied. He was curious at the change in her manner since he had returned from training; before he had signed on she was charming and almost friendly, but now she was brisk and cold.

"See Lorna for an expenses advance to get you down to Devon and underway but first, the Commodore wants to see you in ten minutes time, you know where his office is."

She left without waiting for any acknowledgement. Vaughan carefully packed the paperwork before hefting the fat tube containing the charts onto the table. He was tempted to open the tube to see what Lieutenant Penny Heathcote had supplied, but decided to wait until after his meeting with the Commodore. There also the relationship had changed. As Commander Campbell, he had shown something of a paternal side, especially during the initial break-up of Vaughan's marriage, but now promoted, first to Captain then rapidly to Commodore and back inside MI6/SIS, he showed a much colder side to his personality.

"Come!" Vaughan heard in response to his knock on the Commodore's office door.

"Ah, Vaughan, come in, take a seat over there at the table, I will be with you in a minute."

Vaughan took a seat facing the door and looked about him. He was surprised to see that Campbell was wearing full dress uniform, the broad gold ring on the jacket sleeve the result of a well earned promotion. Until now Vaughan had only seen Campbell in suits, the uniform changed his appearance dramatically. Though the office décor had not changed the atmosphere within it definitely had; it wasn't just the uniform, it was the man himself.

"I had to fight hard to get you on this one Vaughan. There were those in the FCO and that agoraphobic expert of ours, Allsopp-Stevenson, wanting one of their so called, trusted old hands, doing this," announced Campbell, as he strode round his desk and across the office to sit opposite Vaughan at the table. "My reasoning is that you are an unknown in the dirty world of backroom diplomacy. Therefore you are more likely to appear genuine in your approach to Al Djebbar, who is no fool when it comes to assessing people. There are three major reasons why we need this North African Unification Conference and Al Djebbar to succeed. The first is to hold back the tide of Islamic fundamentalism and its associated extremist groups, the second is to reduce the influx of illegal immigrants from that region, and finally to loosen the stranglehold that Russia is gaining on European energy sources."

"Yes, sir, Allsopp-Stevenson was very clear on all of those issues."

"Because of the location of the conference it is impossible for any of the European countries to form any type of sideshow for fear of upsetting the parties involved, it is all a very delicate situation at the moment."

"Yes, sir, he mentioned that too," replied Vaughan, aware that the Commodore was trying to say something but was having trouble selecting the words. *For God's sake, Campbell, stop faffing about. What's this dancing around leading up to?*

"Initially we want you to concentrate on re-igniting Al Djebbar's old affection for this country. I understand that whilst he was here he made some close friendships, all of whom he has kept in contact with over the years. Mostly this has been the occasional letter of polite news between them; it's only with this chap Stanthorpe-Ogilvey that he has kept in really close contact. When you meet him tomorrow get as much out of him as you can, you have to make it appear that you are a longtime friend of his and the current set that he moves in. Don't make the mistake of basing all your knowledge on his university group or you will be rumbled in seconds. Get to know about Stanthorpe-Ogilvey's sailing pals and also the shooting set he moves about with in the winter."

"Yes, sir, but won't he dislike the use of his friendship in this way? I mean, it is almost disloyal."

"I think you may change your mind when you meet the FCO's rising star himself," responded Campbell, with an expression on his face that made Vaughan suspect that Stanthorpe-Ogilvey was not held in Campbell's highest regard.

"Friendships don't impede ambition I take it."

"No, not in this case, fortunately for us," replied Campbell. "Basically what we want you to do is to get close enough to Al Djebbar to see what other visitors he and the conference representatives have, especially any Russians hovering around the Moroccan team."

"Do you want me to liaise with this Arthur Claremont who is living out there?"

"No, definitely not. If you two were seen together it would be obvious who you were actually working for. I had to let the 'old guard' thinkers use Claremont, who may get something useful, but I don't hold out any real hope."

There was a knock at the door and Lieutenant Heathcote appeared. "The Admiral has arrived sir, I have shown him into the interview room and given him a cup of coffee."

Campbell frowned.

"Mr Vaughan," Lieutenant Heathcote said coolly. "Would you clear your things from the meeting room so that the Commodore and Admiral can get to work? Better take your things to interview room four where your next appointment is waiting."

"Certainly, sorry I had no idea that the room would be needed," Vaughan replied, leaping to his feet. "Er, was that all, sir?"

"Yes, Vaughan, that was all," said Campbell, brusquely.

Bugger, he was leading up to something and Heathcote's interruption stopped him from spitting it out.

Struggling with chart tube, briefing folders and briefcase, Vaughan bumped into Lorna, the office's talented receptionist, as he emerged from the meeting room. "Excuse me Lorna, but have I done something to upset the lieutenant?"

"No, her change in attitude is to avoid any, even slightly close relationships. You people get involved in things that she may also wish to help with unofficially if she were to form a friendship; such actions could endanger you both, and the outcome of the operation you were involved in," came the cool response.

"Yes, I understand," replied Vaughan. "I should have worked that out for myself."

"I won't be giving you my phone number either," Lorna said with a deadpan expression on her face, before turning away towards reception.

As she walked away, Vaughan could not see her face but was sure that she was grinning.

On reaching the interview room he used his elbow to open the door and almost fell into the room, dumping his load on the table. A lady stood at the window with her back to him, her perfume immediately recognisable as being the same as the lady's on the train.

"Do I understand that we write for the same publisher?" Vaughan asked.

She turned and smiled, that polite smile which doesn't touch the eyes. "Yes we do but I am actually the final part of your training."

Vaughan smiled, "The 'honey trap'. It was not until the train passed a field of horses that I made the connection. A very handsome chestnut stallion you ride, what's his name?"

"Brigand," she replied, unsmilingly. "A field of horses was not the most flattering of connections to make, but you are the first for a long time to make it."

"If it is any consolation to those that failed, you do look very different with your hair in a net and wearing a riding hat and jodhpurs."

I wonder what her reaction would have been if my response to her on the train had been different? I bet she would have had a good put down line.

She nodded. "We thought your telephone trick was quite good. Be aware that they may be using phone hacking devices, though."

"At 'The Manor' they mentioned that the 'honey trap' maybe wired for the first contact and any later meeting place bugged. I confess I didn't think about phone hacking," Vaughan replied.

"I wouldn't let that bother you too much. It is quite difficult to arrange for one of our phones to be hacked. Places like restaurants perhaps would more likely be direction microphone listening," she said, sounding a little less icy. "Just a few pointers; one, don't kill the contact so quickly, it looked too er, nervy, if you see what I mean. If they think you have tumbled them it would confirm in their minds that you are just using a cover. Sometimes they are not sure that you are not who you are pretending to be. Two, they may be a former enemy asking for help. It has happened in the past and we have gained a great deal of information as a result. Three, try thinking of a way to turn them; as almost a bachelor you have little to lose by having an affair or friendship."

The comment made Ian Vaughan's hackles rise. Despite the current state of his marital relationship, he would not consider starting an affair; he was still hurting too much.

"The important thing," she continued. "Is to recognise the trap, then to use it to our advantage, not theirs, whoever they may be. By the way, always make sure you report the contact. That way later blackmail attempts can be properly managed."

Remembering J.T. Marshal's lecture on personal ethics, Vaughan limited his response to nodding his understanding.

"You passed by the way, I guessed that you had recognised the approach when your eyes swept the rest of the almost empty carriage as I sat down," she said, this time with a friendlier smile.

Vaughan nodded. "I don't flatter myself that an attractive woman would choose to sit opposite me when almost a whole empty railway carriage is at her disposal."

"I would not be that hard on myself if I were you," she said, twitching her lips momentarily into a pout and smiling.

*

Charles Stanthorpe-Ogilvey had been well briefed as to what information Vaughan required. There were copies of photographs taken during his student years with Al Djebbar, details of his family home and pictures of ex-girlfriends and the student group both men were part of. Some two hours later Charles smiled across at him and said, "Take that lot back to your hotel and study it. We should meet again in the morning before you go down to Devon and I will test you on it. You had better be good, Walid is no fool, and for God's sake don't lose any of it."

To Vaughan's surprise he had taken an instant liking to Charles Stanthorpe-Ogilvey, whose greeting the following morning showed a similar regard. The meeting had lasted even longer than the previous day's, and Vaughan was relieved when his new friend Charles said, "My word you have been busy, did you get any sleep last night Ian?"

"Yes, a couple of hours at least," Vaughan replied, returning the warm smile.

To Vaughan, Charles Stanthorpe-Ogilvey came across as a man who understood his role, and the implications that would result in failure to impart the fullest of information. His attitude had therefore produced a deeper exchange of background knowledge than a straightforward, bare facts briefing, could possibly have achieved.

"Fancy you knowing Rebecca the huntress," said Charles, shaking his head in almost disbelief, "and she married Jerry Johnson-Lacey you say; poor old Jerry, it must have been like a rabbit caught in the headlights. He was never very quick on his feet where women were concerned."

"I didn't know that she was at Oxford," said Vaughan, incredulously. "She never struck me as being that bright."

"She's bright all right, in finding a potentially rich husband," replied Charles, smiling. "She studied some lightweight degree at Warwick and spent her weekends husband-hunting in Oxford. Jerry was a year behind Walid and I so he must have been entrapped in his finals year. Poor old Jerry, I wonder if she's emptied the bank account yet."

"Will Walid remember her?"

"Oh yes, he will, she thought he was a prime target until he mentioned that he already had five wives," Charles roared with laughter at the memory. "Apparently her face was a picture of shock and disapproval."

"Just checking, Walid is not married is he? There is nothing about that in the briefing notes."

"No, he is not married, but I understand that he has his eye on a young lady dentist from Jordan. Sorry, I should have mentioned that before, not that you should know about her, but you should definitely be aware that he is currently single."

"It is often the most obvious thing that's missed when trying hard to impart even the smallest of detail," replied Vaughan.

As he left, Vaughan wondered why he had not mentioned that it was 'Rebecca the huntress' who was mainly responsible for the break-up of his own marriage. Why she had worked so hard to poison Sarah's feelings for him he just could not understand. Then it dawned on him that if she had emptied Jerry's bank account maybe she felt she could get her hands on his. *No chance, you scrawny witch.*

*

On his way to Devon that afternoon Vaughan conducted imaginary conversations about his friendship with Charles Stanthorpe-Ogilvey. It helped reinforce his knowledge and confidence in the cover. One thing continued to puzzle him, however, and that was why Campbell had shown some dislike towards the man.

Getting off the train at Taunton Station, Vaughan walked to the warehouse where he had left his van, and drove the rest of the way to Kingswear's Darthaven Marina where he kept his yacht, *La Mouette sur le Vent.*

At 0700 hours the following morning Vaughan was at the helm of his boat motoring downstream on the last of the ebb tide, under a mainsail with two reefs set in it, ready to face the blustery south-westerly force 5 to 6 winds out in the English Channel. As the yacht approached Henry VIII's defensive castles near the mouth of the river the steep waves, caused by the outgoing river and tide running into the wind-driven waves rolling in from the English Channel, had the boat bucking as it rode out to sea. Setting a small area of foresail, he steered a course to clear the Mewstone and Black Rock, finding that the yacht's motion settled now that it was running almost abeam of the seas. Once clear of the Black Rock, Vaughan adjusted his course again to strike out across Lyme Bay towards Portland Bill. Now with the wind on the stern quarter he eased the mainsail and increased the area of foresail until the yacht felt balanced with just a small amount of weather helm. In the quartering sea, the yacht took on a corkscrew motion and Vaughan remembered Sarah, his wife, insisting on a change of course when their old boat took on that unsettling gyration. It was the first time in weeks that he had thought of her in a fond way, the divorce proceedings and her new life in Derbyshire blocking the many pleasant memories of their years together. Strangely, he still could not find it in himself to really blame her or criticise strongly her crazy reactions that had brought about the break-up of their previously solid marriage.

The sun broke through at last and soon he was losing himself to that almost spiritual experience he felt when helming a yacht. The sense of oneness with the elements of wind and water, and isolation from the land and the pressures of modern living were, for him, calming and immensely therapeutic.

As the flood tide started to take effect the waves became less steep and, as the tide increased in strength, his progress improved with the passing of each hour. To Vaughan's great pleasure, and some amazement, he found himself passing Portland Bill at 1300 hours, well ahead of schedule, and with still almost two hours left of favourable tide in which to push on and pass Anvil Point, Durlston Head and Peveril Point. Vaughan anchored the yacht off Swanage shortly after high tide, enjoying a good lunch and a doze before hauling the anchor at 1730 hours in the now gentler conditions of force 4 winds and clear skies. Enthusiastically setting full sail, he took the inshore passage, past Studland and Bournemouth, before entering Christchurch Bay to arrive at Hurst Narrows at slack low water just after 2100 hours, successfully avoiding the worst effects of the ebb tide. After passing through the narrow inshore channel he gybed the yacht and, slowed by the last of the ebb spilling from the western Solent, passed another of Henry VIII's defences, Hurst Castle. Crossing astern of the Yarmouth to Lymington ferry Vaughan noted his yacht's speed over the ground increasing as the new flood tide took effect, carrying him up the western Solent to Cowes in just over an hour. By midnight the boat was tied up alongside the visitors' pontoon in Haslar Marina with Vaughan sat eating a sandwich and sipping hot soup, amazed that, thanks to a good wind and favourable tides, he had completed the trip in just seventeen hours.

CHAPTER 2

CARRIER

The following morning Vaughan donned his standard issue camouflage kit and boots and sat at the chart table thumbing in DELCO's number on his mobile.

"May I speak to Penny in editorial please?"

"Putting you through, sir."

"Editorial."

"Ah Penny, I'm at Portsmouth, who should I contact?"

"Go to the Firm's main gatehouse, they will have someone waiting for you," replied Lieutenant Heathcote briskly.

"Thank you Penny, I'll be on my way." Vaughan ended the call without waiting for any further response; it was obvious that Heathcote was also concerned about phone tapping. In training he had been told never to use surnames or rank when calling into DELCO on an unsecured line.

Leaving the yacht he walked out of the marina and along the Millennium Walk to the ferry ticket office, purchased a ticket, and went down the ramp to the Gosport ferry as it arrived from the Portsmouth side. As the green and white vessel thundered its way back across the harbour Vaughan could see 'Lusty' berthed with the fuel barge alongside and a quayside crane loading stores.

Light rain began to fall as Vaughan strode up the ramp from the ferry jetty to find himself in a crowd leaving the harbour station. Hurrying, he reached the rank in time to get the second to last taxi.

"Trafalgar Gate please," Vaughan said, as he closed the taxi door.

On arrival he paid the driver and made his way into the red brick reception building and was about to select a queue ticket from the dispenser when he was intercepted by a lieutenant commander.

"Are you from DELCO?" he asked quietly.

"Yes," replied Vaughan, taking in the smart fresh faced thirty something year old in front of him.

"I have all the necessary paperwork, so if you will come with me, I have my car outside to take you to the ship."

"Lead the way," replied Vaughan noting the absence of any further introductions.

Cleared through the gate his escort relaxed as he weaved the car through the maze of dockyard roads. "I'm James Folette, onboard you will be known as Dave," he said giving Vaughan a wry grin. "We regularly have a Bob or Dave on board, though we've never had one that wants to bring his own boat with him."

Vaughan smiled, "Oh that's just in case yours sinks – well, it sounded humorous at seven o'clock this morning." Folette gave a broad grin.

Walking the last few yards from the car to the gangplank Vaughan realised just how big *HMS Illustrious* was, as she towered above the quayside. Though small by comparison to her American counterparts she was huge compared to the pair of type 45 destroyers lying forward of her.

Marine sentries brought arms to the alert as Folette and Vaughan reached the head of *Illustrious's* gangplank. "Can you flick me back on?" asked Folette, as he signed in.

A young marine turned to a board on the bulkhead behind him and slid Folette's name tile from the 'off' to the 'on' column.

"We'll go this way and then I can give you the Health and Safety chat and show you part of the arrangements we have made for your craft."

A few yards along the starboard side companionway Folette threw the catches on a bulkhead door leading into the aft hanger. "Basically the principle of one hand for yourself and one for the ship is the rule. Watch carefully where you are putting your feet, as there are many trip hazards. Restrict your time out on the flight deck to a minimum, as it is a dangerous place with potentially two damn great holes in it. A pilot concentrating on inspecting his aircraft parked up there," Folette said, pointing up to the flight deck, "stepped back without looking and landed face down over there. I doubt if he will ever fly again."

"I'm surprised that he is alive, there can't be much bounce in a steel deck," remarked Vaughan, looking at the lieutenant commander in astonishment.

"We are going to lower your yacht down here and use the Terex mobile crane to remove the mast, which will be stored on the flight deck. When you leave us we will just reverse the process."

"You are aware that it's a keel stepped mast and not a deck stepped one?" replied Vaughan.

"Yes, our chief engineering officer, Commander Howard, swore when he was told, but he said it would not be too much of a problem."

Vaughan suddenly felt anxious. Taking a mast down was relatively easy but re-stepping it again, especially as this one passed through the deck and rested on the yacht's keel, was not. All boatyards considered that to be a specialist job, as was the setting up of the rigging again.

Leaving the hanger Folette led the way forward, then turning towards the centre of the ship they reached the flight of steps to the officers' quarters. Looking at his watch he said, "Perfect timing for you to meet the captain. He likes to see all the Daves and Bobs if he can."

The officers' quarters appeared far less claustrophobic than the rest of the vessel, though Vaughan was still very aware of being on a fighting ship. Along a short corridor to port they came to the captain's cabin, the door of which was open.

"Excuse me, sir, your visitor has come aboard," said Folette standing to attention and snapping a smart salute.

"Excellent, show him in."

"This way," said Folette, turning to Vaughan.

Ian Vaughan stepped into the captain's harbour cabin as Captain Andrew Stroud rounded his desk holding out his hand. "Welcome aboard Dave," he said shaking Vaughan's hand warmly. "May I offer you some refreshment?"

"Thank you, a black coffee would be most welcome."

"Can you rustle up my... Ah there you are Matthews, can you bring some coffee for us please."

As both Folette and the steward left, Stroud indicated a chair for Vaughan, and then returned to his own seat. "You're not the first agent I have delivered to a foreign shore, but you are the first that has brought his own yacht. I've been given a rough outline of your mission, I won't ask for any details as I don't want to be told to mind my own business." Vaughan smiled, instantly warming to Stroud.

A knock at the door preceded Matthews entering, expertly holding a tray with cups, saucers and a plate of biscuits with one hand, and clasping a full pot of coffee and a jug of hot milk with the other.

"Just leave them there Matthews, I'll pour it in a moment," Stroud said, as he nodded in the direction of a side table near the door.

42

"Right sir. Lunch is Chicken Marrakech, would you like two meals brought here sir?"

"Do you have time to join me for lunch? You would be most welcome."

Vaughan looked at his watch, it was just after ten o'clock. "Thank you, but no, I have rather a lot of preparation work to do," recognising that the invitation was only a politeness by the captain.

"That's just one then, sir," said Matthews retreating out of the cabin.

Stroud waited for the door to close before crossing to pour the coffee. "Black coffee, did you say?"

"Yes please," replied Vaughan, looking around him and taking in the few items that could indicate his host's personality. Photographs of a minesweeper and two frigates were hung on the walls, together with three rugby team photographs and a picture of a young Stroud in kit receiving a cup. On the desk was a picture of, Vaughan guessed, Stroud's wife and two sons. Vaughan's mind flashed to his yacht's cabin with its single photograph of his two daughters and his mood dampened slightly.

"Right, what do you need from us Dave?"

"First of all a support cradle for the yacht."

"Already done and loaded aboard this morning. It has four adjustable braced supports, one at each corner of a rectangular frame, with a central beam for the keel to rest on. The pièce de résistance is that we have mounted it on heavy-duty castors so that we can manoeuvre it around the flight deck. Our plan is to lower it down into the aft hanger for the voyage and throw a cover over it. Anyone being nosy will think it is some piece of top secret kit we are testing," Stroud said, smiling wryly.

"How do we get her onboard?"

"You bring her up astern of us and the dockside crane will hoist her using a vehicle lift frame and strops. Our Chief Engineer, Commander Howard, has got it all in hand. When we drop you off we will use the starboard side crane. Just pray for a calm sea."

"During the passage I would like to be left alone as much as possible. I need to get into a lone sailor sleep pattern of twenty minutes rest followed by twenty minutes activity. I would like permission to take meals from the wardroom during their normal meal times, but eat them alone either in a cabin or a secluded area high up on the superstructure out of everyone's way."

"That can be arranged, we have made the flag officer's cabin available for you and I will put the word round that you wish to be left alone. Staying undisturbed anywhere outside of your cabin will be difficult though as all areas are regularly inspected."

"Even the deck areas between the funnels?" queried Vaughan.

"On that deck level are several equipment cabinets that have to be inspected hourly to ensure that they are safe and not overheating. Fire risk you know," replied Captain Stroud.

"Of course, every square foot of this vessel has to hold either equipment or personnel, I should have thought it through before asking."

"In fact you are only in the flag officer's quarters due to a lack of accommodation elsewhere. We have taken onboard a company of commandos and a full helicopter complement. That's nearly seven hundred men, double the naval personnel on board, so space is at a premium."

Vaughan looked shocked. "Ye Gods where do you put them all?"

"It's a very tight squeeze but we are used to managing it now. At first, our new role as Commando Carrier was something of a challenge, but my people have developed new skills and devised very imaginative ways of dealing with the problems."

Coffee drunk and the arrangements agreed for the lift-out and voyage, it left only the area for the drop to be established. Stroud produced a chart and unrolled it over his desk.

"I've been giving some consideration to your departure point, and thought that somewhere around here would be good. It is away from the shipping coming out of the Med, the only thing you may see is the Lisbon to Madeira ferry or a cruise ship."

Vaughan leant across the desk to study the chart, noting where Stroud had made a mark and written the co-ordinates. "Yes, that looks fine to me, 37 degrees north by 9 degrees 30 minutes west would be ideal. I should pick up a bit of the trades there."

On leaving Stroud's cabin, Lieutenant Commander Folette gave Vaughan a further tour of the ship. "Here is the ship's bell from the previous *Illustrious*." Vaughan stared at the large bell, shot through in several places, the metal around the holes molten from the heat generated by the bullets. "The Germans did their best to sink her during her time in the Med on Malta convoy duty."

Vaughan's only previous experience of a fighting vessel was a US Navy's patrol launch. Onboard that, one expected conditions to be somewhat cramped, but he was surprised to find that there was little or no more room given to companionways and ladders on this much larger ship. Everywhere was festooned with heavily lagged pipes and cable trays almost buckling under the weight of miles of cabling. *Unsightly, maybe, difficult to clean around, definitely, but in response to damage control, instantly identifiable and immediately accessible. This is first and foremost a fighting ship.*

In the heart of the ship, the operations room, with its amazing arrays of radar screens and computers, demonstrated just how much warfare had changed for this ship compared to her predecessor.

"Nowadays we can pretty much identify anything entering response range. Our antennas, being high up, give us a good view beyond the visual horizon. It is relatively easy to see aircraft at a great distance, but to see low-level missiles coming at you, height of antenna is critical. You have only seconds to identify them in time to track course and launch interception," informed Folette, as he flashed up a screen that showed numerous airborne targets, each tagged with an identification code. "Nearly all of these will be commercial aircraft emitting their own unique identification signal. If I interrogate, say this one," he said pointing to a red cross on the screen with a code alongside it, "I will be given flight number, speed, course, route and aircraft type instantly."

"Very impressive, it operates in a very similar way to the AIS radar on my boat that picks up nearby shipping. A good spin-off for the yachtsman that is, provided you don't rely on it too much," replied Vaughan.

"You mean picking up the vessels not issuing AIS signals."

"Exactly."

Leaving the fighting nerve centre of the ship, they climbed up several deck levels to the flight deck. There the sense of exposure was instant. "A windy place this I imagine when she is up to cruising speed," said Vaughan.

"Yes, a very hostile environment for those whose duties require them to be out here in all weathers," replied the lieutenant commander. "Even on a sunny day this place is no picnic spot when we are at sea. By the way, there's your yacht's cradle parked up against the superstructure." They walked across and Vaughan inspected it.

"Very good, looks more than strong enough to do the job."

They then walked round to the starboard side crane that would be used to put Vaughan's yacht back into the water. "It's a lot bigger than it looks from the dockside," said Vaughan, as he assessed the length of the jib.

"Whilst we are alone out here would you mind telling me if there is any chance that someone will want to stop you from getting off this ship?" Folette asked.

"No, my job is not that important. Why do you ask?"

"Oh it's just that I want to know if we need to be especially watchful on radar that's all. It's not the big stuff like planes that are the problem, it's the little targets like missiles as I explained earlier. I'm cleared up to STRAP 2 if you need to tell anyone anything should the captain not be available."

"Yes I know you are. I'm sure your normal watch keeping will be more than sufficient whilst I am aboard," Vaughan replied, smiling at the thought of being wanted by an enemy that badly.

Ian Vaughan had also been cleared up to STRAP 2 and had been briefed as to who on board had been cleared, and to what level. Even then one only talked business when the need to know time had arrived.

"Can you point me in the direction of the HRFM?" Vaughan asked.

"Certainly, this way. Do you need to make contact with anyone now?"

"No, but I may during the voyage, and I would like people to think that I know my way around."

"Of course, I understand. Strangers asking directions create curiosity and speculation."

After leaving the ship Folette drove Vaughan back to the gatehouse. "Do you want them to phone for a taxi?" he asked.

"No thanks, I have a lot to think about, I'll walk back, the exercise will help to clear my mind," replied Vaughan, really wanting the open air and space around him to throw off the claustrophobia of the warship.

*

At 0130 hours the following morning Vaughan put *La Mouette* alongside the farewell jetty astern of the aircraft carrier. In moments two sailors descended quayside ladders to pick up the yacht's lines and carry them up to those waiting above. Returning to the yacht's deck they took over the guiding of the lifting strops, checking with Vaughan the exact points for lifting. Five minutes later the yacht was being lifted clear of the water and swung over the flight deck and onto the waiting cradle. After the frame support arms had been adjusted and timber wedges tapped in to spread the keel load area, Vaughan was invited to climb down and check that he was satisfied before the strops were removed.

"Excellent, Commander, have you done this many times before?" asked Vaughan.

"No, but Leading Seaman Duncan over there has. His parents run a boatyard on the East Coast."

Vaughan, catching the eye of Duncan, gave him the thumbs up then backed away as the Carrier's tractor unit started to tow the trailer forward to the aft lift platform, with Duncan walking alongside, anxiously checking that the castors were taking the load.

Watching the yacht slowly disappear down into the hanger was a rather strange experience. Looking down from the flight deck, Vaughan was very impressed with the way Duncan used red tape to mark the rigging's bottle screw threads and checked the mast rake before starting the process of removing the mast. When he saw the care that Duncan took as the mast was withdrawn and hoisted onto the flight deck, Vaughan's earlier fears were dispelled.

Like the trailer, the tarpaulin canopy was well designed, and spread over a plastic pipe frame that prevented the canopy snagging on the yacht's deck stanchions. The final touches were to prop and brace the yacht to points on the Carrier's hanger deck and bulkhead to prevent it toppling in a rough sea, and to firmly chock the trailer's wheels.

Looking about him, Vaughan realised that the operation had been conducted with only five of the ship's personnel involved. Even the hanger had been deserted when the deck lift descended.

In company with Commander Howard, Vaughan made his way back along the flight deck, into the ship's superstructure and down two deck levels before passing the wardroom on his way to the flag officer's quarters.

Entering the cabin Vaughan was taken aback.

"Good morning, Vaughan."

"Good heavens. Good morning, Commodore, I didn't expect to see you here."

"Just a final briefing before you set off," said Campbell. "But first of all this document."

Vaughan took the envelope and opened it, inside was his 'decree absolute', the defining end to his marriage. Vaughan sat on his bunk staring at the opposite wall with a feeling of desperate sadness, with the realisation that the woman he still loved had actually pursued divorce proceedings to the bitter end in just short of five months.

Campbell waited for some time to allow Vaughan to collect his thoughts before interrupting him. "I'm sorry Vaughan that it worked out like this; Caroline also sends her regrets to you, she has visited your wife several times, but was unable to counter the influence of Mrs Johnson-Lacey."

"In the face of that bitch there was little anyone could do, even Sarah's parents came round to understanding my situation and tried to talk her out of this divorce, but she wouldn't listen. At least I have reasonable access to the girls so hopefully all is not lost. Financially it's been damned unfair though, despite the work of Colin Dewar."

"Have you seen your daughters recently?"

"I went up the weekend before last and spent a couple of days with them in the Lake District. They seem very confused by it all."

"I'm sure they are. Anyway, I'm sorry I must get on," said Campbell looking at his watch. "You'll be underway in an hour and I need to give you the latest intelligence we have regarding Walid al Djebbar and Al Bashir."

"Yes of course, go ahead."

"Al Djebbar's team have arranged a charter flight to get them to Madeira and have arranged for an American security firm to provide protection at the venue, much to the annoyance of the Portuguese Authorities. It goes under the name of 'Total Cover Security' and has provided protection for a number of congressmen and political events that don't involve the President and senior politicians over there. In fact they have a good track record and employ several retired FBI and CIA men, plus the usual front muscle."

"Is the venue fixed?"

"Yes, they are taking over the east tower of the Vidamar Hotel, which is an elegant five star hotel with an excellent conference centre within its grounds, only twenty yards from the hotel's main entrance; from the security point of view it could hardly be any better. The security team move in there next Monday week and from past experience of these outfits the hotel staff will be run ragged with demands for security cameras and lights," said the Commodore, with a chuckle.

Vaughan smiled with the knowledge that if UK security services had been used the effects would have been much the same.

"Any news of this guy Al Bashir?"

"Yes, he is currently in southern Libya recruiting, in company with another extremist cleric who has appeared from Iran, called Mohammed al Ben Said. He has spent some time in Mali and in particular Timbuktu where for some time virtual sharia law reigned. They are being closely watched, but bearing in mind their location and the cross-border movement available to them, the Libyan authorities can't guarantee to keep tabs on them. This photograph is of Al Ben Said, when you've studied it sufficiently to recognise him, destroy it."

"Allsopp-Stevenson mentioned Russian interests."

"Yes, the two you know of, Sarkis Kazakov and Ulan Reshetnikov, who reside on the island, have been joined recently by a negotiator from STATGAZ called Gleb Smetanin. He is a high-level, backroom wheeler-dealer who has been part of the Russian team that regularly visits Algeria. Quite why he is talking with Kazakov and Reshetnikov is something of a mystery, we would like to know much more of what the discussion is about. Kazakov has, as you know, been linked to arms' dealings and Reshetnikov was purely a thug that made money from buying up steel workers' shares on the cheap. The thing that foxes us at the moment is why a Russian gas field development company is in contact with two minor oligarchs. It seems to us to be very much against their interests to try and derail the talks, especially as they are already well established in Algeria."

"Would they want to keep the borders with the rest of Africa demilitarised in order to maintain the illegal immigration issue with Europe as a block to further diplomatic and economic ties?" asked Vaughan. "Or maybe they are as interested as we are in keeping Al Djebbar's dream alive."

"We just don't know and that is what we would like you to try and find out. Two of our technical staff are on board your yacht at the moment, delivering some listening equipment for your use and some kit for Claremont which you are to deliver. Here's the address and phone number of an apartment we have rented for his use, his cover is that his house is being completely redecorated. There are also a few other tools of your new trade that you may find useful. It will be very obvious what they are for and all of them were introduced to you at 'The Manor'."

"How do I make the delivery to Claremont?"

"Contact him by phone and arrange for a street exchange, he will know what that is about."

"Does the other kit include any upgrade of radio communications?"

"No, if anyone with any knowledge got on board it would be pretty obvious that such a radio was not the normal yachtsman's kit."

"How do you want me to keep in touch?"

"Through the British Consul. She has a 'bullet-proof' hard-wired system that, since the closure of the Consular Office in town, she operates from her private address."

"Does she know I'm coming?"

"Oh yes, she has been informed. Only make personal contact if you need to use the secure phone line; coded email reports on a memory stick enveloped and dropped through her letter box should suffice for this op, alright?" said Campbell, standing in preparation to leave. Vaughan nodded his understanding. "By the way, I will be taking some time off whilst you are in Madeira, but we are sending Leonard Staunton to Lisbon to act as liaison. Sir

Andrew Averrille put him in charge of this one, he will convey your reports to Sir Andrew direct." The Commodore's voice had a decidedly sour edge to it.

So that was it, thought Vaughan. *That was what you were faffing about the other day, but I bet it hadn't been finally decided at that point. Your tone, Commodore, suggests that you didn't want this Staunton character in on this, not one of your team I suspect. Does that mean that I am?*

There was long silence in which Campbell was deciding how much of his doubts regarding Staunton he should reveal to Vaughan. Past experience led him to believe Vaughan to be totally trustworthy, but this matter was very delicate indeed.

"Apparently Staunton has other tasks in Lisbon that he is required to attend to in connection with an operation we conducted in Angola," Campbell explained. An image of young Patterson's mutilated remains flashed across his mind. "Should you need his direct support he will be close at hand. He also speaks perfect Portuguese."

Vaughan had been studying the Commodore's face and listening very carefully to what the man said. *There's that tone again, that sour edge to his voice.*

"Oh, I see, sir, hopefully I won't need to pull him away from this other work of his." *I don't think Campbell believes that Staunton's presence in Lisbon is really necessary for this Angola business and I'm sure he doesn't want him involved with the conference. It's not my concern though, so best leave well alone. There is something to do with that Angola op though, that has the Commodore concerned.*

*

Six hours later Commodore Campbell was sat at his desk reading a CIA briefing on Russian infiltration into European and American political circles, when there was a knock on his door and Sir Andrew Averrille came in.

"Don't get up, Alec, I understand that you've been up all night seeing your protégé off from Pompey."

"Good morning, Sir Andrew. Yes, all sorted and underway. He seems to fully grasp the situation and what he is required to do."

"I hope you are right, Alec. As you know, I think you are taking a hell of a risk sending someone with such limited experience in on this one. The game has changed considerably since Vaughan joined us."

"It is exactly the unorthodox approach that I think will work. Walid al Djebbar is no stranger to our world, and would sense one of our, so called, 'trusted hands' in seconds. Vaughan is very different and still retains that open honest persona that years in this game sadly destroys."

"Did you go down to 'The Manor' to monitor any of his training?" asked Sir Andrew.

"Yes, Lieutenant Heathcote and I spent several hours there early on in his course and were very impressed by the reports received. We watched, on the monitor, one of Adrian Creswell's disguise sessions, it was quite amusing. Since then there has been nothing but praise for Vaughan's effort and aptitude."

"Alright, I'll let you get on. You are sure that you don't want to abort this one and send Staunton to Madeira instead?"

"Yes, Sir Andrew, I am quite sure," replied Campbell firmly.

"Good, that is all I need to know."

*

With a police launch leading the way and an Admiralty tug keeping the bowline just slack, *HMS Illustrious* glided past the old signal tower and through the harbour entrance into the Solent. Following the deep-water channel she weaved around Spitsand Fort having dropped her bowline from the lead tug. At that time of day the Solent was almost deserted, with only a few fishing boats at work, their attendant gulls crying, pleading for a share of the catch. Ian Vaughan stood on the short upper deck just aft of the bridge structure looking across at the Isle of Wight glinting like a jewel in the early morning sunshine, every detail clearly defined as if some magical power had enlarged the view and brought it into sharp focus. Crossing to the flight deck side he looked down at the Apache and Merlin helicopters in neat lines, with their rotors and wheels anchored to the deck. Small groups of 'off duty' sailors, reluctant to leave their saluting stations stood staring at Southsea seafront, no doubt thinking of loved ones left behind.

Glancing at his watch, Vaughan noted that his activity session was finished and rest period due. He had chosen to divide his time afloat into twenty minute 'on watch' and twenty minute 'off watch' periods. This would ensure that when on board the yacht he would see other vessels in time to take avoiding action should that be necessary. The time spent on board the carrier would allow him to train his body to accept the routine. Hurriedly he went down to his cabin and, lying on the bunk, closed his eyes, trying hard to block out the sound of shipboard activity outside. It would be days before the ship's tannoy messages ceased to disturb his sleeping segments.

Twenty minutes later he walked into the officers' dining room, forward of the wardroom, and with the minimum of verbal contact walked out again with his breakfast on a tray. After the meal he rested in his cabin again for twenty minutes before returning to the deck as they were passing the Isle of Wight towns of Sandown and Ventnor, *HMS Illustrious* now up to her full cruising speed.

After the first two days his arduous routine became a little easier thanks to his prior planning of each activity session. During the hours of darkness he remained in his cabin writing up the fictitious passage log, whilst during daylight hours his activity slots were mainly 'The Manor' fitness programme and, when possible, sunbathing. As promised, the officers and crew refrained from engaging him in conversation, and it was only when he collected food that words were exchanged with anyone. The mixed weather had fortunately not interfered with the Carrier's progress and on the evening of the third day, work started in preparation to lower *La Mouette sur le Vent* over the side.

"They are ready for you now, sir," said Second Lieutenant Rush, putting his head around Vaughan's cabin door.

"Thanks, I'll be right with you."

The two men walked in silence to the flight deck and forward to where the yacht stood, on its trailer, with the lifting frame suspended above, holding the strops in place, and Leading Seaman Duncan fussing around checking that everything was in order.

The Carrier had glided to a standstill, broadside to what little wind there was in order to shelter the yacht's immersion. Lieutenant Commander Folette, Commander Howard and the Second Lieutenant were the only officers on the flight deck. A seaman stood near to the ladder that was leant against the yacht's hull in readiness for Vaughan's boarding.

"Before we started unwrapping your yacht I instigated 'River City State One' which effectively prevents any use of personal communication with the outside world. We will hold that state for a period after you have left us," explained Folette. I checked in the ops room before coming up here and saw only one radar contact, and she is ten miles away to the west, the *Aida Sol* cruise ship bound for the Canaries."

"Thank you, Lieutenant Commander," Vaughan replied, suddenly feeling nervous about what was to come.

"Good luck for whatever it is you are doing. I trust we looked after you well enough," said Folette, shaking Vaughan's hand. "Let us know if you want a lift back."

"Thank you, if you see a scruffy bloke on the quayside in Gib thumbing a lift, it'll be me."

"We shall wait until you are twenty metres or so away before we get going. We don't want to scratch that shiny hull of yours," said Commander Howard.

"Thank you, Commander, I would appreciate that," replied Vaughan, as the Commander steered Vaughan towards Leading Seaman Duncan.

"Many thanks, Duncan," said Vaughan, warmly. "You took all the stress away from me; I was getting very worried for her being lifted out and now this tricky bit of work."

"Oh no problem, sir. Now remember, start the engine as soon as she is in the drink. I've opened the engine seacock ready, then go below and get all of the air out of the stern gland; after that give those two lads up there on the frame a wave, and they will drop off the strops and we can lift 'em clear, alright."

Vaughan shook Duncan's hand and smiled. "That's great, Duncan, and thanks for the reminder about the stern gland."

"It's easy to forget things like that at launching."

After a quick wave to the onlookers Vaughan climbed the ladder and stepped aboard his pride and joy. Hurriedly he went below and stowed his kitbag in the forward cabin, before coming back into the cockpit as the Carrier's crane lifted the yacht clear of the cradle and swung it gently over the side. It was a strange sensation as he watched the dark hull of the Carrier towering higher and higher above him. He could hear the radio instructions being passed between one of the men sat on the lift frame and the crane operator.

"Down, down, down a bit more. Hold it there, Jacko, she's in."

Vaughan reached for the ignition and turned it on and waited for the diesel heater coil light to go out before turning the key further to be rewarded by the sound of the engine firing up and running smoothly. Going below he crawled head first into the quarter berth tunnel and opened the side hatch that gave access to the propeller shaft and stern gland. Using a screwdriver he loosened the Phillips clip around the stern gland and squeezed the body of the gland with both hands, then slowly easing off until the trapped air was expelled and water started to trickle out. Tightening the Phillips clip again he checked that the water had stopped coming in and quickly shuffled back into the main cabin, then climbing the companionway steps up into the cockpit gave the signal for the strops to be released. Almost instantly two splashes were heard and the order for the crane to lift the frame and strops clear was given.

Easing the throttle lever forward, Vaughan felt the gears engage and sensed *La Mouette* moving gently forward before he steered her clear of the Carrier's side. High up on the Carrier's bridge they let the yacht get well clear before getting underway again; the rumble of the great ship's engines hardly heard by Vaughan as he stood watching her dark shape get slowly swallowed up in the blackness of the night until only her stern light was evidence of her presence.

The breeze was hardly enough to push the yacht along and Vaughan was tempted to hoist the spinnaker, but settled instead for the cruising chute and full mainsail. As it was his first night aboard the yacht, following his lone sailor's routine, he decided to take his rest periods in the cockpit, rather than go below and trust purely on the autohelm to maintain the course. The northerly breeze meant that the yacht was on a fine broad reach with what wind there was coming over the starboard quarter. The breeze increased with the coming of the dawn, and with it a great improvement in the yacht's progress. Porridge for breakfast and a cup of black coffee filled the activity slot and for the first time Vaughan followed this with a rest below deck. When the AIS alarm woke him he was surprised to find that he had actually slept beyond his twenty minute slot, a sign he was more exhausted than he thought. Rushing up into the cockpit he hurriedly searched the horizon and saw a Royal Navy Type 45 Destroyer some two miles off his port bow, the 'tail-end Charlie' of *HMS Illustrious*'s protection screen. Modern weapons travel so fast that no longer do escorts keep in sight of the ship they are protecting.

The sighting though, of a vessel that close shocked him, obviously the alarm had been sounding for sometime before it interrupted his sleep. This had meant that a further ten minutes or so had passed in which time the destroyer had come over Vaughan's visual horizon and got far too close for comfort; a rude awakening indeed.

Going forward, he checked that the mainsail was not in contact with the mast spreaders and that the anchor was still secure on the stemhead with its locking pin in place. The wind was beginning to pick up and Vaughan planned to put a reef in the mainsail during the next activity period. Returning to the cabin, he lifted a floor panel to see if there was any water in the bilges. What small amount had come aboard as he de-aired the stern gland had been mopped up hours ago, and he was relieved to see that all was still dry. Finally he checked his position and entered up the log before another check for shipping, and making a small alteration in course. As he did so a great sense of loneliness suddenly consumed him, and a feeling of almost fear of this voyage and the unknown world of political intrigue he was about to enter. His orders so vague, so reliant on his ability to befriend this Walid al Djebbar and obtain the information London apparently needed, were a completely new experience. Never in his previous engineering career was he ever in a position of having to improvise conversation with each person he met. Even actors have a script to follow; he would have to make his up as he went along, with only this vague cover story and set of instructions to follow. Unable to even consider sleep, after the shock of having overlaid, he stretched out along the cockpit portside bench staring at the fair weather clouds overhead, now pondering on his immediate future.

It was the exercise involved in reefing the mainsail that shook him out of his sense of despondency. The task had gone well and actually improved the yacht's speed through the water. So many times he had been onboard yachts where the sails were over pressed and the rudder angle so off the centre line that it acted as a brake.

Suddenly, alongside, a dolphin broke the surface, then another. Vaughan went onto the side deck and clapped his hands to attract them back, to be delighted on watching the pair play 'chicken' with the yacht's bow as they raced past several times, their backs just clearing the surface of the sea. When the show was over he went below for his next rest period, no longer feeling completely alone.

CHAPTER 3
SHADOWS FORM

As Ian Vaughan adjusted his course out in the Atlantic, Al Bashir and Al Ben Said left their growing group of followers at Oatrun, a small town north of the Libyan/ Niger border, and headed south, successfully outrunning the security team who had been dogging their steps for the last month. Just over the border in Niger, on a deserted airstrip, they met, as planned, Abdelmalek Takkal, the professional assassin they had hired. His price of one million US dollars for the assassination of Al Djebbar included the air transport, starting with him flying them across the border with Mali to another deserted airstrip at Tessalit. After a difficult landing they waited overnight, sleeping under the wings of the plane, for the fuel truck. In the morning Al Bashir and Al Ben Said prayed together, watched over by Takkal, himself not the holiest of men. Six hours passed before a column of dust heralded the arrival of the vehicle, a dilapidated American Dodge fuel truck, which should have been presented to a museum two decades ago. With a blown exhaust system significantly reducing its power, the truck wheezed to a stop, close enough to the aircraft for the leaky fuel hose to reach the filler cap. Two men got out, one, a member of Takkal's organisation, the other the tanker driver. After greeting Takkal, his man, ignoring both Al Bashir and Al Ben Said, turned to help the wizened old tanker driver pump the fuel from the truck into the aircraft's tanks. As they worked the old man cackled away as old men do, complaining about the changes in the modern world. When the aircraft's tanks were full the old man disconnected the hose and hauled it towards the truck.

"Excuse please, Al Bashir, your clothes must not be stained," said the old man, hesitating to throw the trailing end of the hose onto the side rack of the fuel truck.

Al Bashir nodded and retreated a few yards.

Trained assassins are rarely risk takers and it was Takkal who insisted that they pushed the plane a long way down the runway, away from the fuel spillage, before the truck driver started up the truck to drive away.

"How well do you know that man?" asked Takkal, looking at his assistant and pointing at the fuel truck.

The man shrugged and pursed his lips, indicating that he knew him, but not well.

"Well say goodbye to him," said Takkal as he raised a rifle and fired several rounds at the truck as it started back down the track from which it had come. Empty fuel cans are more dangerous than full ones and empty high-octane fuel trucks are even more so. Villagers heard the explosion eight miles away, and the blast made the four men near the aircraft stagger back several paces, and the aircraft rock violently.

"Why?" Al Bashir asked, visibly shaken by what had happened.

Takkal turned to him and said coldly, "Did you not hear him? He called you by name; he knew who you were. He could have talked."

During the onward flight to the Moroccan airport of Moulay Ali Cherif hardly anyone spoke. Except for Takkal, the others were coming to terms with the deadly nature of their mission. Al Bashir and Al Ben Said were determined that the liberalisation of North Africa and the possible Europeanisation of its culture were to be stopped at all costs, however, both were troubled by the way innocent believers like the old driver were being sacrificed. As shocking as it was, however, both clerics eventually concluded that Takkal was probably right in what he did. Their task was too important to risk even the slightest hint of their movements being discovered and they again being pursued as they were in Libya.

Takkal brought the little aircraft into land at Moulay Ali Cherif with hardly a bump, making the approach without the need to over fly three times to check that it was a runway they were touching down on as they had the previous evening.

The airport officials accepted without question the false documents arranged by Takkal. None recognised Al Bashir or Al Ben Said even though their photographs were stuck to the edge of the police desktop. They hired two taxis to get them to a mosque on the western side of the town where Takkal's man had arranged safe accommodation. The town, which stood in a lush valley below a large reservoir, impressed Al Bashir. They passed between numerous fields of crops surrounded by trees, with irrigation waterways creating a localised humidity; so different from the parched deserts over which they had recently travelled.

In the morning, after prayers at the mosque, Takkal met the two clerics in the Nissan Pathfinder four-by-four he had arranged, in which they would complete their journey to the ancient coastal town of Essaouira.

"Where is your man this morning?"

"He takes my plane back to where I live."

"Where is that?" asked Al Bashir, with just mild interest.

"My home."

Al Bashir smiled at Takkal's response. "You have great trust in him."

"He has reason to have great fear of me," Takkal replied, his statement, matter of fact.

The port of Essaouira on the Atlantic coast of Morocco, due west of Marrakech, is one of the most fascinating and photogenic ports on the African coast. Around the harbour, clusters the old fortified town where ancient cannons defiantly pierce the castellated city walls. To the north the Atlantic batters the ancient stonework and sea defences, whilst to the south the offshore nature reserve of Ile de Mogador, that lies just over a mile off the town's long crescent beach, offers a little protection from the ocean's wrath. At the northernmost point of the bay is the port itself, nestled behind a sweeping defensive sea wall with its entrance facing due south into the bay. During the day the harbour is crowded with small, blue painted inshore fishing boats rafted together like rowing boats on an English lake waiting for leisure hire. The deeper water provides space for ancient wooden-hulled fishing vessels of a design typical of that coast, with high prows, smoking diesel engines and curious foremasts surmounted by small crows' nests. Amongst these ancient craft more modern deep-sea fishing vessels lie, a product of the Moroccan/European Union fishing agreement, now a source of much hostility. The waters along the coast of Morocco were once teeming with sardine and tuna, but as a result of the uncontrolled poaching and poorly defined agreement on quotas, fish stocks were now seriously endangered.

Al Bashir and his companions arrived in the town in the early morning having driven day and night in order to keep on the move between safe houses. The host for their stay was himself a fisherman and devout Muslim who, with his son, worked one of the ancient deep-sea craft. Takkal confidently drove through the city to the old port where they sat in wait for Efraim al Filastenee's boat to return to port.

Not for the first time, Al Bashir studied the assassin as the man dozed, his head resting against the vehicle's door pillar. He was lean and surprisingly ordinary in looks without any remarkable feature in either his face or build. One could pass him in the street without affording him a second glance, or consider him worthy to stop and seek directions. In fact he was the ideal assassin who would pass unnoticed, as he had so often done in Jerusalem, Cairo, Beirut, Paris and even New York. Al Bashir had quickly learnt that Takkal held neither religious nor political beliefs and would take contracts regardless of gender or age of the victim. To speak with him was as if one was talking to a man already dead with neither feeling nor emotion.

The snoring to his right switched Al Bashir's study to his religious companion. Large in build, with small piggy eyes set in a fat pockmarked heavily bearded face, this man drew attention wherever he was. Extreme in his beliefs and persuasive in his preaching he represented the ultimate prophet of sharia law. In Essaouira, Al Ben Said could easily have found new converts to his messages of hate and stricture of belief, for the town was in fact two towns. One, the old and poor traditional, with its fishing port and local market place, the other the modern, rich, touristy, expensive western retail and industrialised. Whilst the tourist gift shops in the hotels and smart main street shops made enormous profits from the craft items they sold, the local craftsmen fashioning intricate carvings and excellent lacquer work struggled to survive in the markets and street stalls. French colonial influence still persisted, backed by many western television programmes that were seducing the young into following ever more western ways. It was possible that these influences, combined with the apparent injustices of the fishing agreement and other sharp western business practices, could be the catalyst that turned the country back to a fundamentalist Islamic state. Fortunately for Morocco, Mohammed al Ben Said's stay would be short.

They had paid five dirham to a street urchin who was begging for fish from the boats as they came in, to tell them when Efraim al Filastenee's boat returned and Al Bashir was pleased to see the boy waving excitedly and pointing to the latest arrival.

"He is here," Al Bashir announced.

Takkal was instantly awake as if he had all the time been feigning sleep, whilst Al Ben Said mumbled and yawned before reluctantly stretching and, opening one eye, said, "I have not heard the imam calling the faithful to prayer."

"Nor will you for almost another hour. It is the arrival of our host that starts this day," replied Al Bashir.

The greeting was brief, as the fisherman needed to sell his catch before the traders had filled their trucks and departed. Agreeing to return again in two hours the three men started to make their way towards the Ben Youssef mosque on the Avenue Oqba Ibn Nafiaa. They had not walked far before Takkal stopped them.

"This is as far as we travel together today," he said. "You two must not be seen together, so if you wish to pray, go to separate mosques. I will take a leisurely meal in that café across the square, when I see you walk back to the port I will follow you."

Al Bashir looked surprised. "No one here knows who we are surely?"

"Did you not see your pictures on the desk at the airport?" replied Takkal. "The two idiots checking our papers must have been blind as well as stupid."

Al Ben Said looked about him nervously. "You are sure they were pictures of us?"

"Very sure," said Takkal. "Alone, only one of you risks being arrested, together who knows what will happen to your plan." There was a pause whilst Al Bashir and Al Ben Said digested Takkal's words. "Walk in the shadows my friends and hide in the crowds, on no account leave the mosque by the same entrance you went in," continued Takkal, before he turned and walked away across the Place Mouley Hassan.

*

Ibrahim el Gharbi was lent against the corner of a building opposite the Mosque Sidi Ahmed as Al Ben Said approached. He did not pick him up at first as Al Ben Said was walking with his head bent down looking at the ground only a few feet in front of him with his shoulders hunched relying purely on the call of the imam to direct his steps. Nearing the mosque, and with the sound of the call to prayer all around him, Al Ben Said had raised his head to check his bearings and in the process exposed his face to El Gharbi. Even then, the agent from the Directorate of Surveillance Territorial (DST) only showed vague recognition. The problem was that he was not expecting anyone on his list to arrive on foot. Reaching into his jacket pocket he retrieved a small booklet of photographs and started to flick through them. He had actually passed the picture of Al Ben Said before his brain connected the two images. He looked back across the street but the man had gone, probably into the main street entrance to the mosque. Aware of the recent directive to take care when pursuing suspects who have entered such holy places, El Gharbi entered the mosque like the other worshipers. As he approached the doors he began the ritual of entry, aware now, that the mosque was crowded with the faithful.

Knelt towards the rear of the mosque El Gharbi picked out Al Ben Said several rows in front of him and as the worship continued he became more confident that his suspicions were correct and the man he was looking at, whenever the opportunity permitted, was in fact the radical cleric Mohammed al Ben Said.

Immediately the prayers ended El Gharbi left the mosque to wait at the foot of the steps as if waiting for someone with whom he had an appointment. Two minutes passed then five minutes and with that the realisation that Al Ben Said had left by a different route.

Taking his mobile from his pocket he angrily punched in a number then put the phone to his ear and, as the call was answered, said. "This is El Gharbi put me through to Abdul el Najid."

The phoned clicked a few times then a gruff voice said, "El Gharbi, what's up?"

"I have just seen that cleric Mohammed al Ben Said boss. He was at prayers in the Mosque Sidi Ahmed."

"Where is he now?" El Najid asked.

"I don't know boss, he gave me the slip in the crowd leaving the mosque."

"Well find him again," shouted El Najid. "I will send some men to help you. Where are you now?"

*

After two glasses of mint tea Takkal had switched to mineral water and was just finishing the glassful when he saw Al Bashir hurriedly crossing the square in the direction of the harbour. Ten minutes passed before he sighted Al Ben Said hugging the shadows, his head lowered and shoulders drawn up, rounding the corner leading to the port's ancient gateway. Takkal was about to follow when a grey Peugeot pulled up at the entrance to the square alongside the café. One look was enough to tell Takkal that the occupants were DST personnel and that they were on the lookout for someone. Draining his glass, he placed a fifty dirham note in the saucer with the tab and strolled as nonchalantly as he could manage across the square and along the street to the port gate.

"One of you has been identified," said Takkal, as he climbed into the Nissan. "You," he said to Al Ben Said. "Get down on the floor while I cover you over, and you," he said looking at Al Bashir, "put on those sunglasses and make it look as if you are talking to somebody on this mobile phone. Do not make eye contact with anyone passing this car."

With Al Ben Said hidden and Al Bashir looking and sounding like a tourist describing to a friend the wonders of Morocco, Takkal slipped away across the car park to the quay and Efraim al Filastenee's boat. Within twenty minutes both fugitives had been smuggled aboard the boat without raising so much as a second glance from those working on the quayside and decks. Having hidden his employers in a space in the fish hold beneath a stack of stinking crates and net buoys, Takkal, following directions from Al Filastenee's son, drove to the fisherman's house and, with the son's help, offloaded the luggage before parking the car several streets away. Returning to the house he was again greeted by the son who took satisfaction in ordering his sister to bring tea and food for their guest. Giving her brother a rebellious glare the girl reluctantly complied, shuffling from the room muttering. Al Filastenee's daughter, with her desires to break away from the traditions of her people, was one of the main reasons for the old fisherman to wish for more fundamental adherence to the rule of Islam. Takkal had noted the girl's reaction and watching the boy, as he assumed his father's chair, wondered what the old fisherman would do if he were to walk into the room now.

"Will you follow your father and become a fisherman with your own boat?" Takkal asked, in an effort to make conversation.

"Huh no, I want to buy a truck and buy the fish from here to sell in Marrakech. Traders make big profit with hotels there, one man he say I buy his truck when he retires. He tell me he is ready to retire and he not more than forty years of age."

Takkal nodded, knowing only too well that the truck driver could see a fool when he met one. "Sounds a good plan but take my advice; check whether other traders are so rich they can retire."

"I trust Jammal, he is good strong man and very shrewd trader."

"Then do not just buy his truck. Make sure you buy his business as well. Contacts are the most important thing in business," said Takkal, wondering why he was wasting his time on giving advice.

The tea arrived with bread and a dish of hummus encircled by olive oil. The girl poured the tea and with her back to her brother presented a glassful to Takkal, awarding him a sultry pout followed by a suggestive smile. Takkal leant slightly to his right so that the girl's body shielded him from her brother's gaze and, returning the smile, winked. She reminded him of a girl he had met in Riyadh who had also been desperate to escape a servile future. He had used her for a week before selling her to a brothel in Istanbul. Strange that he should recall her now, after all this time.

It was close to midnight when Takkal and Al Filastenee rescued their employers from their stinking hideout in the fishing boat's hold. Taking them each by different routes back to the fisherman's humble home, Takkal was pleased to learn that Al Ben Said's return journey to Libya had been brought forward and that he would be leaving in just a few hours. The thought of the radical cleric staying for any length of time in Morocco had been a source of some concern to the careful Takkal.

When Al Filastenee's brother arrived to take Al Ben Said south to the border, the cleric spent much time in haranguing the group and the fisherman's household with his message of hatred towards all non-believers before leading them all in prayer. Takkal for once enjoyed a religious occasion having positioned himself slightly behind and to one side of Shada, Al Filastenee's daughter, who showed no objection or resistance to his fondling of her buttocks whilst the rest of the group's attention was focused on the cleric. In the confusion of Al Ben Said's departure Shada disappeared from the group into the kitchen, before Takkal could suggest a place where they could meet alone.

In the heat by the charcoal oven, she stood, breathing heavily, her heart racing, as she tried to analyse her own reactions to his touching her. Was it a caress or just a lustful grope; without seeing his face and looking into his eyes she could not decide. The only thing she could do was to meet with him again, alone, but with her father and mother always watching her, how could that happen.

Frustratingly for Takkal, Al Bashir kept him busy throughout the day discussing their preparation for the voyage and his plans for the assassination.

"My contract was to deliver us to this place, how are we to enter Madeira?" asked Takkal, unaware of the details of the final link in their journey.

"Al Filastenee is to take us to the eastern shore of the Desertas Islands where we will land and wait one, maybe two, days. He has no knowledge of our mission; he believes we are trying to escape arrest. Then we will be collected by a loyal supporter in his boat and taken undercover of darkness to Madeira where more friends wait for us."

"Why did you not tell me that we were to risk our lives aboard that wreck of a boat not fit to float on a puddle of camel piss, let alone make an ocean crossing?" asked Takkal, angrily.

"Calm yourself my friend, to have told you during the journey here when at anytime we could have been identified, arrested and questioned would not have been wise," replied Al Bashir calmly. "Many lives other than yours and mine depend upon the secrecy of our plans. Also believe that Al Filastenee's boat is sound. He has helped many of the faithful safely onto European shores."

Takkal grunted and shook his head. "I have studied the plans and the photographs of the hotel and conference centre. I also flew there and saw for myself and know that the only place from where I can take him out is from the roof above the restaurant over the conference centre itself. Why did you not use one of your many followers anxious to become martyrs and infiltrate them into the mission?"

"Because the blame must not be laid at the door of Islam," replied Al Bashir. "Besides such a method has high risk of discovery and infiltration takes much time."

"If this is to be seen as political, why do you risk to join with me on the contract? Surely if both of us are caught, your presence will ensure that Islam and the Taliban will be blamed," questioned Takkal.

"I must make contact with those politicians who see Al Djebbar as a western influence working against our culture and beliefs. In addition I must persuade certain Russian interests that their investment is safe," informed Al Bashir, defensively.

So the discussions continued throughout the day, covering every detail of Takkal's plan. He had already decided not to stay in Funchal, but to use a house overlooking the village of Boaventura. There he would be able to assemble and test the rifle he had designed and ordered from five workshops spread from

Paris to Naples via Frankfurt. Based on an RPA Highlander barrel, painstakingly checked for bore alignment and accuracy by an engineer at a scientific engineering firm's workshops in Cologne, the gun's parts were shipped individually to Sarkis Kazakov who was to keep the parts hidden remote from his house and safe from prying eyes.

"You are sure that this Russian Reshetnikov will not spread word of your arrival?" asked Takkal.

"Yes, we will pay him enough for his assistance in our contact with the STATGAZ man," responded Al Bashir testily. "Everything has a high price when you are dealing with heathens."

"Does he know of the assassination plan?"

"Of course not!" Al Bashir replied angrily. "Do you think we are stupid?"

"I will choose my timing to take up position," said Takkal, ignoring Al Bashir's reaction to his question. "It is a tourist complex and many people are around late into the night. No one must see me get onto that roof."

"Of course, but you must make the hit on the morning of the third day, is that clear. You are also being very well paid for your work."

"It would be better if you knew his room number. That is a much safer place to deal with him."

"We believe only one man knows that information and he is still in America," replied Al Bashir. "He is person in charge of this conference security, an ex-FBI man we are told. Anyway, Al Djebbar's assassination must attract the maximum world attention and be very public."

"Yes," replied Takkal. "Right outside the hotel, a place where there would be maximum security."

Takkal leant back against the wall of the courtyard where they were standing. "When does this security man arrive in Madeira?"

"In three days, in fact one week before the conference is due to start."

"Can we not get to him in that time?" asked Takkal.

"Too much risk, he would expose any contact requesting room numbers, even if we said we were delivering flowers for Al Djebbar."

Takkal shook his head and looked glumly at the ground.

Al Bashir could see the doubts forming in Takkal's mind and feared that the backup plan that had long been in place would be needed. Now the question was, should he go alone, cancelling the contract with Takkal, and rely only upon Leyla. No, she was too precious to lose but if Takkal walked away from the contract then maybe he would be forced to sacrifice her. In Kabul he had sent several martyrs to their reward in heaven without regret, but Leyla, so beautiful, so young, so desirable, was different. If only Al Ben Said had chosen another, but of course it was the very things about her Al Bashir had found so attractive that had also attracted Al Djebbar and it was that apparent innocence and beauty that would enable Leyla to get close enough.

"You fear that you will not have a safe way out?" asked Al Bashir.

"It will not be simple and is therefore very high risk. I cannot decide until we get there and see how many people pass. Maybe the Russian can supply two men."

"Why would you need two men?"

"Oh just an idea, that is all," answered Takkal, suddenly feeling more confident.

"The time has come for us to leave," said Al Bashir. "Are you ready?"

The question held more meaning than the simple words used.

Takkal returned Al Bashir's questioning look with a cold stare. "Either you or Al Ben Said were seen yesterday by DST. They will still be searching, so you travel with our fishermen in the truck. The DST agents are unlikely to spot you in that. I will follow later by foot."

Al Bashir considered the suggestion carefully, wondering whether Takkal was about to disappear. If he did he would never get another contract, Al Bashir would make sure of that. It would mean sacrificing Leyla though, which would make him very sad.

"Well?"

"Yes, you are right, I will go with the fishermen, but be sure to be at the boat before the hour of eight this evening."

Half an hour later Takkal, standing by the small window in the room he had shared with Al Bashir and the snoring Al Ben Said, watched Shada close the rusty metal gates to the courtyard after the ageing Datsun truck had coughed its way out into the street and head towards the fishing port. Turning from the gate she looked up and saw him smiling down at her. A shiver of excitement, or was it fear, ran through her body as she wondered whether this would be her chance of freedom from her parents' rule, arranged marriage and a life of drudgery. The kitchen was empty, her mother busy in the next room clearing the basins and dishes of the early evening meal, thankful that the guests were leaving. Shada's tiny room was beside that used by her father's guests, at the rear of the small house, and built over the courtyard toilet. As she passed the guest room door, it opened and Takkal stepped out into the corridor taking hold of her left arm above the elbow.

"I think you want to leave this town," he said. "Maybe I can help you."

Shada almost fainted. To dream of freedom was one thing, to actually take that step was for her terrifying. "I do not know," she answered. "Sometimes I yearn to be free to live my life as I wish. To learn to read, to travel, do things without having to ask my father's permission, but I am too scared."

He smiled and with his other hand pulled her round and held her close. "There is no need to be scared. If you came with me I would teach you many things and show you new places." He reached up and gently stroked her cheek before letting his hand descend to her breasts.

Repulsed and frightened she tried to pull away, but he held her too tightly. "No, please let me go."

Suddenly she found herself being spun round and lifted off her feet to be carried into his room, his hand now clamped over her mouth. She struggled and kicked as he pinned her to the bed.

"Shada, where are you? You are never here when you are needed," cried her mother from the kitchen below.

A new fear struck her at the thought of her mother finding her in this man's bedroom, and with a mighty twist of her body she escaped, but only got as far as the doorway before he grabbed her and pinned her against the wall.

"Remember, your only chance of freedom is to use your body. Think about that while I am away," Takkal said in a harsh whisper. "You share your body with me and I will share the world with you."

Letting her go he watched as she scurried to the head of the stairs and, after a terrified glance back at him, disappeared from view. He knew that Shada would not mention what had happened between them. To do so would bring shame on her for allowing even the first touch.

*

Out in the Atlantic Ian Vaughan's progress had been steadily on programme. He had found the routine strenuous and exhausting for the first three days but by day four, with the yacht charging towards the distant island of Porto Santo, hurried along by the north-easterly trade winds, he felt relaxed. How different his voyage and approach to the island had been, he thought, compared to its discoverers, João Gonçalves Zarco and Tristão Vaz Teixeira. Sent by Prince Henry of Portugal in 1418 to explore the Guinea coast of Africa, they had been blown off course by a storm and only by good fortune came across the island haven they immediately named Porto Santo. Whilst they had fought storms, Vaughan had enjoyed sunny days of fair-weather clouds and a quartering wind hovering consistently just over twenty knots. Zarco and Teixeira's voyage had been into the unknown, Vaughan's was to a precise point on the ocean, 33° 02' .7 north, by 16° 15' .5 west; safely south-east of Ilheu de Cima, a small islet close to the main island of Porto Santo.

Checking the compass course of 185° magnetic, Vaughan went below for the next rest session. The yacht's engine mumbling steadily in the background, standing its daily two-hour battery charging duty, did not disturb his powernap and he woke twenty minutes later feeling refreshed. What had appeared to be a cloud formation on the horizon two hours ago, now revealed itself to be the summit of Pico do Facho, the highest point on the island of Porto Santo, rising to over five hundred metres. Carefully he checked his position and line of approach, as it would probably be nightfall by the time he reached the island, and he knew that to run close to the eastern shore was dangerous. Some two miles north-east of the main island is the islet of Ilheu de Fore; without lighthouse or lit marks it would not be seen on a dark night. With the Canary Current running south-westerly, yachts in particular, could be drawn too far west and risk being wrecked.

Throughout the morning the sun's heat was increasing and Vaughan, for the first time, rigged the bimmi canopy to shade his helming position. At seven in the evening he reached the waypoint, altered course, and two hours later motored into the western small craft anchorage, from where he had a good view of Porto Santo's main town, Vila Baleira, at night. Dropping and setting the anchor, Vaughan went below and breaking the seal on a bottle of single malt whisky, raised a glass in celebration of his arrival. The voyage had been achieved in front of schedule, thanks to favourable winds, but for Vaughan it was an achievement of another sort, that of the lone sailor reaching a safe haven.

In the morning sunshine the little town slowly came to life and Vaughan watched as the few early season tourists sauntered around, some coming down to the beach to bathe in the sea.

Vaughan was about to haul in the anchor and head for Madeira when he remembered his cover story. After taking some photographs and a few soundings he radioed the marina and obtained permission to enter and clear immigration.

Presenting full British registration and insurance, plus his Yacht Master's papers, Vaughan cleared the formalities with the minimum of bureaucratic questioning.

"Are you gonna stay long time 'ere?" asked the marina manager.

"Just two nights," answered Vaughan. "Long enough to sail round the island and make notes for my book."

"You write about our island?"

"Yes, I am trying to encourage more sailors like myself to come and visit here and the rest of the Madeiras." *A good marina only really exposed from the west, water, power, not too expensive and a nice stop between Portugal or Spain and the Canaries,* he thought as he looked about him.

"Ah, thank you, we need many more visitors. Times 'ave been very 'ard for us with bad economy in Europe, eh."

Too early for the main tourist season, Vaughan soon discovered the island to be ideal for those searching for peace and quiet. In the season, things would be very different, but at this time of year it was a desert island in the true sense of the word. Generally quite barren, its inhabitants have little to do when there are no tourists and spend their time enjoying the tranquillity of it all. Lunch in the town and a taxi tour of the island in the afternoon completed the first day's schedule. The following day he circumnavigated the island, taking photographs of the impressive sheer cliffs, witness to its volcanic origins, all the time making notes for his book. Dusk was approaching as he steered the yacht alongside the pontoon and made fast the mooring warps again. The day's sailing, combined with the tranquillity of the island, left him feeling more relaxed and inwardly calm than he had felt for a very long time. Changing from shorts and T-shirt into a shirt and slacks he locked the boat and walked out of the marina and barefoot along the sand to the town. The guidebook had mentioned the island's speciality of Camacho Chicken, and taking a taxi he found a small restaurant in the centre of the village from which the dish got its name. His driver, having good English, was a mine of information regarding the island and its shores, so Vaughan invited him to join him for dinner. Arriving back at the marina it took some hard bargaining to get the man to accept full payment.

"No, no, we eat, we talk, and we are friends. Friends do not make a charge for their time!"

"Yes, Paulo, I agree we are friends, but you are in business with a wife, son and two lovely daughters to provide food for. I work only for myself, my books make money enough; please accept what I want to pay you. When I return to this little island of yours I shall want you to drive me again. I could not do that knowing I have cost you much in loss of earnings, whilst I have gained so much."

"Okay, but when you return we eat at my 'ome, you meet my family. There you will be my guest eh! No payment if you are my guest!"

Vaughan smiled at the lean little man who had saved him so much time in research. "That is a deal, I have your card, Paulo. Until the next time my friend you take good care of yourself."

Waving his knowledgeable new acquaintance goodbye Vaughan turned and walked along the sea wall of the marina to the second ramp and down it to the pontoon. Boarding *La Mouette* he was careful in sliding the companionway hatch back, taking it only far enough to get his arm in and turn off the alarm before pushing it fully open. The heat from the cabin wafted up to greet him, and removing the washboards quickly, he hurried down into the cabin and in the darkness picked up the insect screens and slid them in place before closing the hatch. Only now did he put on the cabin light and was pleased to find all apparently just as he had left it. Now in contact with the land he had to be more careful and went forward to check that the equipment delivered to him at Portsmouth was still safely hidden away. During the last two days of his voyage he had studied the items carefully, trying on the night camouflage suit and night vision headset. The compressed air grapple gun he had practised with for over an hour before he felt that he was sufficiently proficient in loading it and pumping air into the launch pressure tank. The tiny radio microphones and recorders that would enable him to eavesdrop from a distance still amazed him, even though he had spent several sessions at 'The Manor' training with them. The other item that had him completely stunned by its ingenuity was his wristwatch with GPS mapping accessed by removal of the watch's back plate.

Whilst the kettle was boiling for a late night drink, Vaughan stripped his Browning L9, cleaned and reassembled it. Strangely he no longer felt uncomfortable carrying a gun.

CHAPTER 4

ARRIVAL

"You write good things about us, senhor," the marina manger called to Vaughan, as he tossed the bowline over the yacht's pulpit and onto the foredeck, where it lay in a loose coil.

"I will do my best to fill this marina with visiting yachts all year for you," Vaughan called back as he eased the throttle forward and turned the yacht clear of the pontoon's head.

After a final wave to the serious little man with the weatherbeaten face, who appeared to be the only employee on duty that morning, Vaughan steered his yacht through the entrance and out into the bay. Earlier he had thought to sail straight to Madeira itself, the peaks of which he could clearly see, but, as he had sat eating breakfast, with the sunrise bringing another perfect day, he realised that he had time now to look at the Desertas as the security people didn't arrive in Madeira for two days. The more information he had in his notebook and draft pages written the better.

After stowing shorelines and fenders he turned the yacht into the wind and hoisted the mainsail, with a single reef set, then ran out the full jib and staysail, sending *La Mouette sur le Vent* on a fine broad reach course of 205° magnetic towards Deserta Grande. To the north-west he could see a large fleet of fishing boats at work but to the south the sea was deserted. In the south-west Madeira towered over the ocean, even at that distance appearing to dwarf the small island of Porto Santo astern.

A steady force 4 to 5 wind, and the Canary Current, pushed the yacht along at a good speed, but it was still 1330 hours before he closed the Desertas and altered course to port by 55° to run parallel to the dramatic shoreline. Rust red and deep purple basalt cliffs thrusting up to over four hundred metres above the ocean greet the visitor, their hostile faces instilling a sense of awe as the observer takes in the harsh barren landscape. Vaughan had noted from the chart that there was no safe landing point or secure anchorage on any of the three islands, a fact that helped maintain their nature reserve status. A haven for the monk seals and numerous sea birds, reptiles and spiders, the islands suffer from few human visitors, and those that do land must have obtained permission to do so.

*

Standing by the playground fence at his school in Funchal, Zeferino de Lima, Zef to his friends, nervously looked around, and seeing that no one was paying any attention to him, slipped through the gap in the chainlink to dash across the road and hide behind a parked car. It wasn't the first time he had skipped the afternoon lesson with boring Senhor Barbosa and, spurred on by the anticipated thrill of two hours on his new sailboard, he ran down the hill to the marina as fast as his legs would carry him.

The board was a gift from Great Uncle Olavo, who had arrived unannounced at his and his mother's apartment one month earlier. At first Zef was a little frightened of the dark swarthy man with the strange Portuguese dialect, who had apparently come all the way from Brazil. His mother also, did not really welcome her uncle, though Zef could not understand why. She kept on telling him that there were dark secrets in the past, but he should not worry himself about them, as Uncle Olavo would surely not be staying long. However the weeks had passed without any sign of the man leaving and during that time Zef had grown to like his generous great uncle.

By contrast his mother, Amelia, had become more concerned about their visitor with each passing day. She did not approve of the late hours he kept, and his returning reeking of cigarettes and wine. More recently there had been other visitors to the apartment, strangers to the island, who would sit with his great uncle on the balcony holding hushed conferences. If he or his mother approached with refreshments, or to clear things away, all conversation would stop until they were out of earshot again.

Hurriedly changing into just his swimming shorts, Zef carefully wrapped his late father's wristwatch in a handkerchief before stuffing it and his school clothing into his school bag. Zef worked quickly, preparing his recently acquired and as yet untried small slalom board and rig. He could not believe how light and easy it was to carry to the water, and having executed his best ever beach start, he was straight into the foot-straps and hooked into his harness. Soon he was speeding across the water from the quay and out past the harbour wall to the ocean beyond. The speed he was achieving frightened him at first and twice he did a spectacular catapult over the nose while he got to grips with the much more responsive board. The water starts he had learnt to do on the club boards were easy compared to using this smaller more twitchy slalom speed machine.

Fresh and full of energy he soon refined his start technique to suit the new board's characteristics, turning his initial fears into thrills, in the sheltered waters of the bay and stiff onshore sea breeze. Soon he was speeding out, on his favoured starboard tack, ever further into rolling offshore swells he had never encountered before, now completely absorbed by that incredible feeling of being truly at one with board, sail, wind and wave – he had never felt so alive! The ideal conditions encouraged him to charge ever further to windward revelling in flying along in the trough of now metre high waves. He had only to think of applying front foot pressure to have the board carving up the face of a wave, before feeling a fraction of a second of weightlessness as the board and he briefly left the water. Somehow, despite being so full of adrenaline, with all the information flooding back through his feet and arms, he touched down on the back of the waves gently enough to stay on and regain his speed by lifting his foot fractionally to bear off, before hitting maximum speed along the trough, all ready to carve gently up the next face again. What a ride, on nature's most addictive roller coaster, just him, his board, the wind and the sea working together in a magical harmony. Like his speed, time passed all too quickly as he blasted along feeling more confident with every passing moment. He had lost track of time and was shocked as he glanced back expecting to be, as usual, just a few hundred metres out. Where was he? Nothing looked the same, why could he see both the great cliff of Cabo Giráo to the west and the airport to the east? He then realised that he must be at least five kilometres out to sea. Fear gripped the pit of his stomach as he also realised that he would not make it home before his mother returned from work!

Suddenly he felt frightened, alone and unsure of even getting back to the harbour before nightfall. Somehow, he wobbled his way through a gybe and in doing so scuffed his arm and chest on the end of the boom, and cried out in pain. The apparent cool breeze and spray had treacherously disguised the effects of the sun and now, running with the wind on his back he shivered, his hot sunburnt skin sensing the contrasting coolness. At least he was now heading back towards the comfort of the bay and as he got his bearings and sensed that he could be home in time his initial moment of fear passed.

The wind however was dying and he soon realised that he could no longer sit comfortably in his harness, just flying along, but was having to start to work the rig to keep the board on the plane. All too soon the breeze died away completely bringing a new and alarming situation for him. His club board, on which he had been taught all the good basic skills that had allowed him to jump so confidently onto this one, had been large, very buoyant and rigged with a larger sail that would propel him along in the lightest of airs. This small slalom board with the smaller sail he had fitted, though ideal for the conditions when he set out, now lacked the buoyancy and sail power required for his return to the shore. Though not overweight for his age and height Zef was heavy enough for the board to sink as the wind died, leaving him no alternative but to let the rig drop into the sea whilst he lay along the board itself. Now, in the windless conditions and with a less buoyant board, he was stranded. He racked his brains trying to recall any advice given by his instructor, and he remembered laying the rig backwards on the deck of his club board with the clew away from the wind. Duate was a good teacher and well aware of Zef's natural ability and enthusiasm for sailboarding, so he had shown him not just the basics, but much more besides, including getting him proficient in the use of straps and harness from a very early point in his training, never dreaming that Zef would get hold of a slalom board and be so adventurous on his first outing. The question for Zef now was could he convert this knowledge into what to do on a tiny board in a rolling swell?

Young heads rarely have great wisdom; Zef was only ten years old and was now about to learn a painful lesson administered by Mother Nature. Such had been his excitement on hatching his plan that he had left the bottle of drinking water unopened in the hut where the board had been stored. That mistake and the run down the hill to the marina, coupled with very energetic sailing and the heat of the day, had left him seriously dehydrated. Feeling very frightened and alone again, he tried hard to 'self rescue' as he had been shown, but although the swell was rapidly dropping, it kept pushing him off the board into the sea, which at least helped him to cool down. He then tried to kick for the shore pushing the board and rig in front of him. After some ten minutes of this he began to really tire, but would have stayed in the cool sea water had his thrashing legs not attracted two bottlenose dolphins. Scrambling onto the board again he lay still, fearing the creatures' nearness, as they came close, their heads above the water looking at him and making that strange clicking noise they use as communication. Even for an adult this experience would not have been a precious moment in such circumstances, and for a young boy, alone in the open sea, it just added to his fear. The dolphins circled around him for some time occasionally coming close, their heads above the surface eyeing him curiously, before finally losing interest, they swam away.

Several miles south-east of Zef, Ian Vaughan was also finding the going slow as the north-easterly trade wind died down in the shadow of Madeira. Anxious to arrive in the port of Funchal in daylight he started up the yacht's engine and rolled in the jib and staysail leaving only the mainsail up. It was nearly an hour later that he saw, away to port, a flash of colour from Zef's sail as the boy and board were once again lifted over a gently rolling wave. Curious, Vaughan reached for the binoculars and searched the waves to try and identify what it was he had momentarily seen. Minutes passed before he caught sight of it again and this time could see the board and someone laid on it. Vaughan instantly realised the sailboarder's plight in the windless conditions and so far from shore, and altering course, opened the throttle taking the yacht to its maximum speed under power. Keeping up regular sightings of the person, Vaughan soon noted that they were not making any effort to even look around for assistance. *Whoever that is they are hardly moving, just enough to keep their head clear of the water. From this distance they look as if they have been thermidored; I hope I'm wrong.* Checking the distance between himself and the casualty Vaughan planned his next course of action. *I've just got time to get the sun lotion and fix up the boarding ladder. This is going to be tricky.* He coupled the autohelm to the tiller in order to prepare for the rescue, but kept frequent checks on the yacht's progress towards the sailboarder. Having fixed the side boarding ladder in place he secured one end of a long warp to the midship's cleat. Recovering someone at sea is not a straightforward procedure, especially if the person is semi-conscious. Back in the cockpit Vaughan disconnected the autohelm and steered the yacht for the last twenty metres bringing it as near as he dared to the casualty. He was surprised when he realised that it was a young boy on the board, and shocked by the effect the sun had had on the boy's back.

Jesus, you're in a mess, young man. I don't know how long you've been out here but it was too damn long that's for sure. Hurrying forward Vaughan tied the loose end of the warp around his waist, climbed down the boarding ladder and pushed off towards the sailboard. Untying the warp he quickly retied it to the base of the board's mast, noting with relief movement from the boy. He now hauled on the warp to bring himself and the sailboard, with boy on it, close enough to the yacht to enable him to grasp the ladder steps.

"This is going to be very painful, my lad," Vaughan said, as he tipped the board, causing the boy to slip off and onto his submerged shoulder. The boy let out an anguished cry.

Climbing the ladder he carried the boy to the safety of the yacht's cockpit and gently sat him down with his back lent against the rear of the cabin and his head lulling against the spray hood.

"You'll be shaded from the sun there," Vaughan said quietly.

Hurriedly applying the sun lotion to the boy, Vaughan continued talking to him and telling him that he was safe and would soon be back in Funchal. He was also aware that he must quickly get some fluids into the lad and as soon as he had given the boy's exposed skin a good covering of lotion he went below and made up some weak squash.

"Here we go, young man, let's see if you can drink this. Slowly does it, just a small mouthful at a time," said Vaughan quietly as he put the mug to the boy's lips and carefully tipped small amounts into his mouth.

In the shade of the spray hood the boy started to shiver but was now taking more notice of his surroundings. When the last drops of squash had been drunk Vaughan went forward and hurriedly hauled the sailboard and rig onboard then set the autohelm on course for the harbour entrance and opened the throttle. Back at the boy's side Vaughan patiently applied some more lotion then went below again to radio the port and arrange for medical assistance.

Selecting channel sixteen and depressing the call trigger on the microphone, Vaughan said, "Mayday, Mayday, Mayday, this is yacht *La Mouette sur le vent, La Mouette sur le vent, La Mouette sur le vent,* over."

He waited maybe half a minute before repeating the call, and then he heard, "Yacht calling Mayday, this is Porto Funchal, what is your emergency?"

"Porto Funchal, this is yacht *La Mouette sur le Vent,* I have found a sailboarder, a young boy who needs medical attention. Can you arrange ambulance to meet us at marina? Over."

Explaining the condition of the boy and the need for immediate medical attention Vaughan waited for the port radio to confirm what arrangements had been made.

The sound of the boy vomiting had Vaughan gathering a clean face flannel and bowl of water, which he took up into the cockpit to spend the next ten minutes cleaning the lad up. Laid on the board it was inevitable that he would have swallowed a lot of sea water. Getting that out of his stomach was a good thing. As Vaughan went to get the boy some water to drink the Marina Captain radioed to inform that an ambulance was on its way and checked on the yacht's progress.

Half a mile out Vaughan's concerns shifted from the boy to the need to keep alert to large craft movements in and out of the port. He could see the superstructures of two large cruise liners towering above the harbour wall and wondered whether either was about to put to sea. It was difficult though not to be distracted by the sheer beauty of the city of Funchal, set out, as it is on the steep slopes of what appeared to be an enormous natural amphitheatre. The predominately white houses with terracotta tiled roofs were an amazing sight in the evening sunshine. To the west, hotels ringed the shoreline and cliff tops, and behind the town the mountains rose spectacularly, thrusting up above the tree line and exposing the dark volcanic rust brown basalt rock.

Since taking the boy on board it had taken well over half an hour before they rounded the massive harbour wall and altered course for the marina to eventually moor-up alongside a pontoon, astern of the police and custom's rib.

The Marina Captain and a tough looking officer from the Policia Maritima took the shorelines and made them fast to the pontoon cleats. The medic from the ambulance team climbed aboard and quickly assessed the boy. After a hurried wave to his partner the other man picked up the stretcher and passed it over the yacht's pushpit.

"I have been giving him squash, er, fruit juice and water," Vaughan explained to the medic, pointing to the empty mug and gesticulating the act of drinking, assuming that the man had only limited English. "I have also been applying lotion to his skin."

The medic smiled and nodded, then asked, "You 'ave er, er, more sol crème, o senhor?"

"Sol crème, ah, yes sun cream, please wait." Hurrying below, Vaughan fetched a second bottle of sun lotion. "Here use this."

"Obrigado o senhor," the medic replied, squirting a large quantity onto his hand and gently spreading it over Zef's back, before carefully, part lifting and part guiding, the youngster onto the stretcher.

A small crowd, mainly tourists, had gathered, curious to see what was going on. The two ambulance men had just got the stretcher onto the pontoon when a young woman pushed her way to the front of the crowd. Immediately she saw the stretcher and the boy she screamed loudly and called, "Zeferino! Zeferino!" then turned towards the ramp to the pontoon and started to push her way along, calling out alternately, "Zeferino!" and "Por favor! Por favor!"

At the steps she waited for the stretcher-bearers to arrive then went with them walking alongside the stretcher crying and talking to the boy, leaving Vaughan satisfied that the lad had been reunited with family and was being properly looked after. As the ambulance pulled away, its siren blaring and blue lights flashing, Vaughan called to the Marina Captain. "Captain por favor, o tubo de água?"

"Sim, senhor," the captain replied, walking away down the pontoon to the hose reel stand, forward of the police rib, returning two minutes later and handing the hose end across. Thanking the man Vaughan cleaned up the cockpit, flushing the remains of the boy's vomit down the cockpit drains, and then quickly hosed the salt off the decks. He was coiling the hose back onto the stand when the policeman returned as the streetlights and lights around the marina came on.

"You stay 'ere long time?" he asked.

Vaughan nodded, "Yes, maybe two or three weeks, I am writing a book."

"You stay 'ere for tonight," the policeman said, pointing to the pontoon. "Then we do paperwork, er, in morning. Okay?"

"Okay, senhor."

Below, in the cabin, Vaughan tidied away the charts and sat rewriting the notes he had made during the day, feeling rather pleased with the amount of information he had gathered so far. It was close to nine o'clock in the evening by the time he had finished and as he put the notebooks away he suddenly realised how hungry he was, so locking up the boat he went ashore to inspect the quayside restaurants. A dish of talapia and perfectly cooked vegetables, washed down with a bottle of the house red wine, satisfied his hunger and gave him the opportunity to observe the passers-by. Groups of both tourists and locals sauntered along the quay, talking and laughing happily in the gentle warmth of the evening, fanned only by the land breeze that formed the night-time part of what the locals call 'God's air-conditioning'. After paying the bill, Vaughan strolled up the ramp from the marina to mingle with the crowds as they strolled along the esplanade, going as far as the cable car station before turning and heading back to the boat for an early night.

*

By nine thirty the following morning Vaughan had cleared immigration and customs and finally the Marina Captain's office.

"When you ready you move here," said the captain, pointing on the marina map to a berth alongside the harbour's outer wall. "You want help with lines?"

"No I should be able to manage, thank you, sorry, I should say, não obrigado."

The captain smiled, "Sim, it is good you try speak Portuguese."

As Vaughan walked from the office, the tough looking policeman that he had met on landing hailed him and guided a tall, athletic looking man in his late twenties towards him.

"O senhor Vaughan, this man he teach the boy to sail eh," the man smiled a broad friendly smile and held out his hand.

"I Duate Gomes I want to say, er, thank you for saving Zef. 'E is best one I teach," he explained as Vaughan shook his hand.

"He was a long way out to sea, is that normal, usual?"

"Não, não, never I teach more than, er, um quilómetro," he replied holding up one finger. "Zef, 'e too much bravo, you understand, eh." Vaughan nodded. "'Is mama she very cross wi' Zef and she stop 'im from lessons now, finish, no more."

Vaughan shrugged his shoulders unable to see why Gomes was bothering to explain about a mother's natural reaction.

"She wait for you by your boat. Please you tell 'er it was just a mistake, Zef good sailor. It will no 'appen again, eh. You tell 'er please."

"I do not want to get involved. The boy, Zef you say, he will persuade her in time unless he is now too frightened by what has happened."

Gomes did not fully understand Vaughan's comment and turned to the policeman and spoke rapidly in Portuguese. "He did not understand what you say. I will explain."

After ten minutes of a three-way conversation Vaughan found himself promising to try his best to help, then walked back to his boat. When he arrived he found the pontoon deserted and with some relief hurried along it and stepped on board his yacht. It was as he was unlocking the companionway hatch that he heard the clack, clack, clack, of high-heeled shoes beating a tattoo on the pontoon decking. By the time he had pushed the hatch back and cleared the washboards his visitor had arrived.

"Excuse me, hello?" she called.

With a sigh Vaughan stepped back from under the spray hood and smiled at her. "Can I help you?"

"Are you the man who saved my son's life yesterday?"

"I, er brought him back to the shore, that is all."

"That is not all," she replied hotly. "Hospital say he was very lucky you came to help him," her expression serious, her arms waving furiously to accentuate the importance of the hospital's statement. "My stupid son would be dead had you not seen him and rescued him." Tears started down her face and Vaughan began to feel embarrassed and annoyed with himself for trying to trivialise the event.

Her actions and raised voice had begun to attract attention, and to spare his and her blushes further, Vaughan invited her on board. Opening the midships gate he fitted the boarding ladder and taking her hand helped her up onto the side deck.

"Please would you take off your shoes; they will damage the decks."

"Of course," she said, instantly bending down to remove them, her shiny, long dark wavy hair tumbling down, hiding her tear-stained face. Vaughan guessed that she was a working mother, as she wore a smart tailored light grey jacket and pencil skirt. Beneath the jacket was a plain white blouse with stand-up collar, fashionably partly unbuttoned to reveal the start of her cleavage.

"Please, follow me. May I offer you a coffee or tea perhaps?"

"I did not wish to take up your time, senhor."

"I assure you it would be no problem, I have plenty of time. Let's go below out of the heat, and we can talk while I make the drinks."

At the bottom of the companionway steps he turned quickly and suggested that she may find it easier to descend them backwards, ladder style, as they were rather steep. She descended with care, her suntanned feet feeling for each step.

"My name is Ian Vaughan by the way," he said, holding out his hand. "And you are?"

"Amelia de Lima," she responded, taking his hand gently. "Zeferino is my son, oh of course you know that," she added with a nervous laugh.

"What would you like to drink?"

"Coffee please."

He turned his back to her, busying himself at the galley stove and allowing her the opportunity to wipe away her tears. At the sound of a compact being snapped shut and a handbag zip pulled, he turned and asked, "Do you take milk and sugar?"

"No thank you, just coffee."

Placing the two mugs on the cabin table, Vaughan sat himself on the porthand settee opposite her. Looking into her face now, he was struck by her Latin beauty. His ex-wife, Sarah, and 'Miss County Magazine' had been English roses, whilst Umeko Morohashi had that uniquely fascinating graceful oriental beauty, but Amelia de Lima was stunningly beautiful and would have graced the cover of any womens' magazine. What was more she wore no make-up at all, able to rely on her natural olive skin gently tanned by the sun. The only thing that spoilt the perfection of her looks was the obvious tiredness around her eyes.

"How far from the shore was he?" she asked.

"Quite a way," Vaughan replied, not wanting to make matters worse for the boy by putting numbers to his answer. "How far is your, quite a way?"

"Well maybe four, five kilometres," he replied, shrinking the actual distance by almost a third.

She gasped and put her hand to her mouth. "My goodness so far," she exclaimed, her dark brown eyes wide with surprise. "I am glad I have forbidden him from sailboarding again, he is too reckless." She reached for her coffee, and after taking a sip said, "Also he skipped his school lessons; I do not know what makes me more angry."

Her rather prim pose and expression when making her last statement had Vaughan smiling. "You of course never missed a lesson at school," he said, gambling that an obviously lively person would have stretched the rules a bit as a child.

"No I did not!" she replied, bristling at Vaughan's implied accusation. Then looking up and seeing Vaughan's broad grin, smiled back. "I was the perfect pupil, well behaved and attentive," she said in an accentuated prim voice.

Deciding that now was not the time to attempt to persuade her to change her mind Vaughan asked, "What did his father have to say?"

"His father is dead; he died in a car accident five years ago, I bring up Zeferino on my own now my parents are no longer alive."

"That must be very hard for you." *At least Sarah's got her parents should she need them, but as far as my involvement is concerned, I might as well be dead.*

"It is not easy, I run the family import, export business with a small staff."

"Family business, eh. Your parents started it?"

"No, my great grandfather on my father's side, he had made good contacts in Europe before second world war and saw the opportunity."

Now that the conversation had moved away from the rescue both of them felt more relaxed and by the time she had finished a second mug of coffee she had promised to show him Funchal. It was only as she stood to leave that the conversation returned to her son.

"When will your son leave hospital?" Vaughan asked.

"Maybe tomorrow, maybe next day, it depends."

"I see. Look if you are going to give up your precious time showing me Funchal, the least I can do is take you to dinner. How about this evening after you have visited your son?" *Hey, steady, Vaughan, you have a job to do.*

She hesitated, and Vaughan guessed that she was trying to find the words for a polite refusal. *Oh, why not enjoy an evening. She could well save me some time searching for information.*

"Please," he said, "I would feel very guilty otherwise. You choose somewhere that has good Portuguese dishes." *Does this rate for cool chat up? I doubt it. God, I'm out of touch.*

"You are too kind. I would invite you to dinner at my home, but I have my uncle staying with me, so it would not be so comfortable to talk."

"I'm sorry, I had not considered you having guests."

"Oh, he will have to look after himself for a change," she replied, a strong hint of annoyance in her voice.

"Where will I meet you?"

"I will come here for you, maybe eight o'clock this evening? I must go now and attend to my office." *Good God, she's accepted.*

"By then I will have moved *La Mouette* across to the sea wall, but I will be waiting for you at the head of the steps over there," Vaughan explained, nodding towards the end of the pontoon.

After helping her over the side, he watched as she briskly walked away, and disappeared amongst the tourists thronging the quayside, then returning onboard he cast off and motored the yacht across to the outer marina wall where he was assisted by one of the marina staff to moor stern-to between two other yachts. As he stood checking the lines he cursed for forgetting to acquire a stern-to boarding platform. The berth at Kingswear had finger pontoons that enabled him to get on and off amidships; here the berthing arrangement required him to leave by the stern, which, being pointed similar to the bow plus having the rudder hanging from it, meant that the distance to jump was too far for safety. So that was to be his first job, find a supplier of aluminium extrusions and make a boarding platform. What appeared to be a simple challenge turned into a major operation but had the benefit of teaching Vaughan some detailed geography of the city. Stopping only for some traditional potato bread and a sausage, washed down with a cold beer, Vaughan completed the platform only just in time to change for his dinner date.

*

Earlier that afternoon Leyla Najjar had stood nervously in the queue at Funchal airport, her passport in hand and hand luggage at her feet. She had left Amman the day before, and flown to Paris using a passport in the name of Nour Kasawni. After clearing immigration and customs there she walked around Paris for eight hours, not checking into any hotel, then, re-entering the airport, boarded a flight to Lisbon on a separate ticket before using a third ticket for the flight to Madeira, travelling now under her real name.

Leyla was the eldest daughter of a wealthy Jordanian building contractor. On the face of it, she had enjoyed a perfect childhood, during which she had received a good education culminating in studying dentistry at the University of Cairo. Like her mother she was a devout Muslim, but would never have been thought of as radical. The change came when, by chance, she attended a mosque near the home of a friend living in the town of Madaba. The preacher was none other than Mohammed al Ben Said and his message had affected her deeply, challenging the shallowness of her lifestyle and awakening a deep longing for commitment. It was months later, after her final university exams, that she heard the preacher again, this time in a suburban mosque in Cairo and delivering his message under the watchful eyes of bodyguards. His message now more fervent and hostile, strangely gave her a sense of belonging to a greater purpose, drawing her into a group of young women whose beliefs were becoming, step by step, more extreme.

Al Ben Said had recruited several suicide bombers in the past and had almost instantly recognised the hunger in Leyla's eyes to become someone whose life had meaning even if it meant death. Like many extremist clerics Al Ben Said would normally speak of women in the same way as he would talk of litter in the street. The cleric, however, was always careful when preaching to his female recruits to avoid insult and instead tell them of their divine purpose. Quick to respond to his teachings, Leyla was soon selected to lead the group, which brought her in contact with Al Bashir, under whose influence she became fully radicalised, much to her parents' concern and distress.

At the desk, the official indicated for her to pull back her hijab and remove the yashmak so that he could see her face properly.

After she reluctantly complied, the official grunted and pushed her passport back at her. At the exit from the custom's hall she saw a young man with a piece of cardboard carrying her name and walked across to him.

"Ismail al Karaki?"

He nodded.

"I am Leyla Najjar."

He looked at her long enough for her to feel uncomfortable before saying, "Follow me."

Crossing the road he walked quickly across the car park, with Leyla lagging behind struggling with suitcase and hand luggage trying to keep up. He stopped by a grey Mercedes and flicking the key fob opened the boot. "Put your things in there," he ordered, before leaping into the driver's seat and starting the engine.

By the time she got into the car she was sweating and breathing heavily. "Thank you for meeting me," she said, "I hope it was not inconvenient."

"It was, but no matter," Al Karaki replied, accelerating the car out of the parking bay, his eyes fixed on the road.

"Have you heard from Al Bashir?" she asked.

"No. My father waited until late last night, but he did not come."

"He will surely come today then. He has much to do before the conference members arrive."

"Oh, really," replied Al Karaki, obviously totally uninterested.

Once away from the traffic near to the airport and onto the dual carriageway, Al Karaki drove so fast that Leyla feared he would lose control and crash. Exiting a tunnel he braked heavily, flinging the car down a spiralling slip road to join the complex road system to the eastern side of Funchal. His driving, and the twisting turning road system had Leyla feeling quite nauseous by the time they arrived at the Al Karaki residence.

Getting out of the car the young man pointed to the rear door of the house. "My mother is through that door," then he turned on his heels and walked down a flight of steps to enter the front door of the house, leaving Leyla to struggle with her luggage, very aware that her presence was not wanted.

Knocking on the rear door Leyla had to wait several minutes before the door opened and a tired looking woman gestured with a side jerk of her head for Leyla to enter. "Why my brother wishes to involve us in his politics I do not know. We wish nothing but a quiet life; that is why we live here and not in Libya amongst his crazy friends. While you are on this island, you will not tell anyone that you are staying here or are connected with this family," Ismail's mother said, her voice hard and heavy with contempt.

CHAPTER 5

INTRODUCTIONS

Shortly after buying his yacht the previous year, Vaughan had got a friend to supply some embroidered T-shirts emblazoned with '*La Mouette sur le Vent*' beneath a silhouette of a gull in flight. Guessing that one of medium size would fit Amelia's son, he searched for a bag, finding only a UK supermarket one vaguely suitable, and thrust the garment into it. Checking that all was in order below he set the alarm before locking the hatch and making his way ashore. Arriving at the meeting point five minutes early he was both surprised and pleased to see Amelia making her way along the promenade towards him. She was wearing a red and gold floral summer dress with a full skirt and bright red high-heeled shoes. As she caught sight of him walking towards her, she smiled and waved then as they came close she said, "I hope I'm not late."

"No, if anything you are a few minutes early. You look stunning, I feel I should change into something much smarter."

"No, no you are fine as you are," she replied. "I am thinking to take you to the 'Real Canoa' at Ponto Cruz; I think you will enjoy the food and the atmosphere there."

"Is it far?" Vaughan asked.

"We need a taxi; come we cross the road."

In the taxi Vaughan asked, "How is Zeferino today?"

"He is not so sick as he was when he left you, but his back has blistered and is very sore. The hospital say he must stay with them for at least two days."

"I am sorry to hear that, I was hoping that it was not so serious."

"It is suitable punishment for his bad behaviour, but I still cried for him when I saw his back."

Vaughan handed her the T-shirt. "I brought him this for when he recovers."

"That is very kind of you, he does not deserve such a thoughtful gift."

The taxi speeding round a roundabout had Amelia grabbing the door handle to stop herself sliding into Vaughan. "Please driver, slow down, I wish to arrive in one piece," she said severely. The driver took little notice and charged the taxi at the steep hill out of the town centre.

"They call this hill 'Cardiac Hill' because it is so steep and long," she said. "Over there is the Governor's official residence and just beyond it is the casino. Do you go to casinos?"

"No, I am finding life itself is enough of a gamble."

She gave him a questioning look, but as Vaughan did not elaborate, she continued her role as tour guide, pointing out the places of interest as the taxi sped along. "The ladies there, sitting on the walls, come in from the villages and sit there knitting or doing crochet work for sale to tourists. The police move them on from time to time as they do not have licence for selling such things."

They passed a giant statue of a man with his arms outstretched. Amelia, seeing Vaughan look at it with interest, said, "We have many interesting statues around Funchal, not just those of famous people, like Zarco or Christopher Columbus, but also those that symbolise something or are just there as street art." Touching his arm to attract his attention she continued. "That pinkish building on the left is the famous 'Reid's' hotel. You must take afternoon tea there, it is considered to be a very necessary thing for English visitors to do."

"Along with being pushed down the mountainside sitting in a wicker chair, I understand," replied Vaughan.

Amelia laughed. "Yes that as well."

A little further along the road she pointed again. "There is the Vidamar hotel," she said, pointing to a smart modern twin towered building set down below road level to their left. "They are preparing to hold big, important conference there soon. We cleared many boxes of security equipment for an American company two days ago. I believe they have the job of protecting the delegates."

The hotel's setting impressed Vaughan, it appeared to command stunning views of the ocean and the distant Desertas from virtually every guest room. *So that's where it's all going to happen, smart looking place, politicians definitely know how to live.*

"Is it an American business conference?" asked Vaughan, knowing full well what the conference was.

"No, it is an important conference between North African nations I understand. The hotel has very good facility for such thing. The manager is very happy because business, since European finance crisis, has been very bad for Portugal and especially Madeira. I think you know we have very big debts, which means our taxes have gone up, but wages are pushed down; for many people times are very hard."

"Yes, I understand that things are tough for you. It is bad enough in England, but there the ratio of debt to population is nowhere near as bad as here. Let's hope that the conference brings in a lot of money for the island."

"If you look up to your right you will see many banana plants growing. Growing bananas was a very profitable business until the EU decided that they were the wrong shape and banned their import to mainland Europe."

"Am I correct in saying that bananas replaced the growing of grapes after the blight destroyed the vines back in the nineteenth century?"

"Yes, that is correct. Some here look upon the EU as another blight."

Vaughan laughed. "There are many in the UK that share that opinion." *A lady with a sense of humour, this is getting better by the minute.*

Just then the taxi braked, and Amelia reached for the door handle again just in time, as the driver turned the vehicle sharp left onto the opposite carriageway then almost immediately right, down a very steep hill. The road swung to the right and passed a line of restaurants, the last of which was the 'Real Canoa'.

Vaughan paid off the taxi and turned to see the manager of the restaurant warmly greeting Amelia.

"Bruno, this is Mr Ian Vaughan, he is the English sailor who saved Zeferino's life yesterday," she said, then, turning to Vaughan said, "May I introduce Bruno, he owns this restaurant."

Vaughan held out his hand and received a warm, firm handshake. Bruno was immaculately dressed in dark well-pressed trousers, shiny black shoes and a brilliant white shirt with a smart grey neatly knotted tie. Vaughan guessed that he looked young for his age and he had an air of likeable charm about him. Alert eyes and pleasant manner spoke of a good restaurateur who looked after his customers.

"I am so sorry we are quite full this evening. You should have phoned earlier Amelia, I would have saved special table for you," Bruno said, politely speaking in English in order to include Vaughan in the conversation. "Please would you mind sitting outside, here by the pavement? I am sorry, inside is full and those two tables are booked for people arriving in few minutes."

Vaughan looked at Amelia. "Is that all right for you? It is fine for me."

"Okay, Bruno, we will sit there," she said with a mock frown on her face.

"I will bring you some drinks, what would you like?"

"I would like a glass of still mineral water."

Bruno smiled and snapped a salute, "Straight away madam."

"I'll have a gin and tonic," said Vaughan, shaking his head and smiling at her. *I like you, young lady; this is going to be a pleasant evening.'*

The customers were mainly tourists, many of them British. Vaughan noted a young couple on a table nearby. The young man had that air of public school about him, with curly, dark, fashionably unruly hair and wearing an old checked shirt and khaki shorts; his olive skinned arms and legs tanned from probably just a few days in the sun. The girl, blond and English rose pretty, sat enthralled by her partner's conversation, her fingers playing with her hair, laughing maybe too readily at his witty comments; her neat embroidered blouse and pea green skirt at odds with her companion's casual clothes. Strange, Vaughan thought, that the man did not seem as interested in her as she obviously was in him, or was it just that it was he who was playing hard to get?

Bruno and Lisa moved from table to table, taking orders and cheerfully talking to the diners, many of whom were, understandably, frequent visitors. Just inside the restaurant a guitarist played appropriately gentle pieces, just loud enough to be heard but not loud enough to intrude upon an individual's conversation. Unlike many restaurateurs, Bruno understood that people came to eat and talk without needing to shout to be heard above an over enthusiastic musician or piped pop music.

*

Olavo Esteves was very much the son of his father. In Brazil he had accumulated a small but comfortable fortune, running a security firm associated with banks' offices and money delivery vans. His partner and the man that had been the business's strategist, Isidro Rodriguez, had travelled with him to Madeira. It was Rodriguez who had taken on the role of coup planner, and had finally persuaded Diago Velo, the political activist, of the need to secure Madeira as the first step that would divide Portuguese Government response and enable an easier mainland takeover. The last in the group now in Madeira was Huberto Pedroso, a charismatic intellectual and disciple of the Salaza concept of economics and government. All members of the group were sons or nephews of men who, back in the nineteen fiftes and sixties, were operating on the darker side of the Salaza regime, and who, after the Carnation Revolution of 1974, had been 'advised' to go and live abroad. Their political beliefs had not died with their departure and their influence had been passed down to the next generation. It was now that those men and a few serving mid-ranking military officers considered it time that the economic situation for their mother country had reached the point where action must be taken to restore its proud sovereignty.

On the Portuguese mainland Pedroso's brother was working with a small group of industrialists, enlisting sympathisers within the civil administration, carefully selected over the years through social conversation that revealed their political leanings. Arguing that it could be possible for Germany to push for similar demands on Portugal as those made on Cyprus. Huberto Pedroso had been surprised to find how many people looked back at the Salaza years as being the most positive in the country's history in terms of national economic security.

At first glance, any rational person would reject instantly the return to the autocratic rule imposed by Salaza and his followers. No one would want to return to the years of abject poverty for the rural working classes and the terrors of the secret police. However, what had taken its place had put the country in great turmoil for years, during which there had been much unrest and hardship. This had been followed by membership of the European Union, which, though initially had brought development and wealth, had also put the nation in debt to such an extent that decades of austerity appeared to be inevitable, before there would be any improvement in personal wealth. To many, looking back to those pre-revolution years of their childhood, when life was simpler, slower and, when looked at nostalgically, golden, the thought of a return to that political blueprint was an attractive one.

It was that nostalgic response amongst some of the exiled families in Venezuela, Brazil and South Africa, that had encouraged the quartet to consider taking the gamble, six months ago, to start a coup in Madeira. Again it had been Rodriguez who had persuaded the group to wait until all attention was on the North African Unification Conference before making their move.

"No one will be interested in anything else," he had said, "and we can spend the intervening time to encourage Major Alves to use his wife's influence to have his 'special team' deployed on the island to assist with the security of such important delegates."

Everyone at the meeting in Brazilia had laughed heartily. Rodriguez had even considered and developed a plan should the mainland coup fail.

"With Alves and his men on Madeira and great uncertainty and nervousness in Lisbon, Madeira can be moved into a fully independent nation and tax-free haven for investors. Our friends in London and New York will be ready to move as soon as the Island is secured. So what if the mainland coup fails? Huh. The Portuguese Government will no longer have the teeth to bite us," he had explained. "As you know there is a plan for the escape of Correia, Benzinho and Pianto, should mainland Portugal not follow our lead. Obviously they would then join us in Madeira."

With the plans carefully laid and the greatest of care taken with security, the quartet felt the time was right to bring foreign influence on side. This had led to Olavo Esteves using his contact with Ulan Reshetnikov, the Russian oligarch with links to STAGAZ and other Russian businesses, to arrange for a social meeting with the Russian, where the group hoped to gauge his character, before they explained their reason for possible involvement in oil/gas and other Russian based trading. All of them were aware of the probability of European trade sanctions in response to the coup.

Up until the evening of the meeting, Reshetnikov had only had contact with Olavo Esteves, and that association had been very different and secretive. So when the Brazilian asked if other members of his group could join, Reshetnikov made enquiries with his other contacts in Brazil, who informed him of vague rumours of the group's political leanings. Politics, and especially those indicating change, had always worked well for Reshetnikov, and he was therefore anxious to form a bond quickly. He knew well Esteves' weakness for expensive surroundings and pretty girls, but for the others he had no idea, unaware that Huberto Pedrosa was also a frequent client of Sònia's escort agency. Considering this he suggested that the meeting be held, away from the old town, in a five star tourist hotel, where it would be unlikely for him to bump into his local friends and business acquaintances. His mistress, Sònia, had arranged for two girls to join the party and for another two, maybe three, to be available if required.

Arriving early at the Grande, Reshetnikov sent Sònia in ahead to check who was in the lounge, and if there were only the hotel guests, to arrange seating for his party near to the cabaret. After ten minutes a young female waitress came out to his car to inform him that all was prepared. By the time Esteves and his companions arrived Reshetnikov was swallowing the last drops of his third vodka. No sooner had the introductions been made and drinks ordered than the escort agency's girls arrived, suitably mini-skirted and flirtatious. Only Diago Velo resisted the temptation to join in with the flirting, dancing and heavy drinking, not because he was the driver in the group, but because for him such entertainment was contemptuously trivial. To him debate and political discussion were meat and drink of a social evening, not banal conversation with airhead girls whose only interests were fashion and partying. By the time two other girls had joined the party Velo had excused himself and gone for a walk around the hotel's immaculate gardens and pool area. Enjoying the evening warmth he sat on a sun-lounger looking out over the sea towards Cámara de Lobos, then taking his mobile phone from his pocket, dialled the number for Major Antonio Alves.

"Is everything for our celebration arranged?" Velo asked, without introducing himself.

"Yes, Diago, all the invitations have been sent and all of our guests have replied saying that they are pleased to attend," Alves answered, instantly recognising the voice.

"Is the flight booked?"

"Oh, yes, we are economising and coming by charter plane."

Diago Velo smiled. "How will you get from the airport?"

"Oh, the charter company has arranged that for us; they have their own transport, it is all part of the deal."

"That is good, Antonio. Have a safe journey, I will look forward to meeting you again, and please give my best wishes to Yvonne."

After the brief goodbyes Velo ended the call and lying back on the lounger stared up into the night sky wondering whether he should call Norberto Correia again, before deciding it best to wait until morning when Correia would be at his desk in Lisbon's police headquarters.

*

Earlier, a short distance away at the 'Real Canoa', Ian Vaughan had been discovering again the pleasures of talking to a beautiful young lady in a relaxed and thoroughly pleasant environment. Unlike the conversations he had endured with his ex-wife over the last six months, where every one of his words had been twisted, and every suggestion challenged, here there was interest, humour and a relaxed exchange of information about each other. Looking across the table at her, as she told him about life on the island and her childhood, it made him aware of that lost part of his life, sharing true simple reminiscences and honest hopes and dreams without it being an act to mislead and conceal. Suddenly he thought of Umeko Morohashi, he had been able to be honest with her. *Would a postcard be the wrong thing to do? Probably. Will I ever get used to this living a lie?*

Bruno and their waitress, Lisa, had been attentive throughout the excellent meal.

"You must have some great influence here," said Vaughan, "We have been treated like royalty all evening."

"Bruno and my late husband were neighbours when they were young, though I think Paulo was three, maybe four, years younger," replied Amelia, her face, for the first time that evening, sad. "Bruno was like older brother to Paulo, and he and his wife were very kind to Zeferino and me when Paulo was killed."

"What happened?"

"Paulo was driving to the north of the island and police think dense cloud caused him to drive over the edge of a steep drop. He was not found for three days."

Seeing tears form in her eyes Vaughan immediately apologised. "I'm sorry I should not have asked, it was very stupid of me to remind you of that time, when this evening should be a happy one." *You prat, Vaughan, why wreck a perfectly good evening by reminding your hostess of an event she is still grieving over?*

"No, it is I who should apologise, it was over five years ago, I have spoilt your evening with my sadness."

Unconsciously he reached across the table and gently took her hand. "Look, let's change the subject and you tell me what that strange pillar is along the esplanade. You know the one that looks as if it is made of giant Lego." *Oh, come on, Vaughan, you can do better than that. You really needed training in chat up lines not code analysis.*

Amelia blinked her tears away and smiled, keeping her hand in his. "Oh, you mean the 'Pilar de Banger'. Well, an English gentleman named John Banger designed it, I think around eighteen hundred. Anyway originally it was over thirty metres high and I think they used it for signalling to ships in the bay; that was before the harbour wall was built. Someone told me that they also had long rope they used for sending packages to and from the ships."

"Did some of it fall down?"

"No, I think it was taken down because it was no longer of use. Some people bought the stones and had them put together again in their gardens."

"They would make a neat folly."

"Folly?" Amelia asked. "What is a folly?"

"In the eighteenth and nineteenth centuries the wealthy people in Britain would sometimes build odd structures like towers or temples to decorate their estates. These impractical buildings were known as follies," explained Vaughan. "Would you like a liqueur with your coffee?"

"Thank you but no, two glasses of wine is enough for me."

It was as they were waiting for the coffees to arrive that it happened. There was a pedestrian crossing outside the restaurant, and frequently during the evening a short queue of traffic would form as people crossed the road. An elderly couple, slowly making their way across, had caused a line of half a dozen vehicles to back up. The second to last in the queue of traffic was a black Range Rover with the side windows down revealing four middle-aged men laughing and joking among themselves.

Amelia glancing across at the line of traffic suddenly looked startled, "So that is why he did not complain when I told him to cook for himself this evening."

Vaughan looked confused and turned to see who she was referring to.

"The man in the back of that big black four-by-four is my Uncle Olavo from Brazil."

"The one sat on this side?" asked Vaughan.

"Yes. He has been staying with us for the last month and treating me like some housemaid. He was the man that bought Zeferino that sailboard."

"Not Mr Popular then."

"No, not Mr Popular, in fact he frightens me a little. He and those friends of his meet in our apartment and have secretive discussions. They are plotting something I am sure, maybe they want to take my business away from me."

"Why do you think that?"

"When they come, which is often now, they spend much time in serious whispered conversation, which stops anytime I come close to them. It is very sinister."

"Well, they have just gone into that big hotel down the road."

Amelia frowned. "Why come all the way out here to have a drink with friends when he says he does not like modern hotels?"

"Maybe they are meeting someone else who does."

Just then the coffees arrived and their conversation changed for a short time, but it was obvious to Vaughan that she was still intrigued as to what her uncle was doing in that part of town, as she kept glancing round, as if expecting him to be coming towards them.

"You are still curious about Uncle Olavo?" said Vaughan.

Her thoughts had been focusing on her late mother. "Oh," her mother would say, "The revolution changed everybody's life back then." Amelia never wanted to question her gentle, and sickly mother about the reasons for the changes, accepting that she, Uncle Olavo's elder sibling, was always more interested in telling her about meeting Amelia's bookish father when he was part of an educational exchange programme visiting Brazil.

"I am sorry but he acts so strangely," Amelia said, her concentration snapping back to Vaughan and his question. "I know very little about that side of my family; my father avoided going into detail, except to say that my maternal grandfather had not been popular when working for the Salaza government of the nineteen sixites." Finishing her second cup of coffee she said, "Excuse me I must, how do you say in English?"

114

"Powder your nose," he prompted.

She chuckled, "Yes, I must powder my nose."

"While you are doing that I am just going to look at something over the road, I won't be long. Tell Bruno not to panic, I will come back to pay the bill," said Vaughan, as she walked away.

Vaughan waited until she had gone before getting up and hurrying down the road and into the hotel grounds. Entering reception he could hear the cabaret performance coming from the lounge on a lower level and crossing to the head of the stairway, he looked down and saw that the lounge was almost empty, except for a noisy group in front of the stage, and three rather disgruntled couples sitting at the other end of the lounge, casting disapproving glances towards the revellers.

Amelia's Uncle Olavo and another man were dancing very closely with two young women, a third man sat smoking and laughing with a skinny girl who was jigging up and down in her seat in time to the music. The fourth, and undoubtedly the host for the evening, was sprawled in a chair with his arm around a stunningly attractive woman, but it was that man that riveted Vaughan's attention; he would have recognised Reshetnikov's grizzly features anywhere.

Sensing that the woman was about to look up, Vaughan stepped back out of sight, spotting for the first time a tough looking man standing in shadows on the other side of the reception area.

"Can I help you, sir?"

Vaughan spun round to face a reception clerk who had come across offering assistance. *Don't be so jumpy, the goon by the stairs will get more suspicious.*

"No, thank you. I was expecting to meet a friend here in reception, but they must have gone on without me," Vaughan replied. "The restaurant is only at the top of the hill."

The clerk smiled and returned the friendly wave, as Vaughan left the building and hurried back to the 'Real Canoa', checking as he did so that the tough guy, probably part of Reshetnikov's protection, wasn't following.

Vaughan was just picking up the bill as Amelia returned to the table. "I am sorry I was so long," she said. "Alicia was quizzing me all about you, so I had to tell her about your rescue of Zeferino. You are now officially a hero."

Vaughan chuckled and shook his head. "Do I go inside to pay?"

"Yes, we go inside and say goodbye to Bruno and Alicia, it is a little quieter in there now."

Bill paid and goodbyes said, Vaughan suggested that they take a walk down to the cliff top promenade that he had caught a fleeting glimpse of on his way to the hotel. The narrow roadway down from the main road to the promenade was steep enough for Amelia to seek Vaughan's arm for support, wearing, as she was, rather high-heeled shoes. "When do you want your guided tour of Funchal?" she asked.

"Whenever you are free. I can take a break from researching my book at anytime."

"Zeferino must stay in hospital for two more days they say, so how about tomorrow we meet for lunch, then I show you the town."

"That would be great, Amelia. Thank you very much."

She then proceeded to point out the various places of interest that could be seen from their high vantage point before looking at her wristwatch and suggesting she call Carlos, her usual taxi driver.

Half an hour later Vaughan was helping her from the taxi outside her apartment block.

"Thank you so much for a wonderful evening," she said, before suddenly going on tiptoe to give him a brief kiss on both cheeks. "It has been a very long time since I have enjoyed myself as much."

"I have enjoyed your company as well, and shall look forward to seeing you at one o'clock at the restaurant, by the Sacred Arts Museum you say?"

"That is the place, good night." With that she turned and stepping into the porch tapped her code into the security lock, unaware that Vaughan had noted the number.

As the taxi weaved its way down through the town towards the marina Vaughan tried to piece together what he had witnessed at the hotel. *What could it possibly be that would bring together Amelia's Uncle Olavo and Ulan Reshetnikov? It must be worth quite a bit for someone like Reshetnikov to provide female entertainment. That would be quite an expense, to say nothing of the drinks bill. Is this something to do with the STATGAZ contact Gleb Smetanin? The timing for them being here ties in with Smetanin's visit. It also fits with the conference and maybe it would also be linked with Algerian and Moroccan oil/gas production, but why would Brazilians be interested in working with STATGAZ on that.* Unable to take his thoughts logically any further, Vaughan decided that he must try and develop his relationship with the beautiful Amelia and her uncle to see if by that route he could learn more about Reshetnikov's business interests.

*

Whilst Vaughan travelled to the marina in the taxi Takkal and Al Bashir struggled in the dark to haul their dinghy clear of the water and into a cave on the east coast of the largest of the Desertas, Deserta Grande.

There had been much nervousness surrounding their arrival off the island's shore. Carefully threading their way between two groups of local fishing boats they reached the specially selected point along the steep rocky shore apparently without being seen. A Moroccan fishing boat in these, strictly Portuguese, waters would undoubtedly attract attention and possible interception and search by the fishery and coastal protection vessel.

"How long we stay?" demanded Takkal. "Why you not arrange your friends to meet that sinking hulk of a fishing boat out there at sea. Why are we to wait here?"

Al Bashir, tired of Takkal's constant complaining, shouted back, "You are being paid one million dollars and you complain about the engine noise, the food, the smell of fish, the waves, everything!"

"You tell me how long we stay here."

"*Inshallah* tomorrow night, maybe next night it depends upon what other boats are out."

"What do you mean, other boats?"

"Normally the fishermen work the nets or lines in sight of each other," Al Bashir replied, this time in a more normal tone. "If a boat leaves the group early or hangs back questions are asked. They will have to have some good reason to leave early or maybe later, and not bring Portuguese crew with them."

Takkal scowled. "All this because you may be recognised. Why you not allow me to travel by normal means I cannot understand. For me to fly to Madeira is easy and comfortable."

"Because those who order me to do this, insist we go this way, that is why!" retorted Al Bashir angrily.

Takkal threw his arms up into the air in thorough frustration and inward concern regarding the hit. He knew only too well that if they were intercepted before landing on Madeira all would be lost and his part in the plot possibly exposed. "Whoever those people are that you work for, I can tell you now they are idiots who have never done more than plant roadside bombs and ambush groups of soldiers." He kicked at a loose stone, sending it out of the cave to bounce once on the rocky shore before splashing into the ocean. "I do not have to crawl on my belly and hide every moment of the day to arrive in any country."

"They insisted we travel together, I am simply following instruction."

"The instruction was made by one with no brain. I did very careful and efficient arrangement to get you to Essaouira and assumed that suitable arrangement was made for the rest of our journey, not…" Takkal flapped his right arm in the direction of Al Bashir in a sign of disgust and contempt. "If, and I mean if, we get to Madeira, we separate. I go my way and do my job, and you do what you have to, is that clear?"

Al Bashir went to protest but Takkal had not finished. "Do not forget that once the hit is made the rest of the money is paid, or you will die painfully, understand?"

With still strong memories of the tanker driver fresh in his mind Al Bashir nodded acceptance and sitting down heavily on the side of the dinghy offered up a silent prayer. It was then that a wolf spider, hunting along the side of the dinghy, bit Al Bashir's leg.

*

The following morning Vaughan hurriedly stowed the provisions he had purchased in the town's supermarket before changing into reasonably smart clothes ready for his lunch appointment with Amelia. He smiled to himself as he realised that the job didn't appear to have any hours of working associated with it and wondered whether such a pleasant leisure activity was permissible. Arriving at the Café do Museu in the Praca do Municip, adjacent to the Sacred Arts Museum, he chose to sit at an outside table, in the shade of an umbrella, as the sun was now hot.

Looking up he saw her as she crossed the square, dressed in a white blouse and full dark blue skirt, walking between two other ladies. As she crossed the road and started to descend the steps to the restaurant her gaze swept the tables and on seeing him she waved and directed her two companions towards him as he stood to greet them.

"I have brought my two colleagues to meet you. This is Suzie and this is Luz," she said, then turning to the ladies said, "Meet my hero, Mr Ian Vaughan."

"I am pleased to meet you both," said Vaughan. "Please forget the hero bit, I just happened to be in the right place at the right time, that is all."

Amelia went to argue that point, but the waitress had arrived with menus and a request for the drinks order.

During the course of a very pleasant lunch the conversation covered a wide range of topics from the history of the island to child education and the burning subject of the day, the economic crisis. Vaughan learnt that Suzie and Luz were in fact Amelia's employees, who had worked for the business since they had left school. They matched Amelia in having excellent English, and tried, with very amusing results, to test Vaughan's Portuguese.

"My school reports stated that I should avoid any career requiring the use of foreign languages," said Vaughan after attempting to pronounce a dessert speciality, bringing tears of laughter from the waitress as well as his companions.

120

"I think that was very good advice," remarked Suzie, as she dabbed her eyes with a handkerchief.

"Ah, he is awake," said Amelia suddenly, looking up at a tall man walking along the pavement.

Vaughan had seen Esteves, now immaculately dressed wearing dark glasses and carrying a black leather briefcase, as the man had crossed the road. In his early fifties Vaughan thought, distinguished and definitely a ladies' man. "Your uncle?" he asked, not wanting her to have any idea that he had recognised Esteves.

"Yes, my uncle," she replied contemptuously. "He arrived home around four o'clock this morning, very drunk and smelling of ladies' perfume," Amelia wrinkled her nose in distaste. "That however was not so bad as the night I had to help him to his bed; he was on his hands and knees that night when he came into the apartment. Whoever he was with last night still has his shirt as he was not wearing it when he came in."

"You wait up for him?" asked Luz, her eyes large with amazement.

"No of course not, he make a lot of noise coming into the apartment waking me. I was quite frightened at first. If it continues I will have to tell him to find a hotel to live in." Angry now, Amelia's eyes flashed and her head jerked as she looked at each of them in turn, her wavy jet black hair tossed from side to side as she sought their agreement. Vaughan put a hand across his mouth to hide a grin. *Now there is Latin temperament for you, I can almost see the flames.*

Like a solar eclipse the shadow of anger soon passed and once more there was the sunshine of laughter around the table. When the bill came Vaughan settled it after much haggling with his companions, each wanting to pay for the meal. Eventually

Vaughan prevailed by taking the bill to the counter and placing the cash in the hand of the manager.

As they left the restaurant, Amelia asked Suzie, "Ooh. Did customs finally release the Russian's Brazilian chocolate spread?"

"Yes, it was collected from the port early this morning, all two tonnes of it," Suzie replied, arms spread to accentuate the size of the shipment.

"Apparently he already has buyers for it," said Amelia, shrugging her shoulders. "Anyway we must begin our tour, I will see you tomorrow morning."

Amelia looked at Vaughan and said, "Shall we?" indicating that they should walk along the side of the museum and down a cobbled pedestrian street.

"Are there many Russians living on Madeira?" asked Vaughan.

"There are several er oligarchs, I think you call them. A few are beginning to dabble in business here."

"Have you done much business with this one with the sweet tooth?"

"Senhor Reshetnikov? No this is the first time. I hope he pays promptly, we spent a lot of time in clearing his cargo."

When she mentioned the name Reshetnikov Vaughan almost reacted with shock, controlling himself just in time to avoid revealing that he knew the name. *Was that the link with Uncle Olavo Esteves?* He was almost tempted to ask but instantly realised that the question would reveal his seeing the two men together. *Two tonnes of cheap chocolate spread is hardly cause to entertain the way Reshetnikov was doing last night. Drugs probably hidden by the smell of the chocolate.*

The tour included the famous market, then onto Fort San Tiago and the old town with its decorated front doors. This was followed by a cable car trip up to the Monte and a basket sledge ride back down. Her shrieks as the basket skidded round bends reminded Vaughan of the times he had taken his daughters on theme park rides. Blandy's Madeira wine museum shed light on another aspect of the island's history, this visit followed by a stroll through the gardens opposite the theatre rounded off the tour, as all too soon the sun was setting and it was time for her to visit her son in hospital.

"Will Zeferino come home tomorrow?"

"Yes, the doctor said I should collect him around eleven o'clock in the morning," she replied. "I will be very relieved to have him home again."

"I'm sure you will, when will he return to school?"

"Oh, that will not be until Monday. Then I think he will have to stand in front of the whole school and explain what happened to him," she said, in a very serious tone. "The headmaster will then inform him of the punishment he will receive for skipping lessons." Suddenly she stepped close and kissed Vaughan on the lips, catching him by surprise. "Thank you for another lovely day. I must hurry. Goodbye." Then she was gone through the crowd gathering outside of the theatre as Vaughan called out to ask if he would see her again, but she did not reply, just waved. *Now that young lady is just teasing.*

CHAPTER 6

THE VISITORS FROM ACROSS THE OCEAN

Whilst Amelia and Vaughan were being propelled down the winding basket route from the Monte, Arnold Benton Metcalf and his team of security personnel from 'Total Cover Inc' were clearing customs and immigration at Funchal airport. Their flight had been delayed for several hours and Metcalf was showing signs of considerable irritation, which failed to impress the immigration official or the coach driver who had patiently waited for them.

When the coach arrived at the entrance to the hotel Metcalf was the first to get off and then ordered his team to, "Come here and listen up everyone. Once you have checked in I want you to report to Ms Kowalski and Ms Pollard here with your room numbers. They will issue you with radio kits and your person ID code. Memorize the ID, do not write it down."

The group moved off into the hotel's spacious reception area, the men holding back, allowing the two ladies to check in first. Metcalf was next in line. "I am the head of the security team, and my name is Arnold Benton Metcalf."

"Ah yes, Mr Metcalf, could you please fill in this registration form for us."

"Sure. In about an hour I would like to talk to your group co-ordinator and the person in charge of the hotel security. We will need to discuss some work that must be done before the conference delegates arrive."

"Ms Venancio has left for today, but will be here tomorrow morning. She was expecting you three hours ago, apparently your flight was delayed."

"Can you contact her and tell her to come back in?" replied Metcalf, sounding annoyed that she had not waited to greet them.

"I am afraid not, sir, she has meetings with others that she must attend to," replied the receptionist, stiffly.

"Damn, a whole day wasted. What about your security guy?"

"I will see if he is available, sir."

An hour later Metcalf was seated in the foyer with notepad in hand scribbling furiously notes regarding camera and security light location that he thought were required. Having been briefed by Nelson, the receptionist, Franco Serrano approached Metcalf with some caution.

"Mr Metcalf, my name is Franco Serrano, I am responsible for security here."

Metcalf looked up from his notes, taking in the smartly dressed, alert looking young man in front of him. Getting to his feet he thrust out his hand. "Hi, I am Arnold Benton Metcalf. Tell me, do you have much experience of handling this type of conference?" Serrano went to confirm that the hotel was frequently host to conferences, when Metcalf continued, "I doubt it because there is little sign of effective security surveillance around here."

"Madeira is very peaceful island where there is very little crime, Mr Metcalf," replied Serrano, hurt by Metcalf's comment. "This is not New York or Washington. The people of this island are friendly, welcoming people."

"That is as maybe, but the people attendin' this conference have enemies and it is our job to protect them, you understand?"

"I have been asked by my manager to report to him what it is that you require."

"Okay, let's take a walk."

Outside the entrance Metcalf stopped. "When the delegates start to arrive, only their vehicles are to be allowed beyond this point." Serrano went to protest, but Metcalf had held up his hand. "Look just write it down will you, I know that the police will support it. Car bombs are a favourite weapon in the Middle East and North Africa." Serrano shook his head. "The delegates will, on arrival, check in here," continued Metcalf, pointing back at the reception area. "Each person or group will be escorted by my men through the link corridor to the east tower and their rooms. During the conference they will enter only the east tower, and the link corridor will be closed to all."

"I understand that you have brought metal detection arches and X-ray equipment for baggage and hand luggage."

"That is correct. We will be settin' those up in the foyer of the east tower and the entrance to the conference building tomorrow, which means that we will require your maintenance staff to be on hand to ensure sufficient power outlets."

Serrano nodded, at least that job did not sound too difficult. Like most modern hotels the Vidamar reception areas were well equipped with power points.

"Now this is the urgent item that needs to be addressed today, not tomorrow, you understand?" Serrano sighed and nodded again. "We have brought security cameras which need to be installed, one in the centre of the conference entrance canopy, one on the west tower corner looking up the approach road, one on the side of the west tower and one on each front corner of the east tower. Got that?"

"That will take weeks to do," replied a shocked Serrano, "And who will pay for such things?"

"All you will have to do is provide a power supply to each camera. There is no other cabling involved as they are wireless transmission."

"Even so, that is much work. I do not think my manager will agree."

"Well tell him that he will be getting an updated security system for free, 'cos we won't be takin' it home with us."

"I will tell him, but I do not think he will be very grateful."

"Now, except for the conference canopy the cabling must allow for a security light to be installed above each camera. I will work with your people in zoning the light pool when the installation is being done," said Metcalf firmly. "Now let's move to the conference hall."

By the time Serrano's meeting with Metcalf was over it was late evening, and he still had to contact electricians to see about the work required for the cameras and lighting.

Picking up his office telephone he dialled Carla Venancio's home number to tell her about the demands of the 'Total Cover Inc' boss.

*

In the lounge of his Palheiro home Reshetnikov popped the cork out of a bottle of champagne and hurriedly filled three glasses. "This, good cause for celebration," he said, handing glasses to Olavo Esteves and Sonia. "The shipment arrived two days ago and the customs with their normal suspicious nature took samples from every tub of nut chocolate spread and found nothing unusual."

Sonia looked confused and shook her head. "I do not understand why you are so happy about the good quality of nut chocolate spread?"

"Because this genius man here, my friend and business associate Senhor Olavo Esteves, arranged for four tonnes of the spread to be stolen in Brazil and two tonnes exported to Madeira."

Sonia shrugged. "Well," she said, obviously unimpressed. "So you got some cheap nut chocolate spread."

"Here," roared Reshetnikov, "try some and tell me what you think of its flavour?"

Sonia looked at the small dish of dark brown chocolate spread on the table and spooned some into her mouth.

"It is okay."

"Was the flavour strong, as strong as say er coffee?"

"Ah," she replied, "I now understand, drugs were concealed in the tubs. Custom's sniffing machine could not detect drugs over the smell of nut chocolate and it would be a determined custom's officer to stick his hand into a drum of a food product to find anything hidden."

"You are a clever girl Sonia. Fortunately you do not work for customs," said Reshetnikov, putting his arm around her waist and kissing her on the cheek. "I told you, Olavo, that two tonnes would not be too much. They took samples, yes, but I show them that I already have sales for more than half the quantity to patisseries here in Funchal and other places on the island." Reshetnikov took the champagne bottle from the cooler and refreshed everyone's glass. "Your family here get some benefit from the business; for the first time I used your niece's company to clear the goods, they were very efficient."

Olavo Esteves almost choked, put down his glass quickly, coughing into a dark blue handkerchief he had snatched from the breast pocket of his jacket. Recovering, he glared at Reshetnikov. "You did what!" he demanded to know, shouting loudly. "You involved my niece in this illegal business. If the customs had found anything, she, a totally innocent person, would be ruined and probably jailed, how dare you do such thing!"

"Calm yourself, Olavo, there was little chance of any risk to anyone but me."

"Understand this. She is never to be involved in either of our businesses, is that understood?"

Reshetnikov shrugged. "If you prefer it that way," he said, waving away his minder, who now stood filling the doorway to the room. Reshetnikov, realising his mistake may jeopardise future shipments threw out a placatory offer. "In a few minutes I will introduce you to my friend from STAGAZ. You had expressed a desire to talk to him."

"Yes," replied Esteves, quickly adjusting his manner, not wishing to miss the opportunity of establishing himself as the group's lead contact man in connection with Russian business. "I have heard some rumours that I would like to discuss with him, and put forward a hypothetical case for him to consider."

"I will ask him to join us. You will need someone to translate I think. Sonia would be happy, I am sure, to assist."

Esteves hesitated, correctly recognising that Reshetnikov would then almost instantly be informed of his group's plan. "Thank you for your kind offer, but I think we will manage just between the two of us," he said smiling at Sonia. "If we do require assistance may we call for you?"

"Of course," answered a disappointed Reshetnikov.

On greeting, and greatly to Esteves' relief, it was obvious that the talented Smetanin spoke good English. Following the introductions and usual pleasantries, Esteves suggested that, as it was a warm night, he and Smetanin take a stroll around the garden and pool area and talk as they went. In this more confidential environment Esteves presented himself as a business investor, new to Madeira, who had heard, since his arrival, rumours of unrest and dissatisfaction with European economic pressure. As a future significant investor he was anxious to protect his and his business associates' stake in the island's future, should the situation develop into outright rebellion and the island break away from mainland Portugal to become independent. For example would STATGAZ involve itself in energy support in the form of oil to, what would undoubtedly be, a beleaguered community? So carefully and subtly had Esteves introduced the subject and developed the scenario that at first Smetanin had not fully grasped the significance of what was being said to him. It had been a very clever presentation and when Smetanin did comprehend Esteves' message he realised that the man had in no way suggested that he was in any way involved in such a dramatic move. Smetanin was however no fool, and accurately judged Esteves as one of the ringleaders, and as such, someone to remain in contact with, at a distance of course.

*

In England the following morning there was a knock on the bathroom door in Caroline Tucker's flat. "The hairdresser has arrived Caroline, are you out of the shower yet?"

"Just coming, Penny," a nervous voice replied from behind the door.

"I'll answer the door then make some coffee."

"Thank you, I could really do with a cup."

Letting in the hairdresser Penny Heathcote then went into the tiny kitchen and was busying herself making a pot of coffee when the telephone rang.

"I'll get that, Caroline, you just concentrate on getting ready."

Picking up the receiver she said, "Hello," and waited.

"I think I've got the wrong number, sorry to bother you," a voice said.

"I'm just a visitor here, who did you want to speak to?" Penny replied.

"Caroline Tucker if she is available; it's Sarah Vaughan, I'm just phoning to wish her well."

"Oh right, she's just come out of the bathroom, I'll get her for you."

When Caroline took the phone she could tell that Sarah Vaughan was struggling to keep her emotions in check. On finishing the call, which had only taken two minutes, Caroline turned to Penny, her eyes brimming with tears. "I hope the rest of this day is happier than that phone call."

"Good God, what did she say to you?"

"Oh, it was only to wish Alec and I many happy years together, but Penny she was so close to breaking down, I could hear it in her voice. Why she allowed that horrible woman Rebecca to talk her into a divorce I will never understand."

"Neither will I," replied Penny hotly. "Since the divorce absolute was issued that wretched woman hasn't been near Mrs Vaughan; I think Rebecca was after her husband, though she has no chance there, that's for sure. Come on, cheer up, you're getting married to my favourite boss in three hours' time and we have the make-up to follow the hairdo."

The buzzer from reception sounded again. "It's either the bouquets or the dress, hopefully the dress," said Penny as she hurried to the intercom.

An hour and a half later Caroline Tucker and Penny Heathcote stood together in the tiny lounge of Caroline's flat whilst Annette Craven tweaked their dresses then started to take photographs.

"Would you mind if I used a couple of these on my website? You both look absolutely gorgeous, you could both take up modelling. When Mum sees these she'll burst into tears, I'll guarantee it."

"It'll cost, and we models are used to earning large fees," replied Penny trying hard to produce a haughty expression on her face, before spluttering into laughter.

"If you don't mind, Annette, I had better ask Alec first, just in case. I don't quite know how public I can be, bearing in mind the work he does," said Caroline, realising for the first time how careful she would have to be as the wife of one of Britain's senior Secret Intelligence Service officers.

"It shouldn't be a problem, Caroline," said Penny. "His public image is that of a Royal Naval Officer. We make sure he is seen in uniform at several official events in the year, but, yes, it would be best to check."

Another buzz from the reception intercom announced the arrival of Caroline's parents and the bouquets. On seeing Caroline, her mother immediately produced a handkerchief and started dabbing her eyes saying, "You look so lovely dear, are you sure you are going to be happy?"

"Of course she will, stop fussing Elizabeth, I liked the man as soon as I laid eyes on him," cut in her father, a little irritably. "You must be Penny, Caroline has told us a lot about you, I'm Arthur and this is Elizabeth, we're delighted to meet you at last."

When the cars arrived Penny travelled with Caroline's mother in a large Jaguar with Caroline and her father following in a Rolls Royce.

"I had to stop your mother from twittering on otherwise she would have had you all in tears. Having said that Caroline, this has been something of a whirlwind romance. There is no doubt that he has fallen for you, hook, line, and sinker. He made that clear to me when he and I dined at his club a couple of weeks back. How do you really feel about him?"

"I thought that I would never love another man as much as I loved Colin, and when I realised how much I do love Alec I felt as if I were being horribly unfaithful to Colin's memory, but I couldn't help it. I know Colin would want me to be happy Dad, and I am. For the first time in years the cloud that settled over me when Colin and the boys were killed has lifted, and I feel life is starting again."

"I am so pleased to hear that my dear, and so will your mother be. We know how difficult these last few years have been for you, and have been in awe of how bravely you have coped. We desperately want you to be happy and hope that this marriage to Alec will bring you all the happiness in the world."

Later she could remember every moment of the marriage service at St Barnabas Church, Dulwich, where friends and relatives filled every pew. After that however the day became a blur of happy smiling faces, hugs, advice and laughter, with somewhere in-between the wedding breakfast. Her clear moment was of the speeches, the words of which she knew she would remember forever. Then it was time to change and leave the evening celebration for Heathrow and their flight to St Lucia as Mr and Mrs Alec Campbell.

*

On Deserta Grande, Takkal sat morosely at the entrance to the cave, staring out at the ocean, occasionally throwing stones at a pair of inquisitive monk seals. Behind him, lying on a blanket, was a feverish Al Bashir, muttering prayers to Allah. The wolf spider bite, though not deadly to humans, was poisonous enough to create a sizeable red rash and induce a mild fever and nausea. Al Bashir, convinced that death was close at hand, had worked himself into a state of near hysteria and exhaustion. Takkal having at first been sympathetic, had now lost patience with his companion. His dark mood deepened by the fact that no boat had appeared on the previous night to take them off. In fact the only vessel they had seen was a yacht sailing about half a kilometre away going south. Today also, the sea had remained deserted and not for the first time Takkal considered leaving Al Bashir and climbing over the central spine of the island in search of rescue on the other side.

Getting to his feet he stepped back into the cave and rummaged in the bottom of the dinghy for a fresh water bottle.

"You want more water?" he asked.

Al Bashir pushed himself into a sitting position with apparent great effort and held out his hand. "Takkal, you are a kind man. Guided by Allah you have kept me from death, may He bless you."

"We will both surely die unless your friends arrive soon. There are only two bottles of water left and no food," replied Takkal. "You should pray for our rescue from this hellhole you have brought us to. Here, make this last or you will surely die, but not from the bite of a spider," he said before turning away and moving back to his lookout position.

As darkness was falling Takkal struggled to get the dinghy launched, then brought it to the shallows where they could wade into the sea and get on board. Securing the painter under a heavy rock he then went back into the cave and supporting Al Bashir sat him on a rock close to where the dinghy was moored.

As they sat, the lights of fishing boats appeared to the north of the island and started to drift towards them. Three hours passed before a dark shape appeared on the water some distance off and the thump, thump, thump of a marine diesel engine could be heard.

Suddenly a torch flashed twice in their direction then, after a gap of ten seconds, flashed again. "That is the signal," said a relieved Al Bashir. "Please help me into the boat."

Struggling to keep from falling as he supported the shaky Al Bashir, Takkal finally got them alongside the dinghy and held it while his companion got in; with a sharp pull Takkal freed the painter, stepped on board and rowed them out to the waiting fishing vessel.

On their arrival, Takkal was further put out by being almost totally ignored, whilst Al Bashir was almost fêted, the fishermen showing great concern over the bite. The two fishermen were brothers, originally from Algeria, who had crossed illegally into Spain before entering Portugal, where they had obtained false papers. After three years working in the fishing industry they married local girls and therefore received legal status as Portuguese nationals. Their family ties with Algeria had remained strong, even when they moved from the mainland to Madeira. This had been the link through which Al Bashir's leaders had planned their clandestine arrival.

Moving away from the shore the boat went for some distance before showing navigation lights. Apparently the men had hauled sufficient catch for them to return without raising any suspicion. When Takkal complained and demanded to know why they had not come the previous night, he was simply told that they were not fishing in that area then. There was no moon and apart from the glow of the boat's lights there was just an inky blackness, broken only by the occasional light from other boats in the fleet, until they cleared the northern tip of the island where they sighted for the first time the lights of Madeira to the north-west. Rounding Ilhéu Cháo the full glittering array of Madeira's lights came into view holding both men's attention for several minutes.

After four hours, half of which the boat had spent running almost due west, they turned north, heading directly at a small cluster of lights on the shore.

"Where is place you take us?" asked Takkal.

"Cámara de Lobos," the elder brother replied. "We have arranged place for you to eat and sleep. Tomorrow you make your own way. We cannot afford to help anymore, which please you understand."

Takkal had no problem with that as he had already a plan to meet Sarkis Kazakov to collect his packages. He then would travel to the village of Boaventura and the house he had leased. In Al Bashir's case things depended upon the tenuous contacts made between Islamabad, Moscow and Funchal. He was nervous about meeting Ulan Reshetnikov, but the Russian's links with STATGAZ made the contact essential. He was also very unsure of the reception he would receive from his sister, who now lived in Funchal. They had fallen out years before over his beliefs, but the tie of family appeared to be strong enough for her to accept him as a guest for a few days. His only sure contact was Mohammed el Kamal, the junior member of the Moroccan delegation, who had been the source of their papers for entry into Morocco.

Takkal stood looking at the maze of shore lights in front of him. "How you know your way into this harbour?" he asked the younger brother who was helming the boat.

"I look for light," came the answer.

"Yes, but which light?" asked Takkal, not trusting in the will of Allah for guidance.

"You see red flashing light, little bit high over there?"

Takkal looked along the line of the man's arm. "Ah, yes I see."

"We keep this side of that until we see low down flashing green light, then we follow that in. If we lose sight of it we go little side to side until we pick it up again."

The green light he was referring to was set three metres up on the wall of a restaurant in the street leading into the village from the slipways. The street, being narrow, restricted the view of the light from the sea, thus giving sure guidance into the approach channel.

"There, there is the green light you see?"

"Yes I see. Do not lose sight of it," Takkal replied sternly, inwardly, and for the first time in many years, sending a silent prayer of thanks, as his eyes picked out the ragged rocks either side of the entrance lit by the glow of the village lights.

Further into the harbour entrance the helmsman closed the throttle of the engine and pointed to his brother, then to the dinghy. In two quick moves the little craft was launched over the side as the fishing boat slowed.

"We cannot land you at fish quay, too many people to see you. You go in dinghy over there towards where you see green light. Try to be relaxed, we come soon."

Takkal shook his head in disgust and reluctantly made his way to the side of the boat.

The brother helped them over the side and lowered their bags to them. Then the fishing boat moved away and in a few yards turned to port and headed for the quay, whilst Takkal took up the oars again and rowed them ashore.

At one o'clock in the morning the slipways were deserted and their arrival passed unnoticed, much to the relief of both men. Though their jackets and trousers were crumpled and stained they did not stand out, in fact they blended in so well with the few working fishermen about in the streets that their hosts had trouble finding them an hour later, only identifying them by their baggage.

*

Al Bashir was woken the following morning by Takkal shouting into the telephone to someone about a delay in meeting.

"Why must I wait around all day for you. I need a shower and clean clothes; there is no shower here!"

There was a pause as Takkal listened to the reply.

"You want me to visit where?" There was another pause then, "Ahh, I see, then that is okay. You send the car here, eh?" Takkal listened again. "Okay, okay that is good, I wait for Boris at place where Churchill do painting. What time? Ah, ten o'clock is good."

"You have transport?" asked Al Bashir, with fevered perspiration running down his face.

"Yes?" replied Takkal, stretching to ease the stiffness in his back and arms, glaring down at Al Bashir laid on a thin mattress under the window.

"Can you take me to this address in Funchal?" Al Bashir asked, thrusting a crumpled sheet of paper with some Arabic writing on it towards Takkal.

"No, I told you before, from today you go your way, I go mine."

"Please, I need medicine for my leg," Al Bashir said, pulling up his trouser leg to expose a large red inflamed circular rash surrounding an area of weeping pus. "The bite of the spider, not looking good, I need medicine quickly. The brothers, they say they cannot take me until tonight."

Takkal shook his head. "I ask Boris if he help. Maybe I should shoot you and put you out of your misery, eh."

Al Bashir struggled to his feet, obviously not well. Looking fiercely into Takkal's eyes he said with much fervour, "I must do much work before delegations arrive. I have some difficult contacts to make. It will not be so easy for our influence to prevail amongst the nations at this conference. We cannot rely simply upon our beliefs; we must consider the wider aspects of life and living, including economies. Just removing the opposing messenger will not be enough to stop their unholy alliance with western ideology. Yours is not the only part of this mission that must succeed."

For the first time since Takkal had met with Al Bashir he got a sense of the man's belief in his cause. "I neither know nor care about such things," replied Takkal. "All I am interested in at this moment is getting to the meeting place. Can you walk?"

"Yes, for short distance."

"Fortunately it is not far. Collect your things, we must leave soon."

The sun was already hot by the time they left the safe house and started to walk through Cámara de Lobos. Turning onto the Rua S. João de Deus they strolled down to the corner, turning left onto the Largo do Poco. Already the cafés and bars were doing good business but Al Bashir was finding the crowds of tourists too much to cope with as they milled around frustrating his progress. At the top of the street they turned right onto a road that led out of town, and trudged up the ever-steepening incline to a patio on the right overlooking the harbour and village centre. A wall plaque explained that the famous British Prime Minister, Sir Winston Churchill, had sat there to paint the scene.

The wait of five minutes for the feverish Al Bashir was like a lifetime, and when Boris arrived in the black Mercedes he had to be helped from the point where he was leaning against the patio wall, into the back of the car. To Al Bashir's relief, Boris showed no objection to the request to take him to his sister's house in the Socorro area of Funchal.

It was the young Ismail Karaki who answered the door. "I am Mohammed el Kamal al Bashir, your mother's brother."

"She is in the back of the house preparing a meal," replied Ismail, turning away from the door.

Al Bashir was more than a little confused and annoyed by the young man's response. "Please tell her that I am here."

Without turning or making any acknowledgement Ismail walked away down a corridor and, opening a door, put his head into the room and said something. After a few moments he closed the door and crossed the hallway disappearing into another room, leaving Al Bashir leaning against the front door frame feeling weak and faint. Finally his sister appeared, frowning as she approached him.

"You have come then. I hope you are not bringing troubles with you, this house does not want..." suddenly she stopped and looked at her brother more closely. "Are you sick?"

"In my travels here I was bitten by a spider and it has become infected."

"Oh. Oh, come in," she said, in an exasperated tone. "I suppose we must call a doctor to you. You will have to pay his bill, medicine is expensive."

By the time the doctor arrived Al Bashir had washed and changed his clothes. The doctor had almost accepted Al Bashir's story about being bitten while walking in some gardens until he came to describing the spider.

"You say it was how large?"

Al Bashir used his thumbs and forefingers to indicate size.

"There is no biting spider on Madeira of that size, maybe on the Desertas, yes, but not here," said the doctor.

"It was dark, er, bad light, maybe I make mistake with size," Al Bashir replied, too quickly and showing signs of nervousness.

Puzzled and slightly suspicious, the doctor administered an antihistamine injection then cleaned the wound site, squeezed out the pus, then sprinkled penicillin powder over it and applied a dressing.

"Come to my clinic tomorrow, I will have the nurse re-dress the wound and make sure that things are going on all right."

When his sister returned to the room her face was full of anger. "Where were you when the spider bit you?"

"As I said, I was in some gardens."

"You lie!" she shouted back at him.

He rose as if to strike her, his hand raised, when Ismail came into the room. "What is all this shouting in our house?" he demanded to know, glaring at Al Bashir.

"It is nothing, my son, do not alarm yourself. My sister and I had a minor disagreement, that is all," said Al Bashir, looking steadily at his sister.

There was silence in the room for several seconds, before the young man turned and left leaving the two glaring at each other.

"Why are you here, and why is that young woman with you?"

"We are here to help advise some members of the Libyan delegation, the negotiations are very, er, complicated."

"With you everything is complicated, hidden, all behind your hand, never open and set out honestly."

Momentarily Al Bashir thought again to strike her, but controlled his temper. When the conference is ended in confusion and Al Djebbar's call is defeated, then he will teach his sister and her disrespectful son how they should behave to him.

A movement at the door had him looking up. "Teacher, it is I, Leyla. A doctor came to see you, are you not well?" She was dressed in full purdah, with just her beautiful dark brown eyes staring at him with concern.

"On my journey here I was bitten by a spider. All will be well now, I have had the bite treated," replied Al Bashir, looking at her fondly.

Al Bashir wanted to take her in his arms and beg her to marry him, but he dare not for fear of the swift retribution that would come if such action brought failure to his mission. The horrifying reality, was that the young woman he wished above all others to have as his wife was the person selected to get close to Al Djebbar and give her life to destroy him, should Takkal fail in his assassination attempt.

As he looked at her his memory flashed back to the moment Mohammed al Ben Said told her of her sacred purpose. Her face had taken on an expression of great serenity as she nodded acceptance. Al Bashir had wanted to cry out against it, but had been too weak in the face of the charismatic preacher; how he had prayed to Allah that Takkal would succeed.

*

On leaving Al Bashir at the Karaki household, Takkal had been driven down through the old part of the town. He looked across at the crowded restaurants in the Largo do Corpo Santo as the car swung up a cobbled street that led to the Rua de Santa Maria. As they passed a church the driver picked up what looked like a car key fob and pointing it at the windscreen pressed a button on it. The road narrowed as they entered the Calcada do Socorro and seconds later the car swung right through a gated opening in a high wall and stopped in the middle of a cobbled courtyard close to the rear of an imposing cliff top property. Takkal got out of the car and walked a few metres further across the courtyard taking in the surroundings, noting the automatic gate closure as he went. A black Range Rover with darkened windows was parked alongside the wall in the shade of a single palm tree, it was new enough for the tyre centreline markings to be still visible and the paintwork unblemished. Kazakov must be doing well he thought. What looked like a small summerhouse stood close to the cliff edge and a dwarf wall ran from it along the cliff edge past the house to the property's front boundary. The rest of the rear garden was laid to grass with a small border of camellias and strelitzia.

"This way," said Boris, indicating that they should walk round to the front of the building.

Negotiating the uneven steps in the path held Takkal's attention until they came to the front garden where he stopped and looked about him in wonder. A raised circular pond with a fountain in the centre was the main feature, positioned in the middle of a wide patterned cobbled pathway that appeared to flow like a river from an imposing pair of cast iron gates before surrounding the pond, and curving towards an elegant staircase that led to the first floor veranda of the house. To either side of the path were borders of exotic shrubs and flowers, the scent of which hung in the humid air. A tree outside the western end of the property gave a pleasant area of shade to a stone bench amongst the floral scene. It struck him as strange that an arms dealer like Kazakov would live amongst such beautiful and tranquil surroundings. Reluctantly he walked to the staircase and made his way up to the veranda where he stopped again, this time to admire the view of the harbour and the panorama of the city.

"You like my situation here?" said a harsh voice behind him.

Takkal had heard the soft footsteps approach, but had not turned to greet his host. "A soft bed to lay on in a hard world," Takkal replied.

"Not as soft as you may think."

The two men turned and looked at each other and smiled.

"It has been a long time my friend, let me see now, Kabul six months ago. I have wondered many times since why the reporter had to die."

"I do not concern myself with the why, just the fee. That way I can concentrate exclusively on the job."

"How many days do you have before the hit?"

"It depends on when I can get the target in my sights."

"Is it someone attending the conference?"

Takkal shrugged. "I do not have a list of those people, just a name and a picture."

"Huh, yes it is someone at the big meeting. That is good, as it will distract attention from my more profitable transaction." Sarkis Kazakov laughed loudly and throwing a massive arm around the diminutive Takkal said, "Come let us have some food and refreshment, then we go to my favourite club, eh."

"I need a shower and to change into clean clothes."

"Okay, no problema."

Inside, the house was as opulent as its exterior, with polished hardwood floors and intricate plaster mouldings to walls and ceilings that set off elegant crystal chandeliers. The furniture was French antique, much lighter in style than the Portuguese, and obviously expensive. Takkal found it difficult to imagine the bear like Kazakov choosing to live in such delicately beautiful surroundings.

"You like my summer palace?" asked Kazakov, noticing Takkal's fascinated study of the rooms.

"I must congratulate you on your exquisite taste, Sarkis," Takkal replied, slowly shaking his head in disbelief.

"You think as rough arms dealer I am beyond appreciating beautiful things?"

Something in Kazakov's tone warned Takkal to reply with care, the large Russian was known to have a short temper, and when annoyed could be violent.

Takkal turned smiling. "No, no my friend, in truth I am filled with admiration and envious of your situation here."

Satisfied with Takkal's response Kazakov pulled lightly on a brass knob, set in the side of the reception room's chimney breast. A bell rang somewhere in the house and moments later a pretty girl appeared.

"Meet Nadezhda, my daughter."

Takkal smiled at the girl, who seemed vaguely familiar.

"Nadezhda, this man is a good friend of mine, I would like you to show him to the east cliff room."

The girl bobbed a type of curtsey and indicated with her arm for Takkal to follow. The reception room they had been in ran the whole width of the house with wide, polished walnut, double internal doors positioned towards the cliff end. Stepping through the doorway, Takkal found himself in a fully carpeted upper hallway with a short flight of steps leading down to a lower hall at the end of which were a pair of full height doors, presenting a grand entrance from the street that ran down the side of the house. Crossing the hall he followed the girl up a flight of stairs to the first floor where they turned back on themselves along a landing to a window overlooking the sea. Opening the door on her left the girl indicated for Takkal to enter. Walking past her he found himself in a darkened bedroom, the bright sunlight outside dimmed by the closed louvre shutters. He stopped to allow his eyes to adjust to the lower light level, then crossed the room to the far corner and placed his small case on a folding stand. Hearing the girl open another door behind him to his left, Takkal spun round, only to see her gesture for him to look into an adjacent room. She watched him with a strange intensity as he crossed the room again and stepped into the en suite bathroom.

After a cursory glance around he turned to thank her, and went to speak in the hope of starting a conversation, before realising that she had gone, leaving him feeling somehow strange and unsettled by her silent almost ghostly behaviour. That was it; she was a ghost from his past, but from where.

"Your daughter is not a great conversationalist," said Takkal as he placed his knife and fork neatly alongside the fish skeleton on his plate, two hours later.

"A few years ago she witnessed a savage attack on her sister, ordered by some enemies of mine," Kazakov replied, looking down at the table and toying with his silver serviette ring. "She has not spoken since. We have tried everything to unlock her tongue, employed doctors, psychologists, speech therapists, but as you noticed, nothing has been successful."

"What happened to her sister?"

"She died from multiple stab wounds. I have spent much money trying to discover who it was who attacked her."

"If you ever find out and want to er, balance the books shall we say, you know where to contact me," said Takkal.

"I want to balance the books, as you say, by myself," replied Kazakov. "It will not only be the murderer who is punished, but also the person in my organisation who leaked my family's identity."

Takkal gave him a puzzled look. "Identity?"

"At that time there was more turmoil in Russia than there is now, even with the current march back to the days of Stalin and Khrushchev. Many scores were being settled and as a successful business man I had those that felt that they should have what I had worked hard for and achieved." Kazakov picked up the wine bottle and refilled his glass. "You want a top up?"

Takkal put his hand over his half full glass. "No thank you, I cannot drink so much these days."

"Where was I, ah yes, the murdering thieves." Kazakov got up from the table and walked across the room to the window overlooking the rear courtyard garden. "I knew," he continued, "that either my organisation or I was a target of those greedy ex KGB bastards and their friends, so I arranged for my wife and daughters to move away under the false family name of Mosyakov. Everything seemed to be secure, and after six months we arranged a secret meeting. It was fine, they were not happy about being away from Kiev and my wife and I missed each other very much, but they understood why such arrangement was essential. I returned to Kiev to arrange our new life away from Ukraine, happy that they were safe, then, two months later, their apartment was attacked and my elder daughter, Rozalina, brutally killed and my poor little Nadezhda struck dumb by what she saw."

When Kazakov had mentioned the assumed family name it was as if the bottom had dropped out of Takkal's stomach and his chest drawn down into the vacuum created. The shock of this realisation sent the room spinning leaving him feeling faint with fear, for he had been the attacker. He realised now why the girl's face had appeared vaguely familiar, it was the family resemblance to her sister. Had Kazakov finally discovered who the assailant was and used the contact and request for assistance to lay an elaborate trap for him to blindly walk into? His struggle to regain control had taken only moments, but it was a terrified Takkal that had looked at his host to see if his reaction had been observed. Kazakov's thoughts however were many miles away as he stood staring at the little summerhouse, an expression of deep sadness on his face.

As his feeling of shock subsided and rational thought returned, Takkal remembered that subtlety was definitely not one of Sarkis Kazakov's methods, and that Boris would have been ordered to take him out in a drive-by shooting at Cámara de Lobos.

That failed assassination in Russia had haunted Takkal ever since, and had been the drive behind his meticulous planning and cautious execution of the many subsequent contracts. He had been recovering from some illness, maybe flu, and should not have taken the contract, but he was making a name for himself and the job seemed easy enough. He was to kill the wife and two daughters; the apartment was only lightly guarded and had minimal security lighting and alarm systems. Entry had been easy, but the internal arrangement he had been given was wrong, and the elder daughter was sleeping in the room identified as occupied by the mother. His plan had been to use a knife, silence being all-important on a quiet and still night. It all went wrong, as he had moved close enough to slit the woman's throat, the night vision goggles he was wearing restricted the field of vision close to him and he stubbed his foot on one of the bed's castors. Immediately the person sleeping was wide awake and in a flash had reached out and put on the bedside light. The brightness through the goggles blinded him and he had lashed out blindly, missing his target at first, who then screamed loudly. Ripping off the goggles with his left hand he felt his victim's hand push into the base of his neck as she tried to hold him at bay. Still half blinded he had struck again, this time the knife struck home, the blade ripping into the back of her shoulder. The hand at his neck clenched convulsively, the nails tearing at his flesh as she again cried out, this time in pain. Again and again he struck, almost in frenzy, as the girl he could now see clearly, fought back twisting and turning to avoid a fatal blow. He must have wounded her several times before he managed to grab her head and plunge the knife into her throat. Shouts and heavy footsteps on the stairs warned Takkal of the approach of the two bodyguards employed to look after the family, and kicking the window open, he made good his getaway dropping one floor onto the rickety fire escape. He was several kilometres away before he realised that the wetness soaking into his T-shirt was his own blood.

In the room he had rented he cleaned and dressed his wounds hurriedly, before leaving and driving non-stop to the Belarus border then on to Poland. The mission's partial failure had taught him a great deal and to ensure that he never forgot, he kept the scars, now white scores across his tanned skin. Each morning he would look at them in a mirror and swear never to take unnecessary risks.

It was only now, years later, he was to learn that the attack had been witnessed. Trying desperately to appear calm he racked his brain trying to recall whether there was any part of his face that was exposed in the struggle. No, he was sure that his one-piece hood and mask had remained in place; no one could have seen his face. Anyway the girl showed no sign of recognition.

CHAPTER 7

WAITING, WATCHING AND DEATH

The day following Takkal's arrival at Kazakov's home, Vaughan had got down to the serious business of surveillance and at nine o'clock dialled Claremont's home number on the island.

"Arthur Claremont speaking."

"Good morning, Mr Claremont, Ian Vaughan here. Alec Campbell asked me to drop a parcel off to you, but I will need to get a bag for it, do you have any suggestions?"

"Oh, er yes, mm, try the market stall in the little square off the Rua do Sabão, it's called the Praco do Columbo; a stall there sells bags made from large plastic coffee bean packets. The Delta Cafes Diamante ones are nice and strong, they're gold and maroon in colour," replied Claremont. "Oh and whilst you're there try the little tea shop, the 'Loja do Cha', it would be a good place for your elevenses today."

"Thanks, I'll do just that. Alec sends his best regards by the way, he thought you might be in Morocco."

"That's nice of him; no, I have arranged for a visit, in fact I will be going quite soon," informed Claremont. "When you next bump into Alec could you thank him and pass on my best wishes."

Vaughan was impressed, the man was very quick thinking, without any rehearsal he had informed what bag to acquire, the time and location of the swap, and that he had arranged a meeting with his Moroccan friend.

"Of course, Mr Claremont, I'll say cheerio for now, thanks again."

Later, dressed in shorts and plain yellow T-shirt and sandals, Vaughan looked like many other tourists as he jammed a sun hat on his head and headed along the quay to the esplanade. Turning right he walked along to the crossing then found his way up through some narrow streets to the square. The stall was the first one he came to and displayed an amazing number of colourful bags all made from different brands of recycled coffee bean packets.

"Can I help you, Senhor?" asked the lady serving.

"I'm looking for a Delta Cafes 'Diamante' brand bag. It's for my wife, she apparently must have that particular design," said Vaughan, shaking his head as though amazed by his wife's request.

"Please, we have not one on display, but let me look in the box out back."

"That is very kind of you," replied Vaughan, now concerned that a matching bag would not be available. He felt panic rising as he pulled out his mobile phone and checked that he had Claremont's mobile number; breathing a sigh of relief when he found it listed as Arthur M below Arthur H.

"You are in luck Senhor, we have some. Here please, is this the one she require?" said the lady, holding up a maroon bag with gold coffee beans and lettering on it.

Vaughan studied the bag quickly. "Yes that is exactly the same as her sister's, how much do I owe you?"

"Five euro, please, Senhor."

Paying her, Vaughan checked his watch; he had thirty minutes to get back to the yacht, collect the directional microphone and recorder then get back to the tearoom he could see up to his left. He hurried across the square to the road leading to the cathedral, turning left down to the seafront. It was three minutes to eleven o'clock as he re-entered the square and sat down just behind the menu stand by a table outside the tearoom, placing his bag on the ground. At five minutes past the hour, a tall, distinguished gentleman, in his late sixties, crossed the square, arm in arm with an elegant lady, holding an identical bag to the one Vaughan had purchased, just as Vaughan's coffee arrived. Arthur Claremont was more upright than Vaughan had imagined him from the SIS photograph. *Retirement in Madeira must be good for one,* he thought.

Claremont, and the lady Vaughan assumed to be his wife, stopped for a while discussing whether to have a coffee, then they studied the menu board. They allowed just the right amount of time for those at the café tables to look at them, then, losing interest, turn their gaze elsewhere. Making an excuse to get her reading glasses from her handbag the lady put her Diamante bag down close to Vaughan's. After a couple of minute's discussion as to what they would order the lady removed her glasses and sought a table, leaving her husband to pick up Vaughan's bag and join her. A seamless operation that did not attract a single interested glance from anyone at the tables; Vaughan was very impressed. He was even more impressed as he picked up the switched bag to find that it contained two boxed bottles of Blandy's Madeira wine.

Leaving his presents back at the yacht, Vaughan walked out of the city centre, up 'cardiac hill' and along to the Vidamar hotel. His original plan was to lunch in the main hotel restaurant but instead, decided to go to the 'Mamma Mia' Italian restaurant, which was built over the hotel's Sunset Lounge section of the conference suite. He had an excellent view from there of the hotel frontage and the apparently frantic work being carried out. Two basket hoists were in position at the front corners of the east tower with men working to fit security cameras and lighting. Vaughan smiled, Campbell was right, the hotel staff were being run ragged by the security demands of 'Total Cover Security Inc'.

"You like to order a drink, Senhor?" asked a waiter.

"Yes, I'll have a beer, please."

When the waiter returned Vaughan started a conversation with him, asking about the age of the hotel and whether it was one of a large group, and generally showing interest. The pleasant conversation moved onto life in Madeira, the weather, and the numbers of tourists visiting and finally he said, "Excuse me asking but, who is the young lady over there talking to the tall guy in the suit?"

"She is Miss Carla Venancio, she is like, er, manager for group bookings."

"Looks like she has some problems," said Vaughan, as he watched the young woman gesticulating furiously whilst talking to the man, who appeared to be part of the security team.

"I think the company that has been hired to provide security for a big conference to be held here is making many demands," replied the waiter. "I heard they have asked to see employment records of every member of staff, to make sure none of us are criminals."

Vaughan shook his head in apparent astonishment, but thought to himself that the demand was reasonable considering the relative importance of the guests and political interest in the conference.

"Another beer, Senhor?"

"That would be great, er, obrigado."

Vaughan took as long as he could over lunch, hoping to identify if there were any other people anxious to see what security arrangements were being made. He kept looking at the tall man in the suit, apparently in charge of the security equipment upgrade. There was something familiar about him, the way he moved and gesticulated, but Vaughan could not place where he had seen him previously. The man however had his head covered by an incongruous baseball cap and half his face was shielded by sunglasses making it impossible for Vaughan to fully satisfy his curiosity.

Paying the bill and leaving, Vaughan walked down to the west tower reception still thinking about the tall security boss. Hoping to get a better look at the man in charge, he was disappointed, as by the time he had walked down the ramp, the man had disappeared.

Entering the cool hotel foyer Vaughan immediately understood why the hotel had been chosen for such an event. The clean lines of the architecture and polish of the décor spoke of genuine five star luxury. At the desk he made polite enquiries about the room rates and was impressed by the warmth and helpfulness of the response. After expressing his interest in returning to Madeira later in the year Vaughan was offered a tour of the facilities. Like many hotels on the island the Vidamar was built on the edge of a cliff and to get to the pool terrace you took a lift down several levels stepping out onto a large area with three swimming pools close to the ocean's waves. Above the pool level was the hotel's spa, where guests could receive expert pampering followed by luxury lounging, overlooking the outdoors pool terrace and the mighty Atlantic Ocean beyond. Returning to the central lift area Vaughan was shown a suite and a room, both of which were very impressive, before returning to the ground floor and bar area.

Thanking the receptionist for her time and courtesy he elected to stay for a drink in the bar, as a way of extending his stay, and got chatting to the barman.

"They rush around all the time wanting many things done before this er conference starts. I not see much of them, their boss he say they not to drink, as they must stay alert at all time. Sometime some of them creep in and hide in corner over there sipping the 'Jack Daniels'." The barman laughed, then leaning over the counter to avoid being heard by another couple who had just entered the bar, he said, "One man, he comes in every night and drinks maybe half a bottle."

"With that amount of alcohol in the bloodstream he won't be very alert," replied Vaughan taking another sip of his ice-cold beer and wondering whether he should also lay off the alcohol until the job was finished.

As the barman was occupied with other customers Vaughan settled himself in the window corner where he could observe the comings and goings along the link corridor between the two towers. A constant stream of tradesmen were hurrying backwards and forwards carrying drums of electrical cabling or pieces of equipment. *Whoever is in charge of that lot they definitely know how to motivate people,* thought Vaughan, hoping that the hotel was charging sufficient for all the hassle.

Finishing his beer he left the bar and turning right started to walk along the link corridor. He only got five metres or so before a tall muscular 'Total Cover' security guard blocked his path.

"I'm sorry, sir, only those holding pass badges are allowed beyond this point."

"Really, that is very inconvenient," replied Vaughan. "I was hoping to inspect the function rooms in the east tower."

"That will not be possible until after the conference scheduled for next week, sir. In fact, by this evening, this corridor will be blocked off from the rest of the hotel."

"Oh, as I said, that is very inconvenient," said Vaughan trying to look offended by the refusal to allow him access.

Turning on his heels he marched off and rounding the corner into the foyer almost knocked over the diminutive figure of Miss Carla Venancio, the manager responsible for the conference. She looked exhausted and harassed but mustered a smile and apology for getting in the way, before hurrying on down the corridor and past the guard. Vaughan watched her go, feeling sorry for her having to deal with 'Total Cover', who appear to be better named as 'Total Control'.

Back out in the sunshine, the heat and increasing humidity of the day hit Vaughan as he wandered around the area trying to find a location from where he could monitor events at the Vidamar hotel without attracting attention. The problem was that the hotel was set down well below street level and there were buildings along the road pavement frontage that further restricted the view. Over lunch and throughout his visit to the hotel, Vaughan had been on the lookout for other agents like himself, surveying the territory in advance, but had failed to identify any. He assumed that the CIA would have planted at least one agent in the 'Total Cover' team, but the European nations would have to operate in a similar way to himself and Claremont. Visiting a local newsagents and gift shop, Vaughan purchased ten euros worth of bus tickets and using the excellent bus service was back at the marina in twenty minutes, having decided to look at the hotel from the sea. His plan, however, was postponed by the STATGAZ negotiator Gleb Smetanin sitting with a young man at a table in the fish restaurant closest to the entrance ramp. They were in deep conversation as Vaughan casually studied the menu.

"You would like a table Senhor? Please I have a nice one for you here."

"Por favor beer," replied Vaughan, accepting the invitation.

When the waiter returned with the beer he asked, "You like to see our menu, Senhor?"

"Not today, thank you, I ate too much for lunch."

"You eat here tomorrow eh. We give you special discount as you saved young boy from sea few days ago. I see you when you come there and ambulance they come," said the waiter in an overly loud voice.

"Maybe tomorrow," replied Vaughan, anxious now to end the conversation that had attracted the attention of several of the other diners including Smetanin.

To hurry his beer and leave would have drawn more attention, so Vaughan settled back in his seat and looking out over the marina basin waited for the other diners to lose interest in him and return to their conversations. The annoying thing was that the incident had made him known to the Russian who would now be sure to recognise Vaughan if they came in sight of each other again.

After twenty minutes or so Vaughan was about to leave when Reshetnikov and his minders appeared. The waiter almost ran across the restaurant to greet the new arrival and was disappointed when he was waved away and Smetanin rose, bidding goodbye to his young dining companion. Whilst a minder settled Smetanin's bill the two Russians talked quietly, walking away towards the ramp. The young man meanwhile finished his coffee and, picking up a slim package from the table, walked away in the opposite direction.

Vaughan had surreptitiously been studying Smetanin's table companion and concluded that he was a local and probably a hotel worker of some sort. The shoes, pressed trousers and uniform style shirt were of the style he had seen the lower grade Vidamar employees wearing. *Not a restaurant waiter, but maybe room service attendant brought in temporarily to deal with the higher demands of the conference delegates. If that's the case, the Russians have got themselves very well organised.*

Leaving the restaurant Vaughan followed the young man at a distance. The youth had been sitting with his back to Vaughan and at no time turned to look in Vaughan's direction. It was also apparent that he had not been trained in the dark arts of pursuer and pursued, showing no sign of either recognition or suspicion as Vaughan crossed the road alongside him and stood next to him at the bus stop. The shops and businesses were closing at that time of day and the buses were very crowded, so Vaughan found himself hanging onto a roof strap as the bus powered away from the stop and wound its way out of the city centre along the Avenida do Infante to the Estrada Monumental and the Vidamar hotel.

Vaughan's guess was correct, for the young man pushed past him as the stop approached, and followed by Vaughan, got off the bus and hurried across the road and down to the hotel, whilst Vaughan strolled slowly back in the direction of Reid's. The question now was how to combat Smetanin's man without revealing his own interests in the conference. The web of intrigue was getting larger by the hour and Vaughan, not for the first time, wondered whether he was getting out of his depth. His main dilemma was how much direct action he should take, if any, in countering others' interests and attempts to influence the conference outcome. Claremont had obviously made contact with his Moroccan friend, so there was UK influence there, and, if Charles Stanthorpe Ogilvey had done his stuff, then Vaughan at least stood a chance of doing something useful. He continued turning these thoughts over in his mind as he walked back to the marina via the public gardens just down from the President's official residence. He must have been the only person that day not to linger and take in the exotic beauty of the flowers planted in the well-maintained borders and beds. The island, famous for its beautiful gardens and dramatic scenery, lacked only white sandy beaches to make it every tourist's dream.

It was only when he was walking along the sea wall of the marina that his thoughts returned to the moment, as he stopped to look at the yacht logos painted on the wall. Some were just the skipper's national ensign and the name of the yacht, others were more imaginative, and some probably painted by the younger members of the crew. The pictures suggested a type of club with disconnected members, yachtsmen that had called at Funchal on their way, either south to the Canary Islands or south-west out into the trade winds before turning west for the Caribbean. Over the years the artwork had become quite famous amongst the sailing fraternity.

It was too late to set out for the Vidamar by sea so he settled for writing up some more fictitious notes for the book that would never be published to ensure that visitors to the yacht would be convinced that he was who he said he was. By midnight he had typed up on his laptop a record of the leg from Porto Santo via the Desertas to Funchal, with detailed comments about the currents, course taken, port facilities and entry procedure. With Campbell's instructions ringing in his ears, Vaughan finished the evening's work with a coded report that he would send to Staunton in the morning. Sitting back he felt a sense of achievement, not just with the writing and reporting but with a decision made, acceptance of his role as observer rather than action taker.

*

Earlier in the evening Olavo Esteves stood preening himself in front of the mirror. The waiting was getting to him, the months, indeed years, of dreaming for this grasp at power so close and yet so far away. He could hear Amelia in the kitchen preparing food and was tempted to change his mind and eat with her as she kept a good table like his mother used to. *I must be getting old*, he thought, *to think of food as more enjoyable than the pleasures of Diana.*

Adjusting his tie again his thoughts ranged over the planned coup and what his future would be in the new order. His anger over Reshetnikov's use of Amelia's import agency had subsided, particularly after a second meeting with Gleb Smetanin of STATGAZ that morning, as it became obvious that his position as linkman to the oil company was almost guaranteed. Inwardly he hoped for the failure of the mainland coup, as its success would not make Madeira the isolated and independent tax haven that would suit him personally, but how to engineer such an outcome he still had no idea. Those plans could wait until morning; this evening he was going to enjoy himself again with a beautiful creature whose talent for giving pleasure was second to none.

On the way out he put on a friendly smile as he looked around Zeferino's bedroom door. The boy was laying face down on his bed, his back and legs horribly red with thin white areas outlining the burst blisters.

"How are you feeling?" asked Esteves.

The boy painfully turned his face towards his uncle. "I feel still very sick uncle and my back still feels as if it is on fire."

"I am sorry to hear that, Zef, but your momma she look after you well. You will be okay for school on Monday you see."

The comment did nothing to improve the boy's feelings for he knew only too well the humiliation he would have to endure, and the punishment that would inevitably come with it.

Moving along the hallway to the kitchen door Esteves said to Amelia, "I go now. Do not wait up eh, I will be late."

"Try not to wake us all when come home, please," she replied, giving a not so friendly glare.

Ignoring her response Esteves left the apartment and walked down the stairs and out into the street. The breeze off the mountains had brought the temperature down to a tolerable level and Esteves decided to stroll down the hill to the taxi rank, a fifteen minute walk away. In this part of town, where mainly Portuguese lived, the evening streets were alive with the sounds of families; the laughter, the playful screams of children, the radios blaring out the local music station, in fact, the normal sounds of Portuguese family life. At the taxi rank three drivers were stood away from their vehicles holding an animated debate on whether the island's football hero would leave his present Spanish club and return to England to play or join Porto. It was only the sound of the first taxi's rear door slamming as Esteves settled himself on the rear seat that brought the debate to an end, and the driver hurrying back to his vehicle.

"A desculpa, Senhor," said the driver, apologising as he leapt into his seat and started the engine.

"Forum Monumental, Ponta da Cruz, depressa," ordered Esteves angrily, glaring at the driver's reflection in the rear view mirror.

The Forum Monumental, a large shopping centre about five kilometres from the centre of the city, was already starting to close down for the day as Esteves paid off the taxi with the exact amount shown on the meter and hurried down the steps to purchase a bottle of Diana's favourite perfume, some champagne and chocolates. Having carefully placed his purchases in a colourful bag he hurried back up the steps and across the dual carriageway and down the hill to the hotel. Entering the reception area Esteves was pleased to see that the desk clerks were busy

161

attending to a group checking in, and paid him no attention as he passed the gift shop went and down the stairs to the lounge area.

As arranged, Diana was sat at the bar and was deep in thought whilst stirring her cocktail. Reshetnikov's mistress, Sonia, had driven her to the hotel and just as she was getting out of the car had told Diana that tonight would probably be the last night she would have to spend with Esteves. When she had shown disappointment at the news, Sonia had said, "Surely you no like dirty old men like him Diana. You are much too lovely, though he is quite good looking for one so old."

Diana was on the point of blurting out her plan when Sonia said, "Close the door, I must hurry to take Zaza to the party at Machico."

Now, sat at the bar, she realised that she must make the night very special indeed if her plan to return with him to Brazil was to be achieved.

"You have the room organised, my lovely one?" Esteves asked Diana quietly over her shoulder, making her jump.

She spun round smiling broadly with pleasure in her eyes as she looked at him. "You are naughty making me jump like that, but I forgive," she replied, holding his head in both her hands and kissing him. "Yes, Greta has let me have a key and she tell me we have a choice of three rooms. What view would you like to wake up to? The key is for cleaner and unlocks any door," she continued, speaking very quietly.

"The ocean," Esteves replied, reaching down to gently stroke her bottom.

"Oh good, that is what I hoped you would choose."

"Leave the drink," Esteves said, as he saw her reach for the glass. "I have much better refreshment here in this bag."

Slipping off the bar stool, Diana picked up a large shoulder bag and linking arms with Esteves walked with him down the steps and round to the lifts.

In the room, Esteves put the champagne in the icebox of the refrigerator together with the chocolates then presented her with the perfume.

"You are so kind to me, Olavo, tonight I will make very special for you, you see. I go to bathroom, you make yourself comfortable, I will not be long."

In the bathroom Yaroslava let her dress and underwear fall to the floor and stepped into the shower, taking care not to get her hair wet. She knew from past meetings with Olavo that he was fastidious with regard to cleanliness, and tonight she had to ensure that all was perfect for her plan to be successful. She had left Russia five years before, changing her name to Diana Neumann and obtaining a German passport. The German family name, she had taken for amusement, as its meaning, 'new man' or 'newcomer', described both her and her ambition exactly; she was a newcomer on the hunt for a new, definitely wealthy, man. In Russia she had left an abusive stepfather and battered mother, plus a string of offences for shoplifting and other petty crimes. In Germany she found that she had a natural talent for languages and soon obtained work in the east of the country where her initial language deficiencies were not called into question. As her knowledge of the language increased so did her yearning for travel, which had brought her to Madeira one year ago, speaking now, Russian, German and Portuguese. A chance meeting with Reshetnikov's mistress, Sonia, brought her into the escort business, learning immediately that her Russian language was of high value, not that she ever spoke it when working. Reshetnikov's visiting Russian associates, never suspecting her of being anything other than a German girl who spoke

Portuguese, would, as the evenings progressed, become more unguarded in their conversation with each other. Whereas Sonia would be viewed with caution, Diana was accepted as pretty decoration, there to serve drinks and organise food. After only a few months she had risen in the organisation and was no longer expected to supply sexual favours for those who paid for and were demanding of such things.

Her first meeting with Olavo Esteves was one evening when Sonia had asked her to drop off two girls at the casino near to the President's official residence. There she was to ensure that they met the correct client, obtain the payment, then return for further instructions. Little Isabella had recognised Huberto Pedroso and Olavo Esteves standing near the entrance and introductions were made, during which, Diana became aware of Esteves looking longingly at her. Two days later Sonia had offered her a large bonus if she would 'befriend' Esteves, and so the relationship began. What Sonia had not anticipated was that Diana Neumann would recognise in the maturely handsome Olavo Esteves, the sugar daddy she had for years been seeking. Believing Esteves to be telling the truth, that he was a widower and wealthy businessman, Diana had turned on her full charms and was soon meeting with Esteves for lunch or morning coffee, where they would talk happily of worldly things like art, music and sometimes he would even discuss European politics with her.

Stepping out of the shower Diana dabbed herself dry with a large white fluffy towel embroidered with the hotel name and, dropping it on the floor, stepped over to the mirror and repaired her make-up. Reaching into her shoulder bag she pulled out a shimmering gold backless evening dress and stepping into it pulled it up and easing it over her hips she then tied off the halter neck in a bow. The dress fitted as though it had been sprayed on, following the form of her thighs, hips, waist and breasts in creaseless perfection. The dress had cost her almost two months' wages, but it was an investment she had been happy to make, for tonight she hoped would be the night when at long last she could bury her chequered past by enchanting a man of means, someone who had shown that he could treat her like a woman and not just a whore. A second search of the handbag produced a pair of gold drop earrings, and then finally, she removed a pair of gold high heeled slingback shoes that raised her to the perfect height for the dress to swish provocatively as she walked.

Hearing the bathroom door open, Olavo Esteves bent down and, opening the refrigerator, removed the bottle of champagne and two glasses. Turning to face her, he gasped, and standing mouth open in wonder at the vision before him, slowly lowered the bottle and glasses gently onto the table beside him.

She smiled that radiant smile of hers that combined with a twinkling of her eyes expressed pure joy. They stood perfectly still looking at each other for several moments, before, with a twirl as graceful as a ballerina's, she crossed the room stopping close to him, her lips slightly apart and her delicately applied perfume gently wafting over him.

"You like what you see, Olavo, darling?"

"Yes I do, tonight you are a vision of great beauty, Diana," he said, his voice rasping, his throat dry, his eyes taking in her truly beautiful form. "You are like a dream, and I fear to reach out and touch you in case I break the spell and you vanish." It was as if he was rooted to the spot, helpless to move; for that moment the thought of a very different future crossed his mind, a thought that would repeat itself again and again that night.

Slowly Diana reached out for his hand, and drawing it up to her lips kissed his fingers. "Here, you see, these lips are real, I will not vanish at your touch, my darling; hold me close, make love to me."

*

Whilst in port, Vaughan used the yacht's forward cabin for sleeping in. There the double berth allowed him to spread out and enjoy the cool air from the open hatch above him. At sea the quarter berth behind the chart table proved to be an excellent sea berth, but in port, with the companionway hatch closed up, it was too warm. The night had turned hot and sultry, with a feel of thunder in the air. Vaughan slept fitfully, the noises of dogs barking or town traffic unusually disturbing his sleep. A muffled alarm noise appeared to come from the main cabin. He glanced at his wristwatch; it was two o'clock in the morning. Turning himself round and slipping off the bunk he had just stepped into the main cabin when the noise stopped. It had appeared to be coming from the chart table, so sitting down on the bench seat, he searched the surface in the dark for a likely source of the sound. Apart from the logbook, book notes and laptop there was nothing that could have caused the disturbance. He was just about to return to his bunk when from inside the chart drawer came the sound of a mobile phone text receipt alert. His official phone was to his certain knowledge in the forward cabin and it was a few moments before he realised that the sound was coming from his old personal mobile phone, the one he had intended to switch off and leave at his lodgings in Kingsbridge. Taking it from the chart drawer he opened the message, which read, 'We need to talk, meet me at the entrance to Chatsworth House, 12 o'clock Sunday. Sarah.'

He stared at the message unbelievingly for a long time before putting the phone on charge and going back into the forward cabin sleeping fitfully until daylight. In the morning, after a shower and breakfast, he still had not decided whether or how to respond. He was tired, his head ached, and if he was honest, still struggling to find his confidence in carrying out the task he had been given. After half an hour, during which time he had read her message at least twenty times he sent a simple reply.

'What about?'

After the trauma and pain of the divorce Vaughan saw little reason to be overly polite, anyway what the hell did she want, more money? The contact was definitely something he could do without, he had enough distractions without Sarah loading more onto him at a time when he had no chance of dealing with them properly. He wondered whether it was the girls she was concerned about; the thought pricked his conscience, before more rational thought concluded that she would have mentioned that the meeting involved Clare and Louise, knowing that he would respond immediately to any concerns regarding them. Finally he switched off the phone.

*

At around the time Vaughan had been sleepily searching the chart table for his mobile Esteves had been laying exhausted but very content, his eyes half closed as Diana tenderly caressed his expensively suntanned chest, whilst kissing his neck and shoulder. With half an ear he listened to her gentle talk of her happiness and feeling of joy. Somewhere at the back of his mind a thought process was analysing why an accomplished prostitute should be expressing thoughts of joy with regard to their relationship. To Esteves, Diana was just a reward for ensuring Reshetnikov's agent status between the new regime and STATGAZ. Her services were generous, yes, but no more than that.

"When we leave here for Brazil, Olavo, I will be so happy. I am tired of this island and in Brazil I can make you very happy," Diana murmured into his ear, before gently nibbling the lobe.

In his sleepy state he was slow to respond. "We will be always together there, Olavo. There to raise a family together, it will be just perfect," she continued nuzzling his neck, her free hand now stroking his hip and thigh. "It will be wonderful when our first baby is born. I will be so happy."

At last, in Esteves' sleepy mind, the words and intentions were comprehended, his brain in milliseconds filling with shock and fear. What was this stupid girl suggesting? His wife and wealth in Brazil, the potential status in Madeira, the recovery of his family's name and position. Did she think she could share in that!

"What are you talking about, eh? What do you mean a life together in Brazil; you think I would want to be seen there, or here, living with a whore! For all I know you have slept with every one of Reshetnikov's associates, also a wanton gold-digging bitch like you will never bear a child of mine, you hear?" he said menacingly, grasping her throat.

"Olavo, we are good together, you said so yourself. You say I am perfecto, supreme, fantastica. Why you now say such horrible things to me, why!" Diana replied, her voice croaking from his grip on her neck. "Senhor Reshetnikov does not employ me to sleep with you or anyone else, you hear! I work with Sonia in organising the girls and taking the phone bookings. You saw what I do for Sonia the night you tore Isabella's dress and she had to return wearing your shirt."

Sinking her nails into his wrist Diana jerked herself away from Esteves' grip and, half rising, went to lash out at his face, but he was too quick, and catching her wrist forced her arm around her back and pushed her down on the bed, holding her face into the pillow.

168

"You slut; this stops now, you dress and we leave. I no want to see or hear from you again," hissed Esteves, close to her ear. "Understand you will never see or be with me in Brazil, Madeira, anywhere. You understand?"

Diana's illusions of at last breaking away from her former life poured out as tears of frustration into the pillow.

"Yes?" he said louder and more threateningly, twisting the arm further and pushing her face more forcibly into the pillow until he felt her nod agreement. Slowly he eased the pressure on her head and allowed her to rise, releasing her arm.

Following her as she went to the bathroom, he watched as she picked up her clothes and bag from the floor, no longer seeing her as an object of desire but merely another street girl.

"You dress out here, where I can see you," said Esteves threateningly, and watched as she shuffled past him back towards the bed, her face tear-stained, her head hung low to avoid his glare of distain.

Reaching the bed she turned and looked straight at him, her eyes now flashing with anger. "Your wife must never know I suppose," she said, catching the flicker of guilt in his eyes. "Yes, you bastard, you tell me sad widower story, you say you are rich man. You just lie, lie, lie!"

The blow to her face split her lip.

"Shut up and finish getting dressed."

Grabbing his own clothes from the floor Esteves hurriedly dressed, and leaving his shirt tails hanging out from his trousers rammed his tie and socks into his jacket pockets. He strode to the door and opening it carefully, looked up and down the corridor to check that all was clear.

As he closed the door Esteves' thoughts turned to the immediate future and how he was to deal with this girl to ensure she kept quiet. In Brazil the girls he visited never assumed ideas like this crazy kid. Maybe she was looking for money from him as well as from Reshetnikov. 'Well why not, maybe two thousand euros will solve this problem,' he thought.

Turning back into the room he was faced with her charging at him holding something in her hand that flashed; a knife?

The words 'living with a whore' had hit Diana like a savage punch. A whore, that awful word that had haunted her for years, and even as she made a last plea, about how good they were together, she knew that fate was throwing her back, condemning her yet again only to serve men and never receive the true affection she knew other women enjoyed, and maybe even believed was their right. As Esteves had held her arm painfully behind her back and forced her face into the pillow the nightmare of her stepfather returned, the whispered threatening instructions. Even the smells of her stepfather's bad breath and body odour surfaced from her memory, filling her throat with bile and her whole being with loathing. Many men had tried to use her since then, but none had caused such memories to surface. Then the word 'slut' and the blow to her face triggered thoughts she had never held before. She had not felt pain from the blow, just a sense of blind hatred for the man she had trusted her affection to, the man standing in front of her now. A dirty deceitful old man, exactly how Sonia had thought of him, a depraved monster, just like her stepfather.

At that moment she remembered the flat blade screwdriver her stepfather had used to threaten her with, the only thing she had stolen from him, apart from some money. She had kept it almost as a talisman against the evils of the world. It had served her well in Berlin and Porto, but here, in peaceful Madeira, its use had been totally conventional. Stuffing the gold dress into her bag, her hand had reached down to the bottom and grasped the screwdriver handle. Esteves had gone to the door and was just turning back as she rushed at him, the screwdriver held low, aimed at his stomach.

It was all over in a flash. Esteves, no stranger to attempted muggings, instinctively put out his right foot causing Diana to stumble as she closed on him. At the same instant he caught the hand holding the screwdriver and helped by her momentum twisted her hand round and with all the force he could muster pushed outwards and upwards.

Her face, now close to his, changed suddenly from an expression of hatred to shock, before the eyes lost all expression, and her momentarily convulsed body went limp and slid to the floor.

Esteves staggered back and lent against the door, his heart racing, and nausea rising in his throat. "Oh, Diana, you stupid, stupid child. Why did you do this, I would have paid you well. This is such a waste, oh God, oh God why!"

For the first time in his adult life, Olavo Esteves cried, but as he did so his brain formed a plan. Diana's hand still gripped the screwdriver handle, with the blade and shaft buried deep into her body just below the ribcage. So small a diameter was the wound that there was little blood. He knew he must not leave the body in the room, but where could he place it, where it would be sometime before it was found. Huberto had mentioned the roof terraces for the timeshare apartments just one floor up.

Snatching the key from the writing desk, Esteves again checked the corridor, then lifting Diana's body in his arms he carried her along to the stairwell and up to the top landing where he left the body whilst he located an unoccupied apartment. By listening at the doors he was able to discount three apartments and was just opening the door of the fourth when he heard a toilet flush and withdrew hurriedly. Crossing the corridor away from the ocean side of the hotel he listened again at a door and unable

171

to detect any sounds of snoring or movement carefully inserted the key. Slowly opening the door his heart almost stopped as a bedroom light came on and a woman's voice said in a loud whisper, "Harold, there is someone in the entrance, I heard the door go."

"I can't hear anything," responded a sleepy Harold.

"You never can. Now get up and have a look."

Before Harold had donned his slippers and shuffled to the door of the apartment Esteves had closed the door and was hiding back in the stairwell. Hearing the apartment door open then close again he waited nervously for five minutes, just in case Harold had called security.

Trying the west wing of the building's timeshare units proved successful and Esteves, at the second attempt, found an empty apartment. He guessed, rather than knew, that a dead body in a warm room would smell quite quickly, so the roof terrace was the only place. To get there meant carrying her body up a spiral staircase that was quite narrow and tightly curved. The exhaustion of the evening with her now told, and he could only manage two steps before he needed rest. He was now forced to hold her in a fireman's lift and by the time he got her onto the roof and laid her down on a sunbed he could hardly stand.

Going back down the spiral staircase to the apartment, he took a paperback novel from the bookshelf, and returning to the roof opened it over the screwdriver handle before placing the other arm, now beginning to stiffen with rigor mortis, on top to hold it in place. To the casual observer, he thought she would appear to be a young lady dozing in the sun. The final touch was to tuck up the skirt of the dress to make it look as if she were sunbathing and place his sunglasses over her staring eyes.

"Mother of God, forgive me, I never wanted it to end this way. She was so beautiful and so warm. Why did she have to try and kill me? I would have paid her plenty," Esteves said quietly, looking down at her still beautiful form.

He sat for maybe ten minutes on the other terrace sunbed staring at her lifeless form, before fetching her bag from the room, and placing it in the apartment's bedroom. After pulling the bed away from the wall and leaving the mattress askew he upset a table and chair, and pulled a curtain from its rail to make it look as if there had been a struggle before sneaking out of the hotel unseen.

Once clear he had tidied himself up, but in order to hide Diana's blood that had stained his shirt as he had carried her up the spiral staircase to the roof, he was forced to wear his jacket, and soon became bathed in sweat as he hurried along the street back towards the city centre. Several times he considered phoning for a taxi before rejecting the thought as too dangerous. A cruising police car slowed and creeping past him a window was wound down and a torch shone at him.

"Too hot to sleep eh so I go for walk," he said, shading his eyes from the bright torchlight beam.

The policeman made no response and the car pulled away.

As he entered Amelia's apartment he removed his shoes and crept into the kitchen intending to wash the blood from his shirt. He had taken off his jacket and was peeling off his sweat soaked shirt when Amelia entered.

"Uncle, what has happened? You are bleeding!" she said sounding alarmed.

"It is not my blood; that clumsy Huberto, he dropped a glass and then he cut himself, quite badly, picking up the pieces," Esteves replied, with a wide grin on his face, and shaking his head. "Then I think he feel a bit faint eh and grabbed my shoulder to steady himself. The man has too much blood in him for in seconds he make this mess of my shirt."

"Leave it to soak in cold water in the sink; I will see what can be done in the morning. But you are okay, yes?" Amelia said, relieved to learn that it was apparently not serious.

"Yes I am fine, just tired of all these meetings and late nights. Soon the business will be completed thank God," he replied, hoping that the mention of a meeting would help towards his alibi.

"We are all tired of these meetings and late nights, Uncle. You and your friends do not appreciate that I also have a business to run. Today I almost fall asleep at my desk, it is not fair you go on like this," she replied, angry at his apparent attempt to gain sympathy.

Having said her piece, she turned and hurried back to her bedroom, leaving Esteves feeling just a little chastened, but also relieved that she appeared to accept his story. He stood for a full minute looking at the empty doorway thinking about his beautiful feisty niece. He promised himself to reward her in some way after the coup was over and his position in the hierarchy secured. Maybe he should take her out to dinner, he thought as he started to swish the bloodstained shirt around in the water. Looking down at the red cloudy water, cold upon his hand he was reminded of the cold clammy touch of Diana's body in death as he had laid her on the sunbed. The feeling of nausea returned together with the beguiling imagine of her seductively walking towards him, haunting him now and inducing fear. Had he been seen leaving the hotel? Was he picked up on any of the security cameras? If he was identified and questioned would the police believe that he had left her alive? As only his DNA would be found on the body his guilt would be plain for all to see. Sweat was again running down his face and dripping from his chin onto the edge of the worktop. Maybe the police would accept his plea of self-defence. He could say that he had panicked and that was why he had not reported the incident. They would understand, after all she was just a prostitute wanting to rob him of his credit cards and money. Maybe he could say she was very drunk and tripped and fell on the blade.

In a haze of fear and guilt he made his way to his room and stripping off fell onto the bed to lay staring at the ceiling and praying for a miracle. His prayers were answered at five o'clock in the morning in the form of a flash of lightning and the sound of heavy rain that delayed significantly the discovery of Diana's body.

CHAPTER 8

THE CONFERENCE BEGINS

Security was tight at Funchal airport as the conference guests arrived. They had assembled in Tunis during the morning and been flown by two charter aircraft to Madeira's airport on stilts, east of Funchal, in the early afternoon. There the President of Madeira and other dignitaries greeted them, and after long welcoming speeches the conference participants were whisked away in a luxury armoured security coach followed by their staff travelling in conventional tourist coaches. The whole convoy escorted by the police, their vehicles' sirens in full cry and lights flashing, attracted great interest along its route to and through Funchal. At the Vidamar hotel, Metcalf and his little army took over with apparent organised efficiency.

As each delegate registered, the smartly attired ladies of 'Total Cover Security Inc' checked their name against the list and informed the hotel's reception staff of the room number allocated for them to enter all the details onto computer and present the key. Any messages for the guest were also handed directly to them at that time rather than wait for the delegate's staff to enquire after them later. So it was that Al Djebbar, on receiving the key to Room 1034, was also given a personal message from his friend, Charles Stanthorpe Ogilvey, wishing him every success with the conference, and informing him of a delightful sailing author friend, who he thought may be in Madeira on a small yacht called 'La Mouette sur le Vent' writing a pilotage book. The message ended, 'If you have time buy the poor chap a meal, he's hardly got two pennies to his name, you would find the conversation a relaxing diversion.' Al Djebbar smiled as he read the note. It was not unusual for his friend Charles to send such messages and introduce friends or people he knew who maybe needed assistance, thus the message was received on face value and the piece of paper folded and placed in Al Djebbar's pocket.

Metcalf, hovering around the reception desk like some obsequious clerk, approached Al Djebbar as soon as he turned towards the lifts.

"My name is Metcalf, I am in charge of the 'Total Cover' security team here looking after you during the conference. I trust you had a good flight?"

"Yes, thank you, we did," replied Al Djebbar, stepping sideways to go round Metcalf.

"I will escort you to your room, sir."

"Do you think that is necessary?" asked a surprised Al Djebbar.

"Oh yes, sir, my company has received advice from several governments indicating that there is a significant security risk surroundin' this conference and its delegates."

"But I am merely the chairman of the conference and, all right, I am also the person that put forward the proposal, but I am not an elected representative of any government so have no power as such," replied Al Djebbar humbly.

"You must have power to so influence this number of people and to achieve this gathering, sir."

Al Djebbar shrugged and sighed. "Maybe so. Let us measure success by the outcome. It is after all, only the presentation of an idea."

They had arrived at the lifts and one of Metcalf's men pushed the button for a lift to arrive. Whilst they waited Al Djebbar reflected on his new restricted freedom. In North Africa he had moved around without an entourage of security men and only Mehdi Khuldun to assist him. He had met most, if not all, of the current leaders without fanfare and elaborate safeguards, but now he supposed it must all change. What was it that Charles had said in his last email, 'Your time has come to bring order to a world in turmoil, and may all our gods assist you in your endeavours.' Such grand wording he had thought at the time, but now, about to step into the spotlight at a conference that many governments viewed with great interest and expectation, he felt nervous, alone and very small.

The lift doors opened in front of him but he did not move.

"Are you all right there, sir?" asked Metcalf solicitously, pointing to the lift with his left hand and gently steering Al Djebbar with his right.

"Pardon, oh yes, yes thank you," Al Djebbar replied, feeling curiously annoyed at being herded like a sheep.

When they arrived at the room, Al Djebbar inserted the key card and went to take hold of the door handle when Metcalf restrained him. "I need to check the room before you enter, sir," Metcalf said, pulling a pistol from inside his jacket as he opened the door.

Al Djebbar looked on in amazement as Metcalf first checked the bathroom, then the main accommodation area including looking behind pictures and under the bed. Finally after having checked the veranda he indicated that it was safe to enter.

"I will personally check this room twice a day whilst you are here."

"What are you going to be searching for?"

"Bombs or trespassers."

Al Djebbar nodded, Metcalf's tone had been matter of fact and the facts were that this conference was not in everyone's interests.

The reality of this new life now settled unpleasantly in his consciousness.

Alone in the room Al Djebbar looked around, taking in the simple but tastefully styled décor. All his life he had lived simply, even when at Oxford, so these uncluttered surroundings relaxed his mind as if allowing him to breathe more freely. Walking to the patio doors, left open to the balcony, his view was of the vast Atlantic, which that day was a dark grey but almost completely calm. Unlike the dry heat of the desert, here the atmosphere was humid from the rain that still fell heavily from the black clouds above. Rain in an arid land is welcomed and he had learnt to look upon such weather as a good thing that encouraged new life and growth. He stuck his hands in his pockets, a gesture he had acquired and adopted at Oxford, when admiring something of beauty or that gave him pleasure to observe. After a few minutes in which he allowed his thoughts to slow and his body to have a sense of calm he withdrew his hands and idly noticed that he had pulled out the message from Charles. He was reading it again when there was a knock at the door. With Metcalf's performance still fresh in his mind Al Djebbar looked through the spy hole before reaching for the door handle. A large serious looking man stood in front of the door. "What do you want?" asked Al Djebbar, loud enough for the man on the other side to hear.

"There is a person here who claims to be your assistant."

Al Djebbar opened the door and, looking in the direction the security guard was pointing, saw Mehdi standing forlornly near to the lifts.

"He is my assistant and is to be given access at all times, day or night. Is that clear?"

"Yeh, that is clear, but tell him we must search him every time."

Al Djebbar went to protest, but on the assumption that the guard was only following orders he decided to wait until he next saw the man Metcalf.

When both men were alone in the room Mehdi and Al Djebbar talked for a while about the arrangements for the following day and that thorny issue of placement of delegations within the conference hall. Mehdi informed him that there had already been dissent over the seating plan for the evening's welcoming dinner. On the plus side the arrangement committee made up of members from the four nations' government administrations appeared to be working as one team and presenting a solid defence against the egotistical politicians.

"Is there anything you wish me to attend to?" Mehdi asked.

"Not that I can think of at this time, my head is so full of thoughts and ideas that I think it may burst," Al Djebbar replied, holding his head with both hands. "Wait, there is something. Tomorrow the delegations are due to retire for initial consideration at around four o'clock in the afternoon. I must wait before I hear what their basic thoughts are on the issues presented." He looked at the note again, deep in thought. "Yes, yes. Mehdi, I wish you to go to the port in the town here, and find a yacht with the name 'La Mouette sur le Vent' and deliver the message I am about to write." Al Djebbar sat at the desk and hurriedly wrote a brief letter to Ian Vaughan, inviting him to join him for 'afternoon tea' the next day. "There. If the man Ian Vaughan is on board, see what you think of him. I will be interested in your opinion. He is a friend of Charles, they must be close as Charles suggested that I might enjoy this man's company as a diversion to conference issues."

Mehdi smiled, happy with the prospect of a bit of sightseeing. "I will go straight away, I will be interested to meet another of Mr

Charles' friends. He seems to have many very different people with whom he is friendly."

Mehdi's comment made Al Djebbar stop and think more carefully about why Charles had made such an introduction. He was on the point of cancelling his request when he heard the door close as his young assistant left.

*

The organising committee had been clever in placing the tables for the evening randomly around the conference suite's Sunset Lounge ensuring that no one group would appear to be given a higher status than the rest. The delegates' tables were central whilst their support staff occupied the tables around the fringe. Al Djebbar and members of his organising committee moved from table to table greeting people and sharing food with them, keeping the conversation light and away from the issues to be presented and discussed at the conference. At one of the fringe tables Al Djebbar found himself talking with support staff from Libya and Morocco who seemed to be struggling to make conversation. As Al Djebbar worked at generating responses and introducing subjects where he thought there would be common ground, he noticed one young Moroccan eyeing him contemptuously. The man's expression caused him some degree of unease as behind the contempt lay, what appeared to be a deep hatred. Having livened up the atmosphere at the table Al Djebbar made his excuses to leave and immediately went in search of Mehdi, seeing him amongst a group from Algeria.

Mehdi had noticed Al Djebbar's searching look and left his group to meet him.

"You were looking for me?" Mehdi asked.

"Yes. I have just had a strange experience," replied Al Djebbar. "I was at that table next to the far door where the man with the orange robes and turban is sitting. Don't look now, but when you have a chance find out for me who the young man is that is sitting three places to his left."

"Oh that is easy, he is from the Moroccan delegation, his name is Mohammed el Kamal. He apparently works in the border security section of their immigration department. He has been helpful in sorting out their team's accommodation priorities. The Minister for oil and gas exploration has only just been appointed and we had not recognised how important he was from their list, but El Kamal smoothed everything very efficiently."

"Please let me know if he continues to be, very helpful."

Mehdi gave him a questioning look, but before Al Djebbar could explain, shouting from a corner table, that was obviously more than a mild disagreement, diverted both men's attention. Instantly members of the organising committee made a move towards the table, but Al Djebbar stood still and also restrained Mehdi from becoming involved.

"Let others sort that out. If we get involved we would be expected to take sides and at this stage I must avoid any apparent bias."

Though not a good start to proceedings Al Djebbar had expected outbursts such as the one that had occurred. There were many and varied factions in the countries along the north African coast, each with ideals and ambitions that they held dear above all else. This was the political playing field that he had to play on, the game being to overcome the complex web of intrigues, greed and fear, coupled with long held grudges.

At the end of the meal a local dance troupe entertained the guests with some traditional Portuguese dances, accompanied by two excellent guitarists, after which delegates retired for the night.

*

At precisely ten o'clock the following morning Walid al Djebbar walked onto the stage of the Sunrise Auditorium, immediately causing the babble of conversation to decrease and finally stop as he reached the lectern. Traditionally dressed in a fawn djellaba, its hood, seams and cuffs conservatively edged with gold stitching, he wore the red cap known as a bemousse. As he strode across the stage one could see on his feet the traditional yellow leather slippers; Walid al Djebbar was anxious not to appear before this audience looking like a western politician.

"My humble greetings to you all, come with the wish that Allah may bring His blessing to this assembly and guide us through the coming days." This was met with almost a complete silence that would have unnerved most speakers, but not this one.

"It has been a long time since revolution in our region was greeted and given the hopeful title 'The Arab Spring'. I think that we all recognise that the buds formed during those momentous events failed miserably to bloom. The promised spring was cut short by the cold winds of reprisal and political vacuum. What should now have been a glorious summer is descending into the bitterest of winters. Our economies struggle, our southern borders are threatened and we risk losing control of our natural resources. Within our countries acts of terror threaten the much needed technical support from outside of our region, and lawlessness threatens our peoples."

Al Djebbar raised his head to look towards the very back of the auditorium. The silence was almost palpable, his audience stung by the bleakness of his opening comments.

"The purpose of this conference is not to point accusing fingers or wallow in the misery of the present crisis, but to discuss a proposal to unite our nations in a union of states dedicated to securing our political and economic stability together with improving and increasing security and, in so doing, defend our way of life in peace, prosperity and harmony."

He raised his head again noting that there was a sense of optimism appearing in some of the delegates' expressions.

"We have taken considerable time in preparing a regional economic report which I think you will find disappointing, but following immediately on its heels will be a study of export demand considered to be achievable over the next decade."

Picking up a remote control he pointed it towards a laptop computer to start his detailed presentation. Country by country he presented current status and followed it with a considered forecast based on projected demand as assessed by the IMF, IEA and Goldman Sachs.

It was midday when he finally concluded the presentation and suggested that delegates retire to refresh and enjoy some food. At two o'clock in the afternoon Al Djebbar started his assessment of the region's security, carefully avoiding specific threats to the style of religious practice, and concentrating more upon illegal immigration and people trafficking, highlighting the economic and political consequences. At the end of this session Al Djebbar was delighted to see many delegates anxious to ask questions and make statements of their own. Though pleased with such a response he politely declined to open the conference up into a general discussion, suggesting instead, that each group retire to the Sunset Lounge. There, he assured delegates, they would find the area divided by partitions giving each group the opportunity to consider and discuss the proposal and the issues it addressed in private. Assuring them that individual copies of the detailed presentation were available in the rooms for every participant, Al Djebbar left the stage and started to make his way back to his room, accompanied by Mehdi.

"What did you think?"

"It is difficult to say. The Libyan delegation appeared to be very doubtful, whilst I think the Moroccans feared the strong economy of Algeria may cause similar problems to those caused by German economic strength in comparison to the nations with a more rural and tourist based economy during the euro crisis," replied Mehdi.

"Maybe I should emphasise more that I am not proposing a copy of the European Union with a common currency. That would never work. Something more like OPEC where each country maintains its sovereignty, but works together in trade and defence."

Suddenly two of Metcalf's security guards appeared either side of them. "Which direction are you headin' sir?" asked the man next to Mehdi.

"To my room," replied Al Djebbar angrily, annoyed that their discussion was interrupted. He was tired from the long presentation and was still finding it difficult to accept this level of personal security.

"We will escort you, sir."

"If you must," Al Djebbar replied with a sigh.

"I forgot to ask, did you find that friend of Charles, Ian somebody?"

Mehdi smiled. "Yes, I spent maybe one hour with him and a very pretty lady friend of his. We had some tea together onboard his boat and he showed me what he was writing. Many pages of notes about how he sailed here. Over twelve hundred nautical miles he told me, in a boat not so big."

Mehdi's voice was excited. He had enjoyed the meeting with Mr Vaughan who had been very humble in receiving Al Djebbar's invitation.

"Did he accept the invitation?"

"Oh, yes, he said he was very honoured and said he would obviously understand if more important things happened that would require you to cancel."

"It is almost four o'clock now, will you please wait in reception for him and bring him up to my room when he arrives."

As Ian Vaughan walked past the barrier between the east and west towers of the Vidamar hotel, a security guard moved away from the corner of the east tower to intercept him.

"Sorry sir, no one allowed through here during the conference, if you would go back up the drive to get to the road…"

"I have an appointment to see Walid al Djebbar, I am to meet with him at four o'clock," Vaughan said, interrupting the guard.

"Oh. What is your name, sir?"

"Vaughan, Ian Vaughan. He is expecting me."

"If you just wait there, sir, I will go and check."

Vaughan shook his head and shrugged. Turning to his right he stood admiring the pond in front of the link corridor between the hotel's two towers; rectangular in shape it was enhanced by ancient looking olive trees planted in rows on either side. On the pond floated translucent white balls of varying sizes that looked as if they could be illuminated if his observation of power feed cables was correct.

"May I ask what the meetin' is about?"

Vaughan turned and was surprised to see Arnold Benton Metcalf whom he had met in America eighteen months or so before joining the SIS. Metcalf had been a senior FBI agent at that time, but surely no way was he working for them now.

"Good heavens, Metcalf, are you working for the hotel?" *So it was you that was directing operations here the other day that's why there was something familiar.*

"Oh, it is you, Mr Vaughan." The shock of their meeting clearly registering on Metcalf's face, "Er, er no I, I am in charge of 'Total Cover Incorporated' security team, here protecting the delegates at this highly delicate North African conference."

"I see. I'm here at the personal invitation of Walid al Djebbar. He and I have mutual friends in England." *After the Washington inquiry, how in God's name did you get this job?*

"Oh, really," Metcalf replied, staring at Vaughan, apparently trying to weigh up something.

Vaughan knew of the FBI inquiry and dismissal of Metcalf for the falsification of incident reports and wondered how the man could possibly have got another job even vaguely connected with security, then he recognised that the long stare from Metcalf was the man's fear of exposure.

"His personal assistant assured me that my name would be placed upon the official visitors' list for today."

Metcalf looked down again at a list he held in his left hand, as if checking that he had correctly read the name listed. "His assistant may well have made such a promise but he is not responsible for the security of the delegates, I am." With a sigh Ian Vaughan reached into his pocket and produced his mobile phone and started to access the phone list. "If you follow me I will take you to him," Metcalf said, suddenly afraid that Vaughan was about to call Al Djebbar.

Though Charles Stanthorpe Ogilvey had given Vaughan Al Djebbar's mobile number it was only to be used in the most extreme circumstances. Smiling to himself that the bluff had worked Vaughan followed Metcalf, making use of the embarrassed silence between them to look about, taking in the

187

manicured lawns and precision planted graceful palm trees that occupied the area between the hotel's access road and the conference suite, as they walked towards the east tower's reception area.

Once inside he was asked to step through a security arch and was then hand frisked by a Neanderthal-like uniformed guard with hands the size of dinner plates.

"He's clean, boss," said the guard stepping back.

"If you come with me, Mr Vaughan."

Vaughan followed, relieved that he had not been asked to remove his shoes.

On hearing Vaughan's name Mehdi rose from the settee he had been relaxing on, and was going to greet him when the Neanderthal blocked his path. By the time Mehdi had explained who he was and the level of his authority, the lift door had closed with Vaughan and Metcalf the sole occupants inside.

"Er, my presence here is rather hush hush, you understand, Mr Vaughan," said Metcalf, hoping that Vaughan was unaware of his dismissal. "So I would be grateful if you did not indicate to anyone here that you know me."

"FBI, CIA?" asked Vaughan, playing along with Metcalf's lie.

Metcalf nodded affirmatively. "So you see my problem."

Vaughan smiled and nodded agreement. In any event he could not expose Metcalf without endangering being exposed himself. His previous involvement in the defeat of a serious terrorist attack in America would raise questions regarding his presence in Madeira at this particular time, and his personal introduction to the very man responsible for the conference.

Al Djebbar opened the door looking disappointed to see Metcalf but welcomed Ian Vaughan as if he were a lifelong friend. "Welcome, welcome, it is good to see you please come in and join me on the balcony for some tea."

Leading the way Al Djebbar stepped out onto the balcony and proffered a seat to Vaughan.

"Please sit down, I had expected my young assistant Mehdi Khuldun to be with you, was he not in reception?"

"I was so closely escorted that I hardly had an opportunity to look around," said Vaughan, looking up at Metcalf standing in the doorway obviously endeavouring to be part of the meeting.

Al Djebbar looked round and frowning asked, "Did you want something Mr Metcalf?"

"I was wondering whether you need me to attend this meeting?"

Al Djebbar looked confused. "No, in fact I cannot imagine any meeting where I would require your presence. You could however ask my assistant to join us."

When Metcalf was out of earshot Al Djebbar said, "Chaz frequently used the word 'insufferable'. It is a good word and describes that man exactly, but I suppose he is only trying to do his job."

"After receiving your invitation I flashed off a text message to Charles. He's mentioned you several times in the past, normally when swilling cognac around in a glass. You two appear to have had a fair bit of fun together at Oxford. By the way he asks if you've practised punting recently?" Vaughan asked, with a puzzled expression on his face.

Al Djebbar roared with laughter. "Chaz and I, in our first year, decided to invite two very beautiful girls to come punting with us on the Isis. Well Chaz was an expert in handling the punt and took on the upstream passage with great skill, obtaining admiring glances from both of our guests. We picnicked and talked on the bank in the sunshine and I thought that university life couldn't get much better. Then it was time to leave and I volunteered to punt us back down the river. At this point the competitive streak in my youthful personality took over, and after getting the craft out into midstream I decided to give the afternoon a thrill by speeding it back to the boatyard. Thrusting the pole firmly down to the river bed I gave a mighty shove sending the punt off at high speed, but firmly embedding the pole in the muddy bottom, and in an attempt to pull it free I lost my balance ending up clinging to the pole, which slowly started to lean, and as I watched the punt disappear I found myself being gently baptised in the waters of the Isis. Chaz and the girls of course were in hoots of laughter adding greatly to my embarrassment."

Vaughan laughed. "Water pursuits frequently embarrass all of us. Try bringing a yacht alongside when a crowd is watching, lines drop in the water, the crew start shouting in a confusing way, then the engine stops because the line that was dropped in the water is now wrapped firmly around the propeller, just when you need to go hard astern to avoid hitting the pristine yacht in front of you."

"Tell me, Ian Vaughan, what brings you to Madeira?" Al Djebbar asked, suddenly quite serious.

"Oh, unlike Charles, who chose a career in our civil service, I went into engineering but ended up being made redundant. Then I got totally taken up with sailing, but did not want to go down the professional yacht skipper route. I delivered yachts for a bit then wrote a couple of pilotage articles that got printed. That started me on a career of maritime author and I am currently writing a book entitled 'A Tramp's Guide to the Islands of the Atlantic'."

"Are you married?"

"Divorced."

At that point Mehdi arrived together with a waiter carrying a tray loaded with tea things.

"Tea?" asked Al Djebbar. "You know my right-hand man, Mehdi."

"Thank you," Vaughan replied, standing to greet Mehdi. "Yes, Mehdi and I shared a pleasant hour chatting yesterday afternoon."

The conversation, centring mainly on their mutual friend, tested Vaughan's knowledge of Charles Stanthorpe Ogilvey to the limit. Strangely it was the amazing coincidence of both men knowing Rebecca and Jerry Johnson-Lacey that seemed to convince Al Djebbar of Vaughan's authenticity. That was the point at which the conversation relaxed and became worldlier with discussion ranging from Afghanistan to the continuing European economic crisis. Twice the phone rang and Vaughan found himself alone on the veranda as both Al Djebbar and Mehdi attended to the calls.

Almost two hours later, they were on first name terms and after dropping his boat keys onto the bedroom floor, close to the bed, apparently by accident, Vaughan left in the knowledge that a friendship had been made and a listening device successfully planted.

As Walid and Mehdi turned from seeing Vaughan into the lift Mehdi asked, "What did you think of him, did you really like him?"

"Yes, I did, there was something reassuring about him, something that makes you feel comfortable, yes, as nice a guy as I would have expected as a friend of Charles. He also always referred to Charles as Charles not Chaz. Charles Stanthorpe Ogilvey always hated being called Chaz."

"Ah, you were testing him, I thought that may have been the name you called him when at Oxford."

*

Police crime scene tape across the door of the hotel timeshare apartment 1604, and the presence of two policemen turning away idle spectators, were the only visible signs that some crime had been committed. At the request of the hotel management the police were showing considerate discretion. On the roof above the apartment two detectives were questioning the hotel manager concerning the letting of the apartment. Diana's body had been found by, a now hysterical Ursula Platt, two hours earlier after she had clambered up the spiral stairs from her neighbouring apartment. At first she had thought that the girl was sunbathing, but the curious and vaguely sickening smell, had encouraged her to try and start a conversation. Not receiving any response she had looked more closely at the girl noticing a brown stain on the young lady's dress. Ursula was by nature a curious person and was not used to being ignored, so thought nothing of clambering over the low partition wall and approaching the recumbent figure. Touching the girl's right arm, as she asked whether she felt all right, Ursula was horrified to see the arm fall limply off the body, dragging a slightly soggy book with it, and exposing the screwdriver buried to the handle in the girl's midriff. Now sat in her bedroom, shaking and crying, comforted by her husband and a hotel receptionist, Ursula was trying hard to deal with what she had witnessed.

On the roof the two detectives stood waiting for the pathologist to arrive, discussing where to start with their investigation.

*

On leaving the Vidamar hotel Vaughan grabbed a taxi to get him out to the Consul's residence; whilst in the centre of town Mohammad el Kamal was pulling out a chair, at a café in Rua do Bispo, to sit and wait for Al Bashir to finish speaking on his mobile phone. The coffees arrived and delving into his pocket El Kamal handed over a ten euro note and waved the waiter away.

"Has that man from STATGAZ made an approach yet?" Al Bashir asked as soon as he had finished the call.

"Yes, his name is Gleb Smetanin. He is very well connected with the Algerians and obviously has someone helping him with Morocco's delegates. He is staying with a Russian called Ulan Reshetnikov who owns a Quinta; at least, that is what they said it is called. There is the address, it is apparently near the Palheiro Golf Course."

"If I write a message to this Smetanin, what language must I use?"

"He is fluent in Arabic, he has been many years dealing with negotiations in Algeria."

"Allah be praised," replied a much relieved Al Bashir. "Could you, maybe, get a message to him?"

"It will be difficult without exposing you to the rest of the Moroccan delegation. He would undoubtedly enquire whether they know you. My senior boss from the Directorate of Territorial Surveillance, a man named Abdul el Najid is with us, and he will surely know who you are, I recommend your approach is made via the Russian Reshetnikov."

*

Two hours later Ulan Reshetnikov was wondering why suddenly sleepy peaceful Madeira was turning into a hotbed of intrigue and covert interest. He looked at the note again, his not so good

English struggling to cope with the strange word order of the message. One thing that was clear was that the man waiting at the gate wanted him to act as go-between with STATGAZ. He smiled; the smell of profit seemed to fill the air in his beautiful hideaway home.

"Ivan!" Reshetnikov shouted. "Ivan!" he shouted again, only louder.

Hearing heavy running footsteps he waited, glaring at the pool terrace door, which seconds later flew open revealing a two hundred and eighty pound giant of a man.

"Yes, boss?"

"Bring the visitor here and get Sonia to bring coffee."

Out of modesty more than manners Reshetnikov slipped on a pool gown to hide his increasingly flabby form and expanding paunch, thinking to himself that this extended luxurious lifestyle may flatter Sonia but was not making him feel any healthier than hustling an existence on the streets of Moscow.

The meeting with Al Bashir lasted less than half an hour, but the information was most interesting. According to his visitor the North African conference would end in failure and the region, especially Morocco, would move towards a holier status in the Islamic world. His visitor, however, wished to meet with Smetanin to explain the effects on oil/gas development in the region and its effect on Russian interests. This Al Bashir went as far as to indicate that a monopoly would be a possibility.

Smetanin had been in the house at the time and initially Reshetnikov was tempted to introduce the two men, but Al Bashir's inept skills suggested that Ulan Reshetnikov himself could remain between the two parties until his personal understanding of the business became sufficient for him to be included in any 'commissions'. Smetanin knew how such things were done in the business world and Reshetnikov felt confident that the inept Al Bashir could be persuaded without too much effort.

*

Susanne Bevington was a very attractive lady in her fifties, and gave an immediate impression of someone alert, intelligent and thoroughly professional. As Honorary British Consul she had run the office in the Rua da Alfandega, a side street opposite the Fortaleza Palácio de São Lourenço, for some years, but cutbacks ordered by London meant that the office had closed, the local staff made redundant and the day to day working of the office transferred to her private residence. Reluctantly she invited Vaughan in. "I normally conduct meetings with British nationals in their hotels or in the island's prison," she said rather stiffly. "But you are a bit different."

"I am sorry to disturb you but I need to send a report to Lisbon and I understand that you have a secure line."

"You better come through to the office," she replied appearing to relax a bit. "I was warned that you were here but I did not expect you to make contact."

"I was instructed to keep Lisbon informed of progress," said Vaughan. "You may have been told that my presence here is delicate rather than dangerous, and apart from reporting in, I need some information which I hoped you may have to avoid me asking questions around town that may filter back."

"Oh, I see, how may I help?"

"I need two addresses, both of them Russian nationals living here. One is Ulan Reshetnikov and the other is Sarkis Kazakov."

"Um, are you sure that this is just 'delicate'?" she asked as she crossed the office and crouched to open a small floor safe beside the desk.

"It is thought that they and STATGAZ may have shared interests in approaching some members of this North African conference that's going on here."

"Reshetnikov, yes, but it is not the type of business that Kazakov involves himself in I understand," Susanne Bevington replied, getting up and turning to face Vaughan, holding a thick blue leather bound book in her hand.

She opened the book and started flicking through the pages. "Ah here we are, there are two Kazakov's on the island, and neither of them get up to much good," she continued as she wrote down the address on a piece of notepaper, before carrying on the search for Reshetnikov's details. "There," she said after a few minutes. "Be very careful, their money has bought them several friends here, plus they both have heavies looking after them."

"Point taken. Do you have a town map handy?"

Half an hour later Vaughan left the Consul's house, and wanting to think, decided to walk down into the old town rather than find a taxi. Staunton in Lisbon had been brisk and superior, dishing out unnecessary advice as to how to continue links with Al Djebbar. When Vaughan had changed the subject and asked Staunton if he knew anything about one, Olavo Esteves, the response was very abrupt.

"Who?"

Vaughan repeated the name.

"No, why?"

Vaughan explained that he had seen Reshetnikov affording Esteves and three other men from, he understood, South America, lavish entertainment.

"Look, just stick to the job you're supposed to be doing. God, why Campbell put a novice on this I will never know."

"I just wondered whether there may have been some intelligence come through linking South American interests to

Russia and/or the outcome of the North African conference," replied Vaughan struggling to remain sounding civil.

"No, nothing," replied Staunton. "Is that it?"

"Yes, that is all for now." With that Staunton had put the phone down.

Two hours later as darkness was descending Vaughan sat at a table opposite a café bar just a few metres down the hill from Kazkov's house. The beer he had been sipping for the last half hour was getting decidedly warm. Swallowing the remains of his drink he signalled to the waiter and was in the process of ordering a coffee when a dark Mercedes drove out of the gates at the rear of Kazakov's house and turned to come down the hill past where Vaughan was sitting. Turning to see what Vaughan was interested in the waiter laughed.

"Ha, the Russian is off to his favourite nightspot."

"Where is that?"

"Annabel's just down the hill. Why he does not walk there I do not know. In a minute you will see the car come back and wait until he calls."

"What is Annabel's?"

"It is a striptease bar. Many pretty girls work there, you should go and see," the waiter said, giving Vaughan a big wink.

"Have you been?"

"No, Senhor. A waiter cannot afford the beer in such a place, or the divorce if my wife found out."

When the coffee arrived Vaughan drank it as quickly as he could before getting up and starting to walk up the hill.

"You don't visit Annabel's?" the waiter called after him from the door of the café.

"No, like you I could not afford the beer," replied Vaughan.

Passing Kazakov's house on his right he stopped and spent a minute or two looking through the elaborate gates to the front of the property and was interested to see that security cameras covered the whole area. In addition Vaughan noticed discreet infra-red beam devices attached to the lanterns on top of the gate pillars. Moving on he found that the rear garden was hidden from view by the high wall and sheet metal gates, but here again his trained eye detected the beam devices, set to warn of intruders climbing over the wall. Not wishing to attract attention he walked on and taking the next junction, strolled down the hill to turn left at the Casa Portuguesa then left again before finding the entrance to Annabel's down some steps on the right. Entering and making his way across the darkened room to an empty table, Vaughan managed to order a beer over the noise of disco music, and casually looked around at the mini-skirted girls sitting in small groups at tables. In the shadows near to the entrance stood a giant of a man talking to one of the scantily dressed waitresses, but every now and again he would glance across towards a table near to the stage where Vaughan could see Kazakov sitting shouting animatedly into the ear of a rather nondescript individual dressed in an unusual roll neck lightweight top and who was trying very hard not to be noticed. The giant was obviously Kazakov's minder but who, wondered Vaughan, was the other man?

The waitress appeared with his drink and Vaughan shouted, "What time does the show start?"

"Very soon. Would you like some company at your table?"

"Not just yet, maybe later."

As she left the table a group of young Portuguese men came in obviously on a stag night. One of the group knew Kazakov and called to him across the stage. Immediately Kazakov's guest turned his head away and excusing himself made his way to the toilets, passing Vaughan's table on the way. The man's features were possibly Arab rather than Portuguese but Vaughan was not sure, in fact there was little that made a visual impression other than an obvious desire to appear ordinary. By the time he returned the show had started and all attention was focused on the shapely young lady cavorting around on the stage. Such was the timing of the man's reappearance Vaughan was sure that he had waited for such a distraction, as the shy guest appeared more relaxed now that all eyes were on the stage and more people were in the club to aid his apparent non existence.

Vaughan carefully watched Kazakov and his guest throughout the first and second acts before settling his bill and leaving, thankful for the quiet after the cacophony of noise in the club. Coming out of Annabel's he turned left to get back onto the Rua de Santa Maria. Stopping to admire one of the street door paintings that made the street a small, but interesting tourist attraction, he noted that Kazakov's giant minder was following him, obviously more capable of carrying out beatings than conducting the subtle art of shadowing. Not wishing to increase anyone's suspicions Vaughan chose not to shake the man off by ducking into some alleyway but instead leisurely strolled up to the Casa Portuguesa for dinner. Yet again the strange feeling of being at work but not doing what he thought of as work like activity made him feel tense and unsettled, he was still finding it difficult to act the part of an author, or SIS agent come to that. Even the excellent food, wine and brilliant guitar playing did nothing to improve his confidence. On leaving the restaurant he cautiously looked up and down the street and was relieved to find himself alone. The light breeze coming down from the mountains behind the town cooled the temperature and he took his time on the walk back to his boat, practising all the tricks he had been taught to ensure that he was not being followed.

*

Earlier, in the Vidamar's conference suite, national groups were already forming opinions of the Al Djebbar's plan for the region; for the most part the reaction was favourable and the phone lines had been very busy with international calls. It was evening when the questions were starting to form as to the extent of co-operation and integration. The general fear was that the Organisation could easily turn into something similar to the European Union with its huge and expensive bureaucracy that step by step had eroded individual nations' autonomy. Corridor meetings between the various countries started to occur, widening the discussion and almost inevitably increasing doubt about the proposal. Changes, particularly political change, are usually viewed with mistrust, the cautious conservative route invariably being the preferred path.

The hotel request for delegates to vacate the Sunset Lounges to allow preparation for the evening buffet came just in time to keep the conference on track. It was now that Al Djebbar left his room to start a round of visits to the heads of the four delegations. At each visit he calmly explained the profile he envisaged for the Organisation's administration with its basis being similar to that of OPEC. He also listened to the concerns being raised and assured the leading delegates that all would be covered by the following morning's presentation. The Libyan delegation had been very defensive over the issue of territorial security; fear of insurgency by the old regime at the forefront of their minds. Generally it was the political vacuums that had followed the revolutions in Tunisia and Libya that was the problem; both countries were caught in the trap of having to rely on inexperienced politicians supported by an equally fragmented and inexperienced administration. Some were saying that it was far too early, for what were basically new nations, to be faced with such a proposal that everyone agreed would have long-term effects.

During the evening meal Al Djebbar continued to work tirelessly, moving amongst the delegates, this time with small talk, the charm offensive as Mehdi later described it. Close to midnight Walid al Djebbar was under no illusions when he made his way to his eight-man research team at work in the hotel's east tower's meeting room. Day two of this conference would be the make-or-break of the plan he and they had spent the last two years exhaustively researching and preparing. At two o'clock in the morning he called a halt to their work and ordered everyone to their rooms to rest.

CHAPTER 9

EARLY VISITORS

Whether Mehdi and the rest of Al Djebbar's team managed to sleep Walid al Djebbar had no idea, but he could not. The years of watching and waiting, the planning, the meetings and the constant travelling had all been for this moment in his life. It would have been for many men sufficient to bring this audience together and impart the message, and Al Djebbar admitted to himself that six months ago he would have felt the same, but not anymore. Terrorist attacks on important economic targets in Algeria, continued civil unrest in Libya, significant drop in tourism to Tunisia and undercurrents that he did not fully understand in Morocco, cried out for his plan to succeed. The reactions expressed by the heads of the delegations the previous evening were still too cautious to inspire confidence and he feared total failure. The thought of the chaos that would soon engulf the region bringing terror to its inhabitants loomed like a dark storm cloud in his mind.

As the night wore on Al Djebbar alternated from pacing his room to lying on the bed staring at the ceiling trying to will himself to sleep. The dawn came and he was still awake, his brain buzzing with thoughts; five times he had read through the presentation prepared for the morning session, each time marking it with red pen alterations. Moving out onto the balcony, with the cool breeze from the ocean bathing him like a cold shower, he read the document again and realising that he had changed the wording from a confident call to action to a timid plea, he crossed

202

out most of his corrections. Standing and stretching he looked out across the ocean towards the Desertas, silhouetted by the sun as it rose in a fiery orange sky, and thought of Ian Vaughan, that fortunate man, who leisurely sailed the oceans and wrote about his travels.

Turning, he hurried into the room casting off his clothes as he went and stumbled into the bathroom. He showered and dressed in western casual clothes as quickly as he could and left the room. The guard by the lift looked at him in surprise as he thumbed the call button several times in frustration. Getting into the lift he heard the message of his movement being transmitted to the reception and wasn't surprised to find two of Metcalf's army waiting for him as the lift doors opened.

"Can we help you, sir?"

"Yes, I need a taxi to take me to the marina."

"I'm not sure that Mr Metcalf would agree to us doing that, sir."

"Well, as far as I am concerned, Mr Metcalf and his opinions can go to hell!" replied Al Djebbar hotly, stepping past the guards and making towards the doors.

"If you'll just give us time to check with him, sir."

But Al Djebbar didn't hear having reached the doors and found them to be locked. "Open these doors NOW!" he screamed. "I refuse to be held like a prisoner."

The taller of the two guards started to move towards the doors whilst his colleague conducted a hurried conversation with Metcalf. Al Djebbar waited for the man to reach him expecting his demand to be met, but was to be disappointed.

"We're sorry, sir, but it's more than our job's worth to let you go out alone without having clearance from the boss."

"Then come with me if you must," retorted Al Djebbar angrily.

"Check that past the boss, Micky."

A mumbled conversation followed and then the man with the phone gave the thumbs up sign and put the phone down.

"We are both to go with you, sir. We have a car parked just outside."

In the fresh air Al Djebbar started to breath more normally and calm down.

"If you just wait with me a moment, sir," said the tall guard. "Micky will just carry out some checks."

Al Djebbar heard the locks pop as the guard got within key fob range of the vehicle, and then stood for several seconds, before moving close and getting down on his hands and knees to check the underneath of the car. Opening the driver's door he pulled the bonnet catch then went to the front and raising the bonnet looked into the engine compartment, before closing it again and climbing into the driver's seat. It was not until the car was started that Al Djebbar was allowed to approach. Bombs placed under cars were something that Al Djebbar was all too aware of and he thanked both men for the care they had taken.

They drove in silence to the marina and parking the car at the barrier they left Micky to guard the vehicle while the tall muscular guard walked beside Al Djebbar. Arriving at *La Mouette sur le Vent* Al Djebbar was relieved to find Vaughan up and about busying himself in the galley.

"Good morning, Ian, may I come aboard?"

"Hi, Walid, great to see you. Yes, come on over, but watch your step. I would hate to see you repeat the punting incident. Have you had breakfast?"

Walid al Djebbar laughed and with great caution stepped onto the boarding platform and shuffled nervously across then taking a firm grip of the backstay stepped over the pushpit rail of the yacht and onto the small stern deck, as rain started to fall.

Over a cooked breakfast, which for Walid did not include three rashers of bacon, they exchanged pleasantries about Madeira and the hotel. It was after the coffees that Al Djebbar became serious and started to divulge news of the conference's progress. Now, for the first time Vaughan appreciated the briefing given by Allsopp-Stevenson, as armed with this knowledge he was able to understand and appear well informed on North African matters. Two hours later a mentally refreshed Al Djebbar jumped to his feet, thanking Vaughan profusely for his 'time and good counsel' before wobbling back across the boarding platform and hurrying away with the security guard in close attendance.

*

Had Al Djebbar got down from his room to the east tower's reception area thirty minutes earlier that morning he would have seen Mohammed el Kamal scurrying up the approach road to the taxi rank by the nearby gift shops.

Twenty minutes later El Kamal stood in the garden at El Karaki's house waiting patiently for Leyla and Al Bashir to complete their morning prayers.

"How is the conference proceeding?" asked Al Bashir, as he stood and turned to face his visitor.

"The man Al Djebbar is a powerful speaker who has done much work in preparing his presentation. My delegation was very impressed despite my expressions of concern. Although Ali Khasawni, the head of our mission, told Al Djebbar last evening that he was not so confident, he has told us that on our return to Morocco he will do his best to promote the idea of a union of states."

"What about the other countries?"

"Tunisia is not so positive I believe; being a small nation compared to the others, they fear losing any voice in the region. I have worked hard to encourage such concerns, however, Al Djebbar, being from their territory, has strong influence at very high levels. The Libyans are arguing amongst themselves, more about their internal politics than the conference issues, but they also have people in their delegation who are like us in thought, so I do not know how they could make any decision in favour."

"And Algeria?" asked Al Bashir, inwardly praying for a negative response.

"Oh, they are very strongly in favour; after the attack on the gas plant they fear that having enemies close to their borders endangers their wealth."

To Al Bashir it seemed that the eloquence of this 'contemptuous Berber', Al Djebbar, was succeeding in taking the whole of the North African nations, from the Egyptian border westwards, and delivering them into the hands of the hated Americans and Europeans. Al Bashir reluctantly decided to make contact with the explosives supplier, Kazakov. To purchase the chemicals necessary for a homemade bomb was out of the question, and where could he possibly make such a device, definitely not in the home of his sister who now questioned his every move. She was watching from the window now, no doubt wondering what the purpose of Mohammed el Kamal's visit was. He sighed, if only there had been more faithful followers of Allah at the conference.

"You are troubled, teacher."

The gentle voice of Leyla made him jump. He had forgotten her presence, and now hated even more the task he must perform.

"I have to visit an old acquaintance who deals in death for profit only, in this life, with no thought of glory in the next," said

Al Bashir solemnly. "If he has prepared everything I will take you to him tonight."

Leyla instantly understanding the purpose of such a visit simply replied, "I am Allah's servant." As if in sympathy with Al Bashir's feelings, raindrops like tears began to fall heavily and noisily on the paving around them.

Al Bashir had been putting off the meeting with Sarkis Kazakov, not wishing to accept even a remote possibility of Leyla sacrificing herself. The report from Mohammed el Kamal however had forced him to realise how close the North African territories were to becoming like Saudi Arabia, who in his view was a puppet of western ideology. Dismissing El Kamal he returned to his room and rummaging through his belongings found the address in the Calcada do Socorro.

*

As soon as Walid al Djebbar had left, Vaughan hurriedly washed up and stowed the breakfast things then locked the hatches and made his way ashore. The morning was still cool after the rain storm and he found no problem in running as far as the Riso restaurant on the Rua de Santa Maria. He then slowed to a jogging pace along the level leading to the Calcada do Socorro where he walked up the hill passing, on the right, Kazakov's house, to the 'A Forca' snack bar where he ordered a coffee and positioned himself where he could observe the entrances of the arms' dealer's home. After a while locals drifted into the bar, eyeing him curiously. With the second cup he ordered a small cake and continued his casual vigil trying not to draw too much attention to himself.

So this was SIS work, Vaughan thought, sitting and watching and waiting, gambling that his curiosity surrounding Kazakov's house guest would pay off and prove more informative than a watch on Reshetnikov's dwelling.

He had finished the cake and was about to drink the coffee when the tall metal gates at Kazakov's house clanged and started to open. A brand new black Range Rover edged out into the street and turned up the hill before stopping, then rolling back into a gateway opposite the entrance doors to Kazokov's house. As it came to a stop the little grey man Vaughan had seen with Kazakov at Annabel's, emerged from the house, checked both ways, as if to make sure that nobody was looking, and then hurried across the road and leapt into the rear seat of the vehicle to be hidden behind the darkened glass in the rear door windows of the vehicle. As the Range Rover roared past the snack bar Vaughan saw two young ladies leaving Kazakov's by the front garden gates, waving back to somebody in the house, both were dressed very much for the evening and he guessed that they had spent the night under Kazakov's roof.

Finishing his coffee Vaughan paid the bill and left, walking down the hill past the house, noting again the sophisticated security arrangements that appeared so out of place in Funchal. Vaughan had just crossed the road by the garden's west wall when a taxi sped by and stopped opposite the front doors where the Range Rover had stopped just a few minutes before. Making a show of looking at his watch as if he were waiting for somebody, Vaughan then looked up and down the road and succeeded in getting a good look at Al Bashir as he crossed the road to the house and rang the doorbell. Intrigued, Vaughan strolled down towards the café bar he had visited the day before and sat on a bench appearing to be looking out to sea. Someone was breakfasting on the balcony of the house and as Vaughan stole glances in that direction he saw that Al Bashir had been brought out onto the balcony to speak with his host. The meeting lasted only a short time and as the cleric went back into the house another taxi appeared and whisked him away.

The sighting of Al Bashir had greatly shocked Vaughan as the man was on every European country's watch list, and he would have undoubtedly been identified at Funchal airport had he attempted to gain entry by that route. This was definitely a reason to contact Staunton in Lisbon, and Lieutenant Heathcote as well. Vaughan had been concerned by the reaction of Staunton to his report and inquiry about Olavo Esteves and hoped that Heathcote would consider this and the information regarding Amelia's uncle more seriously than Staunton had done.

Needing cash, Vaughan hurried to the city centre and the banks. As he left the cash machine he sighted Kazakov's heavy, walking towards him from the direction of the cathedral, in the company of a small wiry man Vaughan recognised from the 'A Forca' snack bar; both men were scanning the crowds obviously searching for someone. Vaughan guessed that he needed to find somewhere to hide where he could change his appearance somehow as he was probably the person they were looking for. The consul had been right; Kazakov had been sufficiently generous to enlist the help of some local people.

Using a group of reasonably tall office workers as a screen Vaughan made the short walk to the 'Golden Gate Café' without being seen and on entering headed straight for the toilets. The problem was how to change his appearance as his outer clothes consisted of a fawn casual shirt and a pair of dark blue trousers, not something that could be removed like a jacket or pullover. Entering a cubicle he sat thinking of what to do next. Vaughan felt trapped and would be easily identified if either of his two pursuers came into the café; therefore his only chance was to leave in the hope that they had passed by the café and were searching further along the street towards the theatre. Cautiously he opened the door and made his way down the short corridor to the café itself. A quick scan of the customers sitting inside indicated that all was clear, but as he approached the exit he saw the two men were sat at one of the outside tables, right on the corner where they could see along both the Avenida Arriaga and Avenida Zarco, watching passers by; if he left the café by either of its exits he would certainly be seen by them. He considered making a run for it through the kitchen before dismissing the idea as too much Hollywood, besides where would that lead him to. Vaughan rebuked himself for not using the group of office workers for a few yards further which would have enabled him to turn down the Avenida Zarco, he could have made it to the esplanade and marina by the time his pursuers had reached the café. Looking around for a secluded table he saw there were stairs leading to the upper floor of the café and hurried up them. Like the ground floor there did not appear to be a table available until a young couple got up to leave from a table on the balcony.

Vaughan stood back whilst the waiter cleared and prepared the table for him, providing an opportunity for him to reposition his chair where he could, by leaning slightly sideways, observe the two men below. Ordering lunch and a beer he considered his next move but by the time the meal arrived he still hadn't worked out an escape plan, so took his time eating, hoping that the two would get fed up and move away. When the waiter brought the coffee Vaughan was wondering whether the two men were there for the whole day when a shrill whistle from below made him look down to the pavement tables again. He guessed that it was the little wiry man who had made the noise, as it was he who now stood waving for two other men to join him. As they approached Vaughan recognised them as the remaining customers at the 'A Forca' snack bar and realised that had he turned the corner and gone down to the seafront he could well have been spotted by one of them.

As they gathered around Kazakov's minder there was a lot of head shaking and shoulder shrugging before the big man handed out what looked like twenty euro notes to each of them, and pointed out the direction they were to continue the search. The last to leave was the wiry little man who had escorted the minder as far as the 'Golden Gate Café', and now the minder sat alone to wait for his little team's return. This opened up a new possibility for Vaughan who weighed the likelihood of the snack bar clientele giving only a poor description of their mysterious 'watcher', to ensure that they made more money from the search. *Maybe now is the time to put Adrian Creswell's drama training to the test?*

The bill came and Vaughan settled it in cash leaving a reasonable tip before making his way down the stairs, having decided on audacity as the way out. As he stepped onto the pavement he saw the movement in his peripheral vision as the minder looked up from his table. Vaughan just glanced at the man, then, as if doing a double take, looked at him full in the face and smiled.

"Enjoy the show last night, mate?" he said in his best 'Souff London' accent. The minder looked puzzled. "You know, mate, Annabel's," Vaughan continued, saying 'Annabel's' more quietly as if he did not want the ladies sitting nearby to hear.

The minder nodded and almost smiled as he connected the face of Vaughan, which he had vaguely recognised, with his boss's evening at the nightclub.

"My boss, he go there many time, yes."

"Oh, you were wiv yer boss. I fort you was chatin' up the girl on the door. She was a bit of all right."

"You left before Zeta, you miss best act."

"'Ad to get round to the restaurant to meet the wife. I only dropped into the club while she was 'avin one of those spa fings."

"I no see you in club before," the minder replied now relaxing more as the conversation continued.

"No mate, you wouldn't 'ave. We only 'ere on 'oliday see, so it's been all gardens and dinners wiv the friends she's made at the 'otel. Gawd can't women talk eh."

The minder chuckled and nodded in agreement.

"Then when she does this spa fing I fort I'd go and remind me-self wot a woman should look like."

"Your wife, she not so pretty?" asked the minder with a sad frowning expression on his face.

"She was, mate, but 'avin' five kids 'as knocked 'er out of shape a bit, know what I mean."

"Yeh, oh yeh, I know well what you mean."

"Anyway, can't 'ang about 'ere, I said I'd meet 'er from the 'otel and take 'er to Reid's for afternoon tea. Wiv 'er friends of course."

"Maybe I see you at Annabel's again?"

"Not this year, mate. We goes 'ome in a couple o' days. You take care, cheers."

"Cheers, my friend."

With that Vaughan walked jauntily away towards the theatre, hands in pocket whistling, then, back amongst the crowds, he slipped into and through the shopping arcade next to the theatre. Now his progress was much more cautious as he checked in shop windows for reflections of followers and used tall people to hide behind as he rounded corners. Exiting at the esplanade level, he ran across the dual carriageway between the traffic, checked that no one was paying him undue attention, and then hurried down the ramp into the marina and to his boat. Quickly he changed his shirt and trousers, slipped on the Browning in its shoulder holster and adding a lightweight linen jacket, Panama hat and smart brown shoes, went ashore again. Leaving the marina via the pier, instead of the ramp, he leisurely walked to the crossing point, and patiently waited for the lights to change, no more your chirpy Londoner, more your middle-aged gentleman. At the taxi rank he asked a driver to take him up to the Honorary Consul's house, and spent the journey sat slightly sideways in order to check they were not being followed.

*

Susanne Bevington answered the door. "You must be psychic, I was just about to send Yvonne with a message for you. A rather abrupt and rude chap called Staunton apparently wants to know why you have not been liaising with Arthur Claremont."

"That is simple; I was given very clear instructions not to."

"You had better come through and get on the phone to him. He should at least be impressed by my efficiency in locating you so quickly."

"I don't somehow think Mr Staunton is that easily impressed," replied Vaughan, as he carefully wiped his shoes on the doormat.

Staunton was obviously sat waiting for the call as the extension had hardly rung before the handset was snatched up and a belligerent sounding voice said, "Staunton."

"This is Vaughan. Apparently you wanted to know why I have not made contact with Mr Claremont. Well the…" At this point a very loud interruption cut Vaughan off in mid-sentence.

"Too right I want to know, what the hell do you think you are doing out there, having a holiday! Surely 'The Manor' told you of the importance of collective knowledge! You have, in easy reach, an expert on Anglo-Arab relations and you chose to ignore him."

"I chose to ignore him, as you put it because those were my orders. The Commodore emphatically told me to avoid actual contact with Mr Claremont at all costs. If we were seen together by anyone connected with the delegations my cover would be blown."

"Well I don't agree with that assessment. If your meeting was carefully arranged there would be little, if any, chance of it being witnessed," replied Staunton indignantly. "I appreciate that your past contacts with Campbell may have inspired some loyalty, and you are still wet behind the ears with regard to our methods, but be aware you are there to carry out my instructions on this operation. You're there to observe and report and so far your reports have been damn short of anything of interest."

"Well this may interest you," said Vaughan struggling to keep his temper in check. "An hour ago I witnessed the cleric Al Bashir entering the house of the Russian arms dealer, Kazakov. He only stayed a short time…"

"What the hell were you doing nosing around Kazakov's house, you're supposed to be observing who is trying to influence the conference delegates. Who instructed this, Campbell I suppose."

"Aren't you interested in why a Taliban cleric is making contact with an arms' dealer? Furthermore we are interested in any link between Kazakov and a Russian petrochem negotiator named Smetanin, either he or Reshetnikov is acting as host to him. I am trying to find out if and how they are achieving a link to the conference delegates."

"You have not thought, I suppose, of watching the hotel where the conference is being staged?" Staunton asked sarcastically.

"No need, visitors like Smetanin would be put off immediately by the security control for the senior delegates imposed by the 'Total Cover' security team," replied Vaughan, still struggling to regain his calm. "If any contact is being made it will probably be through more junior staff outside of the hotel's confines. The obvious place for such meetings would be either at Reshetnikov's or Kazakov's house."

"Why on earth do you think that?" demanded Staunton.

"Because, like us, the Russians would not wish to appear to be influencing the outcome in any way. If Smetanin was seen entering the hotel you can guarantee that either the American or French governments would know about it and start shouting the odds. It is thought by London that the Russians are as interested in the conference as we are, but they want the North African region to remain politically fragmented. If their activity is exposed then it is possible that an extreme outcome would occur with either an OPEC style grouping or a plunge towards Islamic fundamentalism; either way it would not be in their interests."

"Humph, I think that's a load of rubbish personally. I'm going to check on your briefing with Sir Andrew. Wait there, I'll get back to you," and with that Staunton put the phone down.

"You did not appear to be enjoying your little chat," said Susanne Bevington, placing a tea tray down on a small table. "Do you take milk?"

"Milk please, and, no I don't hold out much hope for my future relationship with Leonard Staunton. Do you have a secure line to London or is it only Lisbon?"

"I believe I can go via Lisbon, all my previous work has been with our Embassy there so I've never needed to deal direct with London."

"I need you to get a secure line to this number," said Vaughan, hurriedly writing down the DELCO publishing number."

"Oh, are you sure?" replied Mrs Bevington, a little nervously.

"I'll take the blame if there's a complaint."

She lifted the receiver and dialled. "Hello, I need to be put through to DELCO London, do you need the number?" There was a pause. "Oh good, I'll hang on."

Turning to Vaughan she said, "They are putting me through now." Mrs Bevington stood with an anxious expression on her face, listening intently. "Ah, hello, hello. This is the Honorary British Consul in Madeira, I have a Mr Vaughan with me who would like to speak with you." Almost shaking she handed the receiver to Vaughan.

"Could you give me five minutes please Mrs Bevington?"

"Oh yes, of course," she replied and hurried from the room, quietly closing the door behind her.

The call originating directly via the embassy in Lisbon meant that Vaughan was put through to Lorna, DELCO's 'gate keeper' receptionist.

"Is that Lorna? It's Ian Vaughan here. Can I speak with Lieutenant Heathcote?"

Lorna quickly checked Vaughan's identity answers then put him through.

The conversation lasted a good twenty minutes during which Vaughan explained the difficulty he was having with Staunton and requested clarification with regard to whose instructions he should follow. He then asked her to run a check on Olavo Esteves.

"Where does he fit in?" asked Penny Heathcote.

"I don't rightly know, but I do know that he and a group from South America have suddenly shown up here and are holding very secretive meetings on a daily basis.

His father was apparently something to do with the Salaza government of the nineteen sixties and was unpopular enough to feel the need to 'relocate' after the '74 revolution I gather, as apparently were many other Salazaists."

"How does that connect with the conference?" asked Heathcote.

"I frankly don't know at the moment, Penny, all I can tell you is that they were also being lavishly entertained by Reshetnikov a couple of nights ago."

There was silence on the other end of the phone and Vaughan took those few moments to think about the link between Reshetnikov and Esteves. "A thought has just occurred to me. Reshetnikov has just imported two tonnes of chocolate spread. When I heard about it I immediately thought he could have used that substance to hide drugs in? If that cargo came in from South America, Esteves could be the South American shipper."

Vaughan thought of Amelia and the role her company had played in the shipment. Could she be into drug smuggling? Then he remembered that it was the first time that her company had been used by Reshetnikov.

"How do you know all this?" asked Penny Heathcote.

"Overheard a conversation in a café," replied Vaughan. "It struck me that two tonnes of chocolate spread for an island of this size was close to giving the whole population sugar diabetes."

"Yes, I see what you mean. Leave it with me I will make enquiries. Meantime humour Leonard Staunton, but avoid contact with Claremont. Staunton may not have the full picture, it was a bit of a rush getting him there."

Vaughan put the phone down and went in search of Susanne Bevington, finding her reading a book in her lounge. "I've finished my call. Staunton will be phoning back in a minute or so. If you don't mind I will hang around."

Susanne Bevington sighed. "No, there are some magazines on the table there. Would you like some more tea?" Then the office phone rang. "That'll be Staunton. That phone has not been this busy for years."

Staunton was again abrupt. "Sir Andrew agrees with me so get round to Claremont's straight away and pool your intelligence, right."

"Okay I'll get onto it as soon as I can," replied Vaughan choosing his words carefully."

In the lounge Vaughan asked for Claremont's normal address, then left the Consul's home to return to the boat.

Making his way back via the 'Golden Gate Café' he saw the little group of searchers standing around looking at the passers-by, and walked between two of them without either even glancing at him, the change of clothing had worked.

*

Shortly after Mohammed el Kamal's early morning visit, Al Bashir had taken a taxi to the home of Reshetnikov, hoping to meet with Smetanin. Arriving at the gate he was told over the intercom that Reshetnikov was still in bed, but would talk to him if he were prepared to return in one hour. Asking then to see Smetanin he learnt that the STATGAZ negotiator had left to meet someone at the conference. Paying off the taxi he stood for a time, undecided as what to do next. Feeling exposed and somewhat awkward he walked away from Reshetnikov's gateway along the road. Being quite high up above the town centre afforded him a good view of its overall architecture, so different to that seen in Libya and Afghanistan. He felt strangely disturbed as it made him aware that he was in a strongly Christian country where his beliefs were generally feared and held in contempt. They would learn, he thought as he looked down over the city with its neat terracotta tiled roofs, church towers and the blue Atlantic beyond. "The will of Allah is strong and shall prevail," he shouted loudly, surprising himself with his unguarded outburst. He wanted to preach to them now, telling them of the one true faith, direct them to the true path of Islam where sharia law reigns as the only path to heaven.

The two-tone blare of a police siren approaching broke through Al Bashir's thoughts and had him scurrying down the steep bank to conceal himself behind a tree. It was then that he realised how exposed he was to arrest on this island, should he be seen and recognised, and how stupid he was to be walking around in the street. Berating himself he then began to wonder whether his sister or brother-in-law would report his presence. Takkal was right he should not have come, but that had been the orders he had been given, Al Ben Said had been very clear that he must personally ensure that Al Djebbar was eliminated. Later when he arrived back at the entrance to the Reshetnikov palatial grounds and pressed the bell again the black steel gate rolled back to reveal the massive form of Ivan.

"Come." Then after a few minutes walk he said, "Go there," and pointed to the pool gate near the top of the driveway.

Reshetnikov was welcoming and offered Al Bashir tea and some cake from a selection that had been set out on a poolside table.

After some minor pleasantries Al Bashir asked when it would be possible for him to meet with Smetanin. Reshetnikov frowned and apologised saying that he had faithfully explained to Smetanin the importance of such a meeting, but had been told that more details were required before Smetanin could adjust his very busy schedule to accommodate Al Bashir. Currently, Reshetnikov explained, Smetanin was holding multi-million dollar discussions with various important delegates at the conference and would shortly be leaving to report to his head office in Moscow.

Al Bashir was reluctant to offer any further details, but he was being pushed into a corner. He either gave up the information or returned empty handed to face the wrath of Al Ben Said and others. There was no choice and during the next hour he explained how sharia law would soon sweep the North African continent, and the need for those interested in continuing good trading relations with that region to respect that and form mutually beneficial arrangements. At no point did Al Bashir mention the word Taliban, but Reshetnikov's brain was faster than most when it came to listening.

"You have not mentioned who you actually represent," said Reshetnikov, smiling benignly at his guest.

"The one true path of Islam," replied Al Bashir, knowing in his heart that to mention those in the mountains of Afghanistan would bring the meeting to an end.

"Let us be honest with each other please," replied Reshetnikov. "You are Taliban." Al Bashir went to protest and explain that he was a son of Libya, when Reshetnikov held up his hand. "Wait, let me finish for you – by Taliban I believe it is they who give you this task of contact with STATGAZ. They know direct contact at this time would be rejected; too much blood has been spilt in past for such working together now, eh."

Reshetnikov looked across at Al Bashir waiting for his response. It took Al Bashir several seconds before he could formulate a safe reply.

"During our exile from Libya the Taliban offered us refuge, but with the removal of the dictator Gaddafi we have returned, and now enjoy a growing number of followers who will soon outnumber all others that follow false teachings. Our influence is spreading as if it is on the wind and soon all the nations, who now sit listening to the American false promises at the so called conference here, will join us on the path of truth and obedience to the will of Allah."

Reshetnikov nodded, appearing to understand and recognise Al Bashir's independence of Taliban control. Inwardly he smiled, as now he was sure that a meeting with Smetanin would not take place but negotiations would continue with him, Reshetnikov, the intermediary.

"I understand your position, but you do not appear to have a voice at this conference. Maybe it is because at this moment in time your holy cause does not have, let us say, sufficient supporters to get you into the meeting rooms of those currently in power."

Al Bashir sat silently, unwilling to openly accept the truth of Reshetnikov's observation.

"I am sure," continued the Russian, "That there are some at this conference who believe in your path of true worship, but they are few at this time and do not hold senior positions in the debates that must surely be happening."

"The tide is unstoppable," replied Al Bashir firmly. "Those that oppose us will perish."

"I will make a suggestion to you. Let me act as your intermediary in the discussion with STATGAZ, as you see I have good connection. Smetanin is an important man in the formulation of STATGAZ policy, but your direct approach to him will have little influence at this time, but through me, doors will be opened and your message heard."

For a further half hour Al Bashir tried to persuade the Russian that at least an introduction should be considered, but all to no avail. Leaving the house and getting into a waiting taxi Al Bashir realised how impossible the task he had been given was. When Reshetnikov had quoted the numbers of Russian soldiers that had lost their lives in fighting the Taliban and informed him that

Smetanin's own brother returned from the fight crippled, it was obvious that Reshetnikov's offer must be given serious consideration. Al Bashir also recognised that the removal of Al Djebbar had to be achieved, failure meant that he, could never return. It was with a very heavy heart that he instructed the taxi driver to drop him off at the home of Sarkis Kazakov.

*

Whilst Al Bashir had been at Kazakov's house arranging for Leyla to be shown the bomb jacket, Gleb Smetanin was in deep conversation with two junior members of the Moroccan delegation in a pleasant patisserie opposite Reid's Hotel. The head of the delegation, Ali Khasawni, had sent the two young men from the Department of Trade to inform the STATGAZ representative that there was no special treatment available with regard to exploration for oil or gas in Morocco. The work would be put out to international tender. The message had been relayed efficiently by both young men and had been accepted with regret by Smetanin. He then swiftly returned to pleasantries saying how much he had enjoyed his recent visit to their country and starting a discussion about Moroccan society and social conditions. Within half an hour he had suggested to these junior members of the Moroccan team that their personal earnings could be considerably enhanced over the next few years if they were to remain in communication with him on issues relating to the country's natural resources. His company was, he said, very generous to those who provide assistance; he himself drives a Ferrari when he is at his home in Italy. In Russia he uses public transport as Moscow is too busy with cars, especially if you want to park them.

As they returned to the Vidamar to report on the meeting and prepare for the next session of the conference both young men were considering favourably Smetanin's offer.

Not so favourable were Metcalf's comments to Chuck Hayward, the Texan with a penchant for large quantities of Jack Daniels. "If the team had been of the number I said was necessary for this job, you would have been on the plane home by now and your pay cheque cancelled. As it is I am stuck with you, you useless drunk," shouted Metcalf.

"You think I'm the only guy who sneaks a drink from time to time, hell no. If you knew the number that creep into the bar when you ain't lookin' then it would be just you and the girls here."

I'm not talkin' about the rest, it's you I have this problem with. You shape up and I won't drop your pay. You don't and I will. You understand me Hayward."

CHAPTER 10

THE COUP BEGINS

It was mid afternoon as Ian Vaughan approached *La Mouette sur le Vent* to see both Mehdi and Amelia sat talking to each other in the cockpit. The water, even in the marina, was choppy from a strong wind coming off the mountains.

"May I join you?" he asked as he started to make his way carefully across the boarding platform.

So engrossed in their conversation were the two that neither had seen him approach.

"We hope you don't mind us coming on board," said Amelia, quickly standing up as Vaughan stepped over the pushpit rail. "There is nowhere to sit on the quay that isn't covered in bird droppings and dirt. Mehdi has only just arrived but I have been here half an hour."

Looking at her dazzling white dress, Ian Vaughan could understand her reluctance to placing it in contact with the grubby quayside.

"No, of course not. How are you? You're looking great," he replied stooping to greet her with a kiss on both cheeks. "Mehdi, how are you, and how is the conference going?"

"That is why I am here, everything has gone very well today and I have been asked to invite you to the hotel tomorrow morning when the final conference message will be issued," Mehdi replied, obviously delighted to be able to pass this news to Vaughan.

"Please tell Walid that I would be honoured to attend. You say that everything has gone well?"

"Oh yes, very well. This morning after a question and answer session, the delegations were invited to make their own statements and all said that they would return to their countries to recommend in full Al Djebbar's idea. We are so very happy as it has taken much work to achieve this conference let alone have such a positive conclusion."

"That is truly wonderful news Mehdi, really wonderful, please pass on my sincere congratulations to Walid."

"Of course, but if you will excuse me, I must return as there are still many matters to be attended to."

Shaking Vaughan's hand and nodding to Amelia, Mehdi clambered onto the stern deck and over the rail to shuffle across the platform unsteadily and walk away along the quay.

"I thought for a moment that he was going to fall in the drink," said Vaughan, replacing a horseshoe lifebelt he had snatched out of its hanger fearing that Mehdi would fall into the water.

Amelia looked at Vaughan obviously not understanding. "Drink, what drink?"

"Oh it is an English expression we use if someone falls into say, a river or the sea, and they swallow, 'drink' some of the water," Vaughan explained.

Amelia shook her head. "He told me that you were immensely helpful to this man who is head of the conference. He thinks you are very clever person who knows much about their region."

"Only stuff that I have read in the papers," replied Vaughan. "Also Walid al Djebbar and I have a mutual friend, Charles, who, as a close friend of Walid's, takes a great interest in that part of the world. We normally discuss it a bit when we meet as Charles thinks that it is very important for the future peace of Europe."

"Have you known this Walid a long time?"

"I have known of him a long time, we had tea together yesterday afternoon." *This could be tricky, I wonder how much Mehdi told her.* "Then he came here early this morning and we had a good chat, he's a very nice guy, highly intelligent. At the time he thought that the whole conference would be a failure, so he must have been delighted with the change in opinions," replied Vaughan, being carefully vague regarding length and depth of his acquaintance with Walid. "You coming here is an unexpected pleasure, would you like a drink – wine, tea, coffee, you name it?"

"Maybe, er, tea," Amelia said, obviously thinking of how to proceed with something that was bothering her. "Zeferino had a very bad night last night so I called doctor to him this morning. He said that maybe Zeferino has some infection and we had ambulance to take him to hospital. They gave him some medicines and say that they will keep him there for two days at least. That is more time he is away from school and he needs to learn as he is behind in many subjects."

"Did he start back at school on Monday?" Vaughan asked.

"Yes, just two days then more time away. His teachers say he is very bright but getting lazy. He thinks too much of this sailboarding and football."

"That sounds like my school reports," said Vaughan chuckling. "It'll be girls next."

"It better not be," said Amelia, glaring at Vaughan as if he was encouraging the boy. "He has to go to university and obtain a sensible degree. I cannot guarantee to keep the family business going until he is old enough to take over."

"Hey, easy, easy. I was only joking."

"Sorry, I am upset. It is not just Zeferino it is also that uncle of mine that makes me worry so much. These meetings continue and he stays out late several times with women. Day before yesterday he comes back home maybe three o'clock in the morning. I hear him come in so I look out of my room and see him go straight into the kitchen. I go to see if he wants something to eat or drink and see him take off his jacket and there on his shirt is much blood. He tells me that one of his friends had cut himself on a broken glass, but there is so much bloodstain and all on his shoulder."

"Maybe he was helping the man, like taking him to hospital."

"I asked and he said no, they fixed cut with bandage. Then this morning, after I leave Zeferino and arrive at work, Luz tells me that the body of a young girl was found on the roof of a big hotel at Ponta da Cruz. She had been stabbed and left there."

"And you think your uncle may be responsible for her death?" replied Vaughan in amazement.

"I do not know what to think, that is why I am here. If I tell the police they may think it the quickest way to solve the case and charge him. As a visitor, and someone who has been with many women since he has been here in Madeira, he could well be charged with murder regardless of his innocence. I dare not tell any of my friends for fear they mention it to others. You know how rumours spread and become exaggerated."

"And if you face him with it he would deny all knowledge, and it could put you and Zeferino in danger. Look let's go below while I make some tea and we can discuss your options further."

In the cabin, Amelia sat herself at the far end of the starboard settee and removed her sunglasses revealing tear-reddened eyes. Busying himself in the galley Vaughan was also thinking long and hard about what he should do. His duty was to observe, as best he could, the conference, yet so far he had done nothing in terms of watching the actual venue to see who was visiting. With Staunton on his back giving different instructions to those given by the Commodore he had a difficult game to play, as it was obvious that there was contact between Staunton and Claremont. Where did Kazakov's little grey man fit in and why was Al Bashir, a cleric, meeting with Kazakov, an arms' dealer? Why was Al Bashir on the island if it wasn't to do with the conference? Really what he should be doing now is finding out where Al Bashir is staying instead of making tea for a beautiful young lady with a wayward uncle. Amelia had been a distraction from the day he arrived and now this problem. Maybe it was the time to come clean and explain to her who he really was, and why he was in Madeira.

The uncle was, however, another intriguing character, holding these secret meetings. Why was he here in Madeira after spending most of his life in Brazil? Bearing in mind the Portuguese economy as it was with almost daily protests on the streets of Lisbon, there was little sense in investing here, particularly on the island where the main business of tourism was in decline, and taxation was being ramped up. Prioritise, that was the only way and the only way he could convince those in London that he was up to doing the job. His orders from the Commodore was to befriend Al Djebbar and he had succeeded there, secondly he had to see if this Russian negotiator, Smetanin, was now in contact with the Moroccan delegation. Thus far he had only set eyes on Smetanin when he was bribing junior hotel staff, so checking that a contact route had been established was the next priority. He also had to track down Al Bashir and see what he was up to.

The kettle whistled as it came to the boil and Vaughan made a pot of tea and set out the cups and saucers on the cabin table.

"You use china cups and saucers onboard a boat," she said in surprise.

"I hate drinking and eating from anything that is plastic. If you stow it carefully china will survive most things, and it is only cheap stuff, not bone china."

He had been a bit alarmed at the cost of putting the yacht's name onto the mugs, cups and plates, but to him this yacht was very special; after all, it was now his home. Again an image of Umeko Morohashi standing in the galley carefully stowing plates as he helmed the yacht out of the Helford River flashed across his mind.

He went to pour the tea.

"No, let it stand for a little while," she said, raising her hand, palm out like a traffic policeman.

"Yes of course, I wasn't thinking," Vaughan replied, hurriedly formulating a course of action for her that would get her away and allow him to continue with what he should be doing. "Have the police given any details of clues they have found?"

"No, apparently they just say that they are following several lines of inquiry."

"Well I would wait until they knock on the door before you say anything."

"You do not think he is involved in this murder," she said, in a way that suggested he had made up his mind.

"Look, if it was one of his friends who was injured he would still have either a bandage or a plaster over the wound. If they return to your house today you can check."

"I did last night when they came. None of them had any dressing on their hands; I looked carefully," she replied, her voice quaking and her eyes filling with tears. "Ian this is worrying me very much and I do not know what to do."

At that point she burst into tears, her shoulders shaking, her head bowed. "This is all too much, I do not know where to go for help that I can really trust. I am really frightened that I have a murderer in my home."

Vaughan knelt down beside her and took hold of her hands. "Look are you sure that you could not spend a night or two with

Luz or Susie or any other of your friends. What about Bruno and Alicia, surely they will let you stay and maybe by then the police will have cleared up everything and made an arrest."

"They will want to know why I leave a guest in my home unattended. It would look very strange to them and I am not a good liar, I would have to tell them and then I fear what would happen, and I do not want to get them involved in this."

"Do you have a spare room?" Vaughan asked, suddenly.

"Why do you ask?"

"Maybe you could put up an English business associate for a couple of nights."

She pointed at him, her expression questioning.

Vaughan nodded. "It is just an idea."

Amelia stared at him for several seconds contemplating his proposal. "It is very kind of you, but then you will become closely involved in my family's bad behaviour."

"I have the luxury of sailing away from here in a few days, but as I said, it was just an idea," Vaughan looked at her, waiting for her to respond. "I doubt if he would try to harm you in any event, but if you had another guest it is even more unlikely."

"If you are sure that you do not mind," she finally replied, dabbing her eyes with a handkerchief.

They were silent for several minutes, she, sat staring at the cabin floor, as Vaughan thought of the equipment he would need.

"I must shop for food on our way home," she said, suddenly.

"Don't bother on my account, we must go out for dinner this evening, we have business to discuss; and besides I have to repay you for putting me up during my short surprise visit."

"He said this morning that his friends were coming this evening for a meeting, they will expect some food and wine," she replied, as if to suggest that she must stay in the flat.

"Is that a full meal or just snacks?"

"Oh, not a full dinner, just, as you say, snacks."

As they left the marina Vaughan noticed the yacht masts leaning in the windy gusts.

"It is getting very gusty, does this happen often?"

"Oh yes, days like this often mean the airport cannot receive planes. Maybe today is one of those days. Pilots who fly in here have to have special training to avoid accident," Amelia replied, fighting to hold down her skirt as another gust came through.

On the way to her apartment Amelia purchased enough food to feed a rugby team for a week. When they arrived her uncle was in the shower getting ready for his evening guests. Amelia immediately set about preparing the food and setting it out on a sideboard against the wall of the sitting-cum-dining room.

"Where do they normally sit and talk?" Vaughan asked her quietly.

"This evening I think they will sit around the dining table, that is where I have placed the ashtrays. They all smoke heavily as you have probably noticed."

Busy in the kitchen Amelia did not see Vaughan attach microphones to the room's lampshades and the veranda railing or see where he hid the two recorders.

"What jacket was he wearing the night he came in with the bloody shirt?"

"The light blue one, why?" she asked.

"I'm going to try and have a quick look at it. If he comes out of the bathroom start talking to him about the arrangements you have made and our going out for dinner."

With that Vaughan quickly entered the uncle's bedroom and looked into the wardrobe. There was no sign of a light blue jacket. The noise of an electric shaver coming from the bathroom stopped and Vaughan had just enough time to get into Zeferino's bedroom before the bathroom door opened and the conversation start between Amelia and her uncle.

The introductions went more easily than Vaughan had hoped. Olavo Esteves accepted that a surprise business visit would be made without appearing to question it as strange. He looked nervous and tense and seemed relieved that he and his friends would have the flat to themselves. When Amelia apologised for not being around to attend to his guests, he waved her comment aside, saying. "Amelia, Amelia, we can manage well, you must go and enjoy the evening, eh."

When they were alone Vaughan said, "Take your time getting ready, we need to leave as the others are arriving."

Amelia gave him a questioning look. "I'll explain later," he said.

Vaughan was waiting in the entrance hall to the apartment when the taxi bringing Esteves' friends arrived. He stepped out of the building. The sun, though low in the sky, gave more than enough light for him to take several pictures of them with the mobile phone he had been issued with. Then calling to attract the taxi driver's attention, he requested the man wait for two minutes whilst his companion came down.

Amelia's exit from the apartment building justifiably brought admiring looks from Esteves' three associates as they stepped aside to let her pass. The off-the-shoulder, dark blue wild silk, figure-hugging dress worn by Amelia would stop traffic in any city. Add to that her natural beauty, and a spellbound moment was guaranteed.

"I must come here on business much more often," said Vaughan, loud enough for the still enraptured visitors to hear.

"Thank you kind sir. Is this taxi ours?"

Vaughan opened the taxi door for her, and then closing it, walked around the front of the taxi and got in alongside her. "Por

favor leve-nos a restaurante Mamma Mia em; a Vidamar o hotel,"
he requested.

"Sim, senhor," the driver replied, promptly putting the vehicle
in gear and pulling away.

"That was very polite Portuguese you used," Amelia said,
teasingly. "Are you always that nice to taxi drivers?"

"Being polite doesn't cost anymore, and in a strange city
possibly costs less."

"Good point."

At the restaurant he chose a window table for two looking
down onto the access road and the Vidamar's reception. From
there he could see, standing outside of the east tower, groups of
men in traditional Arabian dress smoking and talking amongst
themselves.

Moving amongst the gathering was Al Djebbar greeting each
group and exchanging a few words before moving on.
Occasionally he would spend a little more time talking to one
particular member of a group. Never far away from him stood
Metcalf and three of his men, looking out from the crowd for
potential threats to Al Djebbar's safety. Vaughan was impressed
but thought Metcalf to be far too close to the probable target.
*That's your men's job, Metcalf, not yours. You should be standing
where you get an overall view. Show yourself to be in a place
where you can command the situation, you will not impress Walid
al Djebbar by being amongst the cannon fodder.*

"Who are you looking at?" Amelia asked.

"You see the man in the fawn djellaba and red bemousse,"
Vaughan said, "that is my friend Al Djebbar doing the 'press the
flesh' bit."

"The man with the red hat?"

"Yes."

"I cannot see him so well from here. Would I like him if I met him?"

"Yes, I'm sure you would. He is not a rabble-rousing politician espousing hatred and biased views. As I said earlier he is very worldly and not extreme when presenting his region's opinions and ambitions but firm. Above all he listens to what you have to say carefully, and gives you the opportunity to voice your own thoughts. I am very impressed by him, he would make a great statesman given the platform and support."

Just then the delegates and their staff started to file into the conference suite for their evening meal, with the exception of one young looking man who hung back. After a few minutes he looked about him and then walked across to the west tower reception entrance where he dithered awkwardly obviously waiting for somebody, but not wanting to be seen doing so.

Amelia and Vaughan's food had arrived and was half eaten by the time the furtive delegate's visitor arrived. The taxi driver pulling up outside the reception doors was having an argument with his passenger who eventually appeared to give up, then getting out turned and shouted something at the driver, who shrugged his shoulders and speedily reversed the vehicle back to where he could turn it round. The passenger looked about long enough for Vaughan to get a good look at her and identified her as the lady he had seen with Reshetnikov the night he had slipped away from Bruno's restaurant to the nearby hotel.

"I don't think she was very polite to that taxi driver," said Amelia, who had followed Vaughan's gaze. "No tip, I think."

"Overcharged, I hope," replied Vaughan, noting the meeting between Sonia and the delegate. *So that's the Russian route in, I wonder if it is the Algerian or Moroccan delegation the contact bats for?* "By the way I forgot to mention there wasn't any sign of a light blue jacket in your uncle's wardrobe. He's probably taken it to the cleaners."

"I looked in the washing basket for his shirt," replied Amelia. "There was no sign of that either. Do you not think that is suspicious?"

"I agree, it does look a bit odd, but if the jacket was bloodstained innocently then why not have it cleaned, and maybe he can afford to throw shirts away."

"You are still not convinced are you?" she said frowning at him.

"There is something going on, he was very nervous when you introduced us."

"You see! It must have been him, but what do we do about it?"

"What time do his friends normally leave?" Vaughan asked.

"Sometimes they stay till after midnight. Why do you ask?"

"No reason really, it's just that it may be better if we return after they have left, they obviously upset you by being there." *If he had murdered this girl and was smart he would have got rid of both the shirt and the jacket. Would he just dump them in a dustbin or has he managed to destroy them? I can hardly go snooping around in the dustbin store if they are still about, it will be difficult enough with her uncle there.*

"Maybe you are right, but it may make it a very late night," she replied, inwardly happy that she would be alone in his company where she felt safe and relaxed.

They lingered over desserts and coffee leaving the restaurant around eleven o'clock. Outside she slipped her arm through his as they walked towards Reid's Hotel, weaving their way through the homeward bound tourists coming from the direction of the city centre. Crossing the road near to the Pestana Village complex entrance they hired the only remaining taxi, which dropped them off near to Amelia's apartment.

The glow of two cigarettes on the veranda showed that Uncle Olavo's friends were still there. "Once round the block?" suggested Vaughan.

Amelia nodded. "I hope they will not be much longer, I feel quite exhausted with all the tension of the last few days, and with this wind still blowing I am feeling cold."

Vaughan slipped off his jacket and put it around her shoulders.

Returning to the point where the taxi had dropped them it was obvious that Esteves' friends were still at the apartment. They sat in a bus shelter, out of the wind, and he told her about his imaginary voyage out from England and his next planned voyage south to the Canary Islands. Now was not the time to be honest with her, now was the time to either, lose or take, more interest in Olavo Esteves and friends. They had been sitting quietly talking for half an hour when an empty taxi sped past and turned down the hill towards the apartment.

"His guests are leaving," said Vaughan. "We had better give him another quarter of an hour to get to bed."

"He may well go out drinking and chasing women, he has done that before. I feel so sorry for my aunt."

"We had better check then, come on, quickly."

They reached the corner of the street just in time to see all four men get into the taxi and a suitcase being put in the boot. "That's good, they are all going and it looks as if your uncle is not intending to return tonight."

Amelia's heart gave a little joyous leap, maybe it was worth wearing her most provocative dress after all; reaching out she took Vaughan's hand.

In the apartment they found a note from Esteves explaining that he and his friends were going to Porto do Moniz for two days.

Amelia looked puzzled and looking at her wristwatch shook her head.

"Why would they think to go to Porto do Moniz at this time of night, the hotels will be mainly closed up for the night with only night porter on duty."

"They probably have phoned ahead to make a reservation, and if they have paid by credit card a porter would be all that is needed," replied Vaughan.

"But so late at night, why they not wait until morning? That would be much more sensible." Her elation of a few minutes before dispelled by renewed concerns regarding her uncle and his friends.

Vaughan chose not to tell her that Esteves had no intention of going to Porto do Moniz that night. *They want you to think that they are staying the night anywhere else than in Funchal.* He was absolutely sure that whatever the group had been plotting all these weeks was about to be hatched.

"Have you got a torch handy?"

"In the bottom cupboard by the door."

"I'll be back in a few minutes, I'd really appreciate some coffee if you wouldn't mind making some." *Let's see if he has left anything incriminating in the dustbins.*

"You can drink coffee at this time of night?" she asked with surprise. "I would not sleep if I had coffee now."

"Neither will I," Vaughan replied, then checking that the torch was bright enough asked, "Do you know of anyone in this apartment block who is away for a long time?"

Amelia frowned as she thought about his question. "Yes, Mr and Mrs Grenville from number seven are away until August, they've gone to see their daughter and her family in New Zealand. Why do you ask?"

"Their bin should be empty." Amelia looked puzzled.

The waste bins were enclosed in a store, built against the rear wall of the small rear gardens with louvre doors opening both onto the garden and the service road running behind the properties. Finding number seven's bin Vaughan flipped up the lid; it was empty.

Just as I thought, he would have been a complete idiot to stash it in this one, he thought, before working his way along the rest of the line, peering into each bin without success, until he got to number three. Beneath two large bags of household rubbish he could make out the corner of a posh looking shallow box. Quietly removing the bags, he then reached into the bin and lifted out the box, turning it the right way up. It was a shirt box and the label was that of a menswear shop in Funchal; tape had been hurriedly applied to keep the box closed and, using the small Leatherman multi-tool he always carried in his pocket, he cut the tape and opened the box. The bloodstained shirt was inside and had obviously been placed there having defied attempts to wash away the stain. Taking the rest of the rubbish from the bin Vaughan found at the very bottom a thick black polythene bag containing the jacket. After closing the bin's lid and store doors, Vaughan hurried back to the apartment with the shirt and jacket.

"I found these in number three's bin."

"What do we do now?"

The last thing I can afford is to get further mixed up with this. Staunton would have a field day.

"That can wait a bit, first I want you to listen to some recordings I have made," said Vaughan, putting off telling Amelia why he was really in Madeira. "I'll just go and fetch the kit."

In the sitting room he recovered both recorders and was plugging in headphones to the unit picking up the signal from the lampshade microphone when Amelia came in with his coffee.

"You're not joining me?" Vaughan asked, looking at the single coffee mug in her hand.

"Oh, we have to stay awake?"

Vaughan nodded. "I think that listening to this recording is a matter of great urgency. I used some special equipment of mine to record the conversation your uncle and his friends were having in here this evening. You will understand what they are saying, I won't."

Amelia looked shocked and alarmed when she fully digested what he had said. She was about to demand an explanation when Vaughan, anticipating her questioning, held up his hand and said, "Amelia, I think the meeting here tonight was very important and may affect your business, so it is essential that you hear this as soon as possible. Sit down there and listen while I get your coffee." *You dimwit, Vaughan, why didn't you explain to her what you planned to do? Done properly, she would have understood.*

By the time he returned to the sitting room Amelia was engrossed, holding the earphones tight to her head. Suddenly she looked extremely shocked and annoyed taking off the earphones and glaring at them.

"That awful man Pedroso. He thinks I... well I won't tell you what he thinks."

"Listen to the recording."

"There is nothing so far other than very rude comments."

Vaughan frowned at her; pouting like an unhappy child she jammed the earphones on again.

It was Rodriguez, the strategist, who had taken charge of proceedings, insisting that they get down to business straight away. Within half an hour he had set out the operations schedule detailing the key persons controlling the Lisbon end of the coup, then had started to question each member of the group as to their individual part in the takeover of power in Madeira.

Tears were rolling down Amelia's cheeks as she listened and wrote down the main points of what was being said. After a further fifteen minutes she begged Vaughan to let her stop. "I cannot listen to anymore, it is so terrible this thing they are planning. To think it has been done in my home; I never want to stay here another night."

"What were they saying? I could not understand your notes."

"They are planning a coup. They are working with some of the army to takeover the country," she cried, the words tumbling out, her voice trembling with fear.

"Slow down and explain to me carefully."

Amelia gasped several times then began to explain more calmly what she had heard. After five minutes Vaughan stopped her.

"Pack some things and we will get you into a hotel."

"We must go to the police with this."

"There is every possibility that they have infiltrated your police force here, maybe at a high level, I don't know, but I do not think it is worth taking the risk," said Vaughan, wondering what Susanne Bevington's reaction will be to being woken up at one thirty in the morning.

"What do we do then, march to the Governor's house and stand guard. Of course we must tell the police."

"No, it is too much of a risk to take when the coup is probably already underway," replied Vaughan. "I know the person we must contact and she has direct links to the British Embassy in Lisbon and the Government in London. The orders to stop this will have to come from the very top."

She looked at him suspiciously. "Who?"

"The Honorary British Consul," Vaughan replied, "She and I are old friends; come on get some clothes together and phone for a taxi, hurry we do not have time to waste."

After packing his own things and recovering the microphones Vaughan went through and helped her pack.

"Taxi?"

"I will phone now."

Ten minutes later they were leaving the building and hurrying across the pavement to the cab. Vaughan gave the driver the address and settled back in the seat, not surprised to be immediately challenged by Amelia as to why he had not asked her first before planting the recording equipment.

"I look at tiny microphone and recorder, I never seen anything that small. How come you have such thing?"

"A friend of mine is an electronics engineer, his whole life is specialist sound recording. Normally high fidelity kit, but he occasionally plays with making micro stuff just for fun. He let me have it so that I can record some of my research interviews. It saves me making notes which sometimes puts people off."

She gave him a very sceptical look but did not push anymore, except to tell him firmly that he should have told her before as she may have had 'legitimate objections'.

All he could do was apologise profusely and hope that she would forgive him, though why her forgiveness was so important to him he could not quite understand.

*

As Vaughan and Amelia's taxi sped up the hill towards the Honorary British Consul's residence, Takkal and two of Reshetnikov's minders were putting a ladder up against the western side of the 'Mamma Mia' restaurant. The normally busy road was deserted at this time of night and the three men, wearing black clothing and hoods, screened by a line of olive trees from the road, felt secure as they worked. Carefully and silently they

241

hauled a long narrow bottomless box covered in roofing felt up and onto the restaurant's roof.

The box had been carefully made and the felt dirtied to match the rest of the roof's covering. Takkal's attention to detail was his most valuable asset, nothing escaped him. Checking the strength of the stanchions supporting the screening to the air-conditioning equipment, he chose the corner one and attached the end of a black rope leaving the coil close by the screen and out of sight. Then, with the help of one of the minders, carried the box across the roof to the far corner from where he could see the entrances to the east tower of the hotel. After reminding the minders of their orders for the morning Takkal dismissed the men and carefully lifted the hinged end to the box and unrolled a thin mattress in front of him, as he slithered headlong inside. The box itself had been carefully designed and contained, clipped to the inside, the rifle, a pistol, a loaded cartridge gun of building adhesive and a bottle of drinking water. Before the delegates had arrived on the island, Takkal had spent several hours observing Metcalf's preparations and equipment installation. None of the security measures interfered with his plan, but he did fear that the wind, which swirled around the hotel towers, could be strong enough to blow the box off the roof. Unclipping the building adhesive, he lifted first one side of the box then the other, squirting a thick line of glue along the line where the box would sit, then pushed it down onto the glue.

The local TV station had headed most of their news programmes with pictures of the conference delegates moving backwards and forwards between the hotel and the conference suite and events within the conference hall, enjoying the revenue gleaned from global distribution. Takkal had been an avid viewer, timing with a stopwatch the movements of Al Djebbar as he came from the hotel towards the conference suite steps. In the grounds

242

below the house he had rented he rigged a series of pulleys, like aerial runways, that carried moving targets for him to practise with. Like the hotel area, his practice ground was windy; an advantage in establishing offset and drop over the varying ranges. As the conference progressed and the interest in Al Djebbar increased, Takkal noticed that the sector of clear sight was being increasingly reduced, as enthusiastic delegates surrounded the man almost immediately he reached the pavement edge. Past experience had taught him that when a bullet struck and the target went down most people around them would duck then flee. Here, however, were supposedly trained bodyguards whose job it was to block further bullets and retaliate with defensive fire if the assassin's location was established. His employers had insisted that it must be a kill so he had designed the rifle to have a five bullet magazine; he prayed that the first shot would be enough.

*

At the Consul's residence Vaughan held his finger on the doorbell until the hall light came on. The inner door opened enough for a man to peer out. "What do you want at this hour!" he shouted.

"I urgently need to contact the embassy in Lisbon and DELCO London. I am Ian Vaughan, your wife will know me."

The door closed, then after a few minutes Susanne Bevington opened the door wearing a silk dressing gown, and let Vaughan and Amelia into the porch.

"I knew you were trouble the moment I saw you," she said angrily. "What the hell has happened for you to come barging in at this hour?"

"We have firm evidence that a coup has been planned both here and in Portugal and is about to be triggered," replied Vaughan, holding up the recorder.

"You can't be serious," Mrs Bevington replied, her expression a mixture of shock and disbelief. "How did you get this information, it must be a prank that you have overheard."

"My humour does not run to waking important people up at this hour without being sure of the need to do so. I can assure you, Mrs Bevington, that the group heading this have been on the island planning the final stages for the last month."

"Come through to the office."

Unlike Amelia, Susanne Bevington's comprehension of the recording had her reaching for the official phone after just five minutes of listening. After establishing contact with the embassy security in Lisbon and being put through to the night watch at DELCO she proceeded to impress both Vaughan and Amelia by giving simultaneous translation of the recording. After half an hour it was obvious that several people at the London end were listening, and by the end of the first hour the diplomatic phone lines between London and Lisbon were red hot with traffic.

The detail obsessed Isidro Rodriguez had named all of the mainland leaders of the coup and soon most would be arrested and quietly taken away to avoid public disturbance. Airports and harbours were about to impose extremely tight security checks in order to prevent those industrialists and other commercial supporters from going abroad. Anyone working for the companies mentioned, regardless of their status, was to be held until the authorities were satisfied that they were not directly involved.

Much later Vaughan was sitting in a comfortable armchair in the lounge of the Consul's residence sipping at another cup of black coffee. He felt strangely exuberant, but had no idea why; maybe it was the reaction of Staunton. The man's annoyance upon learning what was happening, apparently under his very nose in Lisbon, was almost amusing, as was the hostile reaction of the Honorary British Consul to Madeira when he telephoned and challenged her for reporting direct to London.

Amelia, sitting opposite Vaughan, was staring at the floor wondering what would happen to her when it was realised that the plot had been hatched in her own home. Visions of having to sell the business and leave Portugal crossed her mind. She would leave the business to Susie and Luz, maybe they would believe that she was not involved and let her act as an agent for the business, say in Britain or Germany.

"Lisbon inform that the Portuguese authorities have started arresting the military personnel involved in the coup there, on the mainland, but it appears they were reluctant to take action here in Madeira until they have confirmed that none of our local senior rank army or police individuals are involved," announced Susanne Bevington as she came into the room. "I've just been on the phone with London again, this has put them in a right tizzwas. Nobody had any intelligence that suggested a coup was likely in Europe, though now with Brazil in the state it is in and the Portuguese economy going into severe recession, it does apparently fit some profile they have for assessing these things."

"You say that they are not taking action here?" said Vaughan. "So they have 'limited' confidence in the Military and Police senior ranks. An island is an ideal location, for some hothead with more ego than sense, to try some bid for independence and power I suppose. It makes it essential to choose the right personnel, in order to avoid that scenario; let's hope that the Government on the mainland appreciated that when they made the staff choices, and got it right. There will be a lot of people not looking forward to what happens next."

The Consul shrugged her shoulders. "I'm out of my depth in this situation. There is nothing in our training that goes even close to what is happening here."

*

The only part of the coup scheduled to have started operations was Major Alves and his company of one hundred and twenty men. They had taken off from Montijo airbase near Lisbon with government and military headquarter's approval late the previous afternoon, thanks to Yvonne Alves' persuasive political abilities, but the strong crosswinds had forced them to abandon landing at Madeira's notoriously difficult Santa Caterina airport after three attempts, and they were forced to divert to the island of Porto Santo. It would be dawn at the earliest before they could attempt another landing at Madeira, and Major Alves was becoming very nervous indeed. He had immediately contacted Diago Velo who, relaxing in a comfortable armchair at Reshetnikov's home, reassured him that the delay, though an irritation, did not mean disaster. Such assurances though, did not calm the Major's anxieties and throughout the night he had phoned regularly to seek further assurances. Alves was also regularly phoning his wife, who was the co-ordinator between the mainland and island groups, and at two o'clock in the morning was finishing packing her suitcase and putting her return air ticket to Caracas, in Venezuela, into her handbag.

Marrying someone stupid but rich, helps you get on in the world, but a woman always needs to be prepared to escape at the right time. The very beautiful Yvonne Alves looked at herself in the mirror and noted that she looked tired, but no matter, if things do go wrong she will be able to sleep on the plane. Should the madcap plan of her husband and the six other majors, whose careers had stopped when they had reached their level of incompetence, succeed, then she would enjoy the rewards for the risks she had taken. Idly she thought of Diago Velo; like her he was every inch a politician and very ambitious. If the coup succeeds, she will return from Venezuela, her husband will somehow disappear and she and Diago will at last be together. No more short meetings of deep political discussion and hot passion, at last they will be together as a powerful team set to challenge the former soft socialist order and bring their country to its senses. If only they did not have to rely on the army for support, if only she could dispel that nagging fear of failure, if only Diago were there now beside her.

*

In the lounge of Reshetnikov's quinta, five men anxiously studied the computer screen on which the weather forecast for Madeira was being brought up to date.

"The conference is due to close at midday with the issuing of a joint statement. That is our moment to strike, when all attention is focused there," said Rodriguez. "By the time the speeches are finished we will be in charge here and waiting for Correia to confirm that Lisbon is in their hands. With that the rest of Portugal will join within days, there is no strong government support outside of the capital."

Velo's mobile chimed again. "Oh God, Alves, what is it now?" He answered exasperatedly.

The others heard Alves' angry response.

"Of course there are no weather information persons at the airport. Wait a while and we will tell you what is happening, here they will shortly be updating the forecast," replied Velo, irritated by Alves' frequent calls. "Wait something is happening. Yes, according to this latest information the weather here should improve in the next two to three hours, enough time for you and your men to arrive and get into position."

Huberto Pedroso turned from the window overlooking the city. "You are sure that at precisely quarter past twelve you will have gained control of the President's official residence."

"Yes, Huberto. I will expect you to be arriving in the newsroom of the radio station at exactly that time. You will have six soldiers making the way for you so you should have no problem," replied Isidro Rodriguez. "By the way, I heard you rehearsing your speech earlier, it was good, very good. It should bring cheer to all listeners on the island who feel that yesterday's administration has deserted them."

The others nodded agreement and gave a short round of applause, which Pedroso humbly waved away with both hands and a mildly embarrassed smile.

Diago Velo clapped his hands again to gain their attention. "Today is the most important day and we must ensure that we all do our part in bringing about its success. Olavo and I will shortly be in contact with London and Paris, then later, New York to trigger the financial support we will need for the initial period of our administration. I suggest that you Huberto and you Isidro get some rest if you can." Then he turned to Reshetnikov. "Ulan my friend, you have been a most generous host to us and be assured that we will remember your services to the new Portugal. I understand from Isidro that you have arranged for some supporters to be on hand when the crowds congregate in the square and outside the residence."

"We have made several recruits who have loud voices and, shall we say, strong personalities," replied Reshetnikov, chuckling at his own humour. "Sonia will have breakfast prepared for you at seven o'clock, so you will not face the day on an empty stomach."

The laughter that followed Reshetnikov's announcement had a hollow nervous tone to it. The condemned prisoner's last meal connection had crossed their minds.

Rodriguez and Pedroso left the room together with Reshetnikov, leaving Velo and Esteves alone. They were checking through sheets of contact names and telephone numbers when Sonia entered the room.

"Excuse me, Senhor Esteves, but tell me have you seen Diana recently?" she asked. "I was expecting to see her with you this evening when you came. She has not been at work for two days."

Even though Esteves had rehearsed his response, knowing that Sonia would undoubtedly ask such a question, it still made his stomach lurch.

"No, I have been very busy these last two days and after I leave her about, oh eleven maybe a little later the other evening, I have not seen her," he answered, a puzzled expression on his face. "She seem very well that evening and we had much to laugh about. So very strange she not contact you, maybe she unwell, I am sorry I do not know."

Sonia smiled and thanked him, but she had caught the flicker of fear in his eyes when she had asked the question, and knew he was holding something back. She feared that Diana was the girl who had been stabbed at the hotel; the police had not yet identified the body. The problem was what should she do if it was Diana. Ulan would not thank her if she caused trouble by accusing one of the island's new leaders of murder. She must wait and see whether these crazy people were successful in their attempt to take power. Ulan had made sure that whichever way it went he was safe, so she must do the same.

As Sonia left the room Velo turned to Esteves and said, "Olavo, please do us a favour and stay away from the girls until we have this all in our hands, eh. These nights you and Huberto spend womanising make me very nervous. So please, eh."

"Of course I leave them alone; I know when not to play, you should know that," Esteves replied, angry at the rebuke.

Later that morning, when told to rest, Esteves found it impossible to get Diana's death out of his mind, and lay nauseous and sweating in fear, the scene haunting him every time he closed his eyes. Would Velo, for example, accept that she was just a prostitute and of no importance, or would he take the high moral ground that he occasionally did? What about the others? Huberto would support him, but who else?

CHAPTER 11

IN HARM'S WAY

At five o'clock in the morning Funchal's Santa Caterina Airport was still broadcasting that it was closed on the orders of Lisbon, due to strong crosswinds. The early shift ground staff were curious and constantly asking senior staff why, when there was hardly a breath of wind, the airport still remained closed. The answer given was 'security' which only served to make them nervous.

At the same time three Portuguese military transport aircraft were taking off from Lisbon's Montijo airbase, heading for Madeira, to land and discharge three companies of soldiers and equipment then take off again for airports on the Canary Islands. Flight time was scheduled to be two hours and twenty minutes.

On the other side of Lisbon, Yvonne Alves saw the lights of a car pull up outside her home and picking up her suitcase opened the front door. A smartly dressed young man smiled at her appreciatively and took her case.

"It is nice to see a taxi arriving ten minutes early instead of ten minutes late," she said, noting the smile with satisfaction. "I hope the roads are clear at this time of day. Please take me to Portela Airport, I have a flight to catch in two and a half hours."

Stepping towards the car her brain noted that something was missing, but the handsome young man opening the rear door and gently guiding her by the arm distracted her. It was not until she had gracefully seated herself and adjusted her dress hemline that she noticed another smart-suited man alongside her. Instantly she reached out and pulled on the door handle but the door would not open. This action coincided with her realising that what was missing was a taxi sign on the roof of the car.

"What is this?" she demanded to know. "Why have you come to my house? Who are you?"

"We are police officers, Senhora Alves," replied her back seat companion, flashing his warrant card. "We are here to arrest you in connection with an attempted military coup. We are taking you to the police headquarters where you will be questioned. Meantime I take your handbag, and the contents of your pockets."

The chill that gripped her stomach almost caused her to have an embarrassing accident. Reluctantly she handed him the bag, relieved that she had followed Diago's advice and flushed her old mobile phone down the toilet. Her computer was clean as well, she having only ever used the one in a rented office near to the airport for work in connection with the coup.

Yvonne Alves had a quick brain from years of political debate, and with a shocked expression on her face turned to the man and said, "You say, a military coup, does that mean that my husband is suspected of being involved in such a ridiculous thing?"

"You will be able to hear details of your arrest when we reach Police Headquarters."

"That is not acceptable I demand to know now," Yvonne Alves replied angrily. "You obviously have no idea as to who I am."

"Senhora Alves," her back seat companion replied, "we know well who you are. Our orders are just to arrest you and deliver you to headquarters. There you will be able to try and impress whoever you think will listen. So please do not ask us anymore questions, eh."

Leaning forward he said to the driver, "Put the siren and lights on, I no wish to sit in here longer than I have to." Then turning to

Yvonne Alves he grabbed her left hand and handcuffed her to his right wrist.

She gasped but said nothing having determined at that moment that she would remain silent until she could speak with her lawyer.

With the siren blaring and lights flashing the car sped through the sparse early morning traffic, slowing only when the lights at junctions were at red. Yvonne had little idea where they were taking her; involvement in a coup against the Government was not an ordinary crime. It was not until the driver flung the car left onto the Rua Tomas Ribeiro that she knew it was going to be the Direcâo Nacional da Policia Judiciára. The car slowed only momentarily crossing the Avenue Fontes Pereira de Melo then accelerated rapidly approaching the Portugal Telecom building. Ahead, men were coning off the right-hand lane, apparently to protect an articulated lorry that was parked at the side of the road with one rear door open and hazard warning lights flashing. A small group of people, whose appearance looked vaguely familiar to Yvonne Alves, stood in a furtive huddle on a street corner, but she did not get a chance to look more carefully as a yell from the driver brought her attention rapidly back to the road ahead.

The police car had been travelling at about one hundred kilometres an hour as it passed the side street and it was at that moment that a large dump truck pulled out from in front of the parked lorry to block the road. The young driver's reactions were like lightning, but he had chosen to try and stop the car rather than spin it round and drive off.

"Ambush!" shouted the more senior arresting officer alongside Yvonne. "Turn us round!"

His warning was almost drowned out by Yvonne Alves' piercing scream as her terrified eyes fixed upon the lorry and her hands grabbed the seat in front. Such was the fear driven force of her movement that she dragged the handcuffed right hand and arm of the officer forward to a point midway between the two front seats, just as he was reaching with his left hand to retrieve his Glock 9mm pistol from its underarm holster. Taken completely by surprise with the strength of her action the policeman now found himself slightly with his back to her as the driver of the car spun the steering wheel in a desperate attempt to turn the vehicle anticlockwise in the opposite direction, but his manoeuvre was not well controlled and after spinning two hundred and seventy degrees the car slammed broadside into the dump truck's rear wheels. The truck's thick steel rear tub tore into the upper side and roof of the police car shifting the deployment of the side airbags to a point where they dropped between Yvonne Alves and her back seat companion, effectively saving her life. Neither of the police officers survived the impact, both killed instantly by the head injuries they sustained, and the driver from a bullet fired at close range through the seat back and into his spine, accidentally fired by his colleague.

After the noise of screaming tyres, impact crash, gun shot and tearing metal the sound of voices seemed distant and strange to Yvonne. Slowly the world came into focus and she was aware of a man leaning across her apparently searching for something behind a white curtain. When he pulled back, she could see he was holding a bunch of keys, and selecting one lifted her left hand; the pain the movement caused made her cry out.

"I think she has broken arm and maybe ribs," the stranger said almost nonchalantly.

"The policeman is dead. God rest his soul, he no deserved to die; I know him, he was okay. The driver, he also no longer in this world," he continued, making the sign of the cross across his chest.

Yvonne Alves passed out with the pain as they pulled her from the wreck and the next thing she was drowsily aware of was being sat in a vehicle along with three other members of the coup, with her left arm in a sling. A young man was knelt in front of her applying a dressing to a deep graze on her wrist, presumably from the handcuffs. Painfully turning her head she looked across at a dejected Norberto Correia.

"What went wrong, Norberto?" she asked. "How did they know?"

"Two hours ago British Government agents in Madeira apparently overheard something and alerted our security service. One of my men, he phone me with warning, and told me of your arrest. I managed to get to Jose and Gabrielo here, but I could not contact Marcos and Leonardo. I left messages on their phones, but I fear they will be arrested. Then I had to dispose of the phones so we can do no more for them."

"I think Marcos Benzinho planned to visit Porto yesterday for meeting with some bankers," Yvonne informed. "He tell me on Sunday when he and his daughter came to my house."

"Roadblock ahead," warned a disembodied voice over a speaker in the corner of the wood panelled compartment they were travelling in.

Yvonne Alves cautiously looked around noting that there was no door to their dimly lit container, just six seats bolted to the floor and a cold box strapped to the vehicle's sidewall. In the opposite corner was a chemical toilet, that she now realised she needed to use.

"I need to use the toilet," she said.

"Not possible until we are clear of the roadblock Yvonne. We must remain absolutely quiet, not a single sound or we will be discovered," replied Jose Pianto, the member of the team that had been responsible for the escape plan.

The vehicle came to a stop and voices could be heard together with the sound of a dog. A few minutes passed and they heard the sound of the trailer's rear doors being opened and the tap and scrape of the dog's paws upon the steel decking the other side of the partition that hid them. Then it was over and the doors closed, and after some friendly shouts the vehicle got underway again.

"I am sorry, I not know your name. Can you help me get to the toilet?" Yvonne said, looking down at the man kneeling in front of her.

"Certainly Senhora Alves. I am doctor Franco Goncalves; please you call me Franco. If you use your good arm to guide you along the walls I will support you."

"Please, you all look away, I find this embarrassing enough as it is."

Much to her further embarrassment Yvonne Alves found that she had to request the young doctor to provide more intimate assistance before she was able to regain her seat.

"Thank you er doc… er Franco," she said, blushing more than she had ever done in her life before.

Dr Franco Goncalves smiled and just politely nodded, hiding the despair he felt at having sacrificed his career and marriage for a high-risk chance of a leading position in the nation's healthcare future. He had told his young wife of the coup plans the previous evening and was shocked by the anger of her response. For the first time in their five-year relationship she revealed the horrors her family had endured under the latter years of the Salazar regime. Ordered out of the house her family owned, Goncalves had taken sanctuary at the apartment of Jose Pianto, arriving only minutes before Correia's frantic telephone warning. Now inexorably trapped within the leader group, Goncalves decided to throw his lot in with them in the hope of escaping and avoiding the public humiliation his wife had threatened her powerful family would bring down on him. He had tried to beg for her forgiveness and ask for her family's protection, but calling him a pathetic creep who had brought shame upon her and her family, she had promptly telephoned her father. With the threat of her brothers coming to evict him, Goncalves had gathered up his doctor's bag, checked its contents and fled.

"Everything now depends upon the success of your husband Yvonne," said Pianto, breaking the silence that had settled over the group since the roadblock.

"Even the weather was against us Jose, nothing seems to have worked for us despite Rodriguez's careful planning. If Antonio manages to reach Funchal before the garrison is reinforced then maybe there is a chance."

"He must hold the airport, that is the key, until Huberto Pedroso and the others can mobilise support. I speak with Rodriguez two days ago and he tell me they were making some progress in the town, but the rural people not so keen to listen. They not mention action like coup of course, in case potential supporter became frightened, but they think many want to see big changes," said Pianto, sounding confident and assured. "Many time they tell me of people wishing this socialist rubbish be swept away and businesslike government brought in to rescue our nation."

"I repeat what I said to you over a month ago, Jose. I say to you then that there has not been sufficient preparation and persuasion done. Here the people were more annoyed by the government austerity, but still they only peacefully protest. In Madeira we no hear of any public disturbance, so conditions were not good at this time. We needed people throwing stones, demanding change, then it would have been right time for us," said Norberto Correia, with some feeling.

"Diago, he seemed very confident that they would gain hold of Madeira," interjected Yvonne Alves haughtily.

"Diago is sometimes a little reckless," replied Correia. "I have known him for many years and admire his political views and knowledge, but recently I have been thinking that the wait has been too long for him, and his impatience has got the better of his senses."

"No, I not accept that. Diago he is very good with the politics," Yvonne snapped, defending her lover despite the now obvious failure of the plan. "We would not be in this lorry now had British spies not been lucky."

Just then the lorry slowed and again the group was warned of another roadblock. This time however the search took much longer as the dog drew the attention of his handler to the front right-hand corner of the trailer nearest to where the toilet was placed.

"Sergeant, the dog, he find something here in this corner, you come and look eh."

More scuffling and noise of heavy footsteps from the other side of the partition brought frightened expressions to the faces of those concealed.

"There is nothing to see. Hey, you. What load you carry last time?" asked, presumably the sergeant.

There was a short delay then the driver could just be heard to say that he had four chemical toilets in that corner and the rest of the space was chairs and staging.

A muffled conversation followed in which the two police officers appeared to be satisfied, but the dog was not, and had started scratching at the floor of the trailer against the partition. It was not until the handler called it away that the dog stopped its attempts to dig through to the group sat nervously in their hiding place.

Only when the lorry's engine was started again and the vehicle moved off did the group's tensions ease, but no one spoke.

Suddenly the driver's voice came through on the speaker. "Senhor Pianto, I tell them I go to Serra d'El-Rei for next load. I have friend there who let me park and maybe we put some cases of olives in the back. Please you understand I must make a small extra charge."

"I see no problem with his idea Jose. That was too close to be comfortable," said Noberto Correia, with a nervous laugh. "Are you sure that the seal around this partition is good?"

"It was good enough at the first checkpoint, but maybe the movement of the trailer has caused a small gap," replied Pianto. "Alberto, the driver, he very quick thinking back there. I think no problem." However Pianto's attempt to restore confidence amongst the group belied his own thoughts and fears. "Serra d'El-Rei is very near to place where we switch to cars."

On leaving Lisbon the lorry had joined the A8 going north where it had soon came across the first roadblock. The second roadblock had been set up at the Vale Covo, Cintrao turn-off and was under the command of the very experienced Sergeant Sousa, whose team were very thorough. Sergeant Sousa, as feared by Jose Pianto, had remained suspicious of the lorry and given instructions to a police motorcyclist to follow the vehicle at a distance. The rider was then to report at intervals by mobile phone, not radio, about the lorry's progress and any stops made. There was something in that trailer, Sousa had thought, was not right but he could not quite put his finger on what it was. Before he could give any further consideration to the trailer, however, another lorry was pulled in for inspection, this one loaded with tomatoes.

On completion of the check on the load of tomatoes Sergeant Sousa phoned his Inspector and informed him of his actions regarding the surveillance and was just putting the phone back into his pocket when it rang.

"Sousa."

"Sergeant, the lorry has turned onto the IP6 just as the driver informed. You want me to continue? Only I go off duty in half hour."

"Stay with them. If they turn off at Serra d'El-Rei it okay. Then you come back," replied Sousa. "If they don't, phone me straight away."

In the trailer the group sat, each with their own thoughts, looking at each other anxiously every time the lorry turned a corner. When it left the tarmac and started down a rough track there was, strangely, a palpable sense of relief.

The arrangement and loading of the olives took sometime and Pianto started to look frequently at his watch, as the drivers of the cars had been told not to wait more than one hour at the rendezvous.

At the entrance to the track the police motorcyclist watched as the lorry turned into the farmyard then turning the motorbike around headed back to the station and the end of his shift.

*

In Funchal, Vaughan thanked the Bevingtons and hurried to his taxi. Dealing with this coup was no longer his business, he had to meet Al Djebbar and he was running late.

Amelia had finally fallen asleep in the Bevingtons' guest bedroom, her tear-stained face paled by exhaustion. Vaughan had explained Amelia's innocence sufficient for Susanne Bevington to promise to look after her until Vaughan returned.

At the 'Vidamar', Metcalf greeted Vaughan like a long lost friend and whisked him through the security procedure and up to

Al Djebbar's room just as the man himself was stepping out onto the landing, accompanied by Mehdi.

"Ian, good morning, good morning. I am so glad that you were able to join me today. I could not explain in detail in my note, but I would be delighted if you would sit in the conference today and record the events in writing for Charles to read. As you are an author I could not wish for a more appropriate and accurate chronicler of this event. I know he will hear today the formal announcement, but I feel he would appreciate a more intimate report."

"Walid, you do me a great honour, but I am really a technical author, not as competent as say a journalist would be, in describing the mood and attitudes expressed. Also I doubt if I would understand a word of what is being said."

"Regarding translation that is no problem, I will arrange for Rami Younis to sit with you. He is an excellent English speaker," replied Al Djebbar, with a flourish of both arms. "Regarding your ability, I read some of your notes whilst you were preparing our meal yesterday. Your descriptions of making landfall on Porto Santo and the entry to the bay of Funchal are excellent and would do great credit to any guidebook."

Vaughan winced; the passages Al Djebbar was referring to were intended for his daughters to read, in the hope of convincing them, and Sarah, of the 'peaceful work' that he was employed in doing.

"Walk with us across to the conference hall," invited Al Djebbar. "I have had a text from Charles to wish me luck on this final day. Let us pray that the attitudes of the delegates has not changed overnight."

Vaughan smiled as he shook both men's hands. "Mehdi here seemed very confident yesterday and I suspect has already been canvassing opinion."

"I would rather wait and see, my friend. As you say in England. 'There is many a slip twixt cup and lip'. Or would 'counting chickens before they are hatched' be more appropriate."

"Being confident, that you, Walid, would not have made a slip in all of this, I would probably go with the chickens to be safe," Vaughan replied, feeling more cheerful than he had for the last nine hours.

In the lift Al Djebbar gave Vaughan a curious look. "You look tired, Ian. Does this writing career give you sleepless nights or is it the pretty company you keep?" asked Walid.

"Ah, Mehdi, what have you been saying, eh?"

As the lift doors opened Mehdi was about to answer when Metcalf interrupted. "Excuse me, but we have just cleared a path through the crowd so if you could hurry before the crush overwhelms my men."

As they stepped out onto the pavement applause and cheering broke out; for many the conference signalled a move towards stability in a region that had been in turmoil for many years. The concept offered a way towards the peace and economic growth that many had dreamed of at the start of the 'Arab Spring'. This realisation was now being expressed with enthusiasm.

The press were at the forefront holding out microphones and shouting questions, as the group came through the doors. Vaughan had been close to Al Djebbar's left with Mehdi and Metcalf close behind. The crowd barriers protected by Metcalf's little army were in danger of being overturned and Al Djebbar hesitated to move forward into the narrow pathway left.

Not wishing to appear in front of the world media so close alongside Al Djebbar, Vaughan moved to the side, his eyes watching Walid al Djebbar's face with its changing emotions as the man prepared himself to run the gauntlet.

Metcalf was about to move forward to a screening position slightly in front and to the right of Al Djebbar when his radio sprung into life.

"What is it Hayward?" Metcalf shouted over the hubbub of noise. "What, what black box, you been on the sauce again?" There was a pause during which Al Djebbar took a step forward. "On the roof of what?" Metcalf asked, now taking a step forward himself.

Vaughan, suspecting that something was wrong, stepped forward to intercept Al Djebbar and get him back into the foyer, but as he did so he saw a red mark the size of a five pence piece appear on the side of Al Djebbar's head and hover around his ear.

"Down, Walid!" Vaughan shouted. "Sniper!" At the same time Vaughan launched himself at Al Djebbar, to knock the man to the ground. He had only just made impact when he felt something pass close to his head and heard Metcalf cry out.

The crowd panicked, ducking and running in all directions. To their credit Metcalf's men immediately screened the heap of bodies. Al Djebbar, bruised but alive lay on his side, half covered by Vaughan with Metcalf lying limply on top. Vaughan heaved Metcalf's body to one side, seeing as he did so a large ugly hole in the man's chest.

"The boss is down, get an ambulance!" yelled the first of the door guards to arrive on the scene, as he knelt beside Metcalf's body.

"Shit! I think he's dead," said the guard looking up in dismay, before laying his MP3 pistol down on the pavement as he tried to rearrange Metcalf's limp limbs.

Vaughan rolled off Al Djebbar. "Walid, get inside the foyer. There is nothing we can do here."

"Is he dead, Ian?"

"Yes, I am afraid so."

Suddenly one of Metcalf's men forming the screen fell backwards as blood and skull fragment sprayed over Vaughan and Al Djebbar. Then the return fire started and moments later the cry, "He's making a run for it."

Leaping to his feet Vaughan followed the pistol line of the guard closest to him who was rapidly discharging bullets towards the roof of the 'Mamma Mia' restaurant. It was only a fleeting glimpse, but he felt sure that the man turning to run across to the main road side of the roof, was the man he had seen in the company of the Russian Kazakov.

Impeded by the slower members of the panicking crowd, the guards gave chase. Four men rushed towards the western exit whilst three went east, in an attempt to capture or take out the assassin, closely followed by the four police officers whose presence, until that moment, had been considered as just a political token of co-operation.

With the immediate heavy cordon of protection dispersed Leyla Najjar found it easy to step forward, lift a barrier to one side, and approach the group, whose attention was now returning to the two dead bodies lying sprawled across the pavement.

Vaughan had knelt and was covering Metcalf's chest and head with his jacket, tucking it under the man's shoulder to stop the wind that had been swirling in gusts along the front of the building, from blowing the jacket away. He noticed, as he did so, the guard's gun near to Metcalf's chest.

The movement of Leyla, dressed all in black, the wind tugging at the material around her legs, caught Vaughan's eye and he looked up. At the same time Al Djebbar saw the girl who then reached up and pulled back the yashmak covering her face.

"Leyla?" said Al Djebbar, hardly able to believe his eyes.

In her response, Vaughan noticed that she did not smile, and as her hand released the yashmak it moved down to a point just below her breasts where she appeared to fumble with the garment, endeavouring to reach beneath it. The action triggered an alarm in Vaughan's brain, to be confirmed by another gust of wind that pinned the garment's material tight to the girl's body revealing unusual bulges around her waist.

"Bomber!" Vaughan shouted, as he made a grab for the pistol.

Leyla Najjar took two more paces towards Al Djebbar pulling her outer garment open as she did so. Beneath was revealed the deadly jacket of a suicide bomber and her hand searching for the cord that would detonate the explosives. Vaughan had only moments to grab the weapon from the pavement, aim and fire two shots.

The hole in the girl's face did not destroy the expression of hatred that had disfigured it a second before. The force of the first bullet's impact knocked her backwards onto the road, to lay dead and unmoving. The second shot had gone over her head and into one of the palm trees on the banking the other side of the road.

Two of the three security guards left at the scene grabbed Vaughan and Al Djebbar and dragged them back into the hotel, with Vaughan shouting repeatedly, "She is wearing a bomb!! She is wearing a bomb!"

"Okay, Mac, they heard," said the guard pinning Vaughan to the floor. "She better be or you will be looking at a very long prison sentence."

"Check her for a mobile, quickly," said Vaughan loudly. "For God's sake get someone out there searching. And get the police while you are at it!"

In the background Vaughan could hear the two 'Total Cover' receptionists crying uncontrollably as hotel staff tried to usher them away from the glass doors overlooking the road.

With a fair amount of undue force the MP3 pistol Vaughan had used was taken from his grasp and the weight on the knee in his back increased. Mehdi and Al Djebbar were holding a heated discussion with their support team and Vaughan wondered whether those in the actual conference hall were aware of what had happened.

"It's okay, Wayne, let him up, she was carrying enough explosive to take everyone out within a hundred yards, by the way the detonation was by pull cord, I nearly shit myself finding out," said Metcalf's second in command, Patrick Murphy, pushing his way through the mêlée of people gathered round, anxious to see who was being held. "Get everybody the hell away from here as fast as you can."

Ian Vaughan got to his feet, and was brushing himself down, when Walid al Djebbar stepped in front of him. "Who exactly are you, Ian Vaughan?"

"Like you a friend of Charles, why do you ask?"

"How did you know what was about to happen? For a friend of Charles Stanthorpe Ogilvey, who is supposed to be only a technical author, you know a great deal about terrorism and assassination. I will thank Charles for suggesting I invite you to tea," Al Djebbar replied, giving Vaughan a quizzical look. "My guess is that you are an expert in the darker side of foreign relations." Vaughan thought for a moment that Walid al Djebbar was going to reject him and possibly expose him, but instead the man said, "Ian, my dear friend, shall we now go and finish this conference's business."

Al Djebbar's coolness in the aftermath of an assassination attempt took Vaughan quite by surprise.

"Are you sure you are up to that after what has just happened?"

"Ian, I have been expecting such actions for months now. It is something that I, and many more in positions like mine, have to live with," Walid replied calmly. "Today Allah sent you for my protection and I pray that He will give me the gift of others, like you, in the future. Come, let us get on with this."

As Al Djebbar and Vaughan, closely attended by a screen of security and police, crossed the access road and climbed the steps to the conference suite, Vaughan was talking quietly to a police officer. "I think I saw the assassin in a night club in town a few nights ago. I am not one hundred percent sure you understand, but it may be worth you following this up. The man was in the company of Sarkis Kazakov, who I think lives on the Calcada do Socorro, his house is on the edge of the cliff," said Vaughan, trying to keep the message as simple as possible.

The officer looked at Vaughan in surprise. "You say you recognised the attacker?"

"I said, I think I recognised the attacker, I could not be absolutely sure."

"We will make enquiry. Where you stay? Which hotel?"

Vaughan had not expected the question and was about to inform the officer of the name of his boat and the location when it struck him as being rather dangerous. "Oh, um, I have booked in here," he answered, trying to appear casual. "Excuse me, I must catch up with Al Djebbar."

*

Meanwhile Takkal was riding a motorbike past the football stadium on the west side of the Rua Dr Pita. Aware that he must not draw attention to himself he was fighting down his desire to speed together with the cold fury that seemed to fill his entire being. It had all been so carefully planned down to the last detail only to be foiled by some ape of a security guard who was looking at the target instead of looking outward for a potential threat, as he should have been.

The set-up had gone without a hitch and he had even managed to doze during the night, laid in his carefully constructed hide. He had trained himself to exist in such cramped spaces for much longer periods, and as the dawn came he felt surprisingly fresh and ready for the hit. Takkal had even taken a practice shot, having first made sure that the area was devoid of people. His target was a strange mark he could see on the trunk of a palm tree, and after checking the long silencer alignment with the precision score marks made to the barrel and silencer during earlier practice, he opened the flap, and adjusting his breathing, switched on the laser assist, took aim and gently, ever so gently, squeezed the trigger. The gun gave a quiet spitting noise, simultaneously jerking with the recoil. Pulling a monocular from his leg pocket he had studied the target, smiling at the accuracy of the hit. This was the first time he had ever been able to take a practice shot at the scene, and filled with supreme confidence he carefully withdrew the rifle, closed the flap, to relax, waiting for the build-up of activity that would announce the arrival of his target.

A silencer, especially a long one, would normally risk a minor deviation in the trajectory of the bullet, but not under Takkal's watchful care. It had been specifically engineered to be attached to a bought smooth barrel that had undergone polygonal rifling with a right hand twist cut by his specialist in Germany. A composite Kevlar, fibreglass, graphite stock that gave the rifle near perfect stability, completed the weapon. The shells had full steel jackets that on the high velocity impact achieved, would produce a large initial wound and considerable radial internal injury.

As the crowd, gathered outside of the hotel, began to raise cameras ready to photograph Al Djebbar, Takkal had slowly lifted the rifle and opened the viewing slit wider to take in the doorways and pavement area cleared by the security team. To gain the correct angle the matt black silencer had to protrude from the hide, so Takkal had waited until the doors opened and he could see his target about to step out, before setting the rifle to his shoulder and flicking on the laser assist. Just as expected the security men frantically searched the crowd and beyond looking for a potential threat, their backs to the target. The head of the security team, walking behind Al Djebbar, had stopped as he raised his radio to his ear, and then scanned the roof of the conference complex, gymnasium and restaurant. Something had been reported, but that was the moment, the only moment for a clear shot, and concentrating on his target alone, who was standing obligingly still, Takkal had brought the laser dot to the side of his victim's head, adjusted for wind, and gently squeezed the trigger at the precise moment his target disappeared. Whether the target's movement had caused Takkal to hurry the last millimetre of trigger action causing the aim to shift, he did not know; what he did know was that the gun had fired and the bullet had downed the security team's headman, bringing panic and chaos. Hurriedly he had scanned the scene and realised that to make the kill he had first to remove a security guard who was standing resolutely directly in line with Al Djebbar. He had aimed again, adjusted for wind, and squeezed off another round and his target fell backwards, giving only a fleeting glimpse of Al Djebbar before another guard stepped in the way, this one firing at Takkal's hide.

The return fire had been surprisingly heavy and the box hide was being holed. If he remained to try another shot he would almost certainly be hit and frantically he had fumbled to gather up his 9mm Glock that had been hit and knocked from its clip on the side of the hide. Scrambling out onto the roof, he had pointed the pistol towards the security guards and pulled the trigger but the gun was jammed. Throwing the weapon back into the hide he had rolled several times, away from the edge of the roof, before getting to his feet and running, crouched down, to the escape rope. Kicking the loose end of the rope over the edge of the roof, and checking again the strength of the anchoring point, he had walked backwards to the roof's edge, lent back using the rope to support his upper body and lowering himself hand over hand, had walked down the restaurant's front wall to the pavement.

The screaming, shouting and gunfire had most passers-by running for cover, thus no one appeared to give Takkal a second glance. Using the panicked crowd as cover he had hurried west along the Estrada Monumental to an alleyway just before the Florasol Resort Hotel, and ducking into it, ran up the steps and steep pathway to the Rua Velha da Adjuda and the motorbike Reshetnikov's men had previously parked in the entrance to a garage. Sweat was pouring off him as he struggled into the leather jacket and put on the crash helmet. It had seemed to take ages before the machine fired up and he could ride off eastwards and eventually turn north up the Rua Dr Pita.

As he rode along Takkal constantly had images of the scene just prior to him taking the shot. Yes, that was it, the man that had wrecked everything was not a security guard, but someone who knew what the red dot projected from the laser assist signified. Had Al Djebbar organised a personal bodyguard, he wondered, it would be a million to one against the chance of an ordinary person being in the right place to see the target spot and know how to act. Then he recalled that the man was wearing a light cream jacket not the dark grey, like the 'Total Cover' employees, and was not behaving in the normal way when looking for potential threats. The string of curses that erupted from Takkal's lips lasted for a full minute before the ball and boy appeared in the road in front of him.

It was in a section without a pavement and close to the junction with Caminho das Virtudes. A high wall, pierced by occasional gateways to the surrounding properties, edged the road here and from one of these gateways bounced a football followed almost instantly by a small boy. Takkal instinctively braked hard locking the front wheel and causing the bike to skid and drop from under him. Letting go of the machine he hit the road surface in a parachute roll, narrowly missing the now fear frozen boy and ending up colliding with the fallen motorbike, which had slid the other side of the boy before bouncing off the wall to hit the prone Takkal. He heard a screech of tyres as the following car locked up the brakes to stop just in time. Then there was the sound of car doors opening and running feet as he carefully worked his arms and legs checking for any broken bones. A woman appeared from the driveway shouting as she ran to the boy, and gathered him up into her arms. Only then did she turn and look towards Takkal and realise what had happened. Getting to his feet, assisted by the car driver, Takkal was dusting himself off when the woman approached, and after learning that Takkal spoke no Portuguese used her limited English to invite him into her house whilst she called for medical assistance.

"Senhor, you come my house, I call doctor, please."

"I am not badly hurt, just grazing, nothing serious. Water and dressing is all I need."

By the time Takkal's cuts and bruises had been treated news was coming through of the coup. The boy's mother distraught that such an event had happened in Madeira was crying as the news broadcast continued. People were being advised to stay indoors and a curfew was to be enforced at seven o'clock that evening until six o'clock the following morning. During those hours the Portuguese army would be in control and martial law would be in force.

"I must contact my host," said Takkal, when the lady explained what was causing her disquiet. "He will be concerned as he is expecting me to return soon."

"Please you use my telephone, Senhor," the boy's mother offered.

Something made Takkal hesitate to take-up the offer.

"No – er, thank you, it is too expensive to call mobile from a house telephone, I will use my mobile. No problem."

Claiming to get a better signal, Takkal walked out of the house into the rear garden.

"Sarkis?"

"Yes."

"Takkal, I need to stay low for a time."

"Then do not come to my house. A few minutes ago a friend warned me that my home will be visited by police," Kazakov replied. "He tell me that you were recognised by some English guy. Make your way to your own place, no one know you are living there. I will meet you there with Nadezhda, my people will deal with the police here."

"If you run they will search for you," said Takkal, feeling uncomfortable at having someone else wanted by the police near to him. "How sure are you that man who owns house will not contact police?"

"And die?" responded Kazakov, sneeringly. "I know the little grape grower has much more sense than to try and harm me."

"I need a gun, can you bring one."

"I bring you some, Boris is loading the truck as we speak," Kazakov replied. "I no want police to find my personal armoury. I take it you had to leave everything behind."

"I will see you at the house," said Takkal, avoiding the confession of failure.

*

Al Bashir was found hiding in bushes alongside the western access road to the Vidamar hotel. The two Portuguese policemen were surprised at his state of distress, he was shaking and crying, muttering the word Leyla, Leyla, over and over again. When the 'Total Cover' men joined the two officers they confirmed that Al Bashir was not one of the conference members and a search revealed that he had no means of identification. Suspicions aroused, the policemen chose to hold Al Bashir until a senior officer could take charge and interview this strange man more closely.

Taken and held in a ground floor meeting room, behind the east tower reception area, Al Bashir reflected on the catastrophe that had befallen him. He had been at the back of the crowd as the political heathen, Al Djebbar, had come through the doors and stood preening himself in front of these idiot supporters. Except, he reflected more honestly, that the man did not truly look as if he was in any way self-satisfied or triumphant. Indeed, now Al Bashir recalled the scene, the face he remembered showed humility, and yes, even modesty.

Then there had been a sudden movement, and a shot, and the crowd had panicked. He saw his Leyla, alone, standing unmoved, watching the heap of bodies on the ground in front of the hotel doors. The man in the light jacket moved to push the man on top away, revealing Al Djebbar alive and unharmed. A second shot, and a security guard fell, but instantly the others opened fire in return and some ran to chase down the attacker, and as they did so his Leyla started to walk slowly towards the man she was to die with. Taking refuge behind a palm tree, Al Bashir had held his breath, waiting for the seemingly inevitable explosion and tragic conclusion of her holy mission. He had prayed silently for

273

her reception into the next world until he heard a shouted warning and two shots ring out. Peeping fearfully around the tree, he saw his Leyla, sprawled on her back in the road, a pool of blood spreading over the tarmac from behind her head, and he knew that all was lost. They had failed, and he, not for the first time, questioned the will of Allah and his purpose for his people on this earth.

Kazakov had offered him the option of either a pull cord detonation system or the now more common mobile phone link. Praying that Leyla would ultimately fear death more than seek martyrdom he had chosen the pull cord; or was it that he did not want to be the one to destroy her. Now, however, he wished that he had chosen the mobile phone; that would have guaranteed her death had not been in vain.

He could not remember how he got to the bushes or even why he had hidden amongst them. Now caught, he would be questioned, his identity checked, and his inevitable imprisonment would follow. Maybe better that, than to return to face the wrath of those that had sent him.

*

It took Mehdi Khuldun a full five minutes to convince Miss Carla Venancio, the manager responsible for the conference, of the need to have Metcalf's room cleared and the room re-let to Ian Vaughan. During this time Al Djebbar and Vaughan stood in the wings of the stage with Rami Younis whilst Walid explained that every word he spoke had to be clearly translated so that Mr Vaughan could accurately present the world with the true outcome of the conference.

The speech, Vaughan noted, made no reference to the attempt upon Al Djebbar's life. Instead it presented a challenging, yet positive, picture of the North African region's future as a union of independent states (NAUIS). It was hailed by the vast majority of all parties to the conference as the only way to solve the complex issues they faced; even the few dissenters were swept up by the tide of hope and enthusiasm.

Rami Younis had lived up to Walid al Djebbar's promise of having excellent English. Even the man's accent was impeccably British and Vaughan was confident that the report to Campbell would be the most accurate that could be achieved. As guests transferred to the Sunset Lounges for, a later than scheduled lunch, Younis read through what Vaughan had written, correcting spelling and occasionally grammar as he went. Jointly they inserted descriptions of the audience reaction during the speech, as well as the standing ovation given at its conclusion.

"There, Mr Vaughan, I think we have captured precisely the offer available to the various nations involved. May Allah bless us with the strength of purpose to complete this ambitious task," Younis said, leaning back in his chair, looking exhausted from the effort of conducting the lengthy continuous simultaneous translation.

The two men were talking about their joint hopes for peace in the region, when they were interrupted by one of Al Djebbar's support team inviting them to finish with work and join the delegates for some lunch.

"I'm sorry," said Vaughan, "but I must decline Al Djebbar's kind invitation. I have to attend a previously arranged engagement in town in a short time."

*

When the three military transports from Lisbon landed, an unsuspecting Lieutenant Menzies, whose task had been to arrange

275

for vehicles to take Alves and his men into Funchal, met them. The speed of his arrest and the commandeering of the vehicles stunned both Menzies and the two sergeants escorting him. Sat in shock in the back of a garrison bus, handcuffed to the seat, the lieutenant watched curiously as the planes took off again as soon as their cargoes were unloaded. It was not until the single aircraft containing Major Alves and his company landed that Lieutenant Menzies realised that the hurried departure of the other transports had ensured that the trap set for his hero would be sprung successfully.

As Alves and his men disembarked and started to run towards the terminal building they were swiftly brought to a halt by a vastly superior force of Marines and Special Forces troops appearing from behind the parapet of the airport building's first floor level balcony, and firing a volley of shots over their heads.

Alves' men, stranded in the middle of the vast expanse of the airport apron, went to ground and were looking about, seeking to outflank the balcony force, when other units of Marines appeared from both ends of the building, blocking any such manoeuvre.

In charge of the arresting force was Colonel Franco Castelo Lopes, one of Portugal's most highly regarded military figures. In his years of service the colonel had acquired a reputation of leading from the front; a trait that had earned both respect and loyalty from those that served with him. Striding from the airport embarkation exit in the company of ten heavily armed Special Forces men he stepped into the sunlight and raised a loudhailer to his mouth.

"I order you and your men to surrender your weapons immediately, Major Alves."

On seeing his company surrounded, Major Alves was slow to comprehend what was happening. Even the colonel's order to surrender had not fully penetrated his consciousness. Though his men had thrown themselves to the ground, Alves had taken a further twenty paces before stopping. He was now completely isolated, a lone figure on a vast expanse of concrete with absolutely no cover behind which to hide. He looked about, dazed and confused. Where was Lieutenant Menzies? What was Castelo Lopes doing here, he was supposed to be leaving for a meeting of NATO.

"I repeat: I order you and your men to surrender your weapons immediately, Major Alves," boomed the colonel's voice across the airport.

There was no response. The men laying flat on the airport apron, clearly recognising their impossible position, were waiting for the order to surrender to come from Alves.

Major Antonio Alves merely straightened his back and glared at the colonel defiantly.

"Take aim," ordered the colonel, and two hundred weapons were raised and pointed at the rebel troops.

The order stung the major into acting. Pulling the restraining webbing flap clear of the holster the major pulled his pistol and took aim at the colonel.

"We have come to liberate Madeira," Major Alves bellowed. "The socialist trash who have ruined our great country are already being replaced with the new order on the mainland."

"I order you and your men to surrender your weapons immediately. Your co-conspirators in Lisbon are already under arrest Major. The Government remain in complete control," replied the colonel, not flinching at the sight of Alves' pistol being pointed at him, besides the colonel knew that at twenty metres or more a Walther P38 pistol had little chance of hitting the target.

"Never!" screamed Alves as he fired the gun, surprised not to see the colonel fall.

The marksman of the Special Forces unit on the balcony squeezed the trigger of his Heckler & Koch HK417 killing Major Alves instantly.

None of Alves' men moved, all frozen, awaiting the deadly volley of fire that they felt sure was to come.

"Leave your weapons on the ground and stand to attention immediately."

The two lieutenants were the first to respond, followed resentfully by the sergeants and finally the rest of the rebel company.

"You are to place your hands on your heads, right turn and step away from that area immediately," ordered the colonel.

As soon as the rebels were clear of the weapons laid on the tarmac, the troops from the ends of the building approached cautiously and, ordering the rebels to form up a single line, checked them all for any concealed weapons they may have still been holding.

"It is a great pity that he will not face a court-martial," said Colonel Castelo Lopes, looking down at the body of Alves. "A little rich boy with no brain. I wonder whether his wife put him up to this or whether it was members of his polo club. I doubt if he could have thought of this all on his own."

Not getting a response from his aide-de-camp, the colonel turned and looked at the man who was fingering a hole in his flak jacket.

"Holy Maria, are you wounded?"

"No, Colonel, it did not go all the way through," replied the lieutenant, with a nervous laugh.

"Good, radio Major Barosa and tell him to recall one transport from the Canaries and divide that rabble into two groups and get them back to Lisbon. He can have twenty men."

"Yes, Colonel, right away, sir."

"The major can have a further twenty men to secure the airport here. Then the rest of us must hurry to secure Funchal using the transport Major Alves so usefully organised for us."

At precisely 0945 hours the convoy, led by a Pandur II armoured personnel carrier, moved off for the journey into the centre of Funchal. The aim was to secure the local garrison within the Palaçio de São Lourenço, the President's Official Residence and the Police Headquarters. The colonel would establish his headquarters in the Regional Government offices whilst a detachment would take control of the local radio station. Orders would then be issued for the arrest of the four known coup leaders.

Modern warfare uses the tactic of battlefield attrition whereby one hit removes three men from the field, the soldier wounded and the two others required to take him to the field hospital. Using this concept the colonel ordered that all troops armed with the old Heckler & Koch G3 based HK417 rifle that fired the killer 7.62mm bullet be issued with blank manoeuvre training rounds when dealing with crowd control. Marksmen were to be issued with plastic bullets, should it be obvious that the crowd contained rabble-rousers there to incite trouble. Those troops in possession of the more modern Heckler & Koch G36 firing a 5.56mm bullet were to be held in reserve against armed attacks. The colonel's hope was that the plastic rounds and the G36's smaller bullet had a slightly lesser chance of killing anyone, he desperately wanted to end this without further loss of life.

*

Diago Velo had spent much of the early morning pacing backwards and forwards alongside the swimming pool at

Reshetnikov's home trying to contact Major Alves by phone without success. In Porto Santo, Major Alves was also frustrated in his attempts to contact Velo. The security services in Lisbon had ordered that the island's mobile phone transmitters be switched off for the duration of the emergency. Unable to make contact using the military radio equipment to hand for fear of interception, Alves sought to use the conventional landline in the control tower, only to find that too was disconnected and all airport staff absent.

When at half past eight three military transports flew across the bay Velo, believing it to be the arrival of Alves and his men, cheered excitedly and ran into the house to inform the others.

"You say the Major bring one company of men with him," said Reshetnikov, frowning questioningly. "Three transports is much capacity for just one company no?"

"The Major he probably brings much equipment with him. He may have no chance to return to Lisbon for more for some time eh," replied Velo, wanting to sound confident despite the seeds of concern the Russian had planted.

Reshetnikov nodded, his expression changing to understanding, even appreciation.

Reshetnikov's acceptance of his explanation and a call from Isidro Rodriguez for him to join a final briefing, quietened Velo's nerves once more.

A little before ten o'clock the group of conspirators moved out of the house to a point high up in the garden from where they could view the expressway that led from the airport. By ten past ten they were beginning to become concerned when suddenly the convoy appeared, led by the armoured personnel carrier.

"Alves has exceeded his promise," said Rodriguez with delight, admiring the lead vehicle. "The largest group will enter the town by way of Rua da Ribeira de Joâo Gomes and secure those troops not willing to join us, and then continue on to Police Headquarters. Some they go to the Regional Government Office. The rest they go west, two more junction I think, and turn down the Estrada da Liberdade, Avenue Luis de Camões to the Avenue do Infante and secure the President's Official Residence."

The others, having heard the detailed plan many times before, smiled at their detail-obsessed friend whose planning was bringing them the power they had all dreamed of for many years.

"Ulan my friend, will you join us as we take control?" invited Huberto Pedroso, seeing the Russian standing a little distance away watching the convoy through binoculars.

"I regret not, Sonia and I have much to do here with our businesses, please you understand, eh. We will join you later, maybe this evening," the wily Russian replied. "You keep Sonia's Mercedes for as long as you need, it okay."

Then waving, Reshetnikov returned to the house to listen to the news coming through from Lisbon of troops and police on the streets amidst confused reports of a coup. All appeared to suggest that the army had taken over, but whether it was to suppress civilian protests regarding economic austerity was unclear. There was also the possibility that the military had finally rebelled against the further swingeing cuts recently announced, that would reduce their numbers to a level that the senior command viewed as being dangerous.

As he sat listening intently Reshetnikov saw three of his guests depart, apparently in high spirits, leaving Olavo Esteves to effect the banking activity in preparation for the new tax regime.

CHAPTER 12

A GAME OF QUESTIONS AND ANSWERS

Diago Velo was finding it difficult to fully concentrate on his driving in the company of his two excited and nervous fellow conspirators. The traffic was slow and he constantly sounded the car's horn and gesticulated at other drivers to either hurry or get out of his way. Twice he had come close to a collision and now Huberto, sitting alongside him, was pleading for him to be patient.

"Diago, Diago, do not try to hurry so much. Alves will need time to secure things for us eh. If we arrive too soon we will distract him from his duty and that may be critical."

"You have a point, Huberto, but it would be nice we witness the Major at work eh," chimed in Rodriguez from the back seat, his laugh sounding hollow from the nervousness he felt inside.

As they reached the esplanade they could see people looking towards the Palaçio de São Lourenço confused, not knowing whether to stay and watch or run and hide. Passing the building they saw the armoured personnel carrier outside the main gate with fully armed troops forming a screen.

"Antonio should be at the President's place by now," said Velo. "We go straight there and see which men are to take you to the radio station Huberto."

"Remember, Huberto, there is plenty of time, eh. You may even have time for a coffee," added Rodriguez, reaching forward to give Pedroso's shoulder a friendly shove.

The car tyres squealed as Velo sped the car round the roundabout before charging at the steep incline of the Avenue do Infante. To their left they saw two soldiers escorting three policemen down the hill, presumably, they thought, as part of the plan to isolate the police force until its loyalty to the coup could be assured. Armed police could present a problem if they were not on side.

"Alves is working very efficiently it seems," remarked Isidro Rodriguez. "Try and drive into the Residency's grounds, just in case a crowd develops."

Turning off the road and up the ramp to the gate they were stopped by soldiers under the command of a lieutenant who approached Velo's side of the vehicle.

Before the officer could speak Velo said, "We are here to liaise with Major Antonio Alves, your commanding officer."

"Who are you?" asked the lieutenant pleasantly, taking a notebook from his combat dress pocket and consulting a list.

"I am Diago Velo and this is Senhor Huberto Pedroso and behind him is Senhor Isidro Rodriguez."

"I see. Senhor Olavo Esteves is not with you?"

"No he will join later," replied Velo, impressed that the lieutenant was well informed.

The use of Esteves' full name flashed an alarm signal in Rodriguez's mind dispelled by the lieutenant's next statement.

"If you drive through the gate and park on the right I will arrange an escort for you."

As he turned the engine of the car off Velo's phone chimed with a text message. Hurriedly he took the phone from his pocket and bringing up the message froze. "Oh, God, we have blindly walked into a trap. Yvonne says that our plans were discovered."

"What! What does she say Diago?" asked Rodriguez, his stomach suddenly experiencing the same contraction and icy chill as his companions.

"I read it to you, she say, 'British agent overheard your meeting and informed Lisbon Government. Many supporters arrested including we think Gabrielo Pedroso and Marcos Benzinho. Norberto Correia, Jose Pianto and I are safe. You must hide and find a way to leave the island. Yvonne.' I guess they are following Jose's plan now."

Velo was about to start the car's engine, with the ludicrous thought of escape in his mind, when the car doors were thrown open and the three men dragged out, ordered to lay face down on the ground, and roughly searched.

"Take them inside to Captain Zino," ordered the lieutenant, looking interestedly at Velo's phone messages. "And take this to the captain, it will make his day."

Inside the residence the three were lined up against a wall in front of a tall aristocratic looking army captain, who spent sometime scrutinising each of them in turn.

"Which of you is Isidro Rodriguez?"

"I am," answered Rodriguez, his voice no more than a hoarse whisper.

The captain pointed at Rodriguez and a tough looking soldier stepped forward and, grabbing Isidro's left arm, painfully marched him into a room to the left of the staircase. So started many hours of questioning.

*

The radio broadcast informing islanders of the defeat of an attempted coup and the imposition of a temporary curfew between the hours of seven p.m. and six a.m. was quickly issued, resulting in bringing people out onto the streets demanding more information. The President, in a second broadcast, called for calm to be restored and for everyone to return to their homes or places of work and carry on as normally as possible.

As the first broadcast was in progress Sonia was telephoning the police to inform them that her car had been stolen from nearby a hotel, where she and a friend were taking coffee. Cleverly she used the name of the hotel that Velo, Rodriguez and Pedroso had been staying in. Later hotel staff would confirm that the two ladies had been at the hotel at around the time stated.

*

In the foyer to the conference suite Patrick Murphy intercepted Vaughan. "I hear you're taking Metcalf's room for a night or two."

"Yes, I understand that Al Djebbar would be happier with you guys around me with this assassin still on the loose."

"Did you know that some group here on the island actually attempted a coup, whilst this assassination attempt was going on," said Murphy.

"Good Lord, really," replied Vaughan, hoping that he sounded suitably incredulous.

"Yeh, that's why this place is not crawling with the local police; guess they have more important things goin' on," said Murphy, sounding to Vaughan rather relieved.

Both men stood in silence for a while, watching as the four policemen that had been on the scene at the time, covered the area where the bodies had fallen with plastic sheeting.

"Shame about Metcalf and Pascal; I know Metcalf was a pain in the arse to work for and didn't seem to know too much about the job or team management, but he didn't deserve to be taken out like that."

"He should not have been playing bodyguard anyway, surely," said Vaughan. "The guy who everyone should turn to for command in a situation like that should make sure he is not near the obvious target."

"Yeh, you got that right. Say, you seem to know a hell of a lot about this business."

"Oh, it just struck me as common sense that's all."

"Yeh right," replied Murphy, giving Vaughan a suspicious look.

"Tell me, why was Metcalf carrying that brick of radio, when all the rest of you have a cuff speaker and earphone?"

Murphy looked at Vaughan again. "You don't miss much do you."

"It just seemed strange."

"Well, Metcalf reckoned that the ear pieces gave him a headache and ear infections."

"Oh," replied Vaughan raising his eyebrows. "Someone was telling him about a box on a roof just before the shooting."

"That was Chuck Hayward. People might think he was an old soak who put away too much whiskey, but he was the first to notice that box on the roof of the restaurant along there."

Vaughan looked puzzled.

"Come, I'll show you."

Leaving the conference centre they climbed up onto the grass between the palm trees.

"You'll get a better view up here," said Murphy. "See the roof of the 'Mamma Mia' up there. Well that box shape on top was put there maybe last night, maybe the night before. The assassin used it to hide in, it's a neat idea. It was built to blend in exactly with the rest of the roof, so none of us, except for Chuck, noticed

286

it. He had just switched with Dan Acknell and was doin' the overview watch from the west tower sixth floor balcony. You get a good view from up there. Anyways, he noticed the box and havin' done this job for years realised that it was new, therefore needin' investigation."

"That was very smart," said Vaughan, in admiration. "A black roof and then a black box to match. Very few people would pick that up unless they had reason to go onto the roof regularly."

"Sure. Inside we found the rifle, a pistol, water bottle, monocular, a black hood and jacket. That's what made us think it was night-time when the guy started the stakeout."

"It sounds very professional."

"We left it all in place. The police will want to see it when they have the time I guess."

"You're in charge now?"

"Only until our MD gets here. You'll love him," replied Murphy. "Ex CIA with attitude. He'll want to interrogate you that's for sure."

"Why?"

"Shit you were the one guy who knew what was goin' down and when. Beats me how you downed that guy Al Djebbar just at the right time."

"It was strange really, I was just watching Walid's face as he realised the impact that this conference had had. Then I noticed the red dot appear and move around on the side of his head. It doesn't take too many Hollywood films to know what a laser target assist spot means."

"You tellin' us that you tied some Hollywood films in with a real event?"

"When does he arrive?"

"First thing in the morning apparently; an' I was right, Jack Vale is really gonna want a word with you."

"Tell me, how can I get into town?" asked Vaughan.

"I doubt if you can, the Portuguese army seem to have put a clampdown on all movement. I guess they are trying to track down members of the coup," replied Murphy. "According to some hotel staff, the troops were flown in this morning and have got a cordon around a couple of military aircraft at the airport."

Just then an army jeep raced down the approach road and stopped alongside the police officers. A short conversation followed ending with one of the policemen pointing towards Patrick Murphy, and the lieutenant jumping from the passenger seat and hurrying towards them.

"Excuse Senhor, I am looking for a Senhor Vaughan. Please you take me to him," said the lieutenant, obviously in a desperate hurry.

"I am Ian Vaughan, how can I help you?" interjected Vaughan.

"You please come with me to meet Colonel Castelo Lopes. He wish to speak with you and British Consul; she also there."

For some strange reason Vaughan looked at his watch as if to indicate that he had a more important meeting to attend. He then understood why he had used the delaying tactic.

"Please, Senhor, it is very urgent you come."

"All right, but I need to make a call first," Vaughan replied, and then turning to Murphy said, "I can't for the life of me understand what this is about."

Walking some distance away from Murphy and the lieutenant, Vaughan made contact with DELCO. To his relief he was put through to the Commodore.

"Campbell."

"Vaughan, sir. You are probably aware of the situation here and what led to it."

"Yes, you seem to have a nose for finding trouble, but you did the right thing in reporting it as you did. You know of course that an attempt was made on the life of Al Djebbar this morning?" said Campbell, his voice friendly, not the brisk sharpness as at their last meeting.

"Yes, sir, I was standing alongside him at the time."

"You were what?"

"I said I was standing alongside him at the time, sir. I will be transmitting a full report later, sir, but at this moment I need your advice. I have been asked to attend a meeting with a Colonel Castelo Lopes, which I would think is in connection with the coup. Do you want me to declare my SIS status?"

"No, definitely not," replied Campbell firmly. "The situation still appears to be very confused in Portugal so you must be very careful when discussing your part in this."

"Right, sir, thank you. I better go now, as the lieutenant sent to get me is anxious to leave."

"Before you go, that fellow Staunton has suddenly decided to fly over to you. I understand that he has not been particularly helpful, so be careful what you tell him."

With that the phone went dead, leaving Vaughan looking at the instrument thoughtfully. Staunton had received a big put-down from Susanne Bevington, and his appearance seemed to suggest that he wanted to get some form of revenge by using his more senior status to takeover. Campbell's cautionary phrase suggested that this was the game that had been alluded to at 'The Manor', the one that informs you that you have no friends inside the service.

"Senhor, can we go please? We are keeping the colonel waiting," requested the lieutenant who had made his way across the grass as Vaughan finished the call.

"Oh yes, we must not keep a colonel waiting, must we," said Vaughan, receiving a questioning look from the lieutenant who was not sure whether Vaughan was being sarcastic or not.

The journey to the Regional Government Offices was recklessly fast and extremely uncomfortable. Vaughan, sat in the rear seat without a seat belt, found himself being thrown around as the vehicle hurtled along weaving through the traffic. A roadblock near to the casino, above the President's formal residence, was forcing traffic onto a route avoiding the town centre; with minimum delay the barrier was pulled clear to allow them through to hurtle headlong down the steep slope and career, almost on two wheels, round the roundabout at the bottom.

Escorted to a first floor office, past groups of nervous looking civil servants, Vaughan was shown into a spacious office and invited to take a seat in front of a large and imposing desk.

"Colonel Castelo Lopes will join you in a short while. Would you like some coffee while you wait?" asked the lieutenant.

Vaughan was tempted to request a brandy to help recover from the ride in the jeep, but thought better of it and accepted the offer of coffee.

A hard-looking woman, who was obviously upset at being asked to carry out such a menial task for someone other than a senior member of staff, entered the office and dumped a tray of cups, saucers and coffee pot on the desk with a crash then, glaring at Vaughan, stamped out, slamming the door behind her.

The office was large, and as Vaughan looked about him he realised the former occupant's desk had been cleared and the family photograph, blotter and penholder removed and put untidily in a heap on a small corner table; a correspondence file, with letters spilling out of it was on the floor beside it. Vaughan could hear some noisy meeting or other taking place in an adjoining room. Then the interconnecting door opened and a distinguished, uniformed, upright man in his fifties strode across the room extending his hand.

Vaughan stood, and on shaking hands said, "How can I be of assistance, Colonel?"

"First, Senhor Vaughan, I would like to know how you came to be here in Madeira?" Then glancing at the tray and cups asked, "Coffee?"

"Thank you."

Whilst the colonel poured the coffee, Vaughan explained that he was writing a pilotage book about the islands of the Atlantic, to update previous knowledge for yachtsmen thinking of making such passages.

"How you come to overhearing this conversation about a coup?"

"I was a guest of the lady that owns the apartment in which the meeting took place. She was concerned that her uncle, who had been staying with her for the last month or so, was holding secretive meetings there. As part of my work involves interviewing people for details of port facilities and navigation, I find it easiest to tape-record what they say, then later transfer it to paper," explained Vaughan. "So to put her mind at rest I hid the recording device in the room he normally used for such meetings, thinking that it would be some new business venture that he wished to keep to himself, and would be of no great consequence to her. We were both astounded when we listened to what had been said."

"You have been here for not so many days, how you know this lady?"

Vaughan explained how he had come across her son, Zeferino, stranded on a sailboard far out to sea.

"Are you married man?"

"Recently divorced."

The colonel smiled. "And she is a very beautiful young woman."

Vaughan smiled. "Yes, very beautiful. Do you know her?"

"Why you take this information to British Consul?" asked the colonel, ignoring Vaughan's question. "Why not take your information to the police?"

"We thought about that, but thought some members of the police force may be part of the coup."

"I see. Did you think the same about the army?"

"Considering the number of times the army of one country or another has been responsible for a coup, we chose not to take the risk."

"Your answer makes me feel a little uncomfortable."

Vaughan did not answer.

"Were you in the apartment at the time of the meeting?"

"No, we went out for dinner, just as her uncle's collaborators were arriving. When we returned they had all gone, including her uncle," Vaughan replied. "They left a note saying that they were going to Porto do Moniz for a couple of days."

"What did you think of that?"

"I personally didn't believe it and Mrs de Lima just thought that to travel to Porto do Moniz at that time of night was stupid; that was before we listened to the recording."

The colonel was quiet for a time, obviously considering how to proceed with the interview.

"We believe that Mrs de Lima is involved in the planning of this coup. What do you think?"

"I am absolutely sure that she is innocent. Given what I have just told you, do you still believe that she is involved?"

"You normally live on your yacht in the marina here."

"Yes."

292

"Why you move to her apartment? Were you sleeping with her?"

"No I was not," said Vaughan, sounding shocked and annoyed by the question. Why he had not expected it he couldn't say, after all both Amelia and he were free of any other romantic relationships. Maybe it was the shadow of Sarah still preventing him from moving on. "Look, a couple of days ago there was a young woman murdered and her body left on the roof terrace of one of the hotels, near Ponta da Cruz I think. Anyway, it seems that Mrs de Lima's uncle returned in the early hours one morning, around the time of the murder, with a large bloodstain on the shoulder of his shirt. He claimed that a friend, who had cut his hand, felt faint and held onto his shoulder with the wounded hand. It seemed rather unbelievable, and Mrs de Lima was frightened, fearing that her uncle was involved with the murder in some way, so we thought she would be safer if I were to stay until the police had made an arrest."

"Why did she not say anything to the police?"

"She wanted to believe his story, I think, after all the man is her uncle," said Vaughan. "All right, he had been out with several women late at night whilst he was staying with his niece, but well, to be quite honest I thought it was too much of a coincidence, and suggested to her that she wait for the police to reveal more details before she started throwing accusations about." In truth he had not wanted to get involved with police interviews regarding a murder, especially at a time when the opportunity to cement the friendship with Al Djebbar was there for the taking.

The colonel made some notes on his pad. "My lieutenant found you at the," the colonel consulted a note on his desk, "Vidamar Hotel. Why were you there? We have been informed that there was an assassination attempt made on a conference delegate there this morning."

"I was there at the personal invitation of my friend, Walid al Djebbar, who is leading the conference, and who was the target for both of this morning's attacks."

"I have not received the full details yet. Did you say, both attacks?" asked Castelo Lopes. "There were two?"

"Yes, first was a marksman; he missed, but hit and killed the chief of the private security staff, hired to protect the conference delegates, and another member of that team. Then a suicide bomber appeared. She was shot moments before she could detonate the explosive she was carrying."

"Incredible, quite incredible. Senhor Vaughan, you seem to be surrounded or involved in very much trouble since you arrived on this island, and I keep asking myself, why?"

"I've just been unlucky I guess," replied Vaughan, trying hard to show a facial expression of sad resignation. "I sailed here to get information for a book, and all that has happened since my arrival has been murder, attempted assassination and revolution."

A knock at the door interrupted their conversation, or rather the colonel's careful interrogation.

"Veer!"

"Excuse, Colonel," said a sergeant, marching across to the desk and saluting, before placing Vaughan's notebooks and logbook in front of the colonel.

"Obrigado, Sergeant."

"Had you asked, I would have brought my notebooks from the boat. It would have saved your men from smashing their way in through the hatch and drawing attention to me unnecessarily," Vaughan said angrily.

The colonel questioned the sergeant for a few minutes, then dismissing him turned back to Vaughan.

"Calm yourself, Senhor Vaughan, we found the keys to your boat in your bag at the consul's home."

Vaughan frowned, still angry.

"Your consul was anxious to prove that you are who you say you are, as is Mrs de Lima."

"They are both here?"

"Yes. Shortly after our public broadcast, Senhora Bevington, the Honorary British Consul, brought your lady friend here to explain about her uncle and his, as you said, collaborators."

The colonel opened one of Vaughan's notebooks and started to read. After a few pages he flicked on a few more, then stopped to read again. "Interesting Senhor Vaughan, you have an eye for detail and a way with words."

Vaughan said nothing, and sat waiting for the next question.

"Have you finished your researches here in Madeira?" Something in the way the question had been asked made Vaughan suspicious. If he said yes it would link his stay more to the timing of the conference and coup than was purely coincidental. Was that what the colonel was trying to find out, Vaughan wondered?

"No, not yet, I will have to spend three or four more days here checking marina facilities outside of Funchal. Assuming of course that this coup doesn't disrupt that. If you think it will I would like your permission to sail down to the Canaries and survey that region, and return here later on to complete my work; I have a book to write and a publisher wanting it yesterday."

"There will inevitably be restrictions in place until we are sure that this rebellion or coup is dealt with, but I do not wish that you go to all the trouble of sailing a great distance on account of a few troublesome people," replied the colonel, studying Vaughan carefully. "Let me make some enquiry, excuse me."

The colonel got up and strode across the room, opening the door to the landing and stairwell. "Lieutenant Jacome," Vaughan heard him say; then followed a muffled conversation behind the partially closed door. Stepping back into the room the colonel obviously thought of some further instruction, and turning said, "Eu nä acredito que este Homen seja quem ele diz ser. Mantêm os olhos bem atentos nele e reporta-me qualquer coisa qua consideres supeita."

Vaughan smiled to himself. *So, he doesn't believe my cover and is setting someone to keep a close eye on me eh. Interesting.*

"Senhor Vaughan, you were a key part in warning our government and I fear that if some supporters of this plot got to hear of your service to us, they may wish to punish you in some way."

"Really. How would they find that out?"

"Yes, really. This is a small island, information travels very quickly, even sometimes the most carefully guarded information. So I am proposing to assign Lieutenant Jacome to act as your bodyguard and official escort."

Vaughan could see immediately what the colonel was planning, and anticipated that the next move would be for him to allow the release of Amelia. The colonel was assuming that Vaughan had some romantic attachment to Amelia that would bring them together. If she were part of the coup her only chance of survival would be to explain to the others involved that Vaughan had made the recording without her knowledge, and maybe offer herself as bait in a plot for them to take revenge. Alternatively she may herself wish to exact retribution.

"If it means that I can get on with the job then I suppose I will have to agree."

Then, as an afterthought, Vaughan said, "I may invite Mrs de Lima to accompany me sometimes. She has a vast knowledge of the island. I assume you will be releasing her." *There we are, Colonel, my romantic intentions laid bare. Let's hope that our chaperon, Lieutenant Jacome, is on the side of the angels.*

The colonel gave a knowing smile and nodded. "I am sure that will delight Lieutenant Jacome greatly."

Standing, the colonel again put out his hand. "Thank you Senhor Vaughan, you have performed a great service to my country. I am sure we will meet again before you continue your voyage."

Vaughan accepted the handshake and smiled. "Where will I find Lieutenant Jacome?" he asked, acting as if he had not heard and understood some of the colonel's instructions.

"He is waiting for you outside of this office," the colonel said, as he rounded the desk, picking up Vaughan's books and escorting him to the door. "Please you will need these, I look forward to reading the finished work."

Outside stood the lieutenant who had accompanied Vaughan from the Vidamar; he looked very nervous as he snapped to attention and saluted the colonel.

*

It took Vaughan a long time to persuade Lieutenant Jacome of his need to spend some time at the British Consul's home to collect his things, before going with him to the Vidamar. On arrival at the house, Vaughan asked the lieutenant to wait for him in the car.

Mr Bevington greeted him. "When you two turned up last night with that incredible story of yours, I thought that Susanne was mad to believe it and raise the alarm as quickly as she did. It appears, however, that it was all too true, and London and Lisbon have hailed the three of you as saviours of the Portuguese government."

Not particularly interested in the political response, Vaughan enquired whether Bevington's wife and Amelia had returned.

"Oh, I think they are still with the army chaps. My wife called a short time ago and said that she would be back in an hour or so. Not sure about your friend though, they may want to keep hold of her for a time."

Vaughan looked glumly into the middle distance, his thoughts turning back to his questioning by the colonel. "I suppose after an event like this all sorts of conspiracy theories abound. Maybe I should go and have another word with them."

"You've spoken with the army?"

"Yes, my army minder is sitting in that car outside. If he comes wanting to know where I am tell him I'm taking a shower or something."

Vaughan briefly explained about having met the colonel.

"Bearing in mind your status I would have thought you were better off out of the limelight. Besides the young lady was not impressed by your having deserted her this morning."

"No, I don't suppose she was. She doesn't know who I really work for."

"Are you going to tell her?"

"No, definitely not."

"You may be interested to know that they have rounded-up some of the leaders of the mainland coup, according to the BBC."

"What about here?"

"Haven't heard anything yet, though they have broadcasted details of your friend's uncle," informed Bevington, gravely. "A friend of ours, Sue Smith, who works for a travel agency here, said that some army personnel were arrested at the airport this morning and taken back to Lisbon."

"You can't have a coup without any military assistance. Let's hope it is the good guys that are in charge here now."

"Didn't you find out when you were with this Colonel?"

"It's not the type of question you ask is it. You know. Are you on the side of the demons or the angels?"

"No, I suppose not."

"Would you mind if I went through, I have some reporting to do and a couple of calls to make."

"No, not in the least. You know where everything is I hope," replied Bevington, stepping to one side and ushering Vaughan through in the direction of the office.

Pulling the handwritten report from his pocket, Vaughan smoothed it out and was preparing to type it up on the office computer when he saw the fax machine in the corner. Within ten minutes all twenty pages had been sent to both Lisbon and London leaving only the report on the assassination to type up and a note regarding the interview with the army colonel.

*

About an hour after Vaughan's telephone conversation from the Vidamar Hotel grounds, Campbell had gone through to the communication room and asked to see a replay of the Portuguese Television headline making broadcast of the assassination attempt.

"It's not very clear, sir," said the technician. "There was quite a crowd around the man and the camera was too low to see what precisely happened."

Campbell watched the first run intently, and then requested that they play it in slow motion. "There! Hold it there. Back a bit. That's it," he instructed. "Now can someone get me Lieutenant Heathcote?"

As soon as she walked through the door Campbell pointed to the screen and asked, "Who do you think that is, standing alongside Al Djebbar?"

"Good heavens, it looks like Vaughan, sir."

"Yes, it is Vaughan. I knew he could do it, only a friend of Al Djebbar would be that close at that moment," said Campbell triumphantly. "Thank God I won the battle to keep Staunton in Lisbon, he would never have been able to get that close, regardless of the quality of the briefing."

Heathcote smiled.

"That bloke did more than that sir," interrupted the technician. "You watch this as we roll it on slowly. See him step to one side, but he's turned to look at the other chap, right. I think he saw something 'cos he gives the guy a hard push; see the top of his head move and the other bloke disappear. Then all hell breaks loose and the cameraman does a bit of a runner before he turns to film some more."

After some extreme camera shaking, the view from a new angle showed security men running as if to chase someone, and a woman dressed in purdah walk towards a group of men guarding a man crouched down, his back towards the camera.

"That's your bloke, Vaughan, taking his jacket off to cover someone over who's been downed," said the technician. "Shit, did you see that, he turned and shot that Arab woman? I missed that the first time I looked through this." Campbell gave the technician a stern glare for use of bad language in front of female staff.

"Where did that sequence come from?" asked Heathcote. "It isn't on that broadcast over there on the news channel."

"We was watchin' and recordin' this live."

"Subsequent broadcasts would have been censored, that I'm sure of," said Campbell. "In fact I am surprised that got broadcasted. Though nowadays the public seems to be less squeamish about such things, but watching someone apparently being executed, well, it's out there now," he continued.

"Executed, sir."

"How would you describe it; not knowing that she was a suicide bomber?" said Campbell. "We have the advantage of further intelligence, and seeing it in slow motion. The people who saw this in real time would have had an awful shock."

Heathcote nodded, "I see what you mean."

As BBC News 24 repeated the story they confirmed that two of the security team protecting the delegates had been killed, and that shortly after the assassination attempt, a female suicide bomber, whose identity was unknown, was shot dead, as she tried to detonate the explosives she was carrying. The following item concerned the failed coup and confirmed that many arrests had been made including leaders of the group in Madeira.

"Should we recall Vaughan now, sir?" asked Heathcote. "The investigation may compromise his cover."

"No, not yet. I have learnt that he is helping the Portuguese army, I think in connection with the coup. Also I am anxious for him to try and reinforce his position with Al Djebbar. We need all the help we can get in that area of the world, so let us see how this plays out. There is a great deal riding on the success of this conference, not just trade in resources, but also security in the region. If Al Djebbar's southern border protection plan works, it should take some of the strain off southern Europe, and indeed ourselves, regarding illegal immigration."

"Those poor people must be very desperate though, sir. Look at the number that have drowned in the attempt to reach Italian soil, and even if they survive that, they have to cross Europe to get to us."

"I know, Heathcote. I understand how you feel, but our national debt burden is at a critical level. Anymore social welfare commitments would increase government borrowing and that could well send us spiralling into a depression that would take us back to the dark ages. We are on the brink of economic disaster and our politicians are helpless and hopeless; praying instead that bravado will conceal the real state of our economy. It's not just the balance of payments and government borrowing, personal debt levels are in danger of running far too high to prevent personal defaults on a large scale."

Heathcote and the technician looked at Campbell in shock. "Bloody hell, sir. You reckon it's as bad as that?"

"I'm afraid so. If we go under, economically, those poor people you talk of, Heathcote, will not find any welcome here, only I fear, anarchy," replied Campbell, looking tired and distressed. "Anyway our immediate problem is to assist in getting North Africa into a stable situation, so contact Vaughan through the Consul and instruct him to stay with Al Djebbar until the man returns to Tunisia. Hopefully we can then hand the ball back to Stanthorpe-Ogilvey and his team at the FCO."

"I'll try and contact them now, sir."

"This has just come through from Madeira, sir," said a signal clerk, thrusting Vaughan's report of the final conference speech at Campbell.

Taking it from her, he stared at the young lady. "You're new here."

"Yes, sir. Started last Monday. Transferred from HMS Daring, sir."

"Oh, right, well, welcome aboard."

"Thank you, sir," replied the clerk, who then turned away and went back to her desk at the far end of the room.

"Something troubling you, sir?" asked Heathcote.

"Yes, but I am not sure what," replied Campbell. "I've seen that face before, and not so long ago. Get her file sent over for me will you. I would like to have a read of it."

Vaughan was well into the report, typing swiftly, when the phone rang. "British Consul's Office Madeira."

"This is DELCO publishing, could you ask the Consul to phone us back please?"

"Yes, Lieutenant, I will," Vaughan replied, having recognised the voice instantly.

"Is that Vaughan?"

"Yes it is. I am using her office to send in my reports."

Immediately the lieutenant went through the security checks before conveying Commodore Campbell's instructions.

"Okay, Lieutenant. In fact as soon as I had finished this, I was going to return to the Vidamar. I think that the delegates will be allowed to depart tomorrow, they all have diplomatic immunity anyway, so could not be held here."

"The conference is all over then?"

"Yes, closing speech was this morning, immediately after the assassination attempts. My friend, Al Djebbar, is a very cool customer. He seemed hardly shaken by the event and told me that he had been expecting someone to have a go for some months."

"That was you pushing Al Djebbar down."

"Er, yes. I saw the red dot that a laser assist imposes."

"Well done. How did you know the woman was a bomber? She was completely cloaked by that purdah attire."

"The wind blew the garment apart at the front exposing the explosives she was trying to detonate," replied Vaughan, the image of the girl as she stood in front of him, with that terrible expression of hatred on her face, flashing across his mind.

"So you saved him twice, and many others besides."

"That's if it had gone off. Sometimes these things aren't wired up properly, but I didn't have time to think about that, and I don't intend to check now."

"Shame on you, really?" she said, teasingly. "Who's got the explosives now?"

"I don't know. I would think that the police would have taken charge of them."

"Have the police interviewed you?" Heathcote asked.

"No, strange that. The army seem to be in total control of the town centre, and now you come to mention it I haven't seen a policeman since being taken in by the army," replied Vaughan. "Of course the army may not trust the police."

"Can anyone trust the army?"

"The Consul's husband has just asked me the same question. Talking to this Colonel Castelo Lopes, I am reasonably confident that the troops here in the town are the good guys."

"Be careful, it is rarely that cut and dried," Heathcote warned, "By the way the Commodore is reading your fax at the moment. He was in the communications room when it arrived."

"That was the one covering the conference final speech. I will send through the report on the assassination in about half an hour," replied Vaughan. "Couldn't do it any earlier due to the army interview. I've got to hurry, I have an army minder waiting outside for me, the colonel has placed a lieutenant with me saying that he is there for my protection whilst I complete my notes for the book. I told him that I had three or four more day's work to do, not thinking that he would have me closely watched."

"When are you leaving the island?"

"I don't really know. Hopefully in three to four days."

"That should not be a problem, Vaughan. I will explain to the Commodore. We don't have another op for you at the moment."

When the call finished, Vaughan got back to work, and had just completed the report when he heard the return of Susanne Bevington and Amelia.

"Whatever you said to the colonel was enough to get your friend out of custody," Bevington said as she came into the office. "She's gone to the guest room to lay down for a while. Poor thing they gave her quite a hard time of it."

"Pity I could not have been in two places at once today," Vaughan replied. "I gather she did not take too kindly to my absence this morning."

"She was quite upset, yes," said Bevington. "I have, however, impressed upon her that it was my decision she went to the army with her story and that you were not party to it."

"Thank you. Does she know that I am in here working?"

"No, and there is no reason for her to find out, unless you want her to know?"

Vaughan shook his head. "I don't, so as soon as this is off to London and Lisbon I will scoot off to the Vidamar."

"And desert her again?"

"Look, I'm here to do a job, not get involved with a young lady whose relatives are involved in political unrest."

Susanne Bevington gave Vaughan a long hard stare before saying, "You are right, this is not your problem, but I think that you wish it was."

"I'm finding this job to be more difficult each day. When Staunton arrives he will expect me to be latched onto Walid al Djebbar not providing a shoulder for Amelia to cry on," replied Vaughan as he pressed the send button of the email encoder. "I think that the delegates will be leaving the island tomorrow and that my task will have been completed."

"Did you say that Staunton is coming here?"

"Yes, so London informed me earlier," replied Vaughan. "God knows why. As I said the conference is over and the delegates will either be leaving or will have left by the time he gets here."

"Chances are that he will want a slice of the credit regarding exposure of the coup."

"Probably, I get the impression that he is that type of guy," Vaughan said with a cynical smile. "By the way, have you seen any reports go through from Arthur Claremont?"

"Yes he's been posting regular reports including the reports received from a microphone that you planted. He seems very impressed with this man Al Djebbar. Oh and when I spoke to him at church on Sunday he told me that a Russian has been making firm friends with some junior member of the Moroccan delegation. Their normal stuff I suppose."

"I can confirm that the contact is through the Russian, Reshetnikov," said Vaughan. "His wife or lady friend was at the Vidamar last night meeting with one of the junior members of the delegation."

Susanne Bevington raised her eyebrows. "Staunton will be impressed, you don't happen to know the junior's name by any chance?"

"No, but I know a man who does, and I think I know how to phrase the question."

"Really?"

"Yes really. You see I believe that Sarkis Kazakov aided the assassin, because I am pretty sure that the man I saw running from the hide placed on the roof of the 'Mamma Mia' restaurant was the same man that I saw with Kazakov a few nights ago in Annabel's nightclub."

"You've certainly been busy since you arrived. Few men get to the 'Mamma Mia' and Annabel's in the time it has taken you to do so. I bet your expenses claim will be interesting to read," said Bevington, "but what has Kazakov got to do with Reshetnikov's assistance to STATGAZ? Surely the death of Al Djebbar would have destroyed Russian diplomatic interference had Kazakov's role been exposed."

"I don't suppose that the two men co-ordinated their activities," replied Vaughan, "Both, I would think, are motivated purely by greed. No, what I propose to do is suggest that both men were working together, when I meet Al Djebbar and Mehdi Khuldun, Mehdi will certainly be able to put a name to the Moroccan contact, once I have pointed him out. That should be enough to spoil the Russian approach for the moment."

CHAPTER 13
THE END GAMES BEGIN

The lone house on the mountainside high above the village of Boaventura was typical of the area, block built and rendered, with the exterior walls painted cream under a terracotta tiled roof. The village sprawled along and over the high ridge between two valleys and extended down the western slope into the valley below. The northern extremity of the village reached the cliff tops, that look out onto the apparently endless Atlantic Ocean on which the next, equally dramatic coastline due north, is Iceland, over eighteen hundred nautical miles away. Kazakov and his daughter were sat outside on patio chairs staring out over the village to the grey ocean beyond, wishing that by some magic they could transport themselves to that distant and remote shore.

After the telephone warning, Kazakov and his daughter, together with his housekeeper Magda, had hastily packed and made their way across the island in the Mercedes. Meanwhile Boris was instructed to take the weapons, stored in the basement, to the hiding place at Paul do Mar on the island's west coast. Kazakov and Boris were the only two people who knew of the cellar beneath the derelict building close to the harbour, where Kazakov's shipments arrived and departed.

Tonight, Boris would have to work alone, as the island would be under curfew preventing Kazakov from making the journey. Anyway, he had promised to meet Takkal, who seemed to be in a fix having been forced to leave his weapons behind at the scene of the assassination attempt.

The arms Kazakov had brought with him he had charged a high price for, but Takkal had paid without complaint. It meant that Kazakov, his daughter, housekeeper and Boris could eat well for some time to come.

Idly Kazakov wondered why Takkal, of all the marksmen he knew, had missed his target that morning. The assassin's reputation was legendary so what had gone wrong. The target must have been too closely guarded; radio reports had said that two of the conference security guards had been killed. Maybe they were part of a total screen of guards. Takkal would tell him at sometime, but probably not today.

The sun was slowly disappearing behind the high hillside to the west and Kazakov turned to his daughter, "Let us go inside and watch some television, yes?"

Nadezhda gave a weak smile and nodded her agreement as she got up from the chair and stepping close to her father, put her arms around his waist as he put his arm around her shoulder. This act of affection almost brought tears to the big Russian's eyes. His lovely, silent daughter, all that was left of a once happy family.

*

"Ian, you look exhausted, my friend. What has been happening to you?"

"Sadly, Walid, the young lady that Mehdi met on my boat has an uncle who was involved in the attempted coup. I have been helping to provide evidence that she personally was not involved in the plot. Whether or not I have been of any real help to her, however, remains to be seen. The army have released her, but I fear that she will be hauled in again for questioning." *It's nice to be able to tell the truth for once.*

"I wish that there was something I could do to help, especially as you have done so much for me," replied Al Djebbar. "May I thank you again for your services, not only to me personally, but to the whole purpose of the meeting here."

"I am only too pleased to have been able to help, Walid. What you are trying to achieve is something of immense importance for Europe as well as the North African region. Charles keeps on about it, each time we meet, but it is only since I have been here, and met you, that I have really grasped the full implications of your plan," said Vaughan. *That was good, now let's pop the question.*

"Walid, some things have come out of my meeting with the army, and some other bits of information that I have now pieced together. Is Mehdi about? I would like to just ask him a couple of questions about junior members of the Moroccan delegation."

Al Djebbar frowned. "You think that there is a further threat?"

"Maybe. I don't rightly know. It is just that when I was having dinner the other evening, in the restaurant above the conference centre, I saw one of the, I think Moroccan team, meeting with a friend of a Russian oligarch called Reshetnikov."

"You know a lot of people here in Madeira," said Al Djebbar, with a hint of suspicion in his voice.

"Oh, I know Reshetnikov, I heard all about him when he was loudly entertaining some Brazilians at a place I visited. I was just wanting a quiet beer, and he arrived with his guests and girls as well," replied Vaughan, shrugging his shoulders and smiling cheerfully. "Most of the other customers, like me, soon decided to find another bar."

"The police found a strange cleric hiding in some bushes after the attack on me. They had him locked up in one of the rooms behind the reception area," said Al Djebbar, thoughtfully. "The police could not find any identification on the man, but with all this confusion over the coup they have not been able to do whatever they do to circulate his picture. Frankly I had forgotten about him until now."

"Maybe a connection," replied Vaughan. *I wonder whether this man is Al Bashir or Al Ben Said? I mustn't appear to know anymore, otherwise it will be obvious that I am working for the British Government, and Charles Stanthorpe-Ogilvey's careful friendship goes down the tubes.*

"There was a young member of the Moroccan delegation who made me feel uncomfortable," said Al Djebbar, almost to himself. "I wonder whether it is the same one that you saw meeting with this Russian person." Vaughan shrugged. "Mehdi should be returning here soon," continued Al Djebbar. "If you can spare the time and wait for him I would be grateful. Coffee perhaps, while we wait?"

Mehdi arrived before the coffee, joining them just as Al Djebbar was finishing the story of his brief relationship with Leyla Najjar.

"She was so beautiful, but always in the company of her parents or friends when we met. I even went as far as mentioning her to Charles, believing that her smiles and fond looks were genuine. Oh what a fool I was," said Al Djebbar, as he stood to look out over the balcony towards the ocean. "There is Charles, happily married with children, and I, still single, and only attractive to women who wish to kill me or bankrupt me." There was bitterness in this remark that Vaughan had great sympathy for. It was that hollow side of fame that many must fear they are at risk of.

It took only a few minutes walking through the Sunset Lounges to identify both members of the Moroccan team.

"Thank you for your information regarding the contact with this Russian, Ian. We are aware that Russia has a great interest in the future of Moroccan oil and gas development. I think my friend from the Directorate of Territorial Surveillance, Abdul el Najid will be interested to interview both young men."

Vaughan smiled. *There's two guys in for a very unpleasant time. I wonder whether he will be asked to interview this cleric that has been locked up.* "Are you going to ask him to interview this, er, cleric who was found hiding in some bushes?"

"I have already made that request, Ian. El Najid is attending to it at this moment," Walid al Djebbar responded, with a smile that suggested he was pleased to have been apparently one step ahead. "Will you join us for dinner this evening. I am sure that no one will object to your presence." Vaughan, exhausted by the events of the day and the mental gymnastics he had to perform, started to shake his head and was about to make his apologies when Al Djebbar continued, "I would look upon it as a personal favour to me."

"In that case, Walid, I accept your kind invitation and hope that I do not embarrass you with my lack of etiquette."

Mehdi laughed. "Just sit on your left hand and only use your right, that is really all you need to know.

*

At around the time the conference delegates were called to dinner, Kazakov's housekeeper appeared to announce that their food was on the table and they should go and eat.

Takkal, never one to make conversation, was even more taciturn than usual. "You think your employers will not be pleased with your work today," said Kazakov, enjoying watching the discomfort of the little grey man.

"The Berber has not left the island yet, nobody can leave until the army think they have complete control."

312

"You will try again?"

"This is no longer business, it is pride. I have a reputation to keep," Takkal said, pushing his plate away, the food only half eaten. "I go now to my room to plan, I will see you in the morning."

Standing, Takkal reached down and picked up the US Army issue Beretta M9 that Kazakov had brought for him. "Thank you for this, and the carbine."

In his room Takkal meticulously cleaned both weapons and loaded the three magazines supplied with each. Since leaving his Glock 9mm in the hide, on the roof of the 'Mamma Mia', he had felt naked and very vulnerable.

The Beretta, annoyingly, did not fit the holster he was used to and he disliked the standard cheap webbing one provided. Carefully wiping the pistol with a clean white cloth he slid it under his pillow; with it there he would enjoy a better night's sleep.

*

Staunton arrived at midnight having pulled every string in the diplomatic book to land on Porto Santo and had then hired a fisherman to ferry him across to Madeira. When reception woke Vaughan to convey Staunton's demand for an immediate meeting he was far from pleased.

Stepping out from the lift, Vaughan was met by Hayward of 'Total Cover', the man who had raised the alarm about Takkal's roof hide. Together they walked through the link corridor to the west tower.

"I don't know who your visitor thinks he is, but I'll tell you this, if he talks to me that way again, I'll deck him."

Vaughan chuckled. "Please do. After getting me out of bed at this hour I am tempted to deck him myself."

"Say, are you really just a writer?" asked Hayward. "This guy you're going to meet gave me the impression that you work for the British Government."

"No, not me. A friend of mine does, who is also a good friend of Al Djebbar," replied Vaughan, hoping that the explanation was sounding truthful. "Frankly I don't know who this chap is, I've definitely never met him before. He's probably got the wrong end of the stick; nobody seems to take the trouble to listen carefully anymore. I don't suppose he has the first idea why Al Djebbar invited me to stay here."

"It was for your own protection as far as I was told," replied Hayward.

"Exactly."

Rounding the corner into the reception lobby Vaughan immediately identified Staunton sitting glaring at a group of German tourists who were demanding to know when the airport would be reopened and flights out commenced.

"Is that him, the chap in the suit?" asked Vaughan, knowing full well what Staunton looked like from his briefing photographs.

"Yeh, that's the jerk."

"Okay, I'll take it from here, you get back to what you are supposed to be doing," said Vaughan, anxious not to have Hayward witness the initial meeting.

"My orders are not to let you out of my sight until you are safely back in your room," Hayward replied earnestly.

Vaughan gave a dejected sigh. "Really, you think I maybe topped by a British Government official in front of this audience?" he said, nodding at the German tourist group.

"I'll wait here just in case."

Vaughan shrugged and strolled off towards Staunton, trying hard to place himself directly between the two men.

"Mr Staunton?"

Staunton, instantly recognizing Vaughan, appeared to actually leap to his feet. "You realise the diplomatic problems you have created, why...

Vaughan had held up his hand and in a low threatening voice said, "Don't you dare blow my cover, Staunton. Everyone on this island thinks I am an author and am therefore trustworthy. If you expose me, both of us are likely to be the centre of a diplomatic scandal that SIS cannot afford."

"Then let us find a quiet room where I can give you some career advice," replied Staunton acidly.

Oh no you don't, you arrogant bastard. "I doubt if that is possible at this time of night, especially when reception has its hands full with irate German tourists. In fact, as I have the Portuguese Army's Lieutenant Jacome normally escorting me every time I leave my room, plus 'Total Cover's' staff endeavouring to make sure that I do not come to any harm, the chance of us enjoying a quiet chat in the next few days are nil, I would say." *Frankly, old son, I am getting very annoyed with you, and this job, which I may well tell Commodore Campbell to stick when I get back.*

"Portuguese Army?" questioned Staunton. "Have you blotted your copybook with them as well?"

For God's sake, Staunton, which cage did they let you out of? "Colonel Castelo Lopes believes that I may be at risk of reprisals from members of the coup, not yet rounded up. Olavo Esteves for example has not yet been arrested, according to the latest broadcast."

"What a load of rubbish."

"Maybe, but getting back to the moment, I would suggest that you get yourself booked in and get some sleep."

Staunton glared at Vaughan. "This hotel is fully booked."

Vaughan shrugged, inwardly enjoying the situation. "Maybe the reception staff will phone round for you," he said turning away as if to go back to his room.

"You had better go and ask them to."

"As an author, unconnected with the British Government, it would hardly be appropriate, besides, a request like that from me would hardly carry the same clout as I am sure you would achieve," said Vaughan looking back over his shoulder, before walking back to his 'Total Cover' escort.

"That was short and sweet," said Hayward.

"Short, yes."

"The guy looks a bit pissed off from where I'm standin'."

Staunton looks a bit pissed off does he, well I must be hiding my feelings well. "Really, oh I wonder why, but I don't think I will go back and ask."

Hayward gave a snort of laughter.

*

Nadezhda Kazakov woke early the following morning, the strange surroundings and bird song, different from the cry of gulls at her cliff top home, had ensured a disturbed night and early wakening. She got out of bed and crossed to the window to look at the view across the lush green valley towards the farmed terraces on the lower slopes of the high ridge that cut off Boaventura from the neighbouring village of Aro de San Jorge. After a time, the sound of a shower being turned on made her think of preparing for the day, and crossing to the wardrobe she took some time selecting the clothes she would wear. Having chosen the blue dress her father liked her wearing, she reached for her dressing gown and slipped it on, not tying the belt, preferring to hold the gown tightly around her body as if suddenly feeling cold. Many times in her life the family had been forced to hide, it was the nature of her father's work. Smuggling and trading in arms invariably attracts the interest of the authorities and sometimes rival dealers, so this enforced move should not have felt so strange and frightening to her as it did. Desperately she wanted Boris to arrive, she always felt safe when the big man was around. He was like a second father to her, playing chess or cards with her and chauffeuring her around when she visited her one and only friend on the island.

The noise of the shower stopped and other noises could be heard from the kitchen as Magda started to prepare the breakfast.

Leaving her room Nadezhda walked quietly along the corridor towards the toilet. Next door to it the bathroom door stood open, and as she passed, she glanced in to see Takkal with just a towel round his waist standing at the washbasin shaving, a pistol placed on the glass shelf beneath the mirror. Stood with his head bent over to one side, the right side of his neck was fully exposed revealing the scars inflicted by Nadezhda's late sister, Rozalina. Seeing these, Nadezhda froze, not realising at first why, then realisation dawned, and she gasped, the sound attracting Takkal who, turning quickly, recognised the expression of fear on the young girl's face for what it was. Before he could move, she was gone, running terrified along the corridor, her bare feet slipping and sliding on the polished granite floor. Behind her, she heard the double click she knew so well, of a magazine being attached to a gun; with only three more paces to go the first shot rang out, a deafening sound in the confines of the corridor. She felt the bullet tug at her billowing dressing gown before it smashed the glass in the cabinet where the corridor turned towards her father's room. Trying to slow down, as she approached the turn, her feet went from under her as Takkal squeezed off the second round and watched as her body slammed into the base of the cabinet bringing it down over the top of her.

Takkal had only walked two paces, the pistol held out in front of him, his eyes searching the corridor ahead, behind him Magda let out a terrified scream as a pistol appeared from around the corner where the girl lay trapped, held by Kazakov, who fired three times, blind, missing Takkal, but hitting Magda in the shoulder knocking her backwards into the side of the refrigerator. Thinking that he had hit the gunman, Kazakov put his head round the corner to die instantly from Takkal's third shot.

Abdelmalek Takkal had crouched down and waited, the instant he had seen the barrel of Kazakov's gun appear he had accurately guessed what Kazakov would do next. It had taken only a small adjustment of aim when the man's head appeared, to rid himself of the threat. Slowly he stood and cautiously moved towards Nadezhda's body that lay, still, beneath the cabinet. Blood from her cut foot had formed a small pool on the floor, but that was the only apparent injury to the girl. It was with some sadness that he started to raise the gun again to finish the execution, only to hear a man's voice shout, "Neht!", before dying.

Boris kicked the gun away from the apparently lifeless body of Takkal, then felt for a pulse, just in case. Moving down the corridor it became obvious that there was no need to check and see if Kazakov was alive, nobody survives with the back of their head missing. The blooded foot of Nadezhda sticking out from under the cabinet twitched and the big man carefully lifted the piece of furniture off her.

Shielding her from the sight of her father, he very gently moved her arms and then her legs.

"Where do you hurt?" he asked.

Painfully she pointed to her head and ribcage, and then her bleeding foot. Not until she had seen a doctor would it be revealed that the second bullet had grazed the girl's right breast leaving a physical scar to add to the mental scars that she would carry for the rest of her life. Boris nodded, then taking off his shirt, quickly turned and covered her father's head and body with it. Looking back at the girl he saw she was crying her heart out, her eyes fixed on her father's body slumped against the wall, his legs crossed in an improbable pose across the floor.

Having slept in the cellar of the derelict house until first light, Boris had been anxious to get to his post, guarding Kazakov and his young daughter. He had arrived in the truck as Takkal was finishing his shower, and after looking round the outside of the property had stepped into the kitchen as Magda screamed, then fell back wounded to hit the refrigerator with a resounding crash. As the shooting appeared to stop, he had ventured a glance along the corridor to witness Takkal raising his pistol at the fallen body of Nadezhda.

Now he faced the task of protecting the poor child, as he realised that, with the death of her sister, and her mother dying a year later from cancer, he and Magda were the only adults left in the young teenager's life.

*

Vaughan breakfasted with Al Djebbar and the leaders of the four governmental delegations. The occasion was one of the most buoyant and positive that Vaughan had attended for many years, marred only by news of further unrest in Libya. Al Djebbar also insisted that Vaughan was present at ten o'clock when the delegates assembled in the foyer ready to board the coaches for the airport.

"Your plane was given clearance to land then?"

"Yes, Ian, my friend, I think the Portuguese Army will be relieved to see the back of us," said Walid al Djebbar giving Vaughan the traditional farewell embrace. Then the man's face became serious, but also holding an expression of deep sincerity. "Ian, I owe you my life twofold. That is a debt that can never be fully repaid, but please understand and believe, that if ever you are in need, I will provide, if you are ever in danger, I will do everything in my power to protect you. Here is my personal mobile phone number; there are only ten people that know it, Charles being one. Do not hesitate to call either for help, or in friendship."

Vaughan accepted the sheet of hotel notepaper with the number written on it, then tearing a page from his own notebook, wrote his personal phone number down and handed it to Al Djebbar. "True friendship is a two way thing," he said, "I hope that we never have to call in need, but only to discuss the weather, the quality of the wine, and the peace of the world around us."

Vaughan felt strangely saddened as the coach pulled away carrying this charismatic leader that he felt he could really call a friend. He looked around as the other coaches moved off carrying the support staff for the various delegations, waved away by staff of the hotel who had, justifiably, earned some generous tips. Beyond them Vaughan noticed Staunton looking on, his face set in what appeared to be its normal glower.

"When do we take this voyage?"

Vaughan spun round to find Lieutenant Jacome standing behind him. "Oh yes, well as soon as I have thrown my things back into my bag and checked out. Give me twenty minutes and I'll meet you here." *Brilliant, Lieutenant, I was wondering how I could escape the interrogation of Staunton and this Jack Vale character. 'Total Cover' MD he may be, but he doesn't have the right to quiz me or anyone else come to that.*

Half an hour later the two were travelling in an army jeep at a more moderate speed, this time driven by Lieutenant Jacome, leaving Murphy wondering how he could explain Vaughan's absence to his boss and the two CIA men travelling with him.

"Can we see if Ms de Lima wishes to join us?" shouted Vaughan, over the noise of the jeep as they approached the road junction that would eventually lead them up to the Consul's residence.

"Si, I mean, yes, okay," replied the lieutenant. "Please you call me Ramiro, it seem more, how you say, suitable, if we are to spend time together. Also not good for Senhora de Lima to hear lieutenant this and lieutenant that all the time eh?"

"All right, Lieutenant, Ramiro it is. You call me Ian."

Vaughan was surprised by the immediate acceptance of his invitation by Amelia, until she said with some bitterness, "If I at sea on your boat, that horrible colonel cannot bully me into saying things that are not true."

Vaughan looked at her steadily, "And I thought that you were pleased to be in my company."

She looked back unsmiling. "Why did you go off to that hotel, when you knew what had been discovered. It was nothing to do with the book you are writing."

Here we go again, more lies to tell, but must act the part making the script up as I go. "Amelia I had no idea that Mrs Bevington was going to persuade you to go and tell all you know to the army. However, I personally think that she did the right thing. Had you stayed hiding at her home it would have made you look much more guilty." Vaughan could see that Amelia was about to protest when Susanne Bevington re-entered the lounge.

"Also Walid al Djebbar and I are old friends, who do not have the opportunity to see each other and talk face to face very often nowadays," Vaughan added.

"It was a miracle that you were there," interjected Mrs Bevington firmly. "Had you not pushed him out of the way, as you did, the assassin would have succeeded in killing him."

Amelia gasped. "They tried to assassinate your friend?"

"I'll tell you all about it and him later," replied Vaughan, bending to pick up her bag. "Come on, otherwise it will be nightfall before we set off." *Thank you, Mrs Bevington, that was a very timely interruption.*

Amelia glared at him, then turned and left the room together with Susanne Bevington.

"If it is any consolation, the army hauled me in for questioning yesterday as well," Vaughan said, ten minutes later, as they walked towards the jeep. "For my pains, and according to Colonel Castelo Lopes, my protection, we have the company of Lieutenant Ramiro Jacome."

Amelia stopped in her tracks, frowning.

"Before you start protesting, let me tell you that Ramiro is a nice guy and has been told to smooth our way through army blockades and checkpoints, so be nice to him please."

Still pouting and frowning, Amelia started walking again. Her greeting with the lieutenant, though not cheerfully friendly, was, however, polite, though she said little on the journey to the marina, instead, looking at Vaughan strangely, as if she were trying to understand something about him. Vaughan meantime kept the conversation going by explaining his plans, thought up on the spur of the moment, for the sailing trip.

Vaughan felt a great sense of relief as they cast off and he nudged the engine into gear, slowly motoring the yacht out of the marina into the main harbour and turning east. The maritime police and customs rib manned now by army personnel approached, then recognising Lieutenant Jacome, waved them past.

Once clear of the harbour wall Vaughan turned the yacht into the wind.

"Amelia, can you keep her on this course while I hoist the mainsail?"

She looked nervous but took hold of the tiller and after a couple of minor course deviations settled the yacht accurately to windward. By the time Vaughan snapped the clutches home, securing the main halyard, they were almost far enough offshore to be out of the sea breeze zone and into an almost windless Atlantic.

"Okay, I'll take her now," said Vaughan, hurriedly taking the tiller from her and changing course. "We'll set the foresail, then we can cut the engine. Ramiro, you take hold of that rope and put three clockwise turns around that winch. The proper name for that rope, by the way, is a sheet."

Ramiro gave Vaughan a quick glance to check whether he was joking then looked back at the sheet and frowned.

"These names, such as sheet, halyard, line, cable and warp, help the listener identify the order given in a high wind, when maybe only part of the word is heard," explained Vaughan. "Most of them are traditional, but all save time by replacing phrases like 'the thinner one fourth from the left', or 'the one with the knot in the end'."

Ramiro shook his head, rapidly becoming aware that there was a lot he may have to learn whilst keeping an eye on this Englishman.

"Okay, Ramiro, I have freed off the reefing line, now you pull on that sheet until I tell you to stop."

As Ramiro hauled on the sheet Vaughan turned the yacht into the wind again making it easier for Ramiro to unroll the jib fully.

"Okay, that's fine, keep hold of the sheet for a moment while I get us back on course."

As the wind filled both main and foresail Vaughan studied their shape and taking out a winch handle from its bulkhead box, wound the foresail sheet two winch turns tighter taking out a minor flutter at the head of the sail.

"Okay, now wrap the loose end of the sheet once round that cleat and then make a figure of eight over the cleat horns; that's it, magic."

During the next ten minutes or so Vaughan coached Amelia in steering a compass course then hurried below to put the kettle on for some coffee.

As they sipped their coffee, Vaughan elaborated on his story regarding the friendship with Al Djebbar and gave them a brief description of the assassination attempts on the man, leaving both Amelia and Ramiro almost under the impression that he had merely been a spectator to the events.

"But it was you who saved his life by pushing him, according to Susanne. She said it was a miracle that you were there," said Amelia, frowning at Vaughan. "Why do you make it sound as if it were just part of the crowd jostling?"

"Well it really was the crowd and I…"

"No, no no no," Amelia interrupted loudly.

Ramiro Jacome, who was now steering the yacht, looked up at her in surprise.

"You did the same when you saved Zeferino's life a long way out to sea," said Amelia, a cunning smile now on her face. "Susanne told me in great detail, whilst I was packing my things, what she saw on the television news broadcast."

"Well, er…"

"Well, er, nothing. Again you are a hero and very brave to do what you did. Two men were killed, it could well have been you that stepped in the way of a bullet." Her smile had gone now to be replaced by a look of fear and caring. "Who would have been able to protect me then, eh. Alone as a widow, with a son, I can battle through daily life and run a business, but I cannot, alone, defeat a man so powerful as Colonel Castelo Lopes, who refuses to believe that I knew nothing of my uncle's traitorous activities. You are the only person I can turn to for help. Please, I need you to be a hero again. My hero!"

Whether Lieutenant Ramiro Jacome, looking on, believed her, as she burst into tears, or whether he thought it to be just a clever act, as she stood in the middle of the cockpit looking at Vaughan with an expression of absolute desperation on her face, was irrelevant. Vaughan knew that she was innocent, but helping her prove it could well place him at odds with his new bosses. Staunton definitely would cause problems, especially after Vaughan's attitude to him the previous evening. *Damn, damn, damn. Why didn't I play the grovelling sycophant, why do I always have to take a verbal swing at these bullying prat types? Now I've probably got to condemn Amelia to a prison sentence just to save the British political face.*

Reaching out he took her in his arms. "It's all right, Amelia, it's all right. I'll stay as long as I can to help you."

She clung to him for several minutes sobbing before he eased her arms from around his chest and sat her down onto the cockpit's starboard bench, putting a handkerchief into her hands. "Now dry those tears and I will make some tea."

She screamed. "Aaaaaaah! I don't want tea! I want my life back! I want my uncle in prison for the rest of his miserable life! I want the army off the streets! I want my beautiful, peaceful island back again!"

Both men were shaken by her strength of feeling. It was Vaughan who moved first, sliding along the portside bench towards the stern. "I'll take over here," he said, taking the tiller. "Can you open that locker and take out the fenders and the four ropes hanging on the brackets on the forward end." Vaughan adjusted their course, and then attached the autohelm to the tiller. "I'll just put the fenders down and get the lines sorted ready for going alongside."

Ramiro looked at him solemnly and nodding in the direction of Amelia, slowly and sadly shook his head. Vaughan put a finger to his lips, suggesting to Ramiro to be quiet and let her recover peacefully.

When he returned to the cockpit Vaughan checked their course then went below to radio the marina. Back on deck he started the engine and, turning the yacht up into the wind, hurriedly hauled in the foresail and dropped the mainsail.

"According to the marina office, a yacht left from the visitors' pontoon three days ago, so we are in luck. Had they not left, we would have had to sail back to Funchal."

Again it was the presence of the lieutenant that allowed them through the entrance to Quinta do Lorde marina and twenty minutes later they were alongside the pontoon with Vaughan checking the lines and fender heights. The marina, situated near the eastern tip of the island was a good starting point for Vaughan's further research. It was also an ideal starting point for a day sail taking in almost a complete circumnavigation of the island.

Amelia had gone below and shut herself in the forward cabin, leaving Ramiro feeling uncomfortable and in the way of two people who obviously had feelings for each other. The colonel had told him that he had suspicions about Vaughan and his purpose on the island, but so far Vaughan had done nothing that would indicate he was anything other than a writer who had made some important friends in his life.

"Ian," Ramiro said, walking along the side deck and jumping down onto the pontoon. "We need some wine for our meal this evening, I will see what I can purchase."

"Have a look at the restaurant maybe we should… no. No you're right we had better eat here, I doubt if Amelia is up for an evening out," replied Vaughan, turning his thoughts towards the choice of what to cook.

The meal was a subdued affair with no one able to make a start on conversation. Vaughan found it easier to immediately start the washing up as soon as the meal was finished, detailing Ramiro to go to the marina office and pay for the night's stay.

"I am so sorry," Amelia said, suddenly breaking the silence. "You have probably saved my country from fascism, or such unrest that people are injured, and all I can do is cry because my own little comfortable world is upset."

Vaughan picked up her untouched glass of wine and handed it to her then, reaching across to his own glass, refilled it. "You have been through a lot, what with your uncle's activities and young Zeferino…"

"Oh my God, I forgot to phone the hospital today," she said, rushing towards the forward cabin to get her phone.

The call lasted almost half an hour, but when she returned she obviously was happy with the news received. "They say he has made a good progress, but they still think he should stay some more time with them."

Vaughan felt strangely relieved by the news. *Get a grip, you fool. You will be leaving in a day or two. She has enough problems without you making unwelcome advances.*

"Can I stay with you?" she asked, her expression pleading him to accept.

"Yes, of course, but it won't be a lot of fun. I really have a lot of work to do to get back onto my schedule," replied Vaughan. *That stamps out the territory now for the time frame.* "I'm due in the Canaries at the end of next week."

"That is all right, maybe I can help you. What I cannot do is return to my apartment. Well not until that man is captured and imprisoned."

Um, message received and understood, I think. "Did you mention your fears about him being a murderer, when you were questioned by the colonel?"

She sipped her wine. "Yes, I tell him everything, even about you searching for the shirt and jacket."

Thank you, Amelia, I'm sure that helped a great deal. Though thinking about it, maybe it did help. If you told the tale in the sequence that events took place it would appear to the Colonel that I was at first only concerned about the murder suspicions.

"Did you explain everything in the order in which it happened?"

"Well not at first, but he say he could not understand, and insisted I go through everything exactly the way it happened," Amelia replied, nodding her head as if she were on a plodding walk. "Susanne she is nice lady, and she helped me a great deal."

Footsteps sounded on the side deck announcing the return of Ramiro.

You've been a long time young man. Reporting to the colonel no doubt. "Everything all right?" asked Vaughan, standing to let Ramiro pass.

"Yes, they say tomorrow and next day good sailing weather with wind not so strong on north side of island," said Ramiro, studying Amelia's face and receiving a half-hearted smile.

"That's good, it will make our voyage more comfortable. The waves that side of the island, and the swell, are impressive enough without a strong wind behind them."

During the course of a few games of cards they drank the second of the two bottles Ramiro had purchased at which point Vaughan suggested that they turn in for the night. The card games had distracted Amelia from her worries and she appeared to be returning to her former vivacious self.

Amelia occupying the forward cabin and Vaughan the quarter berth, it left Ramiro only the main cabin porthand settee berth, a location almost like that of a chaperon Vaughan thought, as he slid into his sleeping bag. The night was hot and by morning he lay on top of his bedding rather than in it. By seven o'clock he was wide awake, had cleared the heads and was starting to prepare breakfast before either Ramiro or Amelia roused.

*

Two hours earlier, Olavo Esteves had slipped past the dozing army sergeant and corporal, both sat in a hire car overlooking Amelia's apartment, entered the porch and tapping in the security code, had made his way stealthily up the stairs. Once inside the apartment he raided the fridge and food cupboard to satisfy his now ravenous hunger. Idly he wondered where his niece was and how he should handle things when she returned. Somehow he did not believe that she would willingly co-operate in getting him out of the country.

*

Seven o'clock was also the time when Al Bashir was woken in his prison cell by the sound of an enamel plate of food being loaded into the serving hatch by the cell door.

His right eye was still closed and swollen and any movement of his rib cage still caused him to moan in agony. Seeing only with his left eye he surveyed the bruising on his arms and legs careful not to make any sudden movements. A minion from the Moroccan Directorate of Territorial Surveillance had handed over the confessions of Al Bashir and Mohammed el Kamal at the airport, and told the army where they were detained in the hotel. When the storeroom door was opened an hour later the two officers were shaken by what they found; Abdul el Najid did not like extremists of any religious order and neither did he like those who stubbornly refused to answer his questions. In the end he had the complete story and the names of those who had sheltered and assisted the, would be, assassins.

After some concern amongst the Portuguese officials in Funchal and Lisbon as to what should happen to these two undoubted criminals, it was discovered that the United States was keen to receive them in connection with action against American Forces in Afghanistan. The problem now was one of national pride concerning Portuguese legal sovereignty. This however was tempered by the fact that both prisoners had been brutally tortured whilst on Portuguese soil, hastening the decision to allow extradition.

CHAPTER 14

THE SMEAR CAMPAIGN

To Vaughan's surprise Patrick Murphy was standing on the marina sea wall ready to take the yacht lines as he edged the boat stern first between two other yachts. After leaving Quinta do Lorde marina they had sailed east then along the north coast and round the island to spend the second night at Calheta. In the morning, after an early breakfast they completed the research trip around the island by calling in at Cámara de Lobos on their way back to Funchal.

Behind Patrick stood a tall tough looking man Vaughan took to be Jack Vale.

"I want a word with you, Vaughan." The man's tone suggested that there were no other options available. "Get rid of your guests, I ain't got all day."

"That means that we are both busy men, because I don't have any time at all," replied Vaughan.

Vale's expression changed from cold stare to ice cold menace. "I am Jack Vale CEO of 'Total Cover Incorporated', you were involved in the assassination attempt on this Ayerab guy Al Djebbar. What the hell…"

Vaughan had held up his hand. "Come and see me on Thursday, at around ten o'clock, I'll make some time available for you then," he said, as he fed a line through the port quarter fairlead and made the end off around the adjacent cleat.

The icy expression changed again to anger then frustrated fury as Vaughan turned away and went below to the chart table to finish writing up the log and his notes for the book.

"Do you want me to fix the, er, platform for us to get off?"

"Good God, no, Ramiro, that will encourage those men to come on board."

"You really not going to talk with them?"

"No, I am really not going to talk to them, today or tomorrow, and unless Senhor Vale improves his manners I won't talk to him on Thursday either."

Obviously amused by the incident Amelia came and knelt on the starboard settee looking affectionately across the chart table at Vaughan. A movement on the quayside made her look up through the companionway hatch at the two men still standing looking at the yacht.

"Senhor Vale is measuring the gap between the quay and this boat to judge whether he can step over without falling into the water."

Vaughan leapt up and turning to glare at Vale said firmly, "Don't even think about it."

Vale glared back. "I ain't used to bein' kept waitin' Vaughan."

"Really, well get used to it now."

Several seconds passed as the two men held each other's gaze. *You're not going to win, Vale, not now and not on Thursday; you will be told only the cover story, nothing else.* Then Vale turned, and muttering something to Murphy, strode away.

"That wasn't a good start," said Murphy from the quayside, shaking his head.

"Don't tell me, tell your boss," replied Vaughan, pleasantly.

Ramiro stood looking awkwardly about trying to find something to do without getting in the way of Vaughan, who he suspected was not in the best of moods after the encounter with the American Senhor Vale. Amelia, understanding his dilemma, pointed to the cabin table. "Ramiro, you set the places for a meal, then go to shop for some wine. We need two bottles of red and one of white, okay? I will cook tonight's meal for us."

Saluting her Ramiro replied, with a wide smile, "Immediately madam! As you command!"

In five minutes Ramiro had fled, having laid the table and slotted the boarding platform in place, leaving Amelia and Vaughan alone together for the first time since the evening at Quinta do Lorde marina. In the two intervening days she had relaxed a little, and with the news that Zeferino would be ready to leave hospital the next day, she had brightened considerably.

Finishing the last of his notes and stowing the chart away Vaughan sat staring into the middle distance, his thoughts now on how to deal with Staunton. *Obviously you are not a supporter of Commodore Campbell and I suspect that you are after his job. That's politics way above my pay scale, but the chances are that it will be me that is used to damage Campbell's reputation. I need a word with Lieutenant Heathcote, but will she be prepared to give me any advice?*

"Ian, can you unscrew this for me?"

Vaughan only half heard Amelia's request. "Sorry what did you say?"

"I said, can you unscrew this for me?" she repeated, holding up a jar of hollandaise sauce.

"Oh sure," he replied, standing and taking the jar from her. "There we are, one opened jar."

He placed it on the galley worktop alongside her and was about to turn back to the chart table when she slid her arms around him. "Let me hug you," she said, holding him tightly, her head laid on his chest. "I have been horrible to you since that awful night at my apartment, and you have been so kind to me."

Vaughan, taken by surprise, was not sure what to do, settling for lightly placing his arms around her. *Now where do we go from here I wonder?* His question was immediately answered by her standing on tiptoe and kissing him tenderly then firmly then tenderly again on the lips. "Life is too short to miss a moment of our time together," she said quietly as she stared intently into his eyes, the message clear.

Before Vaughan could respond he heard Ramiro call from the quayside. "Ian, the colonel needs to speak with you urgently. He is sending a car for you."

Amelia's arms dropped to her side and she stamped her foot. "Why does he not leave us alone, eh? Why always questions, questions and more questions."

"He only wants to speak with Ian."

"You had better go, I suppose," she said looking sadly up at him.

"You're not going to tell him to wait until Thursday then?" Vaughan asked, smiling down at her. She went to move towards the companionway. "No no, I had better go. Upsetting an arrogant American is one thing; annoying a Portuguese Army Colonel is something else."

"I wait here for you," she said, turning away and going forward to her sleeping quarters and closing the door.

Vaughan stared after her. *Oh, shit, she's going to have to know. The only alternative is to just walk away leaving her thinking what, that I don't find her attractive, that, that. Oh what the hell do women think?*

To Vaughan's surprise the colonel was sitting in the back seat of the Mercedes staff car, and as soon as Vaughan had got in beside him and closed the door he ordered the driver to proceed.

"Your voyage was successful, Mr Vaughan?"

"Yes it was. Viewed from the sea this island has one of the most dramatic coastlines in the world; the north coast particularly.

"That is where we are heading now, a place called Boaventura."

"What is there that is so interesting as to require that I accompany you?" asked Vaughan.

"Two bodies," replied the colonel. "I think you will be able to confirm their identities for me."

"Really? I wouldn't have thought so. You have no idea yourselves, I mean they did not have any identification?"

"No, nothing."

Vaughan raised his eyebrows but said nothing, instead, turning his head to admire the neatly decorated houses either side of the tortuous road leading out of town.

"Lieutenant Jacome tells me that you have written many words about this island and its coastline."

"That is why I am here," replied Vaughan. "Those 'many words' will of course have to be reduced considerably in number before my editor takes his red pencil to them. So they will probably end up as a couple of paragraphs between pictures and charts."

"That I think would be a great pity."

Vaughan shrugged his shoulders. "Well let me just say that is what normally happens."

To get to Boaventura from Funchal involves driving round, rather than over, the central mountainous region of the island, so it was some two hours later that the Mercedes powered up the steep driveway to the house Abdelmalek Takkal had rented. Parked outside were two police cars and a hearse plus an unmarked car.

Inside Vaughan quickly grabbed a handkerchief from his pocket and held it over his mouth and nose to try and reduce the stench of death. At the end of the main corridor lay the two bodies; one slumped with his back against the wall. At a nod from the colonel a man in a set of pathologist's white overalls rolled the other body, that of Takkal, over, so that Vaughan could see his face.

Vaughan needed no more than a glance before nodding at the colonel and walking as quickly as he could out of the building. In the fresh air he breathed in deeply as he lent against the side of the colonel's car.

"Who were they?"

"The one with the back of his head blown away sat against the wall is a Russian named Sarkis Kazakov. He was pointed out to me when I paid a short visit to Annabel's in Funchal. Apparently he was a regular there. The other man was with him, reluctantly I think, because he was trying everything he knew not to be seen. I thought that probably he was frightened that someone would recognise him and tell his wife."

"You apparently saw him on the morning of the assassination." Vaughan was impressed, the colonel had obviously been very busy. "You mentioned to one of the policemen that you thought it was him who was the assassin."

Vaughan nodded.

"Is that a yes?" the colonel asked firmly.

"Yes, I am sure that is the man I saw running from the box hide." *There's no point in playing games but that is all I'm going to tell you, Colonel.*

"Your writing suggests that you have an amazing eye for detail. That is supported by your ability to recognise a man from just the briefest of sightings. Tell me why is my brain telling me that you are not what you say you are."

Vaughan shrugged his shoulders. "I don't know. Can we go now? Amelia was planning on cooking dinner for us, well for Lieutenant Jacome and I." Then after a few moments pause Vaughan asked, "When are you going to let me get on with my job? I'm finished here and my publishers will be straining at the leash for the first batch of writing. All this is taking me away from what I am paid to do, and I need the money."

"If you let me have your manuscript I will personally ensure that it is couriered to your publisher. Just let me know when it is ready."

"But I also need to move on, down to the Canaries."

"I am sure that we will have this man Esteves very soon, so please be patient a little longer."

On the return journey Vaughan learnt that the colonel was a horseman who in his youth had competed at European level. Though not winning any major cups or medals he had numerous awards from secondary events. His two sons, also good horsemen, had followed their father into the army and had served in Bosnia and Angola.

It was dark and eerily quiet as Vaughan approached his yacht. The town, normally abuzz with activity, was silent. A man stood in the shadows of a small Portakabin at the end of the marina sea wall. Vaughan had seen him step back out of the glow of security lights from the empty bar restaurant on the opposite pier, as he was passing a German flagged, British built yacht moored against the eastern sea wall. Vaughan was just about to step onto his yacht's boarding platform when he heard a harsh whisper.

"Vaughan."

"Who is it?"

"Staunton, who else did you think it was?"

Vaughan contemplated a witty response but decided against it, and strolled over to where Staunton hid.

"What was the military wanting to know?"

"Two bodies were found shot at a house in a place called Boaventura on the north of the island. The colonel thought that I could confirm their identities."

"You couldn't of course."

Vaughan looked up surprised. "I did actually. One was Sarkis Kazakov and the other was the assassin who tried to take out Walid al Djebbar."

"What the hell are you doing spraying information like that about? You're in too deep here, I'm ordering you back to London on the next available flight."

"No can do, I have a minder on board in the form of Lieutenant Jacome and orders from Colonel Castelo Lopes not to leave the island. If I even try to leave via the airport or ferries I will be arrested and my cover blown, and British Intelligence accused of breaking the European agreement of non involvement in the North African Conference."

"Rubbish!"

"Fact! So if you will excuse me I will go aboard before the soldier, standing across the marina there, gets suspicious," replied Vaughan, equally curtly. "By the way, you are breaking curfew. If they see you, you will be shot."

Without waiting for a response, Vaughan turned on his heels and walked back to the yacht whistling as he boarded it, leaving a fuming, frustrated, and now slightly fearful, Staunton, unable to break cover for fear of being spotted by the soldier.

*

"Are you sure that you are doing the right thing, Susanne? That arrogant whelp Staunton could make a lot of trouble for you, for us even."

"I can't sit here and watch as he destroys Ian Vaughan like this. I've read his reports they are stuffed full of misleading information regarding Vaughan's work here. The slant he has put upon Vaughan's relationship with Amelia suggests that until the last minute Vaughan had totally ignored his mission and spent his time pursuing a pretty woman; I cannot let that go unchallenged."

"Vaughan struck me as being more than capable of looking after himself, and what about the reports by Arthur Claremont. He was very impressed with Vaughan's ability to plant a microphone in this chap Al Djebbar's hotel room."

"Henry," replied Susanne Bevington, with a note of resignation in her voice. "You know I told you that something fishy was going on when Staunton insisted on reviewing Arthur's reports before they were sent. That nonsense about the procedures being changed since Arthur retired. Well, I've just been back through the 'reports sent' file and am sure that Arthur's reports have been edited."

Henry Bevington gasped. "Are you sure? You're not just imagining these things because Staunton has got to you, annoyed you, you know."

"He's been very clever, Henry. Where I am sure Arthur referred to Vaughan by name in that report, it now just mentions 'our man inside' as if to suggest that Arthur had got one of the hotel staff to plant the device."

Susanne Bevington slumped down onto the lounge settee. "Oh God Henry, I can cope with the odd tourist losing their passport and money, I can even cope with those stupid people who get themselves arrested for drug offences and then think we are there to wave a magic wand and get them off, but I am just floundering in this cesspool they call intelligence services work."

Henry sat down beside her and put his arm around her shoulders pulling her close to him. "There, there, come here, we will sit down together and work through the reports to see what this nasty piece of work has been up to. That is if I'm allowed to look."

"That is very sweet of you, darling, but I am afraid you cannot look. I have to do this on my own. In fact I've probably told you too much already."

"I overheard Vaughan say that he had great respect for someone called Heathfield or Heathcliffe," said Henry, relaxing his hold on his wife.

"I think you mean Lieutenant Heathcote. Yes, Henry, you're brilliant. I will work on these reports until I am confident that I know what Staunton's game is then I will call her in the morning. Thank you, Henry, thank you." Turning she gave Henry a big kiss before pulling away and standing. "Would you mind washing up the tea things? I have a lot of work to do."

It was three o'clock the following morning before an exhausted Susanne Bevington slid into bed and snuggled up against a quietly snoring Henry. Even then sleep eluded her for the next hour, her mind roaming through the reports she had reviewed. She knew that, before doing anything else, she must reinforce the fact that the break in Vaughan's reporting procedure was due to the close surveillance of Lieutenant Jacome, and Vaughan's need to continue to support his cover story until the Portuguese Army allowed him to leave. Olavo Esteves was still on the run, and she doubted that Vaughan would be released from virtual house arrest until the man was caught. If London wanted to blow Vaughan's cover and expose the British Government to another embarrassing spat with Europe then it was up to them.

*

340

Some two kilometres south-east of the small town of Penha Garcia on mainland Portugal, Dr Franco Gonzales had removed the bandages from the left arm of Yvonne Alves. "I think it is only a cracked bone and not a dislocated break; there is much bruising as you can see, but I think if we improve the splint support, your arm will heal in a few weeks."

A tear ran down her cheeks, washing a clean line through the grey dust that had settled in a thin layer over her face. The early morning sunlight shining through the open loft shutter of the barn highlighted the tiredness and anxiety on her still beautiful face.

"I cannot believe that Diago and the others were captured so easily. Why was my stupid husband not there before that jumped-up jockey, Castelo Lopes, and his little army?"

"Your husband gave his life for the cause," replied Gonzales, surprised and a little shaken by her bitterness.

"Only because again he was too late, too slow, too stupid."

The transfer from the lorry to the cars had gone smoothly with each car leaving for the marina at Peniche on the coast at fifteen minute intervals as planned. The only difference being that due to Yvonne's arm needing attention, Gonzales and she had been the last to leave the woodland area where the cars and their drivers had been waiting in hiding. It was the further delay while they stopped for fuel at a petrol station on Peniche's Avenid do Porto de Pesca that saved them from being arrested along with the others.

Sergeant Sousa, the man in charge of the second roadblock had decided to act even as the lorry arrived at the farm near Serra d'El-Rei. He felt sure the dog had found something, and it had not failed them in the past; also something had been wrong with the inside of that trailer, then, it had struck him what it was. The wide battens running along the inside of the bodywork, used to tie loads in position, had been freshly sawn where they butted

341

against the front panel. There had been a false compartment obviously big enough to hide say four, five people but not so big as to be obvious in such a long trailer. Kicking himself for not recognising it straight away, Sousa had hurriedly contacted his Inspector and then the police authorities in Peniche.

Leaving the petrol station Yvonne Alves and Gonzales had been driven along Peniche's, Avenid do Mar, which leads down to the entrance of the marina, where a large 'gin palace' of a motor cruiser was waiting ready to take them north to the Spanish coast. The traffic had been heavy and the slow progress had allowed Yvonne to see two large police vans parked in haste, with rear doors open wide, blocking a side street; and then a sight she knew well, the unmarked police car. Three of them in fact, parked at intervals at the side of the road. Instructing the driver to keep going past the marina and head out of town saved her and Gonzales from being caught in the ambush.

On leaving them at the remote barn, hidden from the road by an orange plantation, the driver had gone into the town to buy them food and some medical items requested by Dr Gonzales. Enjoying a meal at a café near to the supermarket he had seen the television reports of the arrests at Peniche and the police picture of Yvonne Alves who was now wanted for evading arrest. As he reported his findings to Yvonne and the doctor, she had shown no emotion and had just sat slowly shaking her head. Now, three days later, and alone with Gonzales she watched, as he re-bandaged and splinted her arm, idly wondering how they could possibly complete their escape.

*

Commodore Alec Campbell stood staring blindly out of his office window as the rain, driven by a strong westerly wind, harried scurrying office workers as they battled over the puddled pavements of Vauxhall Bridge. His whole attention was focused on what he had just read in a damning report from Sir Andrew Averrille regarding Vaughan's activities connected with the Funchal mission. After what he had seen immediately following the assassination attempt and what the British Consul in Madeira had reported, Sir Andrew's report was hard to believe. Had he, Alec Campbell, personally misjudged Vaughan's abilities? This should have been an easy assignment, ignoring of course the assassination attempt, but even there, Vaughan's amazing assessment and reactions had been beyond the intended remit of his operational duties. The image of Vaughan shooting the suicide bomber still shocked the Commodore.

There was also this business with the niece of Esteves, who was apparently one of the attempted coup leaders; how on earth did Vaughan get involved in that? Agreed he did exactly the right thing in routing the report the way he did, but why get involved in the first place. Yes the PM was over the moon regarding points scored and the relationship with Portugal strengthened, but by being involved, it had brought Vaughan into the scrutiny of the Portuguese Army senior ranks.

Sir Andrew was calling it a fiasco that was in danger of exposing the British Government and its intelligence services, as interfering in an event that European Governments had agreed not to involve themselves in.

That said, Vaughan had twice saved the life of an inspired North African leader in as many minutes and prevented a major disturbance in the European political order by effectively preventing a coup, which would have undoubtedly destabilised the whole of the European economy, including Britain's.

The Commodore turned to his desk and pressed a button on his intercom. "Good morning, sir," responded Lieutenant Heathcote, in her normal bright form.

"Are you busy?"

The question, if overheard by someone in Heathcote's office, would be taken at face value by the listener, but to Lieutenant Penny Heathcote it meant, 'are you alone and can you speak'.

"No, sir, how can I help?"

"Have we had any reports from Vaughan in the last couple of days?"

"No, sir, but strangely enough there was a report waiting for me from Mrs Bevington in Madeira, at pains to point out that Vaughan was still being closely attended by a Lieutenant Jacome on the orders of Colonel Castelo Lopes," replied Heathcote. "The report was sent at 0245 hours this morning with a request that I phone her when I have a moment, as she put it."

"That is very interesting. Has anyone else seen this report?"

"No, sir, I managed to beat Sub-Lieutenant Alice Morgan to it today. Normally she has taken them down and sorted them by the time I make it to the communications room."

"Trying hard to impress?"

"Yes, sir, too hard."

"Umm, thank you, Lieutenant. Make sure you record your conversation with Mrs Bevington, I would like to listen to it."

"Yes, sir, is that all, sir?"

"For the moment yes, thank you, Lieutenant."

Campbell sat back in his chair. What was the link between Sub-Lieutenant Alice Morgan, Staunton and Sir Andrew Averrille? Where had he seen her before?

Leaping to his feet, Campbell left his office, telling his secretary that he would be spending the rest of the day at his office in DELCO, and to have all calls put through there. He needed his special team close, those that he had absolute faith in, and he also needed the distance from which to view the field of battle. This was not about Vaughan; it was his own future that was at stake.

*

"Why are you still following Ian and me around, eh? Why you not with the others searching for that horrible man Olavo Esteves? We are not the problem, he is."

Amelia glared across the cabin table at Lieutenant Jacome, a mug of coffee in her hands.

"Those are my orders, Amelia, I must obey orders. I know I am a nuisance to you both by being here, but I have no choice, so please understand," Jacome replied, looking and sounding very sincere.

Vaughan liked the young lieutenant, totally unsuited for a military career maybe, but a nice guy who had done his best to do his job without being obstructive or too intrusive.

"Let it go, Amelia, Ramiro has no choice. Your uncle can't hide for long with so many people out there asking questions," interjected Vaughan, fearing that Amelia would fly into one of her fury sessions.

She pouted and looked away. Vaughan could tell that she was close to tears. The strain of her uncle's involvement and the implication that relationship had, were bearing down hard on her. *If only I could tell the colonel of the link between Esteves and his gang and Reshetnikov, but I can't without bringing greater suspicion down on me. If London throws the switch then maybe I could.*

"You look very worried, Ian, what is troubling you?" asked Ramiro.

"Oh it is nothing of major importance. It's just that my work here is now complete and I am sure that my publisher will be getting restless. They expected this project to be done and dusted in six months and I still have a hell of a lot of sailing and research to do," replied Vaughan. "Unlike you, I get paid on results, and I still owe money on this boat." Vaughan was confident that the colonel did not have the knowledge or resources to research any personal lending that Vaughan might have. So the lie about owing money on the boat was reasonably safe.

"Did you mention this to the colonel?"

"Yes, but he is still stubbornly convinced that I cannot leave until this idiot Esteves is found. Why, God only knows. Frankly I am just sick and tired of this whole affair. A good friend of mine has been shot at, and two other men killed right in front of me, and then some fanatic girl tries to blow us all up. To add to that misery, your colonel gets me to help him identify two bodies and accuses me of not being who I am apparently pretending to be!" Vaughan's voice had been rising in volume during this speech and his face clearly showed his anger. Amelia looked shocked and shuffled away from him until her back was hard against the midship's bulkhead. The lieutenant just sat, his mouth open and eyes wide. "The next time you phone in your report to your colonel, you can tell him that I have come to the end of my patience, and he can no longer expect any co-operation. I intend to inform my embassy that I am being held without any, I repeat, any, justification. A good friend of mine is a member of our Foreign and Commonwealth Office as well as being a good friend of Walid al Djebbar, so if your colonel wants to avoid a heap of crap landing on him he better let me get out of here. Got it!"

Lieutenant Jacome nodded.

"Well don't just sit there, bloody well get on with it!"

Jacome scrambled to his feet and, after frantically rummaging in his kit bag, extracted his mobile phone and fled the yacht.

"That will guarantee that I am hauled in again I suppose. I better warn Susanne Bevington," Vaughan said bitterly.

Amelia said nothing, she just sat staring at him, her expression a mixture of shock and fear. Also in her heart was deep disappointment, for she had fallen in love with this good looking, capable and kind man, who she now knew for sure would sail away and leave her alone again, now with the added burden of her stupid uncle hanging, like a millstone, around her neck. As Vaughan clambered up into the cockpit, his mobile phone in hand, she slipped into the forward cabin, threw herself onto her bunk, and wept.

Vaughan dialled the Bevingtons' number and waited. "Henry Bevington, who is calling?"

"It's Ian Vaughan, Mr Bevington. Is your wife available?"

"I'm afraid not, she was working into the early hours last night and she is still fast asleep. I would rather not disturb her, she must be absolutely exhausted."

"Maybe you would be kind enough to give her a message."

"Of course," replied Bevington, his voice kindly, sympathetic. "What do you want me to pass on?"

"Can you tell her that I have had a harsh shouting match with Lieutenant Jacome, threatening to involve the British Embassy unless I am allowed to leave. He is now reporting to the colonel, so I am expecting to he hauled in very soon for further questioning and possibly imprisonment."

"Good Lord, really. I jolly well hope not. Demand a phone call if you get taken in; Susanne will do what she can for you, but as you know her powers are very limited."

"Thank you, you've both been very kind and supportive. I will give a call if I need to."

Aware of the tears and sadness in the forward cabin, Vaughan remained in the cockpit. *She had to be given the message, even though it wasn't the kindest way.* He sat mulling over what he would say and how he would say it to the colonel. *I would bet a year's salary that he won't cave in purely on my threat to involve the embassy; but if he pushes me I will have to follow through with it. On the bright side Ramiro hasn't returned yet, so maybe the colonel is giving some thought to being buried in official complaints.* Vaughan stood and scanned the marina quayside; a soldier was sat on the steps of the eastern seawall, that led to the upper level. *Oh, joy, a squaddy on guard, my cup runneth over.*

Lieutenant Ramiro Jacome did not return until late in the afternoon. "The colonel wants to see you."

"Well tell him to come here, I'm busy working."

"Please you cannot expect a colonel to come to you. That would be a great insult."

Vaughan carried on typing up the manuscript from his notes. "Pass me that chart on the table would you?"

"The colonel will be very angry."

"And I won't be? I've run around after your colonel long enough, this time he can come to me."

The lieutenant got up to leave. "The chart?" said Vaughan.

Lieutenant Jacome hesitated, then picking up the chart handed it to Vaughan. "You will be in so much trouble."

"No, Lieutenant, I don't think so."

When Jacome had left, Amelia emerged from the forward cabin her eyes red from crying, her beautiful face drawn. She looked ten years older than she had the day before.

"They will come to arrest you, you know that."

"Somehow I don't think they will. Look, you go and hold a cool flannel to those eyes of yours and repair your lipstick. Our

348

colonel is a talented horseman, he knows when to use a whip and when to use soft words."

"He is not like you, an Englishman. He is a pompous proud colonel with a typical Portuguese male temper. You have been very silly, Ian, to challenge him like this. What harm would another meeting have done, eh?"

"I am not suggesting that a meeting would be harmful. It is just that it will be held here and not there."

Suddenly a thought struck Vaughan, and going on deck he retrieved and stowed the boarding platform. *If some squaddy tries to jump it he'll probably end up in the drink. So they will have to ask nicely.*

"By the way, Amelia, weren't you supposed to be collecting Zeferino from hospital today?"

"Oh my God I totally forgot. What kind of mother am I to do such a thing? What time is it?"

"It's just gone five o'clock, and curfew is at seven."

"Please, if I use taxi can I bring him here for tonight, my home, I er I scared."

"He will have to share with you in the forward cabin, and if I am arrested, well, we will have to see."

"Of course, thank you. I do not know what I could have done had you not been here. God sent you, I am sure of it."

Vaughan re-rigged the boarding platform whilst she hurriedly grabbed her handbag and shoes.

"I pray we have still some taxis on the street."

Vaughan watched her scurry along the quay, and pass unchallenged by the solitary guard. *So it appears to be just me that is the prisoner.*

Amelia and Zeferino returned only five minutes before the cathedral bells rang out the start of the curfew.

"I cook for us tonight. The lieutenant he not return."

"Not yet, I think the colonel is finishing his paperwork before coming over."

It was the first time that young Zeferino had really met Vaughan, and he showed unusual shyness when he was introduced and told firmly that he owed his being alive solely to the sailing skill and care of Senhor Vaughan. His English was very poor, compared to his mother's, and it took sometime, and a lot of prompting, before she was satisfied that he had said enough.

"If I were you I would start the meal. If Lieutenant Jacome returns he will have to be content with baked beans or something," Vaughan said, before putting a sailing magazine in front of the boy, who, after a nervous look, started to turn the pages, stopping to closely study each picture.

Amelia smiled for the first time that day. "That is a good plan. Maybe he will not return."

"That sadly is highly unlikely. By the way how are Susie and Luz getting on without you?"

"They are doing very well as usual. I sometimes wonder why I go to work."

"Hey, they are that good?"

"Well, maybe sometime they need help with regulation. That is really what I do all day, check and double check that wherever we send our customers' goods, we have got the paperwork right. Each country they have different rules and restrictions, even within the EU. So much for free trade."

"What are your plans for tomorrow?" Vaughan asked.

Amelia was tempted to say that she wanted to stay onboard with him and never leave, but after Vaughan's rant at Lieutenant Jacome it was obvious to her that she did not feature in his future plans. "I thought I would try and find a reasonable cost hotel where Zeferino and myself would be safe from Esteves. I think he will want money and help to escape, and I fear he will use force against us if necessary."

"That sounds sensible. If I am taken into custody by the army you would be very vulnerable staying here alone," replied Vaughan. "And frankly I cannot see Lieutenant Jacome being able to protect you, even if he was allowed to stay."

"I would not wish to be alone with him, his eyes are all over me," she shuddered and turned to the galley, lifting the lid of the refrigerator and pulling out a pack of chicken portions. "Chicken okay for you?"

"Yes that's fine."

Zeferino said something and pulled at his T-shirt and shorts.

"Ah, yes. I must visit the apartment and get Zeferino some more clothes and change mine for work at office."

CHAPTER 15

A SHADOW FALLS AND ALL IS DARK

They arrived just as the evening meal things were being cleared away; a call from the jetty announcing the presence of the colonel, and another man who was stood back in the shadows.

"May we come aboard Senhor Vaughan?"

With a sigh, Vaughan stood and climbed into the cockpit, reaching for the boarding platform as he made his way astern. Assuming that the man standing back, well behind the colonel, was Lieutenant Jacome, Vaughan slotted the yoke of the platform in place and lowered the other end onto the quay, without taking any further notice of the shadowy figure. The colonel confidently strode along the platform immediately, and taking hold of the starboard backstay, swung his legs over the pushpit to the stern deck and stepped down into the cockpit obscuring Vaughan's view of his companion. When Jack Vale stepped aboard Vaughan swore.

"Bloody hell, what is this? I told you Vale that I would talk to you tomorrow at ten o'clock. So bugger off until then!"

"Senhor Vaughan, Senhor Vale is here at my request, and I am here, at your request. My government wish me to discuss with you the attempted assassination incident concerning an important visitor to this island, Walid al Djebbar. Senhor Vale's company was in charge of the immediate security to all the delegates at the conference, and you, played a key role in saving Senhor Al Djebbar's life and the lives of many others. I felt that your combined information would make it easier for my report. So please accommodate my request eh."

Vaughan thought for a moment or two. *I've won the venue argument and Vale is on my turf, so what the hell.*

"Oh very well, come below. I'll make some coffee before we get started or would you prefer wine?"

"Coffee would be very welcome, Senhor Vaughan," replied the colonel. Vale, tight lipped, obviously struggling to keep control of his temper, merely nodded his acceptance.

"If you, Colonel, and Vale here, could sit yourselves on the porthand settee, it will enable me to leap across to the galley," requested Vaughan. "Er, Amelia, if you and Zeferino could spend the evening in the forward cabin, hmm. I'm sorry but…"

"Ah so this is Zeferino," exclaimed the colonel, interupting. "The young man who spend much time in hospital." He reached across and ruffled the boy's hair and started to ask him questions, all the time with a big smile on his face and wide eyes and loud laughter at the boy's, at first, faltering answers. Vaughan heard his name mentioned several times, especially after Amelia joined in the conversation. *You're good, Colonel Castelo Lopes, very good. Charm the boy and get the answers to your clever questions.*

The chatter with the boy came to an end shortly after Vaughan had placed the coffees on the table together with a jug of hot milk and a bowl of sugar.

"So you were a hero even before you set a foot upon Madeiran soil, eh Senhor Vaughan."

"Oh no, I wouldn't go that far, it is the rule of the sea to go to the help of other sailors in danger," replied Vaughan mildly. *No, Colonel Castelo Lopes, you are not going to build a superman image in front of Vale, oh no.* "When I told you about the incident, when we first met, I explained how the rule of the sea works."

"Well according to Zeferino and his mother here, you are."

Vaughan shrugged his shoulders and slowly shook his head. "Anyway you wanted to know about the assassination attempt involving my friend Walid al Djebbar." Then looking across at Amelia he said, "If you could go forward with Zeferino. It's not the type of discussion that you or he should be burdened with."

"Of course, excuse me, gentlemen," Amelia replied, then looking at her son and pointing to the forward cabin door she said, "Zeferino!"

As soon as the forward cabin door closed Vale turned on Vaughan and angrily asked, "How did you know what was goin' down?"

"Vale, neither you nor anyone from 'Total Cover Incorporated' has either the right or the authority to ask me any questions. If this meeting is to proceed, the only questions are to be those of Colonel Castelo Lopes."

"You just can't sit…"

"Senhor Vale, please! Senhor Vaughan is quite correct. This meeting is to establish the facts for my government and not to satisfy your curiosity."

Vale glared at the colonel, then at Vaughan, but held his tongue.

"You told me when we met that you are a friend of this Al Djebbar. Tell me, even though you are friends, how you manage to be here at precisely the same time as he. Was that prearranged?"

"No, it was rather serendipitous, so to speak. A great friend of mine in England, Charles, is a very close friend of Walid's. They were at Oxford together and have been firm friends ever since. Anyway, over the years, I have met Walid on a few occasions, enough you know, for us to be on first name terms. Charles knew that I was doing this book and roughly what my schedule was, so when he heard from Walid that he was in Madeira he sent him a text message or something telling him that it was likely I was around and, well Walid got in touch."

"Why were you there on the morning of the assassination, surely he was very busy that day?"

"Well to be quite honest with you, the day before he had visited me here, very early in the morning, in fact he had breakfast here, anyway, he felt that the conference was stalling and that his ambitious proposal would be rejected. Well we talked for some time, I won't go into details, but then he seemed to get a second wind and rushed off back to the conference, and apparently dramatically turned things around."

"And the morning?"

"Ah yes, well the previous evening, after what appeared to be a very successful day at the conference, he sent his right-hand man, Mehdi Khuldun, with an invitation for me to attend his final conference speech. What he wanted was for me to work with one of his translators and send a more personal style translation of the speech off to Charles in England."

"So you met him, when?"

"Well as you know the previous night had been pretty busy with this coup business, but I had done all I could do. Diplomacy at that level is way beyond me, so I left Mrs De Lima in the capable hands of the Honorary British Consul, Mrs Bevington, and high tailed it across to the Vidamar, just in time to meet Walid, as he came out of his hotel room."

"You chose not to support Mrs De Lima."

"Well, yes, I mean she wasn't mixed up with the coup in any way, I felt, that if anything, the revelation of what her uncle was involved in was more of a shock to her than it was to me; and frankly it is not as though we are very close, you know, romantically or anything. I've hardly known her for any time really," replied Vaughan, trying hard to look a bit embarrassed at having let her down.

"A guy with your looks and situation, and you say you haven't made a move on a gorgeous babe like that," interrupted Vale. "Are you gay?"

The colonel went to admonish Vale for interrupting, but Vaughan got in first. "Though it is of no business at all of yours, Vale, I am still getting over being divorced by the woman I still very much love."

"Please, Senhor Vale, desist from asking questions!"

Vale looking a little chastened, apologised.

Then the questioning teased out a very detailed account of the assassination attempts as seen by Vaughan and from what Vale had learnt from his staff. At the end, it was the colonel who asked Vaughan the two difficult questions.

"Senhor Vaughan, you are a writer, yes?"

Vaughan nodded. "Yes."

"The thing Senhor Murphy, Senhor Vale and I cannot understand, is how you, as a writer, not a bodyguard or member of the armed forces, recognised a laser assist red dot on the side of a man's head, for what it was, then had the bravery to take action?"

Vaughan had been expecting this question ever since he first saw Jack Vale, so had prepared his answer with care; even rehearsing the facial expressions, in the head's mirror of a morning, whilst washing and shaving.

"When my wife upped and left me, taking our two girls with her, I ended up in a bedsit in a town called Kingsbridge in England. I was alone and sought something to take my mind off my wife and the messy divorce she was pursuing. My distraction was DVD's of Hollywood thrillers. You know, Harrison Ford, George Segal, The Bourne movies. Five months or more of those and you do recognise what a laser assist target spot looks like," replied Vaughan, sounding tired and depressed at the memory. "As far as action was concerned, I don't know, I didn't think, I just pushed my friend out of the way."

Vaughan could feel both men's eyes studying him as he toyed with the handle of his coffee mug, a glum expression on his face as he stared at the table.

"Then, Senhor Vaughan, you recognised and shot a suicide bomber. Did you learn to recognise her from movies as well?"

"I suppose so. You know it surprised me too afterwards. What it was I think was that her cloak, or whatever it was that she was wearing, was flapping about in the wind. It was quite gusty at the time and suddenly it blew open and I could see all of these pouches and wires. Thinking about it now it was probably news broadcasts that helped me make the link. The bombings in London, and a few similar atrocities; plus of course terrorist dramas on TV. Regarding shooting her that was just, I don't know, but what I do know is that I was bloody lucky to hit the target. Funny, years ago I gave a lift to a British policeman who was part of an armed response unit. We got chatting about what he did, which was mainly training, but one thing that stuck with me was that with terrorists you always aim for the head. If I ever meet him again I'll buy him a pint, probably three or four, those few words saved my life."

"Did he explain why?" asked the colonel.

"Yes, he said that to aim for the body could well detonate any bomb they were concealing. Also he explained that a one shot hit to the body does not necessarily close the brain down quickly enough to prevent the terrorist from reacting. Only milliseconds in time maybe, but enough time for them to pull a trigger of a gun, or detonator," Vaughan paused. "Someone shot in the head loses the chance to react instantly according to him; that was the case with the girl. She just fell backwards, dead and motionless."

Again Vaughan came under the scrutiny of the two men.

"Mr Vale has said to me that his people thought that you knew very much about their business. Do you?"

"No, not really. I remember saying to Mr Murphy that I was surprised their man, er, Metcalf, was keeping so close to the obvious main target. That just seemed a bit stupid to me," Vaughan replied, looking across at Vale. "But I'm no expert, and when he was shot, your guys bravely stood in the line of fire, even after the second man was hit."

"Where would you have been standin' Vaughan?" asked Vale, this time without any reaction from the colonel.

Vaughan blew out his cheeks. "Phew, I think I would probably have stationed myself somewhere where I could see the overall scene. You know, direct the operation without being too close and not be able to see what was going on."

There was silence for several seconds during which Jack Vale appeared to be weighing Vaughan's comments. Then Vaughan said, "Now I have thought about this a bit more, I wonder whether your team should have kept Al Djebbar on the move. You know, not let him stand still like he did."

"Yeh, that's precisely what Murphy said to me, but Metcalf was in the driver position, bein' right behind this Ayerab."

"You mean Walid al Djebbar," said Vaughan, bristling at Vale's derogatory tone.

"Yeh, him."

"I think three things coincided to produce that situation, one was Metcalf being part of the close protection, two was the quite rapturous reception given to Walid, and probably the most important one, was a radio message from one of the team watching the surrounding roof tops."

"Do you know what the message was?" asked the colonel.

"No, not exactly, but I heard something about a box on a roof. Afterwards I heard that one of your men had realised that the first assassin's hiding place had not been there the day before, and was suggesting it be checked out. Too late as it happened, but pretty smart none the less. Stationed where he was he could not have seen the progress of Walid and his protection group so would not have appreciated that the possible target was exposed," explained Vaughan.

Vale made some more notes on his pad, then looked blindly at the bookshelf above Vaughan's head, deep in thought.

"More coffee, anyone?" asked Vaughan.

"Thank you, you are most kind," responded the colonel.

"Vale?"

"Oh, yeh, er thanks."

While Vaughan was in the galley the colonel stood and came to sit at the chart table. "Senhor Vaughan, why are you entertaining Mrs De Lima on your yacht, together with her son, when you say that there is no romance or long friendship?"

The question had been quietly asked as if the colonel had not wanted Vale to hear.

Vaughan turned away from the cooker and sat down on the companionway steps, close to his clever interrogator. "As I told you before, she is very frightened of this uncle of hers, and now she knows of his involvement in the coup she is even more scared."

The colonel nodded his understanding of Amelia's situation.

"Tomorrow Amelia is planning to find a hotel for herself and Zeferino. She does not want to return to her apartment until Esteves is caught. Maybe you could arrange for her to have some protection?"

"I will look into the possibility," replied the colonel, sounding very non-committal.

"Please, as I am assuming that you are one of the good guys who would consider it their duty to protect the innocent."

The colonel's head turned sharply and he gave Vaughan a fierce glare. Then the expression mellowed and he smiled. "I have on my staff a female liaison officer. Please give me a day and then I will be able to assign her to the task, I am sure she will be ideal."

"Thank you, Colonel, I would appreciate being relieved of a task that I am completely unqualified for."

"Um, so you keep saying, Senhor Vaughan."

Vaughan, hearing the kettle whistle, turned, and seeing the milk about to boil over, was just in time to take it off the heat. "That was close."

As Vaughan poured the coffee, the door to the forward cabin opened and Amelia tiptoed past the heads and stepped into the main cabin. "Have you finished your meeting?" she asked.

Vaughan looked at the colonel questioningly. "Yes, Senhora, we have, so please join us."

Vale went to say something, but then thought better of it.

"Coffee, Amelia?"

"Thank you. Zeferino is fast asleep, so please if you can speak softly, I would be very grateful."

"Of course, my dear," answered the colonel, as he slid his notepad out of sight into his pocket. "Senhor Vaughan has been of great assistance to me and, I think, to many other people on this island. His explanation of his, dare I say, adventures here, has shown him to be a remarkable man. We were extremely fortunate that he arrived when he did, and that he met you and your son."

Vaughan gave a deep sigh, but said nothing, noting that Amelia was now giving him a very thoughtful look. *You're not giving up are you, Colonel, you old fox. I haven't convinced you, have I, damn it.*

The conversation, as they drank their coffee, was polite, affording Amelia the opportunity to do her tourist guide act for the colonel and Vale. Vaughan was impressed by, not only her knowledge, but by her obvious love of the beautiful island on which she lived, and noticed that the colonel had picked up on it too. When they left, the colonel, as only to be expected, was generous in his thanks. Vale, however, was a complete surprise, as when he stepped ashore he turned and said, "If you ever need a job, Vaughan, give me a call, I've left my card on your cabin table."

"Thanks, but no thanks. A spontaneous act to help a friend is one thing, but a conscious act to put myself in the line of fire is something way beyond me."

"I meant leadin' a team," Vale replied, only to see Vaughan shake his head and wave goodbye.

Vaughan was about to go down into the main cabin when the colonel called to him. "Senhor Vaughan, tonight Lieutenant Jacome is assisting me on other duties. He will return to you in the morning, but meantime, I have four guards posted for your protection around the marina. So sleep peacefully."

Vaughan waited for the colonel's car to leave before picking up his binoculars and scanning the marina quayside. *Yep indeed you have, Colonel, four squaddies apparently still awake on duty, thank you very much.*

"Zeferino, he fell asleep almost as soon as he got ready for bed, so I was able to listen to nearly all that was said." She had come and stood very close to Vaughan as he put his mug into the galley sink. Suddenly her expression changed and she looked scared retreating towards the forward cabin. "You are not just a writer Ian Vaughan, you are someone who has been trained to be

361

much more. I fully understand why the colonel and Senhor Vale still do not believe you."

Vaughan stepped across and sat down heavily at the chart table and put his head in both hands. "Go to bed, Amelia, just go to bed. Now." A few seconds passed then he heard her movement and the click of the forward cabin door catch as it closed behind her.

*

Across the esplanade, from the marina, at the army's weapons store in the Palaçio de São Lourenço, a sergeant and a corporal were being issued with live ammunition for their guard duty outside Amelia's apartment. The store's armourer sergeant stared at the corporal's HK417 and asked, "You were ordered to collect live ammunition for this weapon?"

The corporal nodded. "Yes, Sergeant."

The sergeant, who had been attended to first, looked up from studying the magazines issued to him, and nodded.

"Oh, all right," the armourer sergeant replied. Shrugging his shoulders and raising his eyebrows he walked away, to return a few minutes later with two 7.62mm loaded, 10-round magazines. He looked at the sergeant, then again at the corporal, waited for a moment, then, shaking his head, said, "Sign here, and here," pushing a clipboard, with a munitions requisition form on it, across the counter.

*

That night Vaughan slept fitfully, waking feeling stiff and irritable at around six o'clock on a cloudy morning. A cool wind swept down from the mountains behind the city and he shivered as he crossed the platform to the quayside where he started a series of warm up exercises. After half an hour of 'The Manor' gym routine he had restored his physical equilibrium but his irritability remained. Reaching for the small towel and wiping the sweat from his head, neck and legs, Vaughan looked up and saw Amelia standing in the cockpit staring at him.

"Does a writer really need to do sit-ups and one arm press-ups to hold a pen or type on a keyboard?"

"No, but a lone sailor needs to stay as fit as possible. Do you have a problem with that as well?"

"No, I am sorry," she replied, looking down at the cockpit sole, not wanting to face him. "I am also sorry for what I say to you last night. I am confused and scared. My lovely island with its beautiful gardens and scenery, friendly, kind people and so peaceful recent history has been turned upside down. I had text from Susie who tell me that many people in the municipal office are being interrogated by the army and many of those managing our banks and commerce are suffering the same. Men from the mainland have come looking at all office computers and many mobile phones have been confiscated." Tears were running freely down her cheeks and dropping from her chin onto her white blouse unheeded.

"Tell me, did they take your mobile from you?" asked Vaughan.

"Yes, all the while the colonel was questioning me," she answered.

"They gave it back to you?"

"Yes."

"It's probably being hacked into, so the next time you speak to Susie face to face warn her not to say or text anymore messages like that. Just stick to business."

Amelia gasped. "Oh God, will she get into trouble?"

"I don't know, so I think it is better that you speak to her quickly, before she feeds you any more, maybe sensitive, information."

"You see that is why the colonel does not believe you. How do you know such things, eh?"

"In England some journalist managed to hack into the mobile phones of some famous people. Spying, looking for sensational stories to print in order to raise their circulation figures, it was a big scandal, to which there was no technical answer that would prevent them from doing the same again. If a newspaper can organise it, I am sure your security services are expert at it. That's how I know."

"Oh," she replied, looking down again. "I am sorry, Ian, so sorry." Then she turned and hurried below.

Placing cereals in front of Zeferino, sat at the main cabin table, and taking coffee and toast up into the cockpit for his own breakfast Vaughan turned his thoughts to how he could force the colonel into allowing him to leave, without success.

He had finished his breakfast and washed up the cereal bowl, plate and cutlery before Amelia emerged again from the forward cabin. Though smartly dressed, her bloodshot and puffy eyes, red nose and expression of mental exhaustion on her face made her look as if she had been in a serious fight, and lost. Her hair, normally immaculately groomed, was tangled and tussled, completing the wreckage of her visage. She wobbled a bit, as if about to pass out, then hurriedly sat on the porthand settee, looking down at the cabin floor.

Vaughan gave a deep sigh. *A lot of TLC required, but will she accept it?* He walked forward and opened one of the drawers built alongside the clothes' locker opposite the heads. Taking out four snowy white handkerchiefs he looked in the forward cabin and picked up her comb and hairbrush from beside her handbag.

Returning to the galley he soaked the handkerchiefs in cold water then sat himself down on the starboard settee. "Amelia, let's do some repairs to the damage shall we," he said quietly. "Come and sit here with your back to me and hold these clean handkerchiefs over your eyes, whilst I attempt to restore your normally beautiful hairstyle."

Zeferino, also with tears running down his cheeks shuffled along the porthand settee close to his mother. "Por favor a mãe, por favor," he said, almost in a whisper.

She sat for some moments, before slowly standing with one hand on the table and the other on the bulkhead handhold for support. Without looking at Vaughan she turned her back to him and with her right hand seeking the support of the bookshelf and her left the table, she sat almost touching him.

"Here, take these," he said, handing her the cold damp handkerchiefs. Then gently, ever so gently, he set about untangling her hair.

It was nine o'clock before Vaughan was satisfied that he had done enough to restore the worst of the damage wrought by a sleepless, restless night. Her eyes were now far less swollen and her nose almost restored to normal colour. "There, that looks better, not as good as you could do I am sure, but with some lipstick I think you are ready to face the world again," said Vaughan trying his friendliest smile.

Her reply barely left her lips, "Thank you, you have done more than I deserve."

"Rubbish, come on, the order of the day is, Susie and Luz, hotel and finally clothes from the apartment."

"I must have some coffee first, please."

"You do the lipstick. I'll sort the coffee."

Nodding, Amelia slowly walked forward into her cabin and reached into her handbag for lipstick and mirror, just as Lieutenant Jacome returned, in uniform.

"You're not marching onto this boat in those boots thank you," called Vaughan just as the lieutenant's left leg was swinging over the pushpit.

"Sorry I no think. I wait here for you."

"There is something else you can do."

"What is that?"

"Arrange for me to meet the colonel late this afternoon. His office will do."

The lieutenant gave Vaughan a long stare, then nodded. "Okay, I try."

Ten minutes later the lieutenant called down to say that the colonel would see Vaughan at six o'clock that evening.

Well I wonder whether he thinks I am going to make a confession. Then considering the schedule for the day he thought. *I doubt if we will be coming back here, so I better leave the Browning behind, the colonel's guard are bound to frisk me, let's just pray Esteves is not at the apartment.*

Coffee consumed and programme for the day explained to the lieutenant, the quartet set off to meet Carlos who, at Amelia's request, had offloaded his bookings for the day to act as their chauffeur.

Her office was on the Rua Camara Pestana, and with just Vaughan to accompany her she led him to the three second floor rooms from which the business was run. When they entered, both Susie and Luz were busy talking on the telephone. Vaughan looked around and saw a portable radio on the table beside Luz's desk. As the girls finished their calls and hurried over to Amelia, Vaughan signalled to Luz to switch on the radio. It appeared to be a news broadcast, and as such would not have raised suspicions to anyone listening in to any bugging devices placed. Luz frowned not understanding Vaughan's intentions. In response Vaughan put his finger to his lips and wrote in his notebook, 'Walls have ears' and showed it to her. Luz stared wide-eyed at him and put her hand over her mouth.

Greetings over, Amelia asked the normal questions that a business owner would ask of their staff with regard to the progress of work and new business. Throughout this Vaughan sat, his back to the window, writing a note warning both ladies of the possibility of Amelia's and their mobile phones being hacked.

Sliding the note across Susie's desk, around which they were now standing, both girls started reading the message as Vaughan casually turned round and, glancing quickly out of the window, saw someone with binoculars standing against the back wall in the semi-darkness of a room in the building opposite. The profile was vaguely familiar. *That looks like Staunton. Oh get a grip – what would he be doing there?*

Having read and comprehended the message, Susie sidled up to Vaughan. "So no more text messages?" she whispered into Vaughan's ear.

"No, I don't mean that. Just avoid any subject other than this business or girls' chatter. Never mention anything to do with the coup clear up," he whispered in reply, before giving her a light kiss on the cheek and laughing; then again whispering into her ear he said, "There is someone in the building across the street looking at us; don't turn round, just wag your finger at me as if I have been teasing you."

After ten minutes during which Amelia explained her programme for the day, she and Vaughan left the building; Vaughan carrying the screwed up notes in his pocket unaware of Staunton in a grey suit and dark sunglasses hurrying to a white Seat Ibiza.

At the hotel in the Rua Ivens, Amelia was fortunate to be able to book a double room for the next fortnight. The hotel staff, at first understandably suspicious of someone with a Funchal address wanting a room in a Funchal hotel, were finally satisfied when she explained that her own apartment had been infested with cockroaches, and the sprays and clear up meant that she needed to find other accommodation for a time. Before leaving, Vaughan disposed of the notes, he had written at Amelia's office, in the hotel's toilets, double flushing the cistern to ensure that the paper was carried away.

Lunch at the café alongside the Sacred Arts Museum was not the jolly affair of the previous visit, and Vaughan knew that Amelia was fearing the return to the apartment.

Lieutenant Jacome's uniform also did nothing to help the situation, as it appeared to intimidate the waitresses. People on the streets looked to be scared by the presence of the army, who now stood in small groups at major junctions, fully armed and looking for any sign of crowd build-up or disturbance. The happy bustling city of the pre-coup days had disappeared, leaving a ghost like atmosphere where people walked hurriedly, eyes down, keeping strictly to their business. Tourist shops stood empty, the assistants looking forlornly out of the windows in the hope of seeing a customer approach.

"Ramiro, is the army in such numbers all over the island?" asked Vaughan, looking at the group standing around a light personnel carrier on the opposite side of the square.

"No, Ian, the colonel believes that the rural population would not have wished for change. Their life under the Salazarists was very hard. Here in the city we have learnt of many coup sympathisers. Not active you understand, but ready to support if change had been achieved."

Vaughan looked at Amelia raising his eyebrows as a request for her comment.

"The colonel is quite correct to make assumptions the way he has. The island government, that my stupid uncle wished to depose, has its power base in the rural community. Out in the countryside they, at present, seem to be unaware of the impact of the European financial crisis and in particular that of Portugal. In honesty our Government has borrowed too much, and spent it on projects that have not yielded a viable return. Here the road programme, intended to open up the whole of the island to tourism has failed, not because it was a bad plan, but because new tourist destinations on the far side of the world have attracted American and many European tourists away from us. In addition there has also been the global economic meltdown. Maybe in a few years the novelty of the Far East will wear off, and our beautiful island will again attract those seeking a pleasant all year round climate near to their homeland, lovely scenery and friendly people."

Vaughan looked up above the roof tops at the majestic mountains that formed an essential part of Madeira's defence against the elements. He sat marvelling at the thought that an island, a little under fourteen miles wide north to south at its widest point, rises above the ocean to some six thousand one hundred feet.

"You are very deep in thought, Ian," said Ramiro, wanting to break the silence between all of them.

"I was just thinking how beautiful and amazing this island is, and how unfair it is that in as short a period as a month, four lunatic men could destroy what is left of its economic stability, and by doing so, summon forces here that are casting fear and unfounded suspicion amongst all of its population."

It was not the answer that Ramiro had hoped for; its bitterness being obviously inspired by a loyalty and affection for the island and its people, which he, did not possess. He had hoped that Vaughan would say something about wanting the capture of Esteves, and an end to the imposed restrictions on the island's population; but his reply had indicated a criticism of the arrival of the Servico de Informações de Segurança, that people were already describing openly as a witch hunt. Suddenly he felt the outsider in a world that really belonged to his three companions at the table. Ian Vaughan was right, the army and intelligence services being here, asking questions and casting doubts, were just adding to the damage that just a few had inflicted with a plan so ill-conceived as to be a thing of ridicule.

Vaughan's gaze fell upon Zeferino, who had not said a word throughout the whole meal. He smiled and winked at the boy, passing the ice cream menu across to him.

"He eats far too many ice creams," said Amelia, reaching to take the menu back.

"He's had an awful day so far, worrying about you, wondering where he will be living next, scared for the future. Let him have some treat at least," said Vaughan, surprised and critical of her reaction.

"You are right, I am sorry, I am not thinking straight."

"No, Amelia, you are not. You need to get a grip; you had no involvement in your uncle's treasonous activities here, so it is about time you lifted your head. Show people that you are still the good mother and capable businesswoman that I dined with at Bruno's restaurant. Believe in yourself, believe in who Susie and Luz know you to be, don't wear a cloak of false guilt because a distant relative chose the wrong path. It is not yours to wear."

She stared at Vaughan in shock, unable to formulate an answer.

Seeing Zeferino looking worriedly at his mother, Vaughan hailed a waitress, and after a quick pointing session between he and the boy, ordered two of the largest ice creams available. Waiting for the desserts to arrive, Vaughan smoothed out a paper napkin and taking a biro from his pocket, started a game of noughts and crosses with the lad.

Ramiro looked on, feeling even more excluded than before. If only the colonel had not insisted he wore uniform. Everywhere they had been, he had received hostile looks that made him feel more uncomfortable by the minute. Had he been in the company of soldiers he knew he would have felt differently, more confident. In the company of Ian Vaughan, Amelia de Lima and her son, he felt isolated, threatened, and vulnerable. Though Vaughan had spoken to him throughout the morning, Amelia had blanked him, making it obvious that she did not want to be near him. Whilst Zeferino had just shown only fear at any attempt he had made at friendship with the boy.

Neither Amelia nor Vaughan had finished their coffees before Lieutenant Ramiro Jacome had left the table and settled the bill. Why he had taken charge of paying the bill, he realised, was his sense of isolation and of not being in control of events. Returning to the table he asked, "Are we ready to leave for your apartment?" his voice now more commanding, than soft and kind.

Vaughan looked at Amelia who was looking down at her handbag obviously reluctant to make a move. "Come on, Amelia, let's get this out of the way, and both of you settled at the hotel," he said, quietly, encouragingly.

She stood and reached for Zeferino's hand, grasping it firmly, then followed Vaughan to where Carlos had parked his taxi, passing Staunton, unseen, sat at a pavement table of the bar on the west side of the square.

Staunton had been following them since they had left Amelia's offices and had been watching them carefully during the lunch, irritated by the constant attendance of the Portuguese army lieutenant. What he needed was for the De Lima woman to take Vaughan to meet her uncle and all his problems would be solved, but that was not going to happen while they had the army with them. He had to get to Esteves before the authorities did and eradicate the man. If Vaughan got in the way, then he would have to go as well, but Esteves must definitely not survive under any circumstances.

Guessing they were returning to the taxi, Staunton left his half-drunk beer holding down a ten euro note in payment, and hurrying the opposite way around the block of buildings leapt into the Seat Ibiza he had hired, just in time to pull out into the traffic three cars behind the taxi. Ideally situated to follow without attracting attention he managed to remain at a discreet distance as the taxi weaved its way up towards Amelia's apartment.

Suddenly Staunton's mobile beeped and taking it from his pocket he studied the screen and was surprised to see that the call was from Alice Morgan. "Yes Alice, what is it?"

"I think you should know that the Consul, where you are, is causing trouble. There is the log of a report from her on the receive list, but I guess Heathcote got to it before I could. Anyway Tracy saw it and told me that it was about inaccurate reporting and your name was mentioned."

"Where are you talking from?" Staunton asked, feeling rising panic.

"A little café round the corner from work, I took a late lunch so I could give you a call."

"Are my reports still coming through via Lisbon?"

"Yes, it was just that I thought you should know about the Consul," Alice replied.

"And they are going straight to Sir Andrew?" asked Staunton, ignoring Alice's comment.

"Well, yes, of course they are, I make sure of that."

"That's good, Alice, keep it that way," said Staunton now feeling less anxious. "Is Vaughan sending anything through?"

"No, not a thing, but funny you should ask because nobody else has, and you know what they are like for regular reporting."

"Well I think it is because he's got official company so might feel that it is too risky; a good thing really, with him quiet it stops London becoming, shall we say, confused."

Staunton heard a giggle on the other end of the phone and smiled to himself. Alice was a good find and remarkably loyal.

"Must go, Alice, I'll call you later."

"Bye, Lenny, darling, take care won't you," she said, but he had already hung up.

Once in the area of Amelia's apartment Staunton gave up following the taxi and, by taking a short detour, parked his car a safe distance up the hill from her home and sat waiting to observe the comings and goings through binoculars.

CHAPTER 16

WHEN BULLETS FLY

As they neared Amelia's address, Vaughan began to feel nervous, almost as if he had a premonition. "Carlos, please do not stop directly outside Senhora De Lima's apartment, park around the corner of the junction, just uphill."

"Sim Senhor."

Amelia looked at him curiously. "You think my uncle is there?"

"I don't know, he may have got in, or he maybe watching," replied Vaughan. "Let the lieutenant and I go in first and have a look round."

She look relieved, and reaching across Zeferino, gave Vaughan's arm a gentle squeeze. "Thank you, I would feel much happier."

"I must first contact our men guarding your apartment," said Lieutenant Jacome, again seeking to set the agenda.

"While you search the apartment may I suggest that your men stand guard over Amelia and Zeferino," said Vaughan. "Just in case this guy Esteves sees them whilst they are unprotected." Carlos gave Vaughan a nervous look.

The lieutenant nodded. "That is what I had in mind."

Vaughan smiled inwardly. *Oh yes, Ramiro? I'm not that sure that your training would have covered this type of situation.*

Vaughan got Carlos to stop near to the spot where Amelia and he had paid off the taxi the evening Esteves and his gang had held their final meeting in the apartment. When Vaughan got out of the taxi and went to follow Lieutenant Jacome the young officer turned and frowned, but said nothing.

"Ramiro, I will come with you and wait outside the apartment while you search it. If it is all clear, I can then come back and collect Amelia and the boy," said Vaughan. "That way you remain securing the apartment, just in case."

The lieutenant considered Vaughan's suggestion for a moment or two. "All right, but you do not enter the apartment until I give you the all clear, understood?"

"Yes, of course."

As they approached the army jeep Vaughan saw the corporal hurriedly wake the sergeant. *Yep, Esteves could have walked in past you two doing a jig and you would not have seen him. I bet that many times when you two are on watch you are both asleep.*

The lieutenant had apparently also noted the sleeping sergeant and spent several minutes reprimanding him before ordering the two men to follow him back to the taxi. Here he gave another firm series of instructions before turning to Vaughan and saying, "A boring duty is still a duty, yes?"

"Yes, you are right, Lieutenant. A guard must remain vigilant."

"You saw our fine Segundo-sargento then, asleep?"

Vaughan nodded. "Yes, but anyway let's get on with it."

In the building entrance porch, the lieutenant stared at the keypad, and was about to turn back to the taxi when Vaughan said, "One, eight, five, four, nine is the code, then press Z."

"Ah, thank you, Ian, I forgot to ask."

"Here's her door key."

"Thank you again, I was annoyed at my men."

"Wait here for a few minutes to get your concentration back to normal."

Whilst the lieutenant stood, eyes closed, forcing his brain back into the moment and fix on what he was to do, Vaughan peered through the clear glass panel alongside the door towards the staircase. *No one about it seems, that's a pity. If he is in the apartment someone may have heard him moving around or even seen him.*

"I am ready," said Jacome, sounding more confident than he felt.

"Just a moment, why not swap this about and get the sergeant and the corporal to do the search?"

"Huh, they are too stupid to be trusted."

Vaughan shrugged. The sergeant though lazy had given him the impression of having, over long service, gained some considerable experience. "You are sure?"

"Yes, of course I am sure."

Okay, my proud lieutenant, in you go. God help you if he is there, as it will be like cornering a wildcat. Esteves knows that virtually everyone on the island is looking for him, and if I were in his position I'd fight like hell.

Code entered they both stepped into the entrance hall and cautiously climbed the stairs to the wide first floor landing. Amelia's apartment entrance was across the landing to the right.

"Please remember you wait until I say all is clear, then please fetch Ms De Lima and her son and tell the sergeant and corporal to guard the front entrance," whispered the lieutenant.

Vaughan gave the thumbs up signal, thinking, *Why didn't you repeat that whilst we were outside in the porch, that whispered in this echoing sound box of a stairwell could be heard yards away.*

Carefully inserting the key in the lock and turning it, the lieutenant gently pushed the door open. It was only then that he thought to reach for his pistol. Vaughan inwardly groaned.

Please, God, let the apartment be empty, now feeling more vulnerable than ever before at not being armed.

The lieutenant's boots, fine when walking on a pavement or carpet, squeaked on the polished ceramic floor of the apartment, enough to warn the wary of his presence. The kitchen to the left of the central passageway was the first room and needed little time to check. It would have been almost impossible for anyone to hide due to the lack of free space. As he crept back into the passage Vaughan waved for him to come close. Taking his notebook from his pocket and pulling the pencil from the book's spine he wrote, 'HAVE YOU CHECKED THE TRASH CAN/WASTE BIN?' then, 'I SUGGEST YOU TAKE YOUR BOOTS OFF, THEY SQUEAK!'

The lieutenant frowned, and then nodding his understanding, removed his boots and returned to the kitchen, only to come back almost immediately, his socks making his feet slip a little on the polished floor.

"It is full of snack packets," Jacome whispered to Vaughan, before taking his socks off.

Vaughan tried to remember how much food had been left over on the table the night of Esteves' meeting. *Bread rolls, yes, they seemed to have just eaten all the crisps and nuts. Amelia put the meats and cheeses back in the fridge I think. That doesn't tell us anything except that no tins have been opened. If only Jacome had let me help with the search.*

The next doorway, the lounge-diner, was on the opposite side of the passage and first checking through the gap on the hinge side of the door, Jacome cautiously entered the room, pistol held at the ready. He appeared to spend a long time conducting the search and Vaughan was beginning to wonder whether or not Jacome was losing his nerve when the man crept back into the passageway and carefully opened the bathroom door, then peered inside. The next was the toilet, which he also cleared with just a cursory look. Opposite was the box room that Zeferino had been relegated to when his great uncle had arrived. Here Jacome took great care before entering and spent a long time searching.

Vaughan had been allocated the box room though had only unpacked and repacked his few clothes on the evening. He remembered having left one of the sliding doors to the room's freestanding wardrobe open.

The last two bedrooms took Jacome ages to work his way through but finally he emerged from Amelia's bedroom smiling with relief.

"It is all clear, Ian, please you fetch the others," he said, as he walked towards Vaughan and put his socks and boots back on.

"When you were in the small bedroom, the one opposite the toilet, was the left-hand wardrobe door open?"

Jacome thought for a moment. "Yes, because immediately I enter the room I could see all the inside of it."

"Okay, I'll go and get Amelia and the others."

In the ground floor entrance hall Vaughan stopped and went through Jacome's search pattern in his mind. *The kitchen, yes, that was okay and the lounge-diner. There is no place to quickly hide in the bathroom, or the toilet, but he only really opened that door and looked in.*

"Something troubling you, Ian?"

"Yes, but I can't think what it is," replied Vaughan before shaking his head and opening the door to step out into the porch and out to the street. *Yes, there was something else, some other clue, but what was it?*

On reaching the taxi Vaughan asked Amelia to instruct the sergeant and corporal to come with them and keep guard in the entrance hall. Orders understood, Vaughan and the two soldiers, followed by Amelia, holding tightly to Zeferino's hand, left

Carlos in the taxi and made their way to the apartment building where the lieutenant was waiting for them in the porch.

*

Olavo Esteves had celebrated with others as they watched the arrival of the army convoy. After his co-conspirators had left for the President's official residence, Esteves had returned to Reshetnikov's study to continue his contact with those senior staff in America's east coast banking and investment firms who had expressed potential support. Like London, Paris and Bonn the reaction had been one of caution, but there had been no real concerns expressed. The general message was one of, wait a few days for the new order to be established, and assurances given that funds were being allocated.

It was when Reshetnikov burst into the room that Esteves learnt of the coup's spectacular failure.

"You must leave here instantly. Collect whatever you need from your room and I will get Sonia to hide the rest until it is safe for you to have them delivered," Reshetnikov had shouted, as the muscular Ivan stood menacingly behind him.

"They will not search for me here, Ulan," Esteves had replied. "How will they know?"

"They will know because your friends will be forced to tell them. As soon as you are gone Sonia and I will be leaving also."

"Please, you take me with you. I can pay you well for your protection."

"No, the price on your head is too high for me to take that risk," the Russian had replied, as Ivan made a move to assist Esteves vacate the premises.

"You cannot leave me without some protection, please!"

"The only protection I can offer you is a pistol. You use one before?"

Surprised and shocked by the thought of being armed, Esteves gaped. "What, you are offering to give me, a gun?"

"That is all I can do for you. Quickly, you decide, we will sort payment later."

Esteves, shaken by the dramatic change in events shrugged and nodded his acceptance. In the room he had shared with Huberto, Esteves rummaged through his suitcase, recovering all the cash and his passport. Huberto's suitcase contained more cash as did Diago's and Isidro's next door, then returning to his room he grabbed Huberto's light rucksack and emptied the contents onto the bed and stuffed his shaving and washing kit into it together with a couple of shirts. Huberto's baseball cap was on the chair and Esteves took off his jacket and shirt, packed them with the other shirts then hurriedly searched for a T-shirt and slipped it on. Throughout his frantic preparations, Ivan had been standing over him silently hurrying him along. Sunglasses and the baseball cap completed the casual tourist look, and swinging the rucksack over his shoulder he left Reshetnikov's house.

At the gate Ivan handed Esteves a battered looking Russian MP-443 Grach 9mm pistol and a box of ammunition. "Here, the boss he tell me I give you these things. Say, why you steal that money from your friends eh?" a sneering expression on the big man's face, clearly showing his disgust.

Esteves' hackles rose at the insulting remark, and he checked the pistol's magazine; it was empty. That was when he noticed Ivan casually holding a fully automatic handgun at his side. Correctly deciding that now was not the time to teach Ivan manners, Esteves put the weapon and ammunition into the rucksack. "They are in jail now, nothing to spend their money on," he replied, and then hurriedly walked away down the hill towards the town struggling to contain his anger.

It was mid afternoon when he saw his picture being broadcast on the local television special news broadcast, following a call for calm from the President, and he was fortunate not to be recognised immediately by those sitting near him in the café.

After wandering the back streets he found a derelict house in the old town where he slept rough that first night. During the second day Esteves was realising that the time he had spent womanising would have been better used in putting a plan in place to leave the island in the event of the coup's failure. Risking a visit to a newsagent he read details of the restrictions that had been put in place by the army. All marinas were now guarded and only bona fide boat owners were allowed to visit their craft, but none were allowed to leave port. Fishing boats were being searched before leaving port and had to declare the location where they would be working. They were also required to return to port within four hours and the number of trips limited to two in any twenty-four hour period. The airport was closed until the following day when strict security would be enforced; and all incoming flights had been diverted to Madrid or turned back to their country of origin.

Esteves had already concluded that living rough out in the countryside was not an option, as obtaining food by stealing would hold too many risks of being caught. His only hope, he thought, was to return to Amelia's apartment where at least there was some food and shelter, but he found it to be guarded by two soldiers. Desperate now, and fearful of arrest, Esteves made his way back to Reshetnikov's house with the intention of breaking in.

It was nearly dark by the time he had reached the property and found the gates and walls fronting it impossible to climb. He recalled there being a tree in a neighbouring garden that overhung the wall by Reshetnikov's swimming pool, and stealthily making his way along the road to the neighbouring property he found a point where he could pull himself up and over the wall to drop, landing clumsily, in amongst some shrubs. Reshetnikov's neighbours were at home and he could see them through the windows, apparently gathering for the evening meal. Carefully keeping to the shadows he made his way along the garden's side wall and had just reached the tree when a car pulled up at the property's large wrought iron gates, its headlights illuminating the driveway. Esteves had just enough time to fling himself to the ground behind a large clump of strelitzia to avoid being seen.

Car doors slammed and someone could be heard talking to the communication box in the wall adjacent to the gates. Esteves, confused by a car arriving after curfew, strained to listen until he heard the caller at the gate announce loudly that he was from the Servico de Informações de Segurança and demanded entry. The Portuguese security agency was questioning neighbours of those suspected of being involved in the coup. Almost immediately the gates started to open, in fear, Esteves coiled himself up into as small an object as he could to remain hidden behind the plant whilst the car drove past. Carefully lifting his head as the car reached the house, Esteves saw four men get out of the vehicle and make their way to the, now open, front door, to be welcomed by a nervous household. As the front door closed he cautiously stood and assessed the climb up the tree to the branches overhanging Reshetnikov's garden. The tree, one of the indigenous laurel variety, proved to be difficult to climb and he fell twice whilst endeavouring to scramble up the tree's trunk. Then he had the idea of tossing his trouser belt over the lowest branch and fastening it to form a loop that he could hold onto while he swung his legs and around the branch. Eventually with both legs and then his left arm holding on firmly to the branch he was able to grasp a higher, smaller branch with his right hand and pull himself further up into the tree's canopy. Fighting to get his breath back he worked his way around the main trunk of the tree to a point where he could overlook Reshetnikov's property. His view was bitterly disappointing as it revealed the main gates open and four cars in the driveway; lights were coming on in the rooms of the house where men appeared to be conducting a search. Esteves swore under his breath, and making himself as comfortable as possible, put his mind to working out his next move; at least here hidden in a tree he was safe.

He had been watching the search for about an hour when the security agents emerged from the house whose tree he was concealed in and drove away. After a time the house lights went out one by one, but still, over the wall, the search of the Reshetnikov property continued. Clothes and other items were being removed, and Esteves wondered how long it would be before his DNA, taken from his clothing, was linked to Diana's body, and the feeling of nausea came over him again, together with a mental image of the girl's corpse lying on the sun-lounger. Soon he realised that the search was going to go on all night and with great care lowered himself to the ground and stealthily made his way to the rear of the garden, eventually reaching the golf course. There he spent some time searching for a place to hide out for the day, before realising that a stray golf shot could expose him as a golfer searched for his ball. Reluctantly he turned back towards the town, eventually finding a house with a well established garden where he could hide, just as the sun crept over the horizon. Here was also the bonus of bananas and avocados, plus a garden tap for drinking water, and with hunger and thirst satisfied he slept for most of the day.

He left the garden when the family had gone to bed, judging that under curfew most people would be indoors, reducing the chance of him being seen as he made his way back to Amelia's apartment. At the end of his three hour journey, during which his nerves had been tested to the extreme, he was finally dodging from shadow to shadow along the road that passed just uphill of the apartment building. Carefully he peered round to see if it was still guarded and was relieved to see the porch and illuminated entrance hall empty. Creeping forward he peered around the corner of a wall to look uphill and thinking the street to be empty of people he prepared himself to run across the road to the shadow of the wall opposite. Then he heard a cough, and peering round the corner again, saw the glow of a cigarette in the front of a car, parked a short distance up the hill. Moments later he heard the sound of the car door opening and a mumbled conversation followed by the noise of footsteps then the scuffing of feet as if someone was adjusting their position. Taking great care, he stole another look and saw a soldier relieving himself against a roadside tree; the guards were still on duty.

Sometime later, having given up hope of getting into the apartment that night, Esteves again concealed himself in the darkness of the derelict building he had found on his first night on the run, hiding out there throughout the day.

Returning to the apartment building, close to eleven o'clock that night, he noted that no lights came on in her rooms and correctly concluded that she was staying elsewhere. He waited and watched the soldiers on surveillance duty, disturbed to see them regularly walking down the hill then round behind the apartment building. He had to wait until early the following morning for his opportunity, given him when he realised that both of the guards had, probably from boredom, succumbed to sleep.

Knowing the entry code and having a door key meant that entry to the apartment was no problem and the food and snacks left over from the meeting were most welcome, but now three days had passed since he had gained entry to the apartment, during which he had had little sleep, fearing a police or army search, and the food in the fridge had run out. It was quite by chance that whilst checking whether the apartment was still under surveillance he witnessed both soldiers leaving their vehicle in the company of what looked like an officer and a civilian. Watching as they went out of sight, he waited, sensing that the situation was about to alter. Maybe Amelia would return and give him the chance of persuading her to help him leave the island. His plan, though ambitious, was to have her use her contacts to smuggle him aboard a cargo ship. He would pay, oh yes, he would pay much money for his freedom, and he would never divulge her part in his escape. These thoughts, however, were cut short by the reappearance of the army officer in the company of the civilian. As the man looked up towards the apartment, Esteves recognised him as Amelia's businessman visitor, and for the first time viewed the man with suspicion. Why would an overseas, so called businessman, be accompanying a Portuguese army officer? Had Amelia learnt of the group's plans and used this man in some way, or had there been a leak across in Lisbon?

Panic caused him to freeze for a moment, then, making a dive for his jacket and sunglasses on the settee, he hurriedly checked that all was tidy then left the apartment, crossing the wide landing to the front door opposite, and rang the bell.

Senhora Miranda was in her eighties and suffering with failing eyesight. As she peeped through her security spy hole in the door she mistook Olavo Esteves for her son Nicolau and thinking that he had forgotten his key she opened the door to discover too late her error, as Esteves' fist smashed into her face.

Closing the door quietly, Esteves dragged the old lady into her bedroom and gagged her with a silk scarf he found in one of her drawers and bound her wrists and ankles with some tights that had been hanging over the wardrobe door. Very frightened, and in pain from a broken nose, it was to be several hours before Senhora Miranda's son would discover her and get her to hospital.

Whilst Amelia's apartment was being searched, Esteves kept his eye glued to the spy hole in Senhora Miranda's front door, watching every move made by Vaughan. When the army officer finally emerged putting on his socks and boots, Esteves concluded that the visit had purely been to search the flat or maybe recover something that Amelia's friend had left behind. A little while after both men left, Esteves slipped out of Senhora Miranda's apartment, listening for any sound from the entrance hall, and when he heard nothing, crossed the landing to quietly re-enter Amelia's apartment. Hurriedly Esteves recovered Huberto's rucksack, forgotten in his initial rush to escape, and was now intent on returning to the old lady's apartment until he was sure that the coast was clear. He was just about to cross the landing again when he heard Amelia's voice from below and that of a Portuguese man, probably the officer. That was also the moment when a draught caused Senhora Miranda's front door to gently swing shut with, what to Esteves was, a deafening click.

Conversation had immediately stopped in the hallway below and Esteves guessed that the people there were straining to listen for any other sounds. Caught standing just outside of Amelia's apartment Esteves stood stock-still, not daring to move a muscle, perspiration caused by fear forming on his forehead and body. A trickle of sweat ran down his spine and he shuddered involuntarily. Then after several seconds the officer said something and a hubbub of conversation started up, allowing

Esteves to retreat, closing Amelia's front door behind him. It was then that Esteves' cold instinct for survival returned and his plan for escape swiftly formulated.

Hostage taking was Esteves' only hope. The boy was too small to act as a suitable shield against an army officer with a pistol so it would have to be Amelia. That decided, Esteves entered Amelia's bedroom and hid behind the far side of her bed, under the window. He had just entered the room when he heard the key in the front door lock and listened as the officer assured everyone that the apartment was empty.

At the front door Vaughan had gestured to the lieutenant to lead the way. The lieutenant confidently stepped inside then made his way along the passageway, explaining as he did that he had personally checked every room thoroughly. Amelia followed a little nervously, with Vaughan immediately behind her. Zeferino, however, hung back sensing his mother's fears.

Again the sensation that he had missed something important came over Vaughan. *Think, man, what was it that worried you?* Stopping at the kitchen door he looked in. *Have a look in the fridge that might trigger something, but what God only knows.* He opened the fridge. *Bloody hell, it's empty, not a bit of food left, he's been here. Esteves has got past those dozy bloody guards and has been living here!* "Amelia!" he called.

"What is it?" he heard her ask from some distance away.

Stepping back into the passage he asked urgently, "Where are you?" *Aftershave, that was it the smell of his aftershave, he's here.*

"In my bedro… ah…"

Vaughan was about to rush towards her room when Zeferino flew past him shouting, "Mama, Mama."

"Zef, stop!" yelled Vaughan. "Come back." But it was too late, the boy had almost reached the bedroom door.

Suddenly Lieutenant Jacome stepped out from the room opposite Amelia's, the one that had been occupied by Esteves, his pistol held out as if taking aim.

Zeferino stopped less than a metre from the lieutenant. "Não, não…"

The rest of what the boy said was drowned out by the massive noise of Esteves' Grach 9mm, as he shot the lieutenant clean through the heart, knocking the man back into the room he had just left, like a cast-off rag doll.

Vaughan rushed to grab Zeferino, taking hold of the boy and thrusting him into the box room and closing the door. Before Vaughan could make another move Amelia appeared, being marched out of her room tightly held by Esteves, now pointing the Grach at Vaughan and jerking the barrel in a signal for him to retreat. Slowly step by step Vaughan walked backwards towards the front door, wondering how long it would take for the sergeant and corporal to make it up the stairs. He had almost reached the bathroom door when Esteves' focus changed and he saw the man look past him and at the same time go to hold the pistol at Amelia's head, a move he didn't complete before Vaughan had grabbed Esteves' hand and twisted it hard, raising the arm and hitting the hand against the wall in an effort to knock the gun from the man's grasp. The pistol fired as Vaughan pinned Esteves' arm against the wall with his left hand, freeing his right to deliver a chopping blow to the side of Esteves' head, causing the man to ease his hold on Amelia. She needed no second chance and spinning her body round, broke from Esteves' grasp; then, pushing her way past Esteves grabbed Zeferino, who had come out of the box room screaming in fear, and rushed with him back to her bedroom. In the doorway to the apartment the corporal stood hesitantly, undecided whether to put down his rifle and join the fight, or wait until he could get a shot at the stranger with the pistol; he decided to wait.

Locked together, Vaughan and Esteves wrestled, each man desperately trying to gain control. The Brazilian fought with all his strength to bring the pistol to bear on Vaughan, and Vaughan equally struggled in his attempt to disarm the man. He soon learnt that his opponent had the skills of a street fighter, as he only narrowly avoided knee blows aimed at his groin, and attempts to poke fingers in his eyes. The man was fighting like a wild animal, fear giving him greater strength than normal, and now for the first time Vaughan thanked Sergeant Instructor McClellan, as this was the moment when he realised the value of those painful lessons. A head butt into Esteves' face broke the man's nose but did not reduce his will to fight, and neither did the blow to the kidneys that brought a pained cry from the Brazilian. Esteves' sweeping flail with his right leg almost took Vaughan's feet from under him, and the man had got through with several powerful punches to Vaughan's midriff with his left fist, whilst still trying to break Vaughan's grasp of his right arm. The gasp of pain from a brutal punch by Vaughan into Esteves' ribcage had actually cracked two of his ribs, but still he fought on.

What the hell has happened to the cavalry? They were in the doorway just now.

"Sergeant, where the hell are you?"

Vaughan's call for assistance caused Esteves to focus again on the front doorway where the corporal stood trying to take aim with his rifle. That momentary lapse in concentration allowed Vaughan to connect the outside of his left shoe with Esteves' left leg at a moment when the man's full weight was upon it. Running the edge of the shoe's welt viciously down the front of the shin, Vaughan stamped as hard as he could on the top of Esteves' foot breaking several bones. The agonised scream was so loud that no one heard the crash as the Grach pistol hit the hard floor as it fell from Esteves' hand as he tried to reach down to his crushed foot, which was still pinned to the floor by Vaughan's full weight. Vaughan instantly pivoted in an effort to bring Esteves to the ground, a move that exposed Esteves' back to the corporal, alert, sighting down the barrel of his HK417. Seeing his target, the corporal squeezed the trigger and watched, amazed by the effect of the bullet's impact, as it floored both men, like skittles in an alley.

The deadly 7.62mm bullet fired by the HK417 had smashed its way through Esteves' shoulder blade and heart to eventually blast right through the man's chest and strike Vaughan's right side a few inches below his ribcage as he fell backwards under the combined impact of Esteves and the now distorted lead slug as it tore into him.

There was a strange silence of several seconds before the sergeant thrust the corporal out of the way and hurried towards the bodies lying in a heap in the passageway. One look at the fish-eyed stare of Esteves was enough to have the sergeant drag the body to one side and look closely at Vaughan. At first he didn't realise that Vaughan had been hit, as there was blood from the huge exit wound in Esteves' chest splashed all over Vaughan's shirt. A door opened and the sergeant heard Amelia scream and rush towards Vaughan's body, laid in a grotesque pose, his eyes closed, his chest unmoving.

Tearing Vaughan's shirt open the sergeant looked at the wound and shook his head. Amelia fell to her knees and, cradling Vaughan's head, cried, "Ian, speak to me, speak to me, and tell me I have not lost you. Please, please speak to me." Her tears came uncontrollably, running down her cheeks and dripping from her chin onto Vaughan's forehead. Vaughan's right eyelid twitched, just once.

"Muito bom," said the sergeant, rotating his hand, indictating that she should continue talking.

Gently the sergeant felt under Vaughan's body and removing his hand inspected it for signs of blood, there were none, the bullet was still inside the man.

"Ele precisa urgentemente de uma ambulãncia. Agora!" the sergeant yelled, looking back at the corporal stood, with a petrified expression on his face, the rifle held loosely in his right hand, the barrel tip touching the floor. He had never fired at anything other than a target before and was now facing the fact that he had shot and killed a man, probably two.

"Agora Cabo, agora!" the sergeant roared again, this time sparking a reaction from the young corporal who ran as fast as his legs could carry him back to their car and the radio on the rear seat. Message sent and acknowledged, he crossed the pavement and leaning against a garden wall promptly threw up.

Back inside the apartment the sergeant had pulled a bedspread off the bed in the box room and covered Esteves' body. Covers from the bed Esteves had slept on were used to hide the body of Lieutenant Jacome.

Looking up, Amelia told the sergeant where some blankets were, and then helped him as they carefully wrapped one around Vaughan. Only then did she go in search of Zeferino, finding him hiding in her wardrobe. Gently she encouraged him out and holding him close returned to Vaughan to resume her pleas for him to live.

Staunton, sat in his car a hundred metres further up the hill, above the soldiers' vehicle, had watched the proceedings with care and now counted the people as they left or were put into ambulances. A sneer of satisfaction crept across his face when he realised that one of the bodies must be Vaughan's and that none of the three stretchers appeared to have a drip rigged up or be given any special attention before the ambulances drove away. After the shots he had heard, he was surprised that there were no walking wounded. Three shots and apparently three kills, was unusual, but not impossible.

"So, Vaughan has been downed, that should wrap things up nicely," he said out loud. "This will take that superior smile off Mrs Bevington's face."